T0381370

A GAY EPIPHANY

HOW DARE YOU SPEAK FOR GOD?

ROBERT K. PAVLICK

A GAY EPIPHANY
HOW DARE YOU SPEAK FOR GOD?

iUniverse books may be ordered through booksellers or by contacting:

iUniverse
1663 Liberty Drive
Bloomington, IN 47403
www.iuniverse.com
844-349-9409

ISBN: 978-1-4502-8020-4 (sc)
ISBN: 978-1-4502-8021-1 (e)

Print information available on the last page.

iUniverse rev. date: 09/14/2022

DEDICATION

This work is dedicated to my beloved friend, John, who was with me through good times and bad and who always saw the best in me. He always thought that I had something unique and important to give to the world and this work is the result of his continual encouragement and inspiration.

On another level, this work is dedicated to all who read it: to mothers and fathers, educators, religious teachers, legislators and to all those struggling to achieve self-acceptance and acceptance from others, to the end that they may lead fully integrated, genuine and fulfilling lives.

This work is also dedicated to my Mom, Doris, my Dad, John and my grandmother, Anna who although not perfect, were loving and caring and did the best that they could with the cards they had been dealt. They instilled within me the values which I still hold dear and which keep me going.

Last, but not least, this work is dedicated to the many wonderful Hindu and Buddhist teachers past and present who touched my being and rescued me from a life of fear and self-loathing. They taught me that I am a son of God, not a wretched fallen creature "born in sin and shaped in iniquity".

VEDIC PRAYER

Om Asatoma Sadgamaya

Tamaso Maa Jotir Gamaya

Mrityor Maa

Amritam Gamaya

Aum Shanti Shanti Shantihi

Lead me from the unreal to the real

Lead me from darkness to light

Lead me from death to immortality

May there be peace everywhere.

CONTENTS

INTRODUCTION

Until now, I have always agreed fervently with the author of Ecclesiastes 12:12 who said that "…Of making many books there is no end, and much study is wearisome to the flesh." New KJV.

There are so many books on the market on every subject imaginable, even on previously forbidden subjects like homosexuality, that there seems little left that hasn't already been said. And yet even in my limited experience in researching various concepts, I have often read several works on the same subject and still come away confused and bewildered, only to pick up another work by someone else who made it all crystal clear in an instant. I hope that by following my journey, you will come away with a clearer understanding of the issues involved not only in my life, but in the lives of millions of gay men and women and those who love and support them.

Having read the life stories of famous gay athletes, Hollywood stars and musicians I came to the conclusion that while their stories show great courage in their publicly "coming out," still they had definite advantages that the average gay man or woman does not have. A famous Olympic swimmer like Greg Loughanis or a famous musician like Elton John who has already achieved greatness, will usually retain the admiration and respect of his fans even after they become acquainted with the revelation of his sexual preference. The knowledge that Alexander the Great and Hannibal were predominantly homosexual does not rob them of their accomplishments nor remove them from their places in history.

But what about the rest of us who have no silver medals, gold records, or military victories to boast of? We have nothing to attest to the possibility that we might be in any way equal to or, unthinkable as it may seem, superior to our straight counterparts. And so I decided that another story needed to be told of just one average gay man with no advantages; no fame nor fortune, no "edge"; just one man with nothing to offer but his honesty and integrity and personal experiences, which in the end, may not be so little after all. This is the story of one man, who like millions of his brothers and sisters, woke up one day to the reality that he was somehow different from his peers and ultimately faced with a life of rejection, ostracism, fear, violence and second class citizenship.

There are still those today, even in what we consider an enlightened age, who maintain that the gay lifestyle is a conscious choice; perhaps they need to "walk a mile in our moccasins" and see if that is true. The only choice we have ever had is the choice that Hamlet contemplated when he said: "To be or not to be, that is the question." We cannot change our basic nature, which may very well have been determined at birth. The only choice open to us is whether to live a life of hiding and deceit or be true to ourselves and those we love by living an honest, genuine and fulfilling life.

I offer you the story of a young child growing up during the 1950's and 60's, the youngest of three siblings, trying desperately to find love and a sense of security in an often alien, frightening and lonely world. I then offer you an in-depth look at the internal struggles of a young adolescent, faced with not only with the normal problems that all young people face, but complicated by the additional terror of dealing with intense homosexual feelings and fearing the hatred and ostracism which will result if those feelings are ever acted upon or discovered.

How does a young adolescent deal with the knowledge that he is radically different from his peers when there is absolutely no one who he can turn to in dealing with these problems? All of his young life he has been socialized into believing that the feelings that he is experiencing and the person that he is becoming are the most dreadful and degrading thing that could possibly happen to him; unacceptable to both man and God. Who can he turn to, faced with this unbearable life-sentence?

But cheer up. Do not be dismayed. I will finally offer you the man, the adult survivor, no, not survivor, but rather VICTOR ! I will finally show you the mature and balanced gay human, who like millions of his brothers and sisters worldwide, has somehow, by God's grace, managed to free himself from the shackles of the "closet-world" and even the allure of the gay world and emerge into the sunlit world of total spiritual, physical and mental integration.

I offer this work as a gift, not only to my courageous brothers and sisters, but also to those whom they love: parents, siblings, friends, educators, priests, ministers, rabbis, sergeants, legislators and numerous others who inter react with them on a daily basis. Every one of you has someone gay in your family whether you realize it or not. I hope that this small work will enable you to realize and respond to their hopes and fears; their needs and apprehensions, and inform you of how very much they love you and need your love in return, not just mere toleration.

I hope that it will educate you so that you think before uttering thoughtless and caustic remarks and epithets in mixed groups when you do not know who you may be insulting. I hope that it will inspire you to think before voting on anti-gay legislation or excommunicating gays from your religious institutions, that the person upon whom you are passing judgement, is someone's son or daughter, maybe even your own. Just because Uncle Joe is married, doesn't mean that he is not gay. Just because Father Jim is a priest doesn't mean that he isn't gay. Just because your daughter has three children and two ex-husbands, doesn't mean that she is straight. Many thousands, perhaps millions of gays, out of fear, have hidden themselves behind unhappy marriages or cleric's frocks, so please, save yourself a lot of embarrassment and your relatives a lot of pain by endeavoring to understand the condition of homosexuality and how to deal with it in a fair and compassionate manner.

Two thousand years ago, this work would not have been necessary. In the Greco-Roman world which we today admire for its gifts to us of art, architecture, law, government and philosophy, homosexuality and bisexuality were the norm and at the core of their lives and family values. Eva Cantarella, in her book "Bisexuality In The Ancient World", discusses in depth the entire social progression that young Greek men would pass through to reach manhood beginning first as a student or disciple and lover to an older mature man; then a father and head of household in his own right and finally mentor and lover to a younger man during his middle years. His young lover usually lived under the same roof with his wife and children and was no secret to anyone. So same-sex love was an integral part in the right of passage from adolescence to adulthood and then resurfaces again in mid-life.

Now there are those who would simply argue that Greek and Roman society was debauched and simply wallowed in orgies and free love, but that is not the case for the most part. The ancient cultures did have standards for moral behavior prior to the arrival of the Judeo-Christian ethic. Adultery and both male and female prostitution were frowned upon, as were incest and child abuse. In those days, heterosexuals, homosexuals and bisexuals all coexisted without any detriment to each other or any social stigma. The Spartans and Greek-Macedonians never questioned whether homosexuals were fit for the military, in fact they were considered the best and most courageous and effective of soldiers.

We were once the pillars of society: the emperors, the conquerors, the philosophers, the artists and artisans, the musicians, the architects. So what brought us down from Olympus and made us second rate citizens and outcasts in today's supposedly enlightened society? What universal "litmus test" proved us to be inferior, unnatural and a detriment to society? It is only the teachings of man-made religious institutions and their leaders during the appropriately named "Dark Ages, who drunk with power, set out to enslave mankind on every level; spiritual, mental, and physical. It was during that and successive periods that we became known as "faggots", named after the kindling wood that was used by self-righteous and "holy" clerics to burn us at the stake along with others who refused to accept their supreme authority and spiritual agenda.

Not content to merely enslave us, they killed us for the sin lf loving one another, yet all the while giving tacit approval of other "sins" such as adultery, child abuse, violence toward women, slavery, and adult and child prostitution. History shows no records of adulterers or wife beaters being burned at the stake. This erosion of public attitude toward gay men and women continued on down though history to the point in the nineteenth century at which Oscar Wilde spoke of gay love as "the Love that dare not speak its name."

There are those even today who will try to convince us that our society and even our U.S. Constitution and system of laws is based upon Judeo-Christian ethics and the Ten Commandments, but that is entirely untrue. Our laws and Constitution are based upon Greco-Roman laws and ethics which existed way before the coming of Christianity into the Roman Empire. I could be wrong, but I have never noticed any mention in the Constitution relating to "keeping the Sabbath" or refraining from making graven images or the like. There certainly are laws against murder and theft, but those laws trace their history back to the code of Hammurabi, long before there ever was a Judaic Law Covenant. Isn't it odd that we, who pride ourselves and base our culture upon the foundations of Greek and Roman law and philosophy, now choose to pass laws to marginalize members of our society who would have been considered pillars of the community by the Greeks and Romans?

And even if some might choose to say: "Forget about Rome and Greece, we're living in America?" Well then, we might ask how did Native Americans deal with homosexuality. Gay Indians? Are you kidding? No I'm not. It's a known fact that Native Americans found the state of homosexuality to be something unique and mysterious. Because male and female qualities are somewhat polarized in most individuals, Native Americans found it special that both sexes could be found fully integrated in one person and considered those persons highly spiritual and usually groomed them to be the medicine men and shamans of the tribe. So they were treated with great respect and not cast out or merely tolerated.

Well enough of that for now. Please be patient and follow me now through one man's journey from fear and repression to human and spiritual wholeness and integration; one gay man's epiphany or perhaps many epiphanies. I think that you will find that real gay men and women go a lot deeper and are a lot more complex than our stereotypes whose only interests in life seem to be show tunes, fashion, Barbara Streisand, Judy Garland, Liza Minnelli and Madonna.

PART 1
THE BEGINNING OF THE JOURNEY WE CALL LIFE

CHAPTER 1
INCARNATION

I arrived in this dimension, prematurely to be sure, on June 3, 1947 at the unearthly hour of 2:07 AM. I guess that I was in a hurry to get started on this new adventure and I have remained a night person ever since. I was the result of Mom and Dad's last desperate attempt to replace their daughter, Jeannie, who had been lost to leukemia several years earlier on the day after her ninth birthday. Mom and Dad had made many attempts since that fateful day, mostly ending in miscarriages and Mom was strongly advised by the doctor to desist in these attempts or suffer the consequences in her future health. Her response to those warnings was that she would rather die than not have this last child, a daughter. So it was with great anticipation that my parents, John and Doris, approached the long-awaited birth of, hopefully, their new baby daughter, Valerie. Unfortunately for them, upon closer inspection, Valerie turned out to be Robert Kenneth, and with that birth died all hopes of them ever having another daughter. During my Mom's pregnancy, irreparable damage was done to her internal organs and general health, resulting in poor health for the remainder of her life and contributing to her ultimate demise. Not a wise or good thing to tell to a young impressionable mind, but I was told it often. I was to have been their new daughter, Valerie.

My Mom had never gotten over the loss of her daughter, Jeannie, and had developed many neurotic compulsions and phobias over the years since that tragedy. She became obsessively germ conscious and spent hours washing her hands and disinfecting everything in the house with Lysol, to the point where our home always smelled like a hospital. If I dropped anything on the floor, I was under no circumstances to pick it up, but must call for Mom so that she could disinfect it first before I touched it. She also developed strange phobias related to the town of Easton where my sister had died. She felt that she could never return to Easton, nor could we have any contact with anyone who had come from Easton, which was pretty difficult because all of my paternal relatives lived in Easton. That means that my Dad couldn't see his own mother, and that I could not see or visit with my grandparents. After the death of my sister in 1942, my parents sold their home in Easton with all of its contents, never to return. But even that didn't seem to help. My Mom had to be sent away for therapy and electric shock treatments and even my Dad later suffered a nervous breakdown himself as a result of the loss and having to deal with Mom's erratic behavior with no support from his family who were still living, you will remember, in the "City of the Damned", Easton.

Consequently, during that period and for some time after, I was deprived of grandparents and any kind of normal family life. My older brother, John, spent most of his time with Dad or neighborhood children. I, on the other hand spent most of those days up to age five in either the crib or a highchair. I didn't have a playpen because Mom didn't want me near the floor. She was absolutely consumed with the possibility of illness, danger and death and began instilling those fears in me from an early age. Even feeding times were accompanied by stress and hysteria. I wasn't a particularly avid eater and Mom was constantly trying to force food down me with hysterical cries of "Eat, eat, or you will die like your sister died." I remember much later fearing my ninth birthday because I was absolutely certain that I would never live beyond that day, just like my sister.

I recall spending what seemed to me insufferable periods alone in my crib with no one nearby anywhere in the house. I think that my Mom rejected the fact that she had not given birth to a baby girl and resented me in those early days. She was lonely and would leave me alone and go next door to a neighbors' house assuming that I was sleeping, but I wasn't always sleeping. Oftentimes I remember being terrified when a wasp or spider was in my crib and my repeated cries for help brought no one. I became painfully aware that Mom, wasn't just in another room, but that she was totally inaccessible to me should I need her. I spent hours having conversations with imaginary people; I had to be resourceful and entertain myself. Years later my Dad verified that he found out that I had been left alone for extensive periods of time during those early years, and that it was not just the exaggerated imaginings of a child's mind. But there wasn't much he could do about it back then when he was at work all day.

Don't get me wrong, my Mom wasn't a bad or abusive mother. Once I finally became old enough where she could actually converse with me and we could have any kind of an interchange of ideas and affection, she became a very loving and self-sacrificing mother, but those early days were very bleak. I'm sure that she resented the fact that I was not a girl; she still missed her daughter and wept often about it, and I could never replace her in my Mom's mind or heart.

Due to her continued compulsion to have a daughter, she improvised and raised me as one. She refused to have my hair cut until I was almost school-age. I never went to kindergarten nor had any friends. I was pretty much raised on a diet of paper dolls and teddy bear tea parties, etc. I also have no recollection during those early years of having any physical contact or rearing by my father. Again, some 40 years later, my Dad admitted that he never played with me or even touched me during those years due to threats from my Mom that she would take me and leave him if he so much as touched me. All of those years of estrangement from my Dad, which I as a child assumed to be his dislike of me or even his displeasure that I was not the daughter he had hoped for, turned out to be my Mom's crazy attempt at keeping me all to herself. The fact that I had no kind of loving or caring relationship with either my Dad or my brother in those early years was always a source of self-doubt and inferiority.

Despite all of the foregoing, I came into this world full of excitement, trust and wonder. I remember vividly, perhaps my first time outdoors and being able to walk with some confidence on my own. The first thing that I noticed were our neighbors' exquisite rose bushes, so I bolted and made a "bee-line" for the roses. The colors were stunning and the scents were intoxicating; I was ecstatic to say the least, but my joy and ecstasy were soon shattered by Moms' screaming impending doom: "Get away from those bushes! You'll poke your eyes out on the thorns or get stung by bees and die." Mom raced to the scene; fastened her grip on my tiny wrist and never let go again for many years. But you know, until this day, I still can't resist a rose. The possible scratches of thorns or bee stings pale with the joy I experience each time I press a rose to my cheek or inhale that divine perfume.

Unfortunately, Mom continued to instill fear in me: she taught me that all of the things which I considered fun and harmless, things that other children did with no concern at all like swimming, skating, bicycle riding, etc. were all potentially lethal. I already saw the world as a strange and often lonely place, but Mom instilled in me that it was also a very dangerous and threatening place. And unlike other parents who usually assure their children that they at least will always have the protection and care of their parents, my Mom constantly reminded my brother and I that she would most definitely NOT always be there for us. Any time that we were unruly, she would proclaim her sentence against us saying: "Well, you just put another nail in your mothers' casket. It won't be long now until God takes me away from you because you don't deserve a good mother like me." Or an alternative might be: "Why did God take my sweet angel Jeannie and leave me with you two thankless children? I wish I were dead.".

So bit by bit, much of my original trust and confidence and security became eroded; my exuberance for life became somewhat dulled. Every time Mom and Dad left the house, I couldn't be sure if they were ever coming back. I remember every morning when my Mom took my brother to school, sitting at home in terror counting the minutes and nervously tracing the route to the school on the irregular patterns of our formica enamel top kitchen table, absolutely certain that they weren't coming back. Children today are often so well trained that should an emergency arise, they will know how to deal with it. How often, one hears of a four or five year, old calling 911 and saving their Moms' life. But my folks, for whatever reason, saw no need to prepare me for anything. I had no idea what my parents actual names were; I had no idea that we had a surname or what it was; I had no idea what our address was. I had no idea of grandparents or how to reach them. So I was totally dependent upon my folks for everything, even my toilet needs and I was five years old at the time.

That brings us to another dismal, but hopefully comic problem. My mother, in her unceasing attempt to protect me from all germs and exposure to anything foreign, absolutely forbade me to use toilets in any way shape or form, even at home. She believed that anything imaginable, even leukemia was transmittable by toilet seats and there was no reasoning with her. Consequently, I was taught to be anal-retentive and make my Mom aware whenever toilet needs arose. Urination wasn't too bad a problem, she would simply make me urinate into a glass jar, but a "number two" was a big problem and source of humiliation. For a number two, she had to spread paper towels on my bedroom floor and have me go to the potty much like a new puppy on training pads. Of course this posed a really big problem if you needed to do a "one" and a "two" at the same time. Now, when finished, my Mom would toss the paper towel wrapped droppings out of my bedroom window. My Dad wasn't stupid; he questioned her as to what was the explanation for all of the "waste matter" outside my bedroom window, to which she replied: "neighborhood dogs" and to which he replied: "they must be very well bred since they're wiping themselves with toilet paper". But of course, he did nothing about it. In order to make absolutely certain that I would not cheat and venture into the bathroom by myself once I became able to navigate the stairs and such, my Mom told me that there was a large furry bogey man in the bathroom that ate little children if they were unaccompanied by an adult.

Of course that belief created other mental issues for me because in my active mind, I wondered where the bogey man went when Dad and Mom used the bathroom. Was he on his way upstairs? Was he outside my bedroom window ready to climb in and eat me while my parents were indisposed in the bathroom ? During those moments I was too terrified to even look in the direction of the doorway or window and simply waited anxiously for the comforting sound of the toilet flushing, which I somehow thought would summon the bogey man back to the bathroom like the church bells in "Night On Bald Mountain" summoned the ghosts and demons into their graves. Somehow my brother seemed to have escaped all that extreme toilet training and restrictions. So you see, right from the beginning, before ever the "gay specter" reared its ugly head, I was always made to feel that I was somehow different from other children and not allowed the same range of freedoms that they enjoyed. Was it that I was incapable of handling those freedoms which other children had? Was there something inherently wrong with me?

CHAPTER 2
SCHOOLDAYS

Needless to say, when my Mom reluctantly decided to loosen the apron strings and send me off to school, I was totally unprepared for anything that I might experience because she had refused to let me go to kindergarten and my socialization with other children, sports or games was minimal. So as you might expect, first grade might just as well have been a trip to the moon or Uranus as far as I was concerned. I remember vividly my first experience with reading and what a state of confusion and alienation that created. The teacher sat us all down on the floor in a semi-circle while she sat next to an enormous open "Tom and Jerry" book with a pointer in her hand. As she pointed to each word, the other children gleefully responded with: "Run Tom, run." Or "See Jerry run", etc. etc. Well, I couldn't imagine what on earth they were doing; the characters on those pages might just as well have been hieroglyphics or cuneiform for me. But I was bright and just as those who can't read music often bypass that problem by simply memorizing songs, I also, quickly learned to memorize the sentences so that I could at least "chant along" with the rest of the "initiates" and feel part of the group. Likewise the same problem occurred when it came to learning to write my name. My name was Bobby, but the placard on the desk read: Robert Kenneth. Well, I insisted that was NOT my name, to the laughter and amusement of the other students.

Now recess is normally every students' favorite subject, but not for me. You have to remember that my mother had thoroughly trained me in the imminent lethal possibilities in all games and sports and playground equipment. Why one child had even had his leg torn off by a merry-go-round you know. Children had in deed fallen from seesaws and struck their heads, never to regain consciousness again. So my pre-school introductions to the harsh realities of life caused me to see playgrounds and games differently than my peers. I was old before my time and my caution and fear was only seen as cowardice and childishness by both my educators and the other children. Of course, not knowing that I had these preconceived notions, my first grade teacher immediately placed me on a seesaw, which was all well and good until she placed a heavier child on the other end, which of course seemed to catapult me, at least what seemed like one thousand feet off the ground . I screamed and tried to get off and in doing so, fell and tore my teachers dress as she caught me in mid air. Of course all this attracted a lot of attention and resulted in my first, but unfortunately not last, experience of being the recipient of name calling and laughter. The other children all laughed and called me "sissy, baby, mommas' boy, etc. etc.

Within days of that episode, I was faced with a new problem; my first school physical. Now remember that everything at home, including bathroom needs was taken care of by Mom; consequently once undressed with the help of a school nurse, I had little idea of how to repeat the procedure in reverse. I didn't do too badly with my shirt and pants; I did seem to know enough to put my underwear on first; but tying my shoes was an absolute impossibility! So I did the best I could; I basically sort of braided my laces, twisting them together to shorten them and kept tying the only knot that I knew of, a granny-knot at the end of the braid. My laces looked rather like a mandarin pig-tail, and when I got home, my Mom had to cut my shoes off. Fortunately, at that point, she decided to teach me how to tie my shoes.

Fortunately, Mom used to pick me up for lunch every day; no eating questionable food with the other children. One blessing of going home for lunch was that I could finally go to the bathroom, so to speak, after a morning of rigid retention. School did help me gain a few freedoms though like tying my own shoes and learning how to read and write. So I began to feel a little bit more comfortable and like part of the group, but it was still apparent to all that I was not like the other children. They all seemed to have so much in common. They enjoyed games and sports and such while I did not. I felt like such an alien and outcast. I simply counted the hours until I could be safe at home, happy and secure with Mom. By this time Mom had become much more attentive and affectionate, so this began a more pleasing period of my home life, which was unfortunately, interrupted by school.

I must digress at this point to introduce you to my Mom and Dad, who up to this point have sort of been nameless, faceless people, but then I guess that's because they were just Mom and Dad to me, no first names. Parents were not on a first name basis in those days.

My Mom, Doris Marian Saunders was born in Plymouth England in 1912 to a poor, but madly in love unwed mother, Mary Georgina Saunders. Mary had all of the best intentions in the world, but she made the sad mistake of trusting and loving someone "above her station" and his parents quickly shipped him off to some remote part of the "Empire" to be certain that he would not see Mary Georgina again, but he did and Mary then had a son in addition to her daughter. Thirteen years later my grandmother's sister , Florence, who was barren decided to adopt my mother, her niece, to relieve her sister of the financial burden of trying to raise two children alone. Of course that wasn't her only motive; she was also looking for a live-in servant and maid. So Aunty Florrie and Uncle Jim took my Mom with them and departed for America in the mid 1920's. Of course, my Mom, being young and impressionable, thought it all a marvelous idea; the thought of America where the streets were "paved with gold" thrilled her. However, that's not exactly what they found when they arrived at Ellis Island in New York; nor when they eventually settled in the East Side of Bridgeport, CT.

It wasn't long before my mothers' guardians began to show their true colors and became very demanding and abusive to her. They lied about her age and got her a 50-60 hour a week job at General Electric. Of course each week they confiscated her paycheck and also expected her to cook and clean and wait on them hand and foot in her "spare" time. Mom soon realized that she was going to have to take desperate means to extricate herself from this Cinderella-like existence. And what could a young woman do back in the 1920's to escape this kind of fate, but find a suitable husband. Respectable women In those days did not get apartments of their own. So Mom began dating, much to her guardians' consternation.

Although she grew up in relative poverty, she did receive an excellent education from the British public school system which would probably equate today with four years of high school and two years of college. She spoke French and Latin and was versed in all of the Classics, history, Shakespeare, etc. so she was not exactly "house frau" material. She was also very beautiful; very petite and refined with long, waste-length light brown hair and large blue eyes. Consequently, she had extravagant taste in men. She was of course attracted to men, who might offer wealth and prestige, but she also had a very definite demand for physical beauty and masculinity; let's face it; she wanted it all.

Well, she certainly did attract many handsome and prosperous men, but they were all dissuaded and chased away by Moms' hostile guardians who didn't want to lose their live-in maid and servant. Only one out of the entire collection of suitors had the sincerity and courage and tenacity to stand up to Moms' guardians and fight for her, my Dad, John, a rather average in appearance, poor, undereducated, unrefined Russian-American farm boy from Easton, CT. He loved her desperately and wouldn't be dissuaded. So given the options of a live of slavery with her guardians or freedom with a new husband, my Mom eloped with her "semi-prince" who did in deed have a horse. Dad wasn't entirely guiltless in the venture either. He had motives too. All of his friends used to tease him that he would never find anyone worthwhile or suitable because he was poor and uneducated, so Mom was a real prize and trophy to him; what an ego builder!

Of course, as we all know, marriage is not always the panacea for all ills and once the initial excitement of elopement, freedom and a honeymoon in Niagara had faded into memory, the stark reality of Moms' new life began. Mom, although born into poverty, was none the less a great connoisseur of all this is beautiful and refined, and life on a dirty dairy and hog farm in Easton in the late 1920's was not exactly her dream of life in the New World. The farm was replete with dirt roads, mud, all non-English speaking marital relations and hired farm help barging in at all hours for water or food. This was not exactly the Life of Leisure and Luxury in the Elysian Fields which she had anticipated. She loathed their country ways and crudeness and she detested what she considered the ostentatious displays of affection that her mother-in-law lavished on my Dad. She considered Dad a Mommas' Boy. She called the family "The Pleasant Peasants". She felt rejected by the family; she believed that her father-in-law would much rather have had a big husky Russian farm girl for a daughter-in-law; someone who could have helped with the farming; not a petite intellectual and she was partly right. I think the family did see her as an intrusion and resented her superiority problem. She was totally isolated and very unhappy.

Dad was a loving and devoted husband, but the needs of the farm occupied most of his time and he was torn between his wife and his family. Mom was miserable and distraught, to say the least, so she did the only sensible thing to knit their marriage; she gave birth to a baby, my sister, Jeannie in September of 1933. My folks were intensely devoted to Jeannie; she was the proverbial "apple of their eyes" and all went well for many years. In fact, they were so completely contented with her alone that they did not have another child, my brother John until almost eight years later.

But as fate would have it, they did not live happily ever after. Jeannie became ill with leukemia; underwent countless blood transfusions and other painful therapy only to die the day after her ninth birthday. My Mom and Dad were totally destroyed. Mom immediately put the house and all of it's furnishings up for sale and decided to flee the town, bringing no memories with them to their new home in Fairfield, CT. But even being in a new home and new surroundings didn't lessen their grief. Even raising my brother was not an adequate substitute for the daughter they had lost; they wanted another daughter. But on June 3, 1947 they ended up with another son instead, me.

Sadly, with the death of my sister, something of Mom and Dad died too. They were never really close again after that. I don't know if each of them had originally seen the other as a rock and a crag to hide in during difficult times and then when they witnessed each other falling apart lost respect for each other or what. They certainly grieved separately rather than together and that was not good. Or maybe they were simply afraid to love again for fear of losing the object of their affection, but things were never the same again.

Apparently my brother and Dad had a reasonably good relationship during his formative years; possibly because Mom and Dad were somewhat estranged so my Dad spent more time with my brother. But for me, Dad was an enigma; I never knew him. All I knew of him at all was from my Mom's complaints about his weight, his lack of education, etc. etc. He was like a stranger to me. He was faithful to my Mom and a good "bread-winner", but that's all that I knew of him; he had long since abdicated his roll as head of household; Mom made all the decisions. My brother had his own circle of friends and Dad, so that left me mostly with Mom and her friends and female relatives. Whenever we visited family or friends, I somehow always ended up in the kitchen with aunts and housewives while my brother was always admitted to the "sweat lodges" and fraternal care of the men of the family.

I mostly entertained myself with my own fantasies and with TV. Sometimes my Mom would leave me alone for periods while she went next door to have coffee and conversation with a neighbor. During those periods I remember watching a wedding show which presented different weddings each day; maybe a Catholic wedding on Monday and a Jewish wedding on Wednesday, etc. I liked to participate by playing wedding along with the show so I would borrow a pair of organdy curtains from the linen closet to use as a veil and a bouquet of plastic flowers from a nearby vase and play the part of the bride. I really don't know why it never dawned on me to play the groom; I could just have easily borrowed a sport jacket from my Dad's closet and put on his shoes, but I just never did. Go figure.

CHAPTER 3
ENGLAND

The summer of 1953 began a whole new and wonderful period of my life with new and better opportunities for education in the "School of Life". My mom was still experiencing a lot of problems and depression and decided that maybe she just needed to get away for a while; maybe if she could just get back to England to see her Mom and try to recapture what was lost in that mother and daughter relationship, maybe that might in some way improve her outlook on things. She also felt that it was high time that the children meet at least one of their grandparents and since Easton was "off the map" we had to go to England to meet a real live grandparent.

So off we went on the H.M.S Queen Mary for a five day crossing to England. Of course at the tender age of five, I had absolutely no idea what or where England was, but anything that would make Mom happy was fine with me. I also figured that with Dad back in the US of A working to pay for this trip, I might have more time to bond with my brother. Upon arrival in the harbor of Southampton, I did I messed up. I was so excited at all of sites and sounds, just like in the rose garden a year earlier; I strayed off and got lost in the terminal. Of course, as I mentioned earlier, I knew nothing of parents' first names or surnames, so when I was picked up by a London Bobby in the terminal, I didn't have a wealth of information to give him. Fortunately somehow, I did know that we were American and I guess even if I hadn't, my lack of accent would have given that away and I did remember that my Mom was wearing a bright yellow coat which in 1953 post-war Britain would be easy to spot among a sea of gray and black coats; to say nothing of my brother in a bright red baseball hat as opposed to a regimental private school uniform.

So the Bobby quickly reunited me with my family to all our relief. Of course I had been missing for a substantial period of time and still under strict orders about public toilets so it was a double relief to be with Mom again.

The ocean crossing had been wonderful; Mom was unusually happy. I had never seen her this way before. She was excessively attentive and playful with me and her joy was contagious. My brother, on the other hand, was not all that happy. I think that he missed Dad and his friends and the privileges that he had at home. I, however, was just beginning to experience the world with its' kaleidoscope of colors, sights and sounds and it was heavenly. A world of castles and horses and breathtaking farmland; a virtual fairyland; what could be more exciting? Of course we had no family in Southhampton and had to travel all the way across country to get to my grandmother in Dartmouth. My mother rented a taxi, because she had a "thing about busses and trains"; germs and all you know. It was a long grueling trip, confining and stuffy, but it had to be done.

I looked forward to meeting my grandmother. I had no idea what to expect, but just by the happiness on my mothers' face, I knew that she had to be someone special. Mom hadn't seen her in seventeen years so the anticipation level was great. The ship had made excellent time, and so had the taxi so we arrived in Dartmouth at around 1 AM about a day and a half early. My grandmother, who had lived alone for a long time now informed the taxi driver that she was not prepared for us due to our arriving a day early and that he would have to take us to a hotel. This seemed a bit strange for someone who had not seen her daughter in 28 years and her grandchildren, never. After much pleading on the part of the driver (my Mom was too shocked to speak) my grandmother relented and allowed us in. I know that this sounds absolutely terrible, but you do need to understand a little of Granny's background before judging her too harshly.

Granny Tillyard, born Mary Georgina Saunders in Cardiff, Wales, circa 1890 was one of nine children born to a quiet religious woman, Ellen and her usually inebriated, authoritarian sea captain husband William who had a penchant for overindulging himself and then beating his wife and children. Ellen had very little to say about any of it and in her quiet religious way, probably spent hours singing hymns and praying that the old boy would one day just get drunk and drown at sea. Mary Georgina envisaged the escape route which was common practice back then; marry well. She was a domestic and fell in deeply in love "above her station". When she became pregnant with my Mom, her lover swore that he would marry her when he had finished his naval duty. So two years later, still hoping and trusting, she bore him a son also. But his high-born parents at that point decided that the entire affair had gone far enough and got him transferred to parts unknown in the "Empire" and she never saw him again. Years later, she did meet a very kind and accepting young man in the merchant marine, George Tillyard, who felt compassion for her and her plight and married her, kids and all. She had one son by him also later, but she wasn't really in love with him and he was gone most of the time at sea so it was a lonely life for her.

Then came WWII during which time, Gran was constantly in fear for her life and the lives of her sons then at war, not to mention the life of her husband who had escaped alive from several torpedo attacks. Gran eventually turned to alcohol to cope with her life; it was not an easy life. So by the time that we encountered her in 1953, she was tired, worn-out, lonely and tipsy; we caught her at a bad time. But she did mellow out during our visit. The next day she was very apologetic and from that point forward, tried to make our stay there enjoyable. Despite her hard life and disappointments, she turned out to be an amazingly funny and likeable person. She had a wealth of funny stories and jokes, to say nothing of her pub songs and ballads which she would sing throughout the day.

The entire experience with Granny Tillyard turned out to be one which I will always treasure and an adventure of inestimable value. She lived on the third floor of an old stone nineteenth century building with neither electricity nor modern pluming. The old house sat atop one of the highest hills in Dartmouth and rather resembled a foreboding, medieval castle keep, due to the curved exterior walls. It had a commanding view of the town and harbor. Dartmouth itself was a town that time somehow forgot, complete with steam trains, steam ferry boats, outdoor farm market days, butcher ships, bakery ships, fish mongers, chemists (drugstores which only sold medicines), iron mongers (hardware stores), blacksmiths and cobblestone streets with gaslights. It boasted a 16th century shopping mall, the "Butterwalk" with wonderful plaster and timber façade, a hotel in which Sir Francis Drake stayed during the time of the Spanish Armada attack on England, and a marvelous 15th century castle at the entrance of the harbor. It was from that point that the Pilgrim Fathers actually finally departed from England on their journey to the New World after having taken on additional provisions after leaving Plymouth, England. The whole experience was "living history" for me. It was like living in two different centuries at the same time. I got to see and live experiences that my contemporaries have only seen or experienced in museums or reproductions. It was like some kind of incredible time machine experience.

Gran had only four rooms in the flat called "Sunnyside"; two bedrooms, a living room or sitting room and a fairly large dining-family room with a tiny pantry and gas stove in an alcove. The flat was heated by a coal fireplace in the dining room and lit with a gas overhead light fixture into which one had to deposit coins regularly or the light would go out and several kerosene lamps. Consequently, most of the time was spent in the dining room since it had a good southern exposure with good natural light with no need to deposit coins into the lamp until after dark. Also Gran had no intention of lighting the other fireplaces; coal was expensive. When it was time to go to bed, Gram would take hot coals off the fire in a warming pan and go heat up our bed before we retired for the night. Then you simply stayed in bed covered with layers of goose down quilts until morning. In the morning, Gran would heat up water on the stove or in the fire and pour it into a standing wash basin where you would wash your face and hands.

Oddly enough, I didn't find any of this inconvenient at all and rather found it all charming. I was experiencing life in 17th and 18th century Britain in a manner that no textbook could equal. Without any TV or radio, time was spent bonding with family, which is something sadly lacking today. My Mom took this opportunity to begin my indoctrination into British history and culture. I took to it all like a fish to water; partly I guess because I saw how happy my interest in these things made my Mom, but also because I genuinely enjoyed it all. I increasingly became obsessed with my roots and evolved a sense of national pride that I did not feel back home in America. In some strange way, England began feeling more like home to me than my real home. Of course, I was not blind to the fact that the more British I became, the more my Mom seemed to love me and our relationship grew in leaps and bounds. Because my brother during this period seemed generally disinterested, all the love and attention shifted to me. Of course that did nothing to improve my relationship with my brother.

And of course the 19th century living conditions and all of this fit well with Mom's quirks about bathtubs and toilets and such. She didn't have to contend with me complaining "why can't I have a bath like other children? Or "why can't I use the toilet like other children?" It was all very simple: one uses a wash basin to wash up portions of one's anatomy and one uses a chamber pot to relieve oneself. That was certainly much better than squatting over paper towels like a new puppy on training pads. One could poop and pee all at the same time; how ingenious, I wonder at it that Mom hadn't thought of that back in the "colonies". You see, this is just one example of how much more civilized I found Britain.

Everything in Britain was wonderful; it seemed like a paradise to me with its' babbling brooks; patchwork quilt hillsides; wild ponies; its' rustic open moors with oceans of purple heather and yellow buttercups; its' quaint fishing villages and harbors teeming with sailboats and the aroma of the sea and fresh fish; the sounds of the ocean lapping at the shore and the cries of seagulls overhead. Couple all of this with the scents of flowers and the aroma of fresh baking wafting from the chimney of the bakeshop and one is struck with sensory overload.

Yes, God was in His Heaven and all was well with the world. Mom was loving me more and more and so was my grandmother for that matter.

Even my Grans' flat with its' 25 layers of wallpaper, dark woodwork and poor lighting (perhaps a blessing in disguise) was a refuge for me. I loved watching Gran heating up her flat irons in the fire and ironing her clothes; I loved watching her stoke the coal fire and heating up water for the wash basin. I watched her skimming the cream off the milk and cutting up fish for her cat, Smutty, which she placed lovingly atop a block of ice in a large bowl in the hall and covered with a tea towel for his dinner later that day. And I enjoyed the togetherness and quiet times listening and learning as Mom and Gran talked about England and relatives and caught up on the lost 28 years of separation. It was far more interesting and intimate than TV because I was learning about my roots and the people that I loved, not watching fictitious characters on some fake Hollywood set. You know, it's amazing how even today, some 50 years later, just the smell of coal or the sound of a steam train can catapult me back to those days and fill me with a sense of warmth and love and security that I don't often feel now.

Perhaps that's part of what is wrong with people today; we have no roots; no knowledge of even our own immediate family histories; no togetherness. We may know every baseball player's batting averages and may have scores of superficial acquaintances on the internet with whom we dare not even share our real names or telephone numbers. We know all the intimate details of some film star's life or some sports hero, but we seem to be progressively running away from real people, from relatives and friends, into a fantasy world of technology and virtual reality, which by its very name is NOT reality. We have more means of communication now than ever before in history: telephones, cell phones, beepers, faxes, internet and yet we seem to have less time and less to say to each other than at any prior time in history. And of course we do not write anymore.

No, we don't want to put anything in writing that we might have to give an accounting for somewhere down the line. Do you realize that most of what we know about the ancient world and history was taken from the personal letters written back and forth between friends and relatives? What will future generations know of us 500 years from now? Only what they get from safely contrived, politically correct books? How will they know what we truly believed and felt deep down when we fail to express ourselves in writing? All they will know of us is that we lived in a highly technological and bellicose society. No, I would not trade those precious months of intimacy with my Mom and Gran for all of the technology and virtual reality you can give me. But I digress.

My Mom was very changed in England; somehow in England it was safe to smell the roses (remember the roses?) and it was safe to play with other children and safe to pick things up off the floor. No harm could befall anyone in England; rather like some of the lyrics to "Camelot", eh? But I guess that's all part of the British mind-set. It's probably what carried them all through World War II in tact because they were defending "…this blessed plot, this earth, this realm, this England" as Shakespeare so aptly put it in "Richard II".

Of course, all good things do come to an end and as Mom and my brother, Roger and I stood on the stern of H.M.S.Queen Elizabeth and watched the last visible stretch of England disappear below the horizon, we wept. It was not like we were "going home", but rather "leaving home". But at least something wonderful had been gained. I now had a new and special relationship with Mom; I had a new grandmother, and I had a magical, mystical island that I could escape to at least in my mind whenever life just got too difficult. Many of Moms' phobias and compulsions seemed to have abated as a result of that trip. When we arrived home I began receiving normal, human toilet training and my first complete bathtub type bath, just like a normal child; amazing. Of course I did not enter into these new rituals without some trepidation, I mean what about the bogey man who normally held court in the bathroom? How could I be sure that he had been properly exorcised? Would I be able to enter the bathroom unattended by an adult?

CHAPTER 4
BACK TO SCHOOL

Now, back to reality; back to school. Somehow my extreme desire to be like other children and do the things that they could do, coupled by a new sense that Mom would now support my efforts, accelerated me above and beyond my peers, at least in reading, history and art. I was very artistic for a young child and very realistic and rigid in my choice of subjects worthy of my skills. Hence, unlike my peers who colored outside the lines and made pictures of red skies and blue trees; my trees were always green with brown trunks and my skies always blue. And unlike the pictures of dogs and cats and such which my classmates did; my pictures were always of God or of H.M.S. Queen Mary or coronation coaches or castles. I continued to fail miserably at recess or should I say sports or anything physical, but I was an artist. So I continued to be some kind of strange alien to my peers at school.

The fact that I was excelling scholastically and drew and painted strange things did not exactly endear me to my classmates either, but at least I knew that at the end of the day, Mom would be there to bind up my wounds and reassure me that the reason other children were cruel and treated me differently was because I WAS DIFFERENT. In fact she assured me that all superior people are mistreated; they were simply jealous. Mom had decided to raise me as a proper, genteel and refined English private-school boy. And while my manners and refinement might not be appreciated by rude, ill-bred American children, eventually she and I would return to England and I would be recognized and highly esteemed there. Meanwhile, she did not want me associating with common, loud, arrogant, competitive, ruffian American boys unless they showed some signs of proper breeding and refinement. Consequently, I had no friends or playmates. I did eventually meet all of those refined "gentlemen" who she wanted me to associate with, only much later in life, but that's another story which we will ultimately get to.

While a lot of my belief system may have come from my Mom; still, I did have my own feelings on these matters too. On my own, I found loud and competitive boys offensive. To me, the only purpose for sports was pure fun and exercise; it didn't much matter to me who won or lost a game, so long as everyone had a good time. Of course that didn't win me any points with my peers and I was never chosen for any teams. I couldn't understand why most boys had to be so aggressive and competitive; why they liked to pick fights with each other and abuse small animals and make fun of other children, especially the little girls or anyone unusual or handicapped.

My Mom decided that the urban area where we lived was entirely unsuitable for the raising of gentlemen so she found a new house in Newtown, CT, a quiet, refined New England town, much like the villages in Britain. The fact that Newtown had been a "loyalist town" (loyal to King George III) during the American Revolution, coupled with the fact that most of the populace were of English or Yankee origin led her to believe that this would be fertile ground for us to grow and flourish in. She was pretty much right.

Newtown was a delightful, friendly little country town. It was safe to leave doors and windows open and to take walks, etc. And the people and children were fairly refined and well mannered. But even there, the boys in school were still competitive with their sports and would argue over who had to take me on their team. So my closest friend, was the little girl next door, Linda, who was three years my junior. My Mom loved watching us play together, so did her Mom. You see Mrs. Cooper had lost her first born son and my Mom had lost her daughter, so each parent, when they saw us playing, would secretly pretend that we were brother and sister and that all was well.

We enjoyed each others company immensely because I wouldn't make fun of her or abuse her as other boys would, and I on my part, could just be myself with her and not have to be competitive. I would take her bland, uninteresting doll houses and decorate them to make them beautiful. Everything that we did together was creative, not destructive. I loved her dolls and toys; it was "summertime and the livin was easy". Life with my little friend was simple and unthreatening. She didn't make fun of me for picking flowers for my Mom or playing with her doll houses. She didn't care if I could throw or catch a ball.

That summer of 1955, something else wonderful happened; we went back to England again. This time I got to meet my Uncle Reginald, Aunt Dolly, Uncle Jack and my two cousins, Vivian (a male) and Valerie, my namesake. Remember that I was supposed to be Valerie had my plumbing been correct. We had a wonderful time that summer, but in some strange way, I noticed that even over there, my uncles and male cousin somehow seemed to bond with my brother, while I was left to have tea and crumpets with my Aunt, Mom and Valerie. Somehow the male members of both my paternal and maternal sides, always seemed to exclude me. Was there something that they knew on a subconscious level that even I didn't know at that time?

But I didn't care, the new and wonderful relationship that I had with my Mom and female relatives more than compensated for my lack of male companionship. And they knew how to do such wonderful things; almost like magicians. They could take a bag of flour and turn it into wonderful, delectable pastries. They could take dirty, grungy clothes and make them new and crisp and wearable again, while all the guys could do is get things dirty. They could arrange flowers and make things beautiful while the guys were forever standing around looking at auto engines or tearing them apart. I spent my eighth birthday in England; it was the best birthday ever. I didn't miss my Dad at all. We went to beautiful parks; went boating; sailed my new sailboat in the sailboat pond; all things that I never did back home.

On this trip my Mom was even more ecstatic than on the prior trip. We left my Uncles' home and traveled back to see my grandmother again in Dartmouth. We were really starting to know our way around and settle in. To accomplish our daily trips to castles and cathedrals in Dartmouth, my mother hired a young independent cabby to take us around. He was very kind and sweet and took us all over; often at no charge. He and my Mom became great friends or possibly more. My Mom didn't want the fantasy to end; nor did I and it almost didn't. Apparently at some point the young man asked Mom to divorce Dad and stay in England with him, or at least that is the impression that I got because she advised me that our stay in England didn't have to end this time, so apparently, she considered it. My brother was against the idea and wanted to go back to America and be with Dad. Mom agreed that Roger should go back, but that she and I would stay in England. The incident reassured me that while I might be about to lose my brother and Dad, that Mom would at least always be there for me and had great plans for me. She fantasized enrolling me in a nice, private boy's school and arranging for me to sing in a boys choir in some lovely English cathedral.

Well, that was a dream to be cherished. I wasn't all that close to my brother, and Dad was still somewhat of an enigma to me so I didn't consider it any great loss. Mom was beautiful and sophisticated and fun to be with and I had won her totally; my victory was complete. However, when the time came for her to send my brother packing, she had second thoughts about it and began feeling guilty. After all, Dad had stuck by her through her nervous breakdowns and treatments and had worked overtime to finance these jaunts to England without him. And even though he wasn't polished, suave, handsome or educated; still, he was faithful and kind to her and a good provider. Who knows how the young taxi driver would have turned out?

So once more, we stood on the stern of H.M.S Queen Elizabeth, watching our dear England disappear before our eyes. Mom and I wept, but not Roger.

CHAPTER 5
MATUSHKA

This time a truly miraculous thing occurred when we returned from England. On the return ride from New York to Connecticut, Mom asked Dad to take us to his parents in Easton, CT. Remember Easton? "The City Of the Damned" from which no one ever returns alive? Mom admitted that it had been wrong for her to have kept Dad away from his parents for all those years and wrong to have kept the children from being with their paternal grandparents and she wanted to make amends. Well, I was overjoyed. Now that I had experienced how nice a grandma can be, how convenient it would be to have a grandma closer to home that my 3,000 mile away grandma in England.

Maybe from hereon in, Mom would now be well, Dad would be happier and we could be like a real family. So I finally got to meet my Russian grandma and grandpa, Anna and John. Geographically, they had both come from a small village, Shambron, in Slovakia, but ethnically, they were Russian and spoke Russian and Slovak. At this point in time, Grammy spoke perfect English, however Grandpa John, who we called Zetto, spoke no English at all which was sad because I would have loved to have heard his tales of coming to America at the turn of the century all on his own on a ship that was half steam, half sail, but I never got to talk to him. Dad wanted to teach me Slovak so that I could at least talk to grandpa a little, but Mom was adamantly against it. Really that would have been a great idea because it would have brought me closer to Dad, but I think that secretly, that's exactly what she did not want.

My Grandma, Anna, was without exaggeration, the ultimate, U.S. Bureau of Standards grandmother. She could easily have been bronzed and put in Washington as a model of everything a grandma should be. She was the epitome of kindness, sacrifice, hospitality and compassion and she was an incomparable cook. I think that she was born with her hair in a bun and wearing a full length apron because I never saw her any other way. From that first meeting forward, she had us to Sunday dinner every week without fail. But to call it dinner is really a misnomer and a disservice to her. It was always a feast and a celebration. She always used her best linen, crystal and cutlery. There was no such thing as informal dining. Every

Sunday was Thanksgiving Day replete with roast beef, turkey, sweet potatoes, corn, peas, beets, fries, coleslaw, fresh-baked bread, carrots, stuffing, and fresh-baked short cake with either fresh strawberries or fresh peaches and cream. Most of the ingredients were from her own garden which she continued to tend into her late 70's and early 80's.

She was married to a not so handsome; not so intelligent; not so successful farmer, but she loved him dearly and waited on him hand and foot for over 50 years. She raised two sons and a daughter, who like in my parents' case, also died. In addition to all the fabulous cooking over those years she did farm work; took in laundry and worked as a domestic for some of the local wealthy people of Easton; she was not a lazy woman. I find it sad that she had to work so hard and take in other people's laundry and clean other peoples' homes when at one point she owned over 200 acres of prime land in central Easton and should have been living a life of comfort and leisure. But fate and circumstances were not kind to her and her heart was bigger than per purse. The farm did not do all that well and granny had many needy relatives who kept arriving from Slovakia. As a result of constantly bailing out hopeless relatives from financial disaster by selling land to unscrupulous land sharks for next to nothing, she ultimately ended up with nothing but a small house on ten aces of land, which she again, sold to her doctor for next to nothing only so that she would have money to give to her children and grandchildren while still alive.

As was always the case on both sides of my family, my grandpa and the male members of the family took little interest in me. Even my Dad always seemed more interested in his nephews and niece next door than in me, but Granny Anna always took me under her wing and would show me how to cook things and bake and plant in the garden. She didn't find my interest in cooking or baking strange or tell me to go outside with the men; she always had time to share with me. She was a strong woman, yet tender and emotional. She never took you for granted. Each week for 14 years, whenever we would arrive at her home, she would run down the driveway and hug us and kiss us and cry as though she hadn't seen us in years.

I wasn't used to that kind of depth of love and emotion. We rarely hugged or kissed in my family; in fact, my father and I never even touched each other at all until years later when I was leaving for seminary and we shook hands at parting. But Granny made you feel loved and special. She taught me patience and forgiveness and the strength to face great sadness and adversity. She taught me that kindness and emotion were not signs of weakness, but that they could dwell harmoniously along with other fine qualities like courage and strength, all in the same person. She rarely complained about her lot in life, but simply accepted the good along with the bad.

Mom was pretty good with all of this, but there was some slight animosity and jealousy there. She saw her mother-in-law as just a little too much of a saint and wondered when she would show her true colors. Part of the animosity was jealousy which she admitted later in life. She wished that she could have been raised in such a loving family herself and have had both a mother and father.

That last trip to England had certainly mended most ills and our life together in Newtown became quite pleasant. Mom was still running a tight ship though and didn't allow my brother or I free rein. My only friends were the little girl, Linda, next door and two other boys my age, Bill and John, both doctors' sons of course, one has to mix with "the right sort of people". I will be forever indebted to Bill who taught me to play chess and John, who attempted to teach me to ride a bike unsuccessfully, but did teach me how to dress up in drag. We spent hours at his house dressing up in his older sisters' clothes and prancing around the house. I don't know why it never dawned on us to dress up in his fathers' clothes. But then this was nothing new to me. As I mentioned earlier on, when I was younger, and my mother would go next door for coffee , I would often stay by myself and watch a wedding program that used to be on TV in those days. Each day would have a different wedding; one day Catholic, next day Protestant and so forth. Just like most children like to play along with TV as either cowboys or Indians, or nowadays perhaps as gangsters, I used to play wedding. I would take my mothers' extra organdy curtains out of the closet and put them over my head like a veil and I would carry a lovely bouquet of plastic geraniums as my bridal bouquet. I don't know why it never dawned on me to play the groom. All that I remember is that I was always the bride. Now take that one to the bed and sleep on it.

My brother and I did not like the tight reins that Mom kept over us. So we made it a point to learn the triggers and switches to pull whenever Mom wouldn't let us stay up late watching TV or wouldn't allow us to go outside with friends. We would usually retort with the cruelest epithets that we could devise like: " I hope England sinks" or "I wish Hitler had won the war" or "Gran Tillyard is a lush". Sometimes these comments were met with light verbal rebuke like: "Go to your room!" or "No TV for you two tonight". But at other times, if our timing was off and Mom was in a particularly maudlin mood, the response might be much more severe, heated and physical.

As much as she had grown to love me, I must admit that I can recall several occasions of her chasing me through the house with a carving knife screaming: " I gave you life and I have the right to take it away. No court on earth will convict me." I remember blockading myself into my bedroom by pushing the bed and other furniture up against the door to protect myself. Oddly enough, my father, who was the one who I thought did not like me, never laid a hand on me.

Probably the worse bomb that was dropped on me during that period was when my brother decided to sit me down and reveal to me what wondrous things awaited me in the future. He postulated to me that it was only a matter of time before Grandma and Grandpa and Mom and Dad would all be dead and he would be married and far away and I would be all alone and quite helpless in the world. What was I going to do then? After expounding on all of this he quietly left the room and left me by myself to ruminate on these truths. Well, until that moment, those thoughts had never dawned on me, and while my life was not perfect, still it held out hopes for the future.

But that one statement crushed me because I somehow instinctively knew that it was true; that at some point I would be an orphan and all by myself. It was like some kind of Déjà vu experience reminding me that this whole sad cycle had happened before and would happen again. I really don't know why my brother said this to me. Was he like my Guru, initiating me into the sad realities of life, or was it just a sad adolescent attempt to rob me of my brief moment in the sun of my mothers' adoration? In either case, it left me with a terrible sinking feeling in my gut for some time. In fact that one statement would tend to color everything in my life after that, because I then knew that anything and everything that I found enjoyable or anything or anyone who I loved would only be short-lived and would ultimately be taken from me. Perhaps it's good that I learned that lesson young and was prepared because within only a few short years, my entire life was to be shaken to the foundation.

CHAPTER 6
SEX REARS ITS UGLY HEAD

Yes, this is what you have been waiting for isn't it? But you will have to wait a little longer because although my sex life began in these adolescent years; it really goes back much further to an earlier period when I didn't recognize what was occurring as being sexual in any way. We need to go back to those earlier days when I was left alone a lot with only myself to amuse and my imaginary friends and Teddy bear cellmates.

I remember as a child, putting milk on my nipples and then pressing my Teddy bears' lips to them and pretending to breast feed the Teddy. I have no idea where I got that from because as a baby, I was NOT breast fed. But I vividly remember nursing my Teddy and I remember that pressing his lips against my nipples or playing with my nipples gave me some kind of arousal which if continued, would actually culminate in some sort of dry climax or relief followed by euphoria.

I also remember having what can only be described as rape fantasies although I certainly had no idea what sex or orgasms or rape was all about. They were always the same. I would sit in my crib (at age four or five !) and wrap the sheets around me in the manner of a sarong. I would then imagine one or more muscular, hirsute men, much like Roman gladiators, fondling me and trying to pull my sarong off. I would act this out with my eyes closed by tugging at the sarong myself with one hand while fighting off the advances with my other hand. Eventually the right hand "gladiator" would always win out and begin squeezing my nipples and fondling me all over until I achieved some kind of non-sexual, non-semen, but nonetheless, sense of orgasm and release. The only reason that I fought the gladiators off was to maintain some degree of modesty and propriety because the experiences themselves were never threatening; I enjoyed them and really wanted to be overpowered by these men, but a "woman" doesn't want to come across as too easy.

Now granted, I had at that time some exposure to centurions and gladiators via TV, but back then there were certainly no fondling scenes nor rape scenes in any of those movies. I remember watching Tarzan and Hercules with my mother and hearing her comments like: "Now that's a real man; how did I ever end up with your father?" So apparently she too liked those big muscle hunks. What can I say? Like mother, like daughter. I remember thinking that Tarzans' Jane was nice and that the Greek women in the Hercules movies were pretty, but I wasn't attracted to them; part of me wanted to BE those women and the object of a virile mans' affection and desire. Now I ask you all, where were these ideas coming from?

The fantasies continued from age 5 to 11. I remember becoming very aroused during the summer months whenever we went to the beach or to a neighbors' house and there were shirtless, masculine men present. I just couldn't get them out of my mind. I began secretly compiling a scrapbook of clippings of any muscular or hairy shirtless men that I could find in "Look" or "Life" magazines. I was very artistic and when the clippings no longer sufficed and I wanted something a little racier, I would do my own sketches of massive, muscular men with a lot more missing than just their shirts. Of course all of my male sketches portrayed overly endowed men, often with women kneeling submissively clutching their massive thighs or biceps. I put the women in because I tended to identify with them and wanted to be a slave to one of my self-created Herculean men.

So now I want to ask all of you fundamentalist experts out there, where were all of these thoughts and desires coming from? They certainly weren't coming from a homosexual school teacher; nor were they coming from a gay uncle or a child molesting neighbor so where were they coming from?

The Christian Right keeps harping on the debilitating effects of pornography or exposure to gay topics in any way shape or form. They attribute the rise in homosexuality to those causes along with "Rainbow Curriculums", etc. But where was my latent homosexuality coming from? I had no exposure to any of those stimuli. In fact it became necessary for me to be creative and create my own stimuli. They say that "necessity is the mother of invention: well I guess it is. My young and presumably innocent mind and body together created what my libido wanted and needed. It didn't need any outside source or help. So the fact is that you can shield a child from porno, shield them from all Non-Christian influences; lock them away in an ivory tower and you will still not be able to keep them from feeling what is right and natural and good for them as individuals. If the seed of homosexuality is there it will grow; you will not be able to stop it. If it is not there, then no amount of exposure to homosexuality will put it there.

Scientists now know that sexual preference is determined at a very early age; not at puberty and nothing can be done later to change that orientation. Some authorities even believe that genetics is involved in it or at least predisposes and individual to being gay. I for one, firmly believe that because I cannot recall a time in my life when I was not attracted to men. Oh yes, I loved my mother and always gravitated toward women, but I could only see women as mothers, sisters, aunts and friends; I couldn't really see them as sexual objects. Of course there were occasions in later life when to conform to social norms, I forced myself to date women and afterward forced myself into prolonged periods of celibacy and countless religious movements to thwart my natural tendencies. But "it's not nice to fool Mother Nature" and you will never win without destroying yourself in the process.

How often I see little seedlings pushing their way up through concrete slabs and rocks and barren soil, against all odds to eventually realize their destiny as an adult tree or shrub. It seems that nothing can stop that little seedlings' progress unless man chooses to kill the seedling because he has labeled it as a weed or because it isn't conforming to what he thinks it should be. But I ask you, is that what parents, governments, religious institutions want to do? If your children don't meet up to your expectations and can't conform to your preconceived notions of what they should be do you prefer to physically, emotionally and spiritually destroy them? Do you want to make them feel so worthless and degraded and isolated hat they would rather die or kill themselves rather than struggle on with no support from family, friends or churches?

Or would you rather help them to grow and mature according to their own nature and learn to appreciate their own uniqueness and special qualities, allowing them to be all that they can be rather than what YOU want them and expect them to be? I wish to God that back in those days I had someone that I could have talked to: parents, a minister, a gay uncle or a counselor at school. Perhaps then I wouldn't have had to endure years of mental anguish, suffering, self-loathing, guilt, and suicidal feelings; all in a fruitless attempt to conquer feelings and tendencies that came from within and are unconquerable. I can't help but recall a religious cartoon that I once saw of a little boy kneeling by his bed praying to God and saying: "I guess I can't be all that bad, cuz God don't make no junk."

In 1958 we moved away from Newtown, it was just too far for my Dad to keep commuting to work. We moved to Trumbull, CT where I encountered a less naïve set of friends than I had hitherto known in Newtown. Now you must remember that up to this point, I had absolutely no knowledge of sexuality in any form; no father and son talk; nothing. Actually there never was to be any father and son discourse at any point, but that's another story. Everything I learned about sex came from friends and my brother. You must remember that in the 1950's there was no sex education in school so where would I get any information from? My first fragments of sexual knowledge came when my older brother slipped up and mentioned to me that he was now fertile and could father children if he chose.

Of course that didn't mean much to me because I didn't know what "fertile" meant. My friends for the most part were just as ignorant as I and told me that they believed that you could get a woman pregnant by urinating in her; they knew nothing of sperm or eggs or anything remotely like that so I pressed my brother further until he reluctantly shared some of the "sacred secrets" with me which suddenly brought me to the grand realization that I too might also be "fertile".

You see for the last 3 months prior to our talk, I had noticed that during my usual self-explorations and manipulations which had always resulted in some sort of climax and euphoria, I was now also experiencing more intense sensations accompanied by an emission of an unidentifiable body fluid. Until my talk with my brother, I had assumed that I had injured myself and was quite concerned because on an earlier occasion when my Mom caught me "touching myself", she had warned me that if I continued in that, I would injure myself and my health. So here, while I had thought that I was indeed reaping the just rewards of my unclean conduct, I discovered that Mother Nature was simply smiling upon me and rewarding me with an early puberty. Eventually, I did evolve a sense of pride in having successfully reached manhood, while at the same time exploding the myth of depleted health and sterility which was supposed to be the end result of " touching yourself". Of course I couldn't share my elation and pride with anyone in the family because then they would know that I had persisted in my sins. That joy was only meant to be experienced some fifteen years later at least on my honeymoon night and not before. But I was able to share my secret with other curious neighborhood boys who were also desperately seeking sex education which they were not receiving at home.

It wasn't long after that when I began experiencing my first limited sexual encounters with neighborhood boys. Oddly enough, at that point, I didn't really know for a fact that I was "gay"; hell, I had never even heard the term. I was just experimenting as all young men will do. Oddly enough, it was straight boys who lured me out and enticed me to have oral sex with them, both giving and receiving. I didn't know anyone who was gay. I thought that I was the only one in the world who was attracted to men and found it comforting to find that there were other boys my age who wanted to have sex with each other.

So for a short while I had my moment in the sun. I had known the sacred secrets which I imparted freely to all who asked. I had ceased being the outcast and weirdo; other boys relished my sexual favors. They didn't care if I was good at baseball or football so long as I gave them pleasure and I was good at that. What I failed to realize was that they were all just using me for practice and experimentation in preparation for the great and awe-inspiring day when they would finally be able to try this all out on neighborhood girls. I had no such fantasies. I was blissfully content just to be with them and satisfy their needs in the hope that eventually one of them would grow to love me. But no such luck.

I thought that I had found kindred spirits, but I was wrong. These same young men a few years later would attack me and ridicule me in the schoolyard; call me "faggot" and such and make my life miserable for engaging in the exact same activities that they had once engaged in. But you see, they realized that I was different. They had now graduated to molesting and abusing young girls and I had not so they were "normal" and I was the "queer". You see it's "normal" to feel up girls in the hallway and make unwelcome comments and advances, but God help anyone who looks at their butt or privates when they are in the shower; that's justification for a thick lip or a broken jaw.

But you know, the whole system is crazy. When you are 10-15 years of age you are supposed to hate girls and have nothing to do with them. If you hung out with girls you were a sissy. But then suddenly as if some atomic clock determines your life, at 15 or 16 you are now suddenly supposed to perform a 180 degree turn and love girls and date them. Hell, make up your mind. Well I'm sorry, but my biological clock did not tell me to change direction at age 16 nor 17 nor 21 nor 35 nor 55. But just remember that even a broken clock is right twice a day.

During that early period one of my male neighbors suggested that he bring his sister over so that we could have a three-some. I was appalled and horrified to say the least. You see young gay males do have their own innate sense of values and proprieties without the need for Bibles, Torahs or Korans. I had no intention of experimenting with my neighbor's sister just to see if I might be a latent heterosexual. Unlike my peers, I did not believe in using people for experimentation. I had hoped for a genuine relationship. Plus there just wasn't any attraction there.

I declined the offer and I felt betrayed and sick at heart. I knew that I had made a big mistake in not following through. Had I followed through, no one would have known that I was gay, but I refused to hide behind girls just to cover up my homosexuality; it's not fair to them; it's just using them. I had to be true to myself, I couldn't justify using other people to cover my tracks as so many others did. Of course I would pay dearly for that mistake later when my neighbor and all his friends were taunting me in the schoolyard, but at least I had maintained my integrity. They were the hypocrites. It wasn't long ago that they were all clamoring to get into my pants, but now they were all suddenly "straight".

It became apparent to me at an early age that morality was not a question of right or wrong; it wasn't a question of appropriate or inappropriate behavior; it was simply a question of power and authority. Because you see even on a Junior High level; the biggest, roughest and toughest guys could freely flounder back and forth between the straight world and the gay world and no one would dare call them a faggot because they had "proved their manhood" by maybe once in their life sleeping with a girl. I could have done the same thing, but I couldn't see sacrificing the girls' and my own integrity. Why do I have to prove that I am a man? I simply am. I don't need to prove anything to anyone. Just because I am refined and somewhat passive and like the finer and beautiful things in life does not make me a woman. No, I was not going to use another human being to prove a point. But I must say that I resented deeply those who used women to hide their real sexual preferences.

And I still do resent them. I resent authority figures who make the rules and yet are somehow above their own rules. I resent generals and admirals who have no problem at all coercing enlisted men into illicit affairs with them while the wife is away and then turning around and saying that gays are unfit for military service. I resent how the military can turn a blind eye to the immorality of enlisted men impregnating half of Southeast Asia and then saying that the presence of a gay recruit under the same barracks roof would be degrading.

I resent clergymen who remove gay parishioners from being lay readers or sacramental ministers while they themselves are molesting children and getting away with it with no sanctioning whatsoever from their superiors who know very well what they are doing. I resent governments legislators which are supposed to represent the needs of all citizens and who are supposed to keep a separation between Church and State who then pass anti-gay legislation based entirely upon Judeo-Christian ethics rather than based upon any valid civil needs or the needs of the community at large.

I resent the double standard that I see on every level of society. When was the last time that you saw a protest rally by priests and the Knights of Columbus protesting adultery or wife beating or the alarming illegitimacy rate of unwed mothers in this country? Never, and you never will because that kind of immoral behavior is "normal". Yet when two homosexuals who love each other dearly, have been in a monogamous relationship for 20 years and now want to legitimize it with a civil union try to do so, all hell breaks loose. "Oh God, it's the end of the world; it denigrates the institution of marriage." Well, I think that those men and women who DO have the right to marry but choose not to and would rather father 5 children by 5 different women or become pregnant by 5 different men and those married men with mistresses and those who abandon their families for a 20 year old secretary have denigrated marriage far more than we could ever hope to. But I digress.

Getting back to my Junior High peers who turned on me and abused me, I suppose that I shouldn't have felt singularly abused because they only treated me exactly the way that they treated their women. I think that's why I have learned such great compassion for women. I feel sorry for these young girls, who legitimately in love with these macho thugs, give themselves freely thinking that doing so will earn his love. While in bed everything is "Oh baby, you're the greatest; I think I love you." Then two hours later they are telling all of their friends what an "easy piece" she was and what a slut she was. It really makes one wonder how much these machos really do love women when they spend all their time just using them and degrading them.

If you ask me, I think that all of this macho womanizing translates into hatred of women not love. It could very easily be a way of covering up other deeper hidden feelings; possibly latent homosexual feelings by coming across as the stud, the lady's man, when in reality they would rather be with another man but lack the courage to make the transition. In my own experience I have met many men and found that the biggest "fag-bashers" and loud mouths on the surface are secretly prancing around at home in women's undergarments. And I say this from experience because I have had many fine, long-term friendships with straight men who were secure in their own sexuality and masculinity who are both respectful of their wives and respectful to me also and have no fear or problems with my homosexuality. Many of them have even attended gay weddings and such and treated them with the same respect that they would show at a straight wedding. God bless them!

The only good thing that came out of those turbulent Junior High School years is that my reputation preceded me and consequently, I finally did meet some other like-minded souls so I finally discovered that I was not alone and not the only "ugly duckling". But it was still difficult because I had been "outed" or exposed and so even other gay young men were often afraid to be seen with me; plus many were switch hitters and preferred to keep a girl handy to cover their tracks. I didn't want anyone like that; nor did I want just casual sexual encounters.

I wanted a love relationship, but it's pretty hard to find someone 14 or 15 years old who is committed. And there was no one that I could turn to for advice or help.

You see, when well–meaning parents turn out in droves to oppose sex education in the public schools or things like the "Rainbow Curriculum" designed not to promote homosexuality but to foster better understanding of the issue, those parents are presupposing that neither their children nor their friend' children are either gay or sexually active, but they are dead wrong and they are making a fatal mistake. They are afraid that their children will become gay if they are exposed to positive gay role models in school. But let's face it, the fact is that just about ALL GAY CHILDREN ARE BORN TO AND RAISED BY STRAIGHT PARENTS. If those parents are displaying a happy and secure marriage and family life to their children isn't it more than likely that the children will want to be like them? How can some minimal exposure to homosexuality and the problems and difficulties encountered by gay men and women suddenly cause a young person to switch boats mid-stream? I hardly think it would. Gay people live in a society that is almost exclusively heterosexual. The Church pushes heterosexuality; the military pushes heterosexuality; advertisers push heterosexuality; most movies and TV shows either display or promote heterosexuality.

Let's get real here. The fact that these parents, churches, educators et al are missing is that some children in Junior High have already identified themselves as homosexuals and are experiencing great emotional stress and turmoil; not because they are gay, but because of the hatred, the mockery, the name calling and the general ostracism leveled against gays by heterosexuals; not to speak of the physical violence. They need good, solid gay roll models; they need counseling; they need to know that they are not dirty and degraded and fit only for hell; they need to know that famous gays throughout history like Plato, Socrates, Hannibal, Alexander the Great, King Richard the Lion Heart, Michaelangelo, Leonardo Da Vinci, King James I, Walt Whitman, Leonard Bernstein, Cole Porter, Tennessee Williams and others have contributed much to the fabric of our society and that they can too.

Isn't the only sane and compassionate thing to give emotional and spiritual support to those young individuals in the public and private school systems who already identify as gay rather than making them feel isolated and lost at a time in life when young people want so desperately to fit in and be accepted by their peers ?

CHAPTER 7
TRANSITION AND LOSS

I can't stress enough the value of at home Moms. My Mom was the love of my life. We became such great friends over those years. While I couldn't discuss my sexual feelings with her at least she was always there for me when I cam home from school to dress my mental wounds and make me feel like I was worth something after suffering rejection and taunts all day long. Mom took a lot of the stress off of me by assuring me that I was, in deed, different from other children, but in a positive way. She assured me that in many ways I was superior to others and that I had to accept the fact that superiority and scholarship go hand in hand with ostracism because others are often jealous.

Perhaps that reassurance didn't make me feel any less lonely or left out, but at least it didn't make me feel inferior and worthless as I might have felt without her support. Whenever I felt unusually insecure or depressed she would let me take the day off from school and we would play chess together or she would have me read poetry to her or sometimes we would just watch schmaltzy WWII British movies together like "Mrs. Minivers' Roses" and we would sit there and cry into our individual cups of tea. Sometimes we would go for rides in the country and other times we would continue my education in British history and Royalty. She never lost sight of the dream that she and I would someday go back to England. She was very unhappy here and felt like a fish out of water; she was so much happier and alive in England. Since I had become so British over the years, I was her pride and joy and she told me often that I was the only reason that she had for living. Unfortunately, that dream of she and I returning to England was never to be realized.

Not long after our move to Trumbull in 1958, during one of our "skip-school" day jaunts riding in the country, Mom momentarily blacked out and side-swiped a city bus. Needless to say, she was very concerned and afraid to drive again until she could ascertain what had caused her blackout. After extensive testing, the results showed that she had developed a progressive and fatal kidney disease called uremia. Of course neither my Mom, nor my brother, nor I were made aware of that diagnosis by my Dad; we believed that her illness could be controlled with medication and that all would be well.

But as time went by, it became increasingly evident that all was not well because despite all the medications, Mom began having unexpected seizures which resembled epileptic seizures. There was no advance warning; no symptoms; they would just materialize out of no where. I had always been spiritual, but became far more spiritual during that period and of course tried to make all kinds of deals with God to make my Mom well. She prayed a lot too and again, longed to be back in England.

Things got continually worse and Mom was having seizures with more frequency from 1960 to 1961. I began losing a lot of time from school because she was afraid to be alone and I was afraid to leave her alone. You have to remember that there weren't all that many home care workers in those days and there was no such thing as dialysis to remove the impurities from Moms' blood and Dad had to work; my brother had just begun college in Storrs, Connecticut so there was only me to look after her. Oftentimes I would be in my room working on a project only to be startled by screams of terror coming from the living room when my Mom felt a seizure taking hold. I would rush to the room only to find her on the floor contorted and foaming at the mouth with her eyes rolled back into her head. It was a terrifying sight for a 12 or 13 year old all alone to deal with, but somehow I always managed to get my composure and call for an ambulance to get Mom to the hospital and then call my Dad to go to the hospital.

My Dad and my brother were always somehow exempt from this duty; they never had to witness her seizures and be alone with her during those hard times; it all fell on me. I lost so much time during the 1961-62 school year that I was kept back a year and never got to graduate with my classmates, but I never regretted the quality time that we spent together during those years and I was glad to have been there for my Mom.

My faith was beginning to erode so I had to make some new deals with God. Instead of asking Him to heal her outright, I promised that if he could just put her in remission and give her 4 or 5 good years so that we could return to England and she could at least have a few happy years and then die, I promised that I would become a priest or minister. But my all-good, Santa Claus-like God of those days who sees even the "fall of a sparrow", yet does nothing to keep it from falling, likewise, did nothing to save my Mom. In May of 1962 while Dad, Mom and I were out for a family drive, Mom went into a seizure; the first ever that Dad had witnessed.

Dad was horrified and didn't know what to do, but I was "old hat" at this and calmed him down and held onto Mom as we rushed to the hospital. She was in hospital for only 3 days and then released. So 3 days later we went to the hospital to pick her up. We were so happy to be bringing her home again and so was she. She wanted desperately to go home. We picked her up at around 11AM and within four blocks from the hospital she went into another seizure. We had to take her right back to the hospital from which she was never to leave again, at least not alive.

During the next two weeks I tried as best as I could to cheer her up. I brought in slides of England and reminded her of her dream to go back, but somehow, instinctively, she knew more than the doctors, Dad, or myself. She wept bitterly and squeezed my hand and told me that she would never see England gain, but that I should go back in her place to see and do all of the things that she had only dreamt of. I promised her that I would and I have kept that promise to this day. I have been to England many times and my home is filled with all of the British finery and memorabilia that my Mom would have loved and been proud of. I guess I sort of lived her life for her vicariously. It was getting very late that night even for the ICU. Mom was in an oxygen tent having difficulty breathing and filling up with fluids. I leaned into the oxygen tent and kissed her and told her that I had to leave but would see her the following day. Her eyes welled with tears; she kissed me and said: "no you won't". I knew what that meant but I hoped for the best.

The following day I was home after school talking with a friend on the phone and waiting for my Dad to come home and take us to the hospital. Dad came in earlier than usual and told me to hang up the phone. When I asked him why he just blurted out: "hang up the phone, your mother is dead." Well I certainly did hang up the phone and proceeded to my room to dismantle the little makeshift shrine that I had built in my room as an offering or perhaps a bribe to God to keep my Mom alive. Well, He apparently wasn't listening or occupied elsewhere; He had failed me and I hated Him. He had lied to me; he had told me in his Word: "If you ask anything in my name, it will be granted" John 14:14. Well I did and He didn't and so I no longer felt obligated to pour my heart out and grovel before a capricious, egomaniacal deity who didn't keep His promises. So I became an Agnostic for a time. I was angry with the doctors, clergy and even my Dad for not telling my brother and I the severity and finality of her illness. Had we known, we might have been able to handle those last 3 years differently, but it was too late now.

Those last four years from 1958 to 1962 had been very difficult and turbulent. For one thing, my brother, who was at that point well into puberty, had begun some heavy dating and sexual encounters; all to my parents' horror. You must remember that back in those days, sex before marriage was frowned upon; not like today where it is the norm. First of all you must understand that in my Moms' mind, there wasn't a woman alive good enough for her boys. In addition, her British background predisposed her to taking a dim view of other nationalities. Consequently, if the girls' family was anything other than British, she was unsuitable. And if she had a past, it was out of the question. So Mom disapproved of all of the girls that my brother dated and she and my brother fought constantly. Whenever my brother "fought dirty" by bringing up our maternal grandmother's questionable past and morals, Mom would go wild and then Dad would get involved in it, threatening to punch my brothers' lights out. On several occasions these arguments did in fact culminate in fist fighting and wrestling between my Dad and my brother.

Our last Christmas together as a family was spent with my brother drunk out of his mind, fist fighting with my Dad and with Mom screaming in the background her usual condemnation: "You just put another nail in your mothers' coffin". It was not pretty. And apparently it left scars on my brothers' mind as well because I have heard that for years, my brother was afraid to visit our mothers' grave; that every time he did, he would have some kind of car accident shortly thereafter and believed that she was reaching out of the grave to "get him".

Then too, when I look back over the years, I can honestly say that I can't recall my Mom ever showing any kind of affection to my Dad. On Saturday mornings he would get up early, put the coffee on and make breakfast for all of us. I still remember the heavenly aroma of that coffee, mingled with that of bacon frying and the strains of polkas playing on the radio. Dad would usually get playful then and run over to Mom and attempt to kiss her and pull her onto our kitchen "dance floor" to dance a polka with him. But she would not have any of it and would always push him away and say that he was being ridiculous. Some 18 years later, when I saw my Dad dancing with my stepmother at a wedding, I broke down crying and had to leave the room because you see, I had never seen Mom and Dad dance together and show affection toward one another, and I would so much have loved to have seen that.

Mom would also purposely stay up watching TV every night until 1 or 2 AM in the hopes that by the time she did retire, he would be sound asleep and therefore she would not have to be intimate with him. And yet despite all of this physical and mental deprivation, Dad continued to love her dearly and never strayed or cheated; he was a saint. Yet Mom didn't seem to appreciate him; she spoke often to me of all of the finer men she could have had. She put down his lack of education, his weight, the way he dressed; just about everything and was continually planning her escape or should I say "our" escape. So you see, this was not exactly a "Leave It To Beaver" situation. Nor was it one which would inspire a young man teetering on the edge of the fissure which lies between hetero and homosexuality to want to make the leap and plant his feet firmly in the heterosexual world replete with a non-responsive, asexual, terminally ill wife and troublesome children.

Now had we all known that Mom was terminally ill, perhaps then, we would have all made more of an effort to pull things together; make amends for past hurts and lead a reasonably balanced and happy life together for those last four years. We would have had some happy memories and no regrets. But as it turned out, we did not know and when the final day came, we were left with nothing but sad memories, guilt and the frustration of never being able to turn the clock back and make up for the unhappiness we had heaped upon Mom and ourselves during her last days on earth.

When Mom died, a large part of me died with her. You see, she was the only one who supported me in my spiritual and artistic pursuits. I had a natural flare for art. I loved painting and building things and Mom would always encourage that and rave to everyone about my talents and the beautiful things that I had created. Dad, on the other hand, would only complain about the smell of the paints and glues and the mess that I had made in the process of creating. He seemed to feel that all of my projects were foolish and a waste of time.

When Mom was sick and could no longer drive, she just about had to beg neighbors and even my brother, to take her places. Consequently I longed for the day when I would be able to drive; I would have loved to have driven her anywhere. I loved making her lunches and her tea; I love waiting on her and playing chess together. There isn't anything that I wouldn't have done for her and I looked forward to the day when I would have a job and be able to buy her all of the lovely things that she wanted and which Dad could not afford what with all of her medical expenses. I wanted her to be at my graduation; I wanted to take her back to England again only in grand style this time and do all of the things that we had never been able to afford in the past. I wanted to buy her beautiful clothes and jewelry and shower her with gifts. But all of those dreams were dashed to pieces and lost forever when she died. It was as if my whole world and reason for being came to and end at that point. I was inconsolable, not that anyone tried to console me anyway. We all grieved separately, but not together, not as a family.

Eventually my brother returned to college and my Dad to his 10 hour work days and I was left entirely alone.

Even visiting with the one or two friends that I had at that time was only a source of mental pain to me because when I saw the at least seemingly happy family lives that they had, I was only reminded of what was sadly lacking in my own life and faced with the stark reality that life would never be the same again. Even when Dad was at home, he would mostly complain about my continual absences and that I was neglecting my duties at home. And of course now, I understand that he was grieving too and felt abandoned, but back then, I simply felt that I had no one to come home to. That period was probably the period of my greatest sexual activity during adolescence and it makes perfect sense, for to quote Blanche DuBois in "Streetcar Named Desire", "… the opposite of death is desire." Having experienced nothing but prolonged illness and death over the last four years, I filled the void with sensuality and the hope that someone would come along who would appreciate me and love me.

CHAPTER 8
FINDING GOD

During the spring break from school in 1963, I was at home and on the phone talking to a friend, in fact, one of my sex partners, when the doorbell rang. I wasn't going to go to the door, it was probably only a salesman, but something prompted me to make an exception this time. So I opened the door and was faced with two very sweet and well-dressed ladies who asked me if I had ever lost a loved-one and how I would feel if I knew that I wouldn't have to wait years until I died to be reunited with them, but that there was strong reason to believe that God was going to bring about His Kingdom on Earth within the next ten years. Not only that, but He was going to resurrect all of our loved ones and they would be able to live eternally along with us on a newly restored paradise earth. Well, that certainly grabbed my attention; they couldn't have picked a better topic so I invited them in.

Now you have to remember that from my Mom's death, I had begun to truly hate God and had turned away from all religious thought. But these two ladies explained to me very convincingly and using the Bible, that God was not my enemy, but that Satan had killed my Mom and that God had only allowed him to rule over the earth for a limited, set period of time and the expiration of that time period was now at hand. They assured me that God would "wipe away every tear" and that death would be no more, "neither mourning nor pain"-Rev 21:4. So you see, according to them, God had not lied to me; He would keep his promise, but all in due time and not according to mans' reasoning.

Well, I was absolutely elated ! It was the first time that I had heard some good news since my Mom had died. I don't know why I immediately believed them; perhaps it was because they handled the Bible with such expertise and spoke with such authority and conviction; perhaps it was because they were so kind and compassionate and seemed to be genuinely concerned with my pain and well-being, I mean it's not like they were selling something or looking for money. And perhaps I believed them because it was what I WANTED to believe, even though there wasn't a scrap of scientific or empirical evidence to prove their theories. Let's face it: God hadn't intervened in the affairs of man for almost two thousand years, if ever. And there was no reason to believe that He was going to do anything now or within the next ten years. But perhaps my loneliness and wishful thinking prompted me to invite them back that evening.

Now that evening I was supposed to be going out grocery shopping with Dad, so when he arrived home, I advised him that I wouldn't be able to go with him because I had invited two of Jehovah's Witnesses to come over and study the Bible with me. My Dad was furious and advised me that I could do whatever I wanted, but that I had made a terrible mistake and that if I ever let Jehovah's Witnesses into our home, that I would never be able to get rid of them. He was right, or almost right; time would tell.

That evening they brought with them a very tall, attractive 30 ish young man; they were astute enough to believe that what I desperately needed was a "big brother" image in my life. They, of course were not aware that I was very attracted to 25-30 year old handsome men, much more than to my peers. In any event, John and I immediately hit it off and he did, in deed, become like a big brother to me and a mentor. He made me feel special and he showed interest in the things that I said and created; much more so than my dad or brother. I was also very attracted to him. He was tall, broad shouldered, lean and strong and always sported a five o'clock shadow no matter how often he shaved, but more than that he was also kind, gentle and sincere and showed genuine concern, which made him even more attractive to me. Of course, knowing how most religious institutions react toward homosexuality, I didn't dare let on to John that I had this problem. I know that he wouldn't have beat me up; that wasn't the problem. What I feared more was that he would feel uncomfortable around me or worse yet, abandon me and I really needed his strength and companionship at that point in my life.

Eventually, without ever asking, I found out the view of Jehovah's Witnesses regarding homosexuality and it was even worse than I feared. Unlike other religions who although not encouraging it, at least have some tolerance; Jehovah's Witnesses have no tolerance whatsoever. Anyone practicing homosexual behavior is promptly excommunicated or "disfellowshipped". Anyone suspected of being gay, even though celibate, is still avoided like the plague and most Witnesses will not associate with them. So I had a real problem on my hands. What to do? It was a question of priorities. What did I need more? Continued casual sexual encounters with people who did not and would not ever love me or reunion with God, the hope of eternal life on earth with my Mom and even now the genuine love of my new brothers and sisters of Jehovah's Witnesses.

I opted for love; genuine love; not temporary love engendered by sexual favors. I felt certain that I could sublimate my sexual desires if only my spiritual and emotional needs were being met. Plus John explained to me from the Bible how the Holy Spirit changed lives and made us all a "new creation". Maybe I could be "born again" and this time straight, not gay. Then I wouldn't have to spend the rest of my life hiding my feelings and living a half-life of strictly monitored and self-imposed celibacy. So I decided to leave my gay life behind and continue my Bible study and association with the Witnesses.

I was richly rewarded when a whole new world opened to me. Most of the other Witnesses were very much like John; warm, loving, caring, and sincere and they all took me under their wings. All of a sudden I went from having no real family and no real friends to having a multitude of fathers, mothers, sisters and brothers. What an oasis of love compared to the dessert of loneliness and rejection that I had been experiencing before. So I threw myself, body, heart, mind and soul into the Watchtower Society. There were some teachings along the way that I found either confusing or irrational and difficult to accept, but I think that I simply put those on the "back burner" certain that they would someday be resolved and because I wanted so desperately to belong to this new family and fit in.

In a short time, I was baptized as one of Jehovah's Witnesses against my father's and brother's wishes; they said that I was out of my mind, but then who were they to tell me what to do? They were never there for me; they weren't interested in anything spiritual at all; they never supported me in any of my dreams and endeavors; it was always all foolishness to them. Needless to say, they did not attend my baptism nor support me in any way, but my new found brothers and sisters certainly did. And they fortified me and prepared me for the future, explaining that I should expect persecution and ostracism by family and old friends because Jesus was doing a harvesting work, separating the sheep from the goats, the worthy from the unworthy. They advised me that it was best for me to separate myself from those who may not be found worthy to live in the Kingdom now, so that I would not be hurt and grieved later on when they were to be annihilated at the coming Battle of Armageddon and the end of the old world.

The Witnesses stressed celibacy for young people and didn't encourage marriage prior to the coming of the Kingdom to Earth; time enough for that then. They felt that we should spend all our time preaching the coming Kingdom and put God ahead of our emotional or sexual needs. So at least there wasn't any pressure on me to date or marry. But of course I would have to continue to bridle my sexual appetite and never let on to anyone the kind of "main courses" that I preferred. So I was forced to live a lie and endure mental pain and anguish every time I had to sit though a scathing sermon on the human degradation and abominable and eternal plight of homosexuals. But of course there was the distant hope that someday God would heal me.

One of the Witness families became especially dear to me; a Norwegian family made up of a mom, dad, three brothers and one sister. They were especially kind to me and had me over for dinners frequently and often over for entire weekends. You see, I was a fast learner and a devoted Witness. I threw my entire life into it and rose rapidly through the ranks. I was conducting Bible studies myself now and even preaching sermons from the pulpit on Sundays. They were all astounded at my spiritual growth and thought that I was a fine example for the young people in the congregation. They were also sad for me that the price I had paid for this was the loss of my own family. So they became my family. They also had some ulterior motives because they felt that since I was so filled with the Spirit, that I would be a good influence on their sons and daughters. At this point, I was 18 and the three sons in question were 10,14 and 16.

I became especially fond of and attracted to the 14 year old son. We'll call him "K" for the purposes of privacy. "K" was just so spunky and full of life; he was such a joy to be with and also artistic like me; he did beautiful water colors of country scenes and still life and also caricatures and cartoons. We took an immediate liking for one another. And when he made the first move and asked me to be his friend. How could I refuse ? I began picking him up from school from time to time and taking him out for snacks and to the movies, etc. In no time at all, he began responding very warmly to me.

As soon as we were clear of the school, he would invariably scoot across the car from the passenger seat and throw his arms around me and give me a big hug and often remain right next to me rather than returning to the passenger side of the seat. He was always making some kind of physical contact with me. Even in the Witness meeting hall, the Kingdom Hall, when he thought no one was looking, he would cautiously lock pinkies with me or pinch my leg or play footsies with me under tables. He really seemed to love me and I knew that by this point I had most certainly fallen in love with him because I had never felt this way before in my life. Oh, I had dated somewhat in High School and had gone to proms and all. Hell, I had even gone on back roads necking, but somehow was never able to feel anything whatsoever. The only way that I can describe my feelings on those dates is that it was as though my body was shot through with Novocain.

I couldn't feel anything and was just going through the motions and acting out what was expected of me by my unsuspecting partner. But with "K" it was entirely different. "K" was magic; he aroused me; he filled me with desire; I wanted to kiss him from head to foot; I longed to be with him; I couldn't think of anything or anyone else but him. I had never felt anything like this, not even with my previous male sexual partners. Oh they were arousing and I functioned much better with them than with women, but this was different. This was the first time that I was experiencing love and I was filled with joy; I felt like a balloon about to burst.

Just as in the case of riding in my car; whenever his parents allowed him to spend a weekend at my place; the sleeping arrangement was supposed to have been that he would sleep in my brother's empty room and I would sleep in my own; there was only a twin bed in each room; not double or full-sized beds. But invariably as the night progressed, "K" would always steal down the hall and end up in my bed. We would tickle each other or wrestle or have pillow fights and would always end up cuddled together for the remainder of the night. He would usually lie in front of me with me behind with my arms around him and he, holding my hands which were clasped around his abdomen. I loved the scent of his hair and having him close to me, but it aroused me and I was very fearful that he would feel my erection. Oftentimes I had to carefully sneak out of bed and "take care of the problem" so that I could get some sleep. I can't say that I fantasized making love to him while I "took care of the problem", that was entirely out of the question and I didn't want to even entertain the thought. I simply "took care of the problem.

First of all, I deeply respected and loved my new found religion and secondly, I could not endanger the eternal welfare of the young man whom I had grown to love so deeply, so I wasn't about to encourage anything. At no time did I ever fondle him or touch him inappropriately. I wanted to keep this relationship on a purely spiritual and unconditional love level; I wanted our love to be pure and beautiful and not motivated in any way by sexual needs. I felt certain that I could control myself and keep it on this level so long as I had his love and I did. His love meant far more to me than sex, which I guess told me that I really was genuinely in love for the first time in my life.

It was unbearable to be separated from him. During the week when we could not be together, I would drive up to his house, turn off my headlights and just sit outside on the street gazing longingly up at his window. I found joy and peace just knowing that he was there and it was the next best thing to actually being with him. Whenever I could not be there, the next best thing was sleeping with one of the T shirts that he had given me, carefully placed on my pillow so that I could smell his scent and fantasize that he was actually in my bed.

I remember one time when we were swimming in a friend's pool, he, carelessly dove feet first into the shallow end of the pool and sprained his leg. I was hysterical. Even though I did not swim very well, I threw myself into the pool, dragged him out and carried him in my arms to my car to take him home. When we got to his house no one was home so I helped him undress and change into his pajamas. Again, I couldn't bring myself to actually look at his naked young body as I helped him change clothes; to me that seemed as though I would be violating him so I sort of looked beyond him while helping him dress. Then I carried him to his bed and deposited him there. I was just about to leave, but felt compelled to go back to his bed and kiss him gently on the forehead before leaving. He didn't seem shocked or surprised; it was probably the same manner in which his mother had often kissed him. It was a pure and holy kiss and something that I needed to do. I had wanted to kiss him for as long as I had known him and this was my only chance and as far as I could go. I told him that I would pray for his swift recovery and pray I did. Actually, I prayed to God that He would take most of "K"s pain and give it to me so that he would not be in any discomfort.

Weeks later when he had recovered, I went out and bought us matching gold rings with our names inscribed inside of each other's ring. I justified in all based on the covenant that David and Jonathan had made in the Bible at I Samuel 20:41, 42 which now, in the light of reality, makes me question exactly what kind of relationship David and Jonathan had. I mean what exactly does it mean, when upon Jonathan's death, David states: "I am distressed for you, my brother Jonathan; you have been very pleasant to me; your love to me was wonderful, surpassing the love of women." –II Samuel 1:26. In any event, since I had the keys to the Kingdom Hall, I arranged a private and simple little ceremony for "K" and I, during which we read the passages relating to David and Jonathan, washed each other's feet, exchanged the rings and promised everlasting love for one another; ending in a warm embrace. Sort of a makeshift wedding to be sure, but of course I couldn't let on to "K" that this was my intent.

Although when I look back now, he must have known and must have been feeling the same things that I was, since he usually initiated everything; I mean it was he who had first asked me to be his friend and he who kept climbing into my bed. Who knows? Maybe in a different world without social taboos and restraints, the normal progress from boyhood to manhood might just be loving one of your own sex first, learning how to love another human fully, and then progressing on to love the opposite sex and the children which result from that union. That's certainly the way it was in the ancient Greek world.

Of course when his mother saw the ring, she became concerned. She thought that it looked odd and was concerned about what others might say. I think that she may have had some mother's intuition as to where this was headed and began scheduling his time so that he was spending more time at home and with other friends. But he got over it quickly; he was a very bubbly and amiable young man; loved and sought after by all. I think that I was much more in love with him than he with me; he was just as happy to be with his other friends who he had neglected, but I was not. Oddly enough, his mother counseled me that it was not fair for me to spend so much time with "K", when her older son, "T" was very lonely and hurt that I didn't have any time for him. In retrospect, "T" might have been the better choice. He was very handsome; far more handsome and physically developed than "K"; emotional, loyal and sincere.

Years later while vacationing with "T" and other friends, in Switzerland, we got separated in the hotel we were staying at. "T" ended up staying with a mutual friend in one room and I was by myself in another. In the middle of the night, "T" came to my room to visit for no justified reason. He was in his pajamas and began playfully tossing around statements with sexual innuendos. He asked me if I was lonely sleeping in that room all by myself. I teased him saying that I would not be alone for long; that I was going to go down to the lobby and see if there was someone who wanted to share my bed with me. He taunted me saying: "Why would anyone want to sleep with you? You probably don't have much that anyone would want. I have more.", at which point he dared me to compare our "manhood", to which I readily agreed. He dropped his pajama bottoms, as did I and we both stood motionless gazing at each other's eyes and then each other's prowess; then each other's eyes and again each other's prowess; each of us afraid to make the next move based upon our religious training and constrictions. We were both at "full attention" and I think he wanted me as badly as I wanted him at that moment, but suddenly he became frightened and said that he should probably go back to his room and that we should forget that this ever happened.

It's a pity that I lacked the courage to make the first move and a pity that what was obviously very natural for both of us was thwarted by our religious convictions because I'm sure that he would have made a marvelous and loyal partner and that we might still be together to this day, because that's the kind of sincerity and loyalty that he exhibited. As it turned out years later, he ended up in a very unhappy marriage; was betrayed by his wife and ended up divorced. And I too, ended up betrayed by several partners who lacked the kind of sincerity and devotion that "T" had to offer. But I digress. We need to get back to my relationship with his brother.

During my relationship with "K", I became overwhelmed and frightened by the things I was feeling. You see, I still entertained some small hope that God was ultimately going to heal me, but it certainly didn't seem as though that's where I was heading. I had never felt the kind of strong, overpowering feelings for any woman that I had felt for "K" and didn't know what to do, so I took a terrible risk and asked to talk to one of the elders who I felt was at least a little more liberal and understanding than the others. After explaining to him what I had been going through, his advice was not to share this information with anyone else and ignore the feelings.

He said that the Devil was simply trying to lure me and make me think that I was a homosexual because I was a valuable asset to God's Organization and he wanted to either drive me crazy and get me to kill myself or at least lure me away from the "Truth" and effectively destroy one of God's chosen servants. He suggested that I immediately apply for service at the Watchtower headquarters in Brooklyn, NY and get myself away from "K" so that I would no longer be tempted. He assured me that in Brooklyn, surrounded by so many "Spirit-begotten Sons of God" and their good influence that I would soon be whole again.

During the interim period, I took on a new Bible student who had been referred to me; we'll call him "E". He was a young chef from New Haven who had become interested in the Bible and Jehovah's Witnesses. It was very refreshing and a joy to spend time with "E". He was older and more mature than my previous object of affection; very attractive; drove a motorcycle and had his own little place with no parents present to get in the way. It wasn't long before I found myself attracted to him. The fact that he looked up to me and admired my depth of knowledge and needed me to teach him was very enticing. So we traded favors. I taught him about the Bible and he taught me the rudiments of gourmet cooking; it was a nice exchange.

There was a great difference in this relationship because while "K" was just an adolescent, "E" was definitely a MAN and I had never had a relationship with a man before. He would take me for rides on his motorcycle and I would ride on the back with my arms wrapped around his abs; loving it all to death. Even though I was deathly afraid of motorcycles, I conquered that fear because if afforded me an opportunity to be physically close to him and hold him without anyone being any the wiser; not even him since he was, presumably straight.

I knew that I was headed for deep trouble again because my feelings for "E" were growing in leaps and bounds. He gave me a pair of his motorcycle boots that I treasured and used to sleep with just to have something that had been next to his body near me. During the Black

Panther riots in New Haven, when the Panthers were rioting and burning buildings, I rushed to New Haven in a blizzard to get "E" out of there because I was concerned that he would be harmed or worse killed. Yep, I was falling in love again and had to nip this one in the bud. That's why when the letter finally came from the Watchtower Society, inviting me to serve at their headquarters for the next four years, I accepted readily and couldn't pack fast enough. I was fleeing for dear life.

Somehow it never dawned on me that living in an eleven story building with approximately 900 other healthy and fit young males would pose a problem. So off I went in February of 1967 to my new home and hopefully new life. My friends all threw me a lovely going away party which my Dad attended. All of the Witnesses told Dad how proud they were of me to which he responded that he was proud of me also and he gave me a big hug. I was deeply moved; it was a touching moment and the first time in 20 years that my Dad had ever touched me or told me that he was proud of me.

CHAPTER 9
RUDE AWAKENINGS

My vision of the Watchtower headquarters home known as "Bethel" was highly overrated and totally incorrect. I guess I thought that I was entering a seminary where I would receive a full and thorough seminary education in exchange for helping print Bibles and religious books and tracts in the printing factory nearby. How wrong I was. The majority of my time was spent in the factory and precious little time spent at education aside from the normal five weekly evening meetings that I was used to back in my old congregation in Connecticut. We worked five and a half days per week in the factory and had one evening class which largely consisted of studying the Bible via Witness related study aids giving their interpretation of the Bible. I had expected a regular course of study like one would have at any normal seminary with courses in perhaps comparative religion, psychology, teaching, philosophy, etc. but I should have known better because they were against all forms of higher education.

While I had been studying with Jehovah's Witnesses back home, I was accepted at and ready to go attend the University of Connecticut. In fact I already had some credits there from advance placement English and history courses which I had taken while in High School. But the Witnesses took a very dim view of secular higher education and warned me that many had lost their faith while in college. They also assured me that God's Kingdom would be established by 1974 on earth so it was pointless to work toward a career in this "dieing old world" when a New World was at hand. So I never did enter college after graduation from High School, much to my father and brother's consternation. Instead, one of the local elders had given me a 3 day per week job at his factory to finance my local ministry and keep me in gasoline; my needs at that point were minimal and very simple. That's why I jumped at the opportunity to go to Bethel because I thought that I could get my education there. Well I certainly did get an education there. I graduated from the "School of Stark Reality" and ended up doing post graduate work in the "School of Hard Knocks".

Initially, I was put to work in the Bethel Home doing cleaning and light maintenance. Since I was highly artistic and good at writing, I had hoped that I might be used in the graphic or writing department. Since I was also good at public speaking and teaching I had also hoped that I might someday become an instructor, but none of that was ever to be. But I was patient. I was well aware that it was common practice in seminaries to be given humble, menial and often degrading jobs initially to break one of the sin of pride; plus everyone had to pay their dues. So I was obedient and steadfast at whatever assignment I was given. Eventually things did change.

I was assigned to the printing factory bindery, which I thought to be a step up and an honor; wrong again. What I hadn't anticipated was the boredom and monotony of working on an assembly line and the stress of trying to keep up with machines that were running much faster than I could. If your ability to feed material into these machines did not keep pace with the machines; they would temporarily shut down, production time would be lost and you would be severely chastised. All day long I had to untie heavy bundles of segments of books which had been stacked and tied under pressure. I had to untie them and then load the signatures or segments into a machine which gathered them into complete books. The boards at either end had slivers and the ropes burned when you loosened them. There was no air conditioning in the factory. So there I stood for over eight hours a day; sweat pouring off of me; hands bleeding from splinters and rope burn; legs and back in pain from bending and lifting while the foremen yelled: "faster, faster, faster". Hell, I couldn't go any faster, I thought that I would pass out. So finally I made another incorrect assumption.

I assumed that Christian brothers would have compassion and patience and realize that I was working as hard and fast as I possibly could and that I was doing my job to the best of my ability. So I begged them to send me back to my old job in the home; cleaning toilets and showers. But they refused. They assured me that God does not make mistakes and that it was His Will that I remain where I was. They suggested that perhaps I wasn't dedicated enough and should perhaps simply be dismissed from the facility entirely.

Now apparently, I wasn't the only one having this difficulty. My roommate, who had at first been a waiter in the Bethel Home was also now working in the factory sewing Bibles together on an old, outmoded 1940's style book stitching machine. He found the pace and monotony so terrible that he did the unthinkable. He thrust his hand into the machine and allowed the needles to puncture his hand just so that he would be taken off of the job. It worked. I should have been so smart.

Now coupled with the frustration of the factory assembly line was also the fact that I was intensely lonely and missed all of my friends back home. There was none of the love and comradeship here that I had experience back home. I had no visits from my family or friends and little correspondence; I was intensely unhappy. I mean when my brother was at college, either we, as a family, would go to visit with him or he would come and stay with us for the weekend every two weeks. Yet when I was at Bethel no one came to see me in almost two years; I was heart broken. My system began closing down. I had been transferred to the sewing department; the same as my roommate and like him; couldn't stand the boredom and began falling asleep at the machine. I just couldn't stay awake. I began missing meetings and classes because I just couldn't stay awake. I finally went to a doctor to see what was wrong. The doctor assured me that there was in fact nothing physically wrong with me, but that he felt I was suffering under deep and chronic depression and should probably see a psychiatrist. Well, that was just out of the question. Jehovah's Witnesses DO NOT go to psychiatrists; God heals all in time.

Of course as I mentioned earlier that Blanche DuBois' remedy for depression and death is "desire", so too, I found myself in the same situation. There is simply nothing more life affirming than desire. Not all of the Bible studies nor Witness propaganda; not all of the prayers and pleadings for God to "remove the thorn" from my side; not all of the meetings or sermons nor the fact of living in this Holy Place were able to help me or quench my thirst. All of the old feelings started coming back with a vengeance. Of course, with the exception of infrequent masturbation, I still couldn't allow myself to act upon any of my desires or fantasies. I began to hate myself for that. Perhaps I just didn't deserve to be in this Holy Place; perhaps I was totally unworthy; perhaps I simply deserved to be cast out into the darkness just like Adam and Eve were cast out of the Garden of Eden. Perhaps I had no right to defile my brothers and sisters by my mere presence there. I was filth; a Sodomite; destined for eternal destruction when Christ returns; I didn't belong here. This is what I had to live with day and night with no one that I could turn to for help. I couldn't dare discuss this with anyone.

I finally did make some new friends at Bethel. They were almost as unhappy and frustrated as I, but at least I now had someone that I could share some of my frustrations with, but certainly not all. We only received a small monthly allowance of $15. 00 per month and a supply of subway tokens so that we could get to our congregation meetings. Most of our needs were taken care of but the allowance was for incidentals like toothpaste, postage stamps, etc. Consequently if you wanted to go to a movie or something and didn't have an independent source of money, you needed to find a part-time job outside of the facility, which was frowned upon by the Society. So my small circle of friends got part-time jobs as cater-waiters and such. We all seemed to love the same things: Broadway musicals; Classical music concerts; art shows;

nice restaurants, etc. so we saved our money so that we could escape the boredom and maybe once every two weeks go out on the town. At other times we would get together on a Saturday night and just get plastered. Oddly enough there were no restrictions against drinking at the Bethel home and the dumpsters were always piles high with bottles and beer cans by Monday morning.

While working as a cater-waiter, I met another fellow Witness who also worked in the same sewing department with me, but I had never notice him there before; guess I was just too busy trying to keep up with the work and keep from sewing my hand into a Bible. But I notice him at the catering facility; he was so strikingly handsome in his waiter uniform; I couldn't take my eyes off of him. He was taller than me with thick, shiny black hair, my favorite 5 o'clock shadow, and a tight, lean frame with broad shoulders. He was part Scottish; part Mexican with flashing dark Latin eyes and beautiful full lips. His name was D---d. You figure it out. "D" was just so suave, worldly and sophisticated. He loved opera, ballet, classical music, cocktail lounges, fine food, fine wines, etc. He immediately asked me if I would like to accompany him to Lincoln Center sometime. Well, of course, I jumped at the opportunity. I was so completely drawn to him and began going places with him exclusively and he with me; so much so that my roommates began taunting me whenever they answered the door and "D" was standing outside. They would whisper to me: "Your date is here" or "Your lover is on the phone". Little did they know they weren't far from wrong, or maybe they did know.

All I know is that I was totally smitten. I couldn't take my eyes off of him and was so proud to be seen with him. We would dress in tuxes and go to the opera; we would go to the botanical gardens and take pictures of each other; he would often put his arm around me or massage my neck. Of course he did tell me that he had been quite the lady's man back in his hometown congregation in San Jose, but he also spoke of his love for San Francisco, so I wasn't sure quite what to make of all of this. All I knew was that he had made my life more full and rich; that he was with me now and I wasn't going to worry about the future.

But then the fateful day came; something that I hadn't planned on and was totally unexpected. He told me that his roommate was leaving Bethel and asked if I would move in with him. Well, is the Pope Catholic? How could I not? I was elated, but at the same time worried. Why was he doing this? Was he feeling what I was feeling? And if he was and we were living together, how long would we be able to refrain from taking this to the next stage? How long could we keep this relationship on a Platonic level? How long could we keep from acting on our feelings and how could we act upon them without jeopardizing our faith and promise of everlasting life in God's Kingdom on Earth? Of course we wouldn't have to tell anyone; we could keep it to ourselves and be discreet. But that wouldn't work. Surely God would ferret us out and expose us for the degenerates that we were. We would be exposed to public shame to say nothing of eternal damnation. Maybe this wasn't such a good idea. What should I do? I didn't want to hurt his feelings; I didn't want to reject him when I needed his company and his love so very much. So I mustered my courage and told him "Yes, I would love to be your roommate."

Well, we got along just famously and really enjoyed living together. We both knew that at the end of a hard day, we had each other to go home to and that we would "lick each other's wounds", not literally of course, and make each other feel good. Living with "D" made life more bearable and worth living. But of course it was difficult being in such close proximity and not being able to touch him or kiss him or fully express myself or enquire as to whether he felt the same way about me. But there certainly was a lot of non-verbal communication going on. Oftentimes when I was lying on my bed reading, I would be aware of him watching me and staring intently at me. But as soon as I looked at him, he would quickly divert his gaze or pretend that he was reading. Also many times when I was shaving in the morning, he would come up behind me and put his arms around me and give me a bear hug and say things like: "you're so squeezable, you little imp".

Whenever he touched me, I would melt; I was really starting to fall head over stilettos in love with him. I would lie awake at night propped up on one elbow just watching the moonlight on his face and wishing that I could be in bed with him and make love to him. And then he made it even worse, he suggested that we make our small room more like a living room by dividing it up into a sitting area and a sleeping area; this meant putting our beds together on one side of the room in sort of an "L" formation. Well of course, now we were sleeping with our heads only maybe two feet from each other and I could almost feel his breath on my face. I was going nuts. I wanted him so badly, but we just couldn't and again, since nothing had been verbalized, I couldn't really be certain if the attraction was mutual. Was he waiting for me to make the first move? Well I just couldn't . I mean this just wasn't Sadie Hawkins Day ; nor was it "ladies' choice.

The next day while I was shaving, he did it again. He came up to me and said: "Gee, Bob, you have small hands." To which I replied: "My Mom always told me that I had surgeons hands; that I would make a good surgeon because I could get my hands into tight places." At that point he told me to hold out my hands and he placed his hands against mine; palm to palm and said: "Look how much bigger my hands are than yours." At which point he then wrapped his fingers around my hands and we stood there motionless palm to palm gazing directly into each other's eyes for what seemed like an eternity though it was only momentary. Finally he suddenly diverted his eyes; released his grip on my hands and almost pushed me away nervously; said he had to go take a shower and left the room. I think that he was afraid of what he saw in my eyes. I think that he was afraid of what he was feeling and that's what caused him to panic. Unfortunately, the moment was lost.

Now you will remember that I told you before about how "D" had related all of these war stories to me about what a playboy he had been and how many hearts he had broken back home, etc. etc. Now once you had been at Bethel for four years, it was sort of like military duty, you were free to leave without any disgrace or any problem. On the other hand, you were also free to stay indefinitely. Now at some point down the line, "D" would also be free to leave, go back to California and break some more hearts. But suddenly one night after work he said to me: "Bob, we need to talk". Now we had been getting along wonderfully, so I was a little concerned about this need to talk; talk about what? Did I talk in my sleep? Had he found out something about me? Oh my God.

So "D" sat me down and proceeded to make me the following offer: "If I told you right now that I am going to write these girls back home "Dear John letters" and tell them not to wait for me. And if I told you that I have decided to stay here at Bethel indefinitely, would you promise to stay here with me indefinitely? Well, I could have been floored. Was this some kind of veiled proposal? What exactly was he asking of me? What did he mean? I didn't know what to say; it was so sudden and so unexpected; plus I wasn't all that thrilled with Bethel. Maybe if he had put his cards on the table and said: "Let's run away from here and make a life for ourselves together in San Francisco." I would have said "Yes, yes, yes." But he didn't say that. Of course I wanted to be with him and would gladly have stayed with him "until death us do part", but I didn't want Bethel as part of the package. So I told him that I would have to give it some serious thought. At which point he seemed to grow cold and distant as though I had rejected him. Things were not quite the same after that.

Now the Witnesses were dead wrong in their definitions of homosexuality. They defined homosexuality as simply an overly exaggerated, animalistic, compulsive sexual drive lacking any sense of responsibility. They said that since these people didn't want to be responsible for a wife or children, they would rather simply have sex with each other to avoid the possibility of commitment or responsibility. But being a homosexual, I was certainly in a better position to know what I was feeling inside than they were. I had already fallen madly in love with three men without the benefit of sexual relations in any of those relationships and yet I loved them intensely and would have died for any one of them had the need been there, so how could anyone say that my love for these men was based soley upon an over exaggerated sex drive? My God, I wasn't even having sex and refrained from it specifically to protect them. I didn't want to defile them or get them into trouble or saddle them with guilt. I loved them enough NOT to have sex with them. Now that's a real twist wouldn't you say? This is why I believe that true homosexuality goes far deeper than sex. Bisexuality is more frivolous and may fit in closer with the Witness definition of someone who "wants their cake and eat it too" attitude; someone who just wants to have fun and not be responsible to anyone. If their girlfriend gives them an ultimatum, they can say " Well, honey, you knew that I was gay and will always want men as well as you. And to their boyfriend, they can say, well guy, you knew that I was straight and will always want women as well as you. It's an easy cop-out. But true homosexuality KNOWS what it wants; it does not vacillate from male to female as the wind changes direction and it goes far deeper than sex. Of course, I guess it would be wrong for me to try to speak for all homosexuals, but speaking for myself, all I have ever wanted is one man; one soul mate to love and care for and cherish for life. It's very sad that in my mid life I have not yet found that and may never, but I will keep hope alive.

Now I have to explain to you that all the while my relationship with "D" was in progress; other like-minded seminarians were also going through the same pain and torment. Of course it never dawned on me that there were others there like me. I had always felt that I was "the only one", but that simply wasn't true. As I said at the onset of my first mentioning Bethel to you; you simply don't take 900 strapping young men in their peak of fertility; tell them not to marry or have sex until the Kingdom Comes; pack them all into one building replete with steam baths and saunas and expect nothing to go wrong. HELLO out there? Is anybody home? This same problem has been going on for centuries in monasteries and convents all over the world. How the Watchtower Society dreamed that it would never happen there is beyond me. But then they believed the Kingdom was coming in 1914 at first and then in 1974. Oh well.

In any event, it appears that quite a few of the young brothers had been pairing up and acting on their homosexuality until one of them went on a guilt trip, confessed to the Elders and "turned States evidence" to get off light by making a list of all of the other brothers he had sex with. Now it was the practice of the day at breakfast to begin the day with prayers, scriptural readings and then comments by the President of the Watchtower Society, Nathan Knorr. To accommodate over 900 Bethelites, there were three large dining rooms connected by closed circuit TV so you could watch and listen to all of this. One fateful morning the axe fell. Nathan Knorr announced that some among the brethren had confessed to loathsome and despicable acts. Yes they had committed homosexual acts ,which was an "abomination to the Lord" and they were being dishonorably discharged from the seminary. He then proceeded to read a list of the names of the offenders for the purpose of public humiliation.

I sat and listened to the names in horror as I recognized many of them as friends of mine; my old buddies with whom I had gone to Broadway shows and concerts. It figures, "birds of a feather flock together." But I had no idea that any of this was going on. No one had ever given so much as a hint that any of this was going on. Now I knew that I would not be on any list per se because I had not committed any "abominations" although I certainly would have like to. There were some really gorgeous, hunky studs at that seminary, but that wasn't what it was all about to me. I wanted love, not just sex. But I was still fearful that I would be implicated in some way since I was a friend to many of the offenders. That's partly why this was not an especially good time for me to say to "D", "Oh yes, I will stay with you forever my love, neither life nor death will separate us." Nor was it an appropriate time for him to say to me: "I love you Bob and I want you to stay here with me." We were treading on some pretty thin ice here. So now the crucible was in place and the witch trials had begun. How many would fall? It was anyone's guess, but each morning after the prayers and scriptures a new list would be read off publicly and I would sit there in fear and trembling. I just didn't know what to do; I couldn't stand it anymore; I had to talk to someone.

Now you have to understand that the Bethel Home was located near the water in Brooklyn Heights. In those days the area was a Gay Mecca. Many gays lived there and others would come there to cruise the hotel swimming pools and health clubs and also, at night, they would walk along a long stretch of park and sidewalk below the home known as "The Promenade". There were also several gay bars not far from there. So it wasn't hard to find other gay men. I began going to gay bars at first just to be with other people like myself. I wasn't there to pick up or be picked up by anyone; I still was clinging to the last vestiges of my faith and couldn't give in now; no, not now; not yet. It would mean dishonorable discharge and possibly even excommunication from my faith; I couldn't bear that. But I did need someone to talk to. So I began meeting other gay men, but I felt like such a jerk, bending their ears with my problems and then declining their offers of overnight lodging and affection. I mean they meant well and they were lonely and needed affection too. I knew that in time I would wear out my welcome. So what was I to do? I no longer really belonged in the Jehovah's Witness world, but I likewise didn't really fit in with the gay world either. I was like a man without a country. I just wanted to die.

Night after night I started drinking; I didn't know what else to do; at least that numbed the pain. Sometimes I would go up to the roof concealing a bottle of vodka under my coat. "D" was asleep so he didn't know, or at least I didn't think that he knew. I would just sit up there and drink and drink and bewail my plight. On several occasions I contemplated suicide. I mean what other way out was there? There just weren't too many options. I just didn't belong anywhere; not in the Witness world and not in the gay world.

Finally the fateful day came, as I knew that it would. I was called into the headquarters office. Apparently the authorities had in deed connected me up with my fallen comrades and had sent spies following me around Brooklyn Heights, watching me going in and out of gay bars. They admitted that they had never seen me leave with anyone and that I had always come straight home, but they still felt that I was a danger to the community. What's worse, my beloved "D", probably in order to throw them off the track and protect himself, reported that he had seen me late at night from our window walking on the Promenade with homosexual men. He wasn't so sure whether or not I had gone home with any of them. I was advised that I would have to leave the institution; they gave me the option of leaving voluntarily rather than being dismissed since they really didn't have anything on me; I had been above reproach. So my name was not to be read off at the breakfast table. At least I had been spared that humiliation.

I went back to our room and encountered "D" who hadn't expected to see me that time of day. He was surprised and uncomfortable to say the least. I asked him how he could do this to me. His only response was that he was sorry and that I had already been framed prior to his statement and there was nothing that could be done about it. He tried to lessen the tragedy of the situation by reminding me of how much I disliked being there and that it was probably all for the best; afterward telling me that he had to go to the library. I sat there alone in the room trying to gather my thoughts. Where would I go? What would people say? How would I explain my return to the Trumbull Congregation before my four years were up? What if the Society contacted my old congregation and alerted them that they had a possible sex offender in their ranks? Then I wouldn't be welcome there either. How would I get a job? I had received no useable education while I had been there. How far was I going to go on the pro-rated $15. that they were going to give me?

I finally mustered the courage and words to call Dad. I knew exactly how to approach it. I said: "Hi, Dad? You were right all along; I should have never come here; they're just taking advantage of me and I am not getting any education. I should have listened to you and gone to college. I'm ready to come home now." Well, it didn't work. My father reminded me that when I CHOSE to move away from home, that was my decision; he never stood in my way and told me then that it was my life to live and no one else's. But in the same token, he now told me that once you make that kind of decision, you cannot then go back on it. In short I could never go home again; I had left home and now I would have to live with that decision. He told me that he would be glad to help me get a place to live and a car, but that I could never go home. Well, I was floored. I didn't know what to say or do. I felt totally crushed and abandoned. It was like the end of the world. I experienced one "end of the world" when my Mom died and now I was losing my Dad; my standing in my religious institution and all sense of security. How much could I endure? In retrospect, my Dad did the right thing; he forced me to become a man; to stand by my decisions; determine my own fate; be self-reliant and independent. I am indebted to him for that; he was a truly wise man; but of course, at the time, all I could feel was crushed and abandoned.

Fortunately, no one at Bethel reported anything negative to my old congregation, so I was able to arrange lodging with a young married couple who were friends of mine. They were musicians and not really "gung-ho" witnesses so they never questioned why I left Bethel and told me that I could stay with them rent-free until I got established. That was a real blessing. And you'll never guess who was already sharing the house with them. You got it. "E", my old heart throb, the motorcyclist and chef was living with them. So hell, things were starting to look up. My friends came to pick me up in Brooklyn which was very nice of them. I could have just come back on the train. As I handed in my room key and walked out the front garden gate for the last time and heard it clang behind me I wept. As unhappy as I had been there; still, hearing that gate clang behind me and not having my key anymore only deepened the sense that I had been "cast out of the Garden of Eden, never to have access again. I did have some fond memories from there and then too, my "D" was still there and I would now be separated from him forever.

CHAPTER 10
BACK TO THE REAL WORLD

I was fortunate to have friends that were willing to take me in; and fortunate that Dad was at least willing to help me get started again, even if he wouldn't let me go home. And I was thrice blessed that the local congregation of Jehovah's Witnesses didn't seem to know anything about why I left Bethel; because you see, despite everything, I hadn't yet given up on my religion.

It was also great to be living under the same roof with my old flame, "E". Of course he didn't know that he was my "flame" and much had changed in my absence. He was now dating a girl in the congregation who was sort of a "half-baked" witness and she was putting him through absolute hell. I felt really bad for him because he would confide in me how much he loved her, yet she was just tormenting and using him; playing cat and mouse and getting as much out of it as she could. Sadly, I had never wanted anything from "E" other than his love and I knew that in a different world, I could have made him much happier than she, but there was nothing much that I could do about it. Plus, I had to get on with my own life, looking for a job, a car and a place of my own.

Initially "C" and his wife taught me the rudiments of playing bass guitar and suggested that I play and sing in their combo since I wasn't a bad singer. So we tried that for a while, playing in small lounges and at weddings and such. But they didn't have much initiative. They rarely scouted out new jobs and spent most of their time at the movies and amusement parks until the money from the last job ran out; then they would look for another job. This was no way to get ahead so I decided that I would have to strike out on my own. Dad got me a used car as he had promised and I began my job search, but as I mentioned earlier, I really had no training to speak of in anything marketable so I really had to take whatever I could get.

My first job was as a room service waiter at the Holiday Inn of Bridgeport, so I decided it would probably be better if I moved to Bridgeport to save money on travel to work. There was another young "fringe Witness "D—" who lived in Bridgeport; we sort of became buddies. I think he picked up on the fact that I was "different" calling me honey and dear, etc, but not mockingly; it was in a light-hearted and good natured way. He said that I could move in with him rent-free until I had a few paychecks under my belt, so long as I didn't "bother" him. So this began a new adventure.

"D—" noticed that I was severely depressed and introduced me to something that he said would take the edge off and make me feel much better; marijuana. Well it certainly did take the edge off and I loved it. I remember back when I was in Brooklyn walking to the Watchtower factory always seeing young hippies with big smiles sitting on their doorsteps. They were always in beautiful, colorful attire with the arresting strains of Hindu chants and the beautiful scent of incense wafting out of their windows. How often I had envied their freedom and seeming happiness. I wanted to be just like them; well maybe now I could. Of course smoking pot was not something that I could afford on a

daily basis; and certainly not on the wages of a room service waiter. Also things were getting a bit dicey at the Holiday Inn; I was only 22; not bad looking; and with an aura of innocence so I had difficulty with middle aged men constantly "hitting on me" and trying to get me to deliver more than just their breakfasts. I was still very religious and didn't appreciate the advances, so I decided to look for another job, as did "D—: who was sort of fed up with his job too. Ultimately, we both ended up working together in the Master charge department at a local bank. Once we felt secure in our jobs we decided to move out of the crime laden neighborhood that we had been living in and found a really nice third floor apartment for only $100 a month, which was a good price even then back in 1970. So things were moving right along.

"D—"eventually met a charming young Mexican seamstress who fell madly in love with him. Before she had come here she had worked for a fashion designer in Mexico City. She was a great boon to me because she would come over weekly and clean our apartment, which was something that "D—" would never do; he was a real slob that way. She was a lovely, articulate, intelligent and refined young lady. I don't know what she ever saw in "D—". Don't get me wrong, "D—" was a nice, kind-hearted person, but a real back woods Maine potato farmer type while she was sophisticated and classy. She saw through me immediately, but she was very accepting and open-minded and we became good friends. Whenever "D—" tried to fix me up with local girls in our congregation, she would lovingly say: "I think that Bob would rather meet some young men. I should take him to Taxco, Mexico with me and introduce him to my former boss, Francisco. He has many handsome young men there who he keeps in style at his villa and would love a blond American."

I often wonder how my life might have been different if I had accepted her offer and gone to Mexico. But I guess that in my childish mind, hope still sprang eternal that perhaps someday, God might "heal me" and that I might be able to lead a normal life, whatever that was. I felt that exposing myself to a banquet of stunningly gorgeous male morsels, when I was supposed to be on a "diet" would be more than I could endure. I may have failed at Bethel, but at least I had not yet totally fallen from Grace. So instead, I did the stupid thing and allowed two of my friends, "T" and his girlfriend, "D" to fix me up with her girlfriend from Norwich, CT. It was a big mistake and the last of that nature that I would ever make, because I deeply hurt a lovely young girl in the process and found it difficult to forgive myself.

M---s, was a lovely, innocent and vulnerable young lady. I liked her immediately, but of course I never came to love her. I also was very fond of her family. Her mother was English, just like my Mom, so we talked endlessly about England over a nice cup of tea. I was invited over every weekend and also brought to all family and extended family gatherings as though I were a prospective son-in-law. I tried desperately to love "M", but whenever we went out dancing at local discos in New London, I felt uncomfortable being close to her. My attention would invariably wander from her to the hunky sailors that I saw either standing at the bar or dancing with other women. Whenever a hot sailor was dancing nearby in close proximity to me, I would instantly tighten my hold on her, which the poor girl mistook for passionate feelings directed toward her. She never suspected that my arousal was due to the close proximity of an attractive man; she would have been crushed had she known because she had fallen head over heels in love with me.

In time, I lost my job at the bank and could no longer afford those long trips to Norwich, but her parents had the answer to that; they suggested that I move in with them and that her uncle would get me a job in Norwich or New London. So the pressure was on now and I knew that I had to escape; this just wasn't working. But what else could I do? I really tried to love her. During those long drives to Norwich, I would try to talk myself into loving her. I would remind myself of how much she loved me and that this might be my only chance at some semblance of normality. I would remind myself of how supportive her family was and how this was the only way that I would be able to remain true to my faith and keep from falling into the bottomless pit of moral depravity that was waiting to engulf me. By the time I reached Norwich I would have myself totally convinced that I could do this. "Yes, I can love her" I said, "Yes, I can make a go of this" I thought, but as soon as she opened the door and threw her arms around me, I felt nothing but terror and a leaden weight in the pit of my stomach. I just couldn't go through with it.

So I lied. I told her that during the fairly long period during which we had been apart due to my unemployment, that I had met and fallen in love with a local sister in my congregation and that I was very sorry that things had not worked out for us. It was a stupid and thoughtless thing to do. I think that she was a sweet enough and kind enough girl to have been able to handle the truth better than the lie that I fed her, but what could I do? If I told her that I was gay and she mentioned it to anyone, I would be excommunicated, ostracized; cast off. She was the kind of compassionate young woman who would probably have married me anyway just to help me cover my tracks, but that wouldn't have been fair to her. So I stuck with the lie.

Three weeks later her mother called me to acquaint me with the mental scars that I had inflicted on her daughter. She told me that "M" couldn't eat or sleep; was presently in therapy and losing time from work. She asked me what "M" or they had ever done to deserve this type of shoddy treatment and betrayal. Well of course I didn't have any answers because they certainly didn't deserve this; it wasn't their problem; it was my problem, but now they were suffering the effects of that. It wasn't easy for me either; I was stricken with guilt and remorse. I never intended nor wanted to hurt another human being. But far better, I thought, to hurt her minimally now, rather than wait until after 20 years of marriage and break it to her then; abandon her with teenage children and destroy several persons lives. And yet that is exactly what religion and society were, and still are forcing people to do.

Wouldn't it be far better for gay men and women to be "out" and accepted by religion and society so that straight, unsuspecting men and women would know enough not to date us or fall in love with us? Wouldn't it be far better to let us live our lives in peace and security, allowing us to marry each other rather than force us to lead double lives of deception and hide behind your daughter's aprons? Thousands of gay men and women over the years have been forced by fear to marry unhappily. And most of those marriages have ended in divorce and broken families when there was no need for all of that suffering. Still thousands of others continue to lead double lives of deception, the gay side of their lives strictly limited to degrading momentary flings with countless anonymous sex partners, spreading disease to each other and to their wives. Is that what religion and society wants? It's the same reason that even in this new century of supposed liberation, that gay servicemen and lesbian servicewomen are forced to marry one another just so that they can keep their careers in the military. Then, behind closed doors they are able to swap partners without the military being any the wiser. What's wrong with this picture in the Land of the Free and the Home of the Brave ?

During the Vietnam era when thousands of healthy young heterosexual men fled this country or married and fathered children so as to not have to serve in the military, thousands of homosexual men and women who would have automatically been exempt from the military due to their homosexuality, in stead signed up and put their lives on the line for this country; often making the supreme sacrifice. Yet if anyone had discovered their secret, they would have been summarily given dishonorable discharges; had their military careers destroyed and would have been treated as degenerates and traitors. What's wrong with this picture?

Why are we continually made into second rate citizens when we are the ones serving our country; we are the ones actively involved in politics and voting; we are the ones paying a disproportionate share of the taxes in this country due to our single status and not having any children in the school systems since we can neither marry nor adopt ? Even under the new "Don't ask, don't tell" era we are still marginalized. Straight military personnel are free to engage in any sort of out-of-wedlock activities that they choose. Brothels are often set up near military bases or women brought in for the amusement of the troops, while gay servicemen are expected to cultivate the "gift of celibacy". Millions of fatherless Amer-Asian children went homeless and starved to death following the Vietnam Era, but that's OK, because that kind of behavior was "normal". It's also "normal" for suspected gay servicemen to be beaten to death by other U.S. soldiers if they so much as look at another man. What kind of double standard is this? Aren't gay servicemen and servicewomen putting their lives on the line just as much as anyone else? Then why are they not entitled to the same privacy, intimacy and sexual gratification as anyone else?

And most importantly, what is the basis of these military prohibitions? Are they secular or religious? If they are religious then they are in direct violation of our Constitution and the principles of separation of Church and State. Do gay men and women simply make poor soldiers? I think not. What about Alexander the Great and his lover who conquered the known world? What about Julius Caesar and Hannibal? What about the Spartans and the Amazons? What about King Richard the Lion Heart ? And what about all of the gay veterans, some of whom I personally know, with Purple Hearts and all manner of military decorations ? But Society doesn't want anyone to know about gay veterans; hell, that would make us equal to straight men wouldn't it? That would dispel the myth that we are all limp wrested sissies who have no rights and shouldn't be spoken of in the same breath as real patriots. Isn't it odd how history has a way of repeating itself?

It wasn't all that long ago during WW I and even into the beginning of WW II that Black servicemen were initially only given menial and mundane positions in the military for fear that they might actually prove themselves victorious and capable soldiers; hell, that might make them look equal to white men. And women, likewise were kept at bay out of fear that they too might someday be considered equal. You see, that's really what this is all about. Society simply wants to keep us as a sub-culture which exists purely as a result of their permission and tolerance. They don't want to outright show intolerance because that is no longer politically correct. But neither do they want to grant us full equality because that, in their eyes, would somehow diminish their superior standing. So they throw us crumbs like civil unions instead of marriage; crumbs like "Don't ask don't tell" instead of "It's OK to be gay in the military".

So many times in the workplace I hear co-workers expressing their joy in making wedding plans or their sorrow at the loss of a spouse. All of their co-workers, including myself, are usually supportive. We plan wedding showers and baby showers; we attend funerals and are there to support one another. It's only right that people want to and need to share their happy and sad experiences with others with whom they spend 40 hours per week out of their lives. But gay men and women don't have those same privileges. We can't share our happy and sad moments with co-workers because as they say: " I don't care what THOSE PEOPLE do behind closed doors, but they should keep it to themselves. Don't throw it in my face"! Well, I don't think that anyone is throwing anything in anyone's face, but I am a human being with the same needs as anyone else; the only thing that is different about me is my sexual preference which is such a small part of my total being. I am your son, your daughter, your aunt , your uncle, your niece, your nephew, your accountant, your teacher; and in some cases your mother, your father. Why are my needs, my joys and my sorrows so unimportant that I must stifle them and sublimate them in order to gain your approval?

It was at this point that I finally took a long, hard look in the mirror and said to myself: "I am Bob; I have blond hair, hazel eyes. I am five foot seven inches tall, I am right handed, not ambidextrous, and I am GAY. It's as simple as that, and I refuse to keep fighting my basic human nature that I was born with. I must be true to myself."

CHAPTER 11
FREE AT LAST

When you look at a beautiful work of art it is usually from a distance, so you aren't really in a position to notice any of the flaws if they are there. But when you get up close, the flaws become evident. Well, let's just say that I had my face mashed into the canvas. During my very close exposure to the Watchtower Bible and Tract Society at it's Brooklyn headquarters and even later in my local congregation of Jehovah's Witnesses, I encountered many such flaws which I suppose I might encounter in any other denominational seminary or monastery; this is in no way meant to be a sinister or diabolical attack on Jehovah's Witnesses, who for the most part, I always found to be sincere, honest, and self-sacrificing individuals and model citizens.

Where I found them lacking was in the fact that their entire approach to theology was entirely insular. While they used the same Bible that everyone else uses (although they did and do have their own version, the "New World Translation") most of their teachings and commentaries were exclusively taken from their own books and tracts written by high ranking Jehovah's Witnesses at headquarters. Outside sources might be used from time to time, but only if they corroborated accepted Witness doctrine. They did not allow the direct study of other religions via the reading of their holy books, say the Koran or the Hindu Vedas. No, you were limited to reading only the Society's versions of what those other religions believed and taught. And you were certainly not allowed to attend or participate in the religious celebrations or teaching services of other religious denominations; that would amount to apostasy for which you could and would be removed from the congregation and that was no small thing.

If a Catholic is denied the sacraments, that is a very serious loss to that individual, but at least they can still attend church, associate with other Catholics and perhaps regain the right to receive communion again somewhere down the line. But when a Witness is disfellowshiped, no other Witness anywhere may speak to him, visit him, write him or communicate with him in any manner. You are totally cut off and shunned. Now I am not certain if this is still the practice now some 30 years later, but that is the way that it was then.

Witnesses were also discouraged from even associating with "non-believers" on a strictly social level. They said: "bad associations, spoil useful habits." You were enjoined to avoid non-believing relatives and family members; you were not allowed to celebrate birthdays, religious or political holidays. You were primarily to spend your time at Witness sponsored meetings or out preaching from door to door to gain converts. There were five weekly meetings to keep you connected. Even the Bible studies which we conducted at no charge in people's homes were strictly monitored from time to time by an elder who would asses the situation. If the student was docile and making progress in Jehovah's Witness teaching, the study could continue. But if the student refuted any Witness teachings and countered them with his own concepts, even if backed up by scripture, the elder would more than likely suggest or even demand termination of such a Bible study. I often wondered why that was, and soon found out.

One thing that the Watchtower Society hadn't banked on was the possibility that during our daily preaching activities on our own, without an elder present, that we might be exposed to people of other faiths who were just as spiritualized as we and just as adept at using the Bible to prove the foundations of their faith. During the course of my preaching activities I met many such fine individuals who manifested high levels of spirituality and who could prove from the Bible that they had just as valid a reason for their faith as I. I was truly amazed at this because I really had never been exposed directly to other religions or philosophies since the Witnesses had discovered me at an early age.

My family had not been all that religious. My Mom was a nominal Episcopalian and my Dad, a nominal Russian Orthodox. Neither really practiced nor truly understood their faiths and they would not compromise and let us attend either of those churches so I did not have any real religious training. Perhaps had I received religious training prior to my first meeting with the Witnesses, I might not have been so impressed and easily convinced of their veracity. And I want you to understand that at this point, we are only talking about exposure to Bible-based, Judeo-Christian based faiths. I was totally ignorant of the fact that there were far older faiths and philosophies with their own holy books that predated Christianity by hundreds and thousands of years and which were just as valid to their worshippers as my faith was to me.

I think that the moment of truth cam one day when I was preaching from door to door in Easton, CT. A young Hindu monk or Acharya as they are called, bearded and clad in a white robe and turban, cheerfully greeted me at the door and welcomed I and my preaching companion in. I explained to him the purpose of our visit, to which he responded by offering us tea and refreshments rather than abruptly showing us to the door as so many others had.

I was young and foolish and repaid this man's kindness by methodically pointing out the irrationality of worshipping cows and monkeys rather than God. I also in my ignorance advised him that the Bible was the oldest and original holy book begun by Adam and ergo, the only true source for religious teaching. He never once attacked back nor tried to use his superior wisdom, which I now know was at his disposal, to fend off my darts, defend his beliefs or simply make me look like the total fool and spiritual infant that I was. No, he was kind, patient, composed, serene and full of love and compassion. He advised me that "Truth is one, though the paths be many", that one day I and my friend would each find our own path and that when that day came, I would remember him. He then embraced us and sent us on our way.

The few morsels of spiritual gems which he had offered us and which I allowed myself to listen to while simultaneously preparing my next defense, made much more sense than what I was teaching. He spoke with such authority and certainty and love, not as one who simply read their faith in a book and got it second hand, but as one who had actually experienced God firsthand. I wished that I had only a fraction of what he had. His faith was able to withstand the assault of differing opinions; he saw no need to convince anyone or win any argument; he didn't need the reassurance of other believers; nor volumes of religious literature to bolster his faith; he simply KNEW. His faith was not from books; nor had it been "spoon fed" to him as a child. No it was the result of years of meditation and searching within which culminated in a direct experience of Reality. I wanted desperately what I knew he had, but I did not know how to go about getting it. One thing, however became certain in my mind; you can't hear when you are talking; you can't learn when you are teaching. The little monk had used the illustration of trying to pour water into a glass already full. It's simply not possible. Hadn't even Jesus said that you "can't put new wine into old wineskins"?

I knew then that I would have to empty myself and approach all of life as a totally new experience. I would have to rid myself of all pre-conceived notions and concepts if I was ever to experience life and see things as they truly are; unfiltered by old concepts and beliefs. Not that those old beliefs are wrong, but they may simply not be accurately depicting the entire picture. The monk had also given me an illustration of three blind men trying to describe an elephant. The first man said: "An elephant is as wide and tall as a small hill". The second blind man said: "Oh, no, an elephant is long and slender", that man having only felt the trunk. The third man said: "Oh no, you are both wrong, an elephant is like a cow because it has horns", having only felt the tusks and not knowing where on the elephant they were located.

None of those men were actually wrong in their descriptions; they were merely describing their own limited experience of an elephant, but they were wrong in insisting that their limited experience accurately depicted the whole elephant. Rather than arguing the point and defending their own individual concepts, they would have done far better to listen to one another. The whole is equal to the sum of its parts. Had the blind men combined their concepts, they would have come a lot closer to knowing or seeing what a true elephant is. I decided then that I needed to be open to all concepts and open to experience life in all of its dimensions. Some things I would be destined to learn from loving teachers like this young monk; others from friends and still others from the "School of Hard Knocks", but in the end, Life is the best teacher. One thing was certain; I had to tell the elders that I could no longer continue preaching, but how could I do that without getting myself into serious trouble.

All of this new understanding was overwhelming for me; it was more than I could handle without a little Jack Daniels. So I indulged myself. As I sat there drinking, I knew that I needed to talk to someone about all of this and who better than my old flame "D" who was still down in Brooklyn. I also wanted to clear up unfinished business with him and finally say the things that should have been said when I was living with him. The Jack Daniels was beginning to loosen my mind and tongue. There was no way of calling him so I wrote him a letter. Initially the letter was sharing with him my newfound faith and philosophy on life, but as the Jack Daniels took hold I became more sentimental and also more emotional and cut right to the quick. I told him that I was in love with him and had been all along, but that I feared what might happen if I had revealed it back in Bethel. I told him that of course I would be glad and honored to spend the rest of my life with him, but that he would need to come here now. I assured him of my undying love and mailed the letter. OOOPS !!! The next day I realized that I had made a BIG mistake. But there are no mistakes in life, merely opportunities for learning; things happen for a reason. Needless to say, "D" forwarded the letter to the elders of my local congregation. But in actuality, my faux pas led to my emancipation. You see, I had too great a sense of loyalty and too great a love for the congregation to ever leave it voluntarily so it would take excommunication or disfellowshipping to finally set me free.

The elders called me to a closed meeting at which they posed the following questions: "Do you believe that the Watchtower Society is the sole repository of Truth on earth?" To which I replied: "No". "Do you then feel that the Society is teaching lies and false doctrines?" I replied: "No, I believe that you are accurately depicting the Truth as you believe it to be, but that in your incessant desire to always be right, you are only seeing part of the picture and excluding anything that does not fit with your preconceived notion of what is Truth." "Are you following other false religions?" I replied: "No", but I resent your labeling other people's belief systems which are far older and established than yours as false religions. All I am doing is searching and seeking for the Truth, for Reality, not part of the Truth and part of Reality." I explained to them that it would have been very easy for me to just lie my way through their hearing and remain a member in good standing, but I could not do that and remain true to myself or to them. I suggested that if they wanted to punish me for my honesty then so be it, but that decision would be on their heads and their consciences.

They said that I was a very serious threat to the security of the congregation and oddly enough disfellowshipped me for apostasy, never once mentioning homosexuality. Maybe "D" had stricken those parts from the letter so as not to implicate himself. I will never know. I felt glad that I had the courage to stand up to them; but at the same time saddened that I would pay a dear price for this. In one fell swoop I lost all the friends and people who I had loved for ten years now. I could never see or talk to any of them ever again. As I left the Kingdom Hall I felt liberated and isolated all at the same time. I didn't know what to do; I knew that I needed to talk to someone but to whom? They were all gone.

Now you must understand that for all of these ten years, I had gone against the wishes of my family. I had avoided family gatherings, birthdays, holidays, etc. I had really turned my back on all of them; not because I didn't love them but because the Witnesses had brainwashed me into thinking that they were all going to be destroyed as non-believers at the upcoming Battle of Armageddon due to hit in 1974 and it was now 1971. I was trying to wean myself away from them so that I would not suffer terribly when they were taken from me. Would they now take me back after all these years? I had to at least try so I called my brother's telephone number.

My sister-in-law answered the phone and I related all that had happened. Well, to my surprise, her response was: "I am sorry to hear that they put you through all this pain, but thank God it's over and welcome home; we have all missed you so much these last years." Tears rolled down my face as I tried to gain composure. I asked her for her forgiveness, to which she responded that there was nothing to forgive. She understood how deeply I had believed in my faith and knew the control my religion had held over me. She was just glad that it was over and welcomed me back with open arms as did my brother and my Dad. She invited me to dinner for the next Sunday. Now you tell me who were the truer Christians?

Well, I hope I haven't totally "bummed you out" at this point. Life does get better as you will see; some parts of my life have been sad and some hilarious so please stay with me as I move into a new dimension of life, sort of like an explorer sailing in uncharted waters. I no longer have the elders to chart my path for me; now it's all up to me, which can be both exhilarating and frightening all at the same time. At this point in time I felt rather like Maria in "Sound of Music" when she closed that convent gate behind her and sang: "I've always longed for adventure, to do the things, I never dared. And now I'm faced with adventure, so why am I so scared"? Life is very scary with no boundaries, no parameters, but that's what I will now have to create for myself: new values, new parameters; a new sense of self and spirituality that will be workable for a young gay man living at the end of the 20th century.

PART II
OUT OF BONDAGE AND
INTO THE LIGHT OF DAY

CHAPTER 1
SEARCHING FOR PARAMETERS

I had always been spiritually inclined, even as a child, but as I mentioned earlier; we were not a particularly religious family. You know, strictly wedding and funeral Christians. Oh we celebrated Christmas and Easter and all, but they were almost more secular holidays than religious. I sort of pursued religion or spirituality on my own by reading the Bible myself or via TV and movie productions. I wanted so desperately to believe that it was all true.

My brother and I were different as day and night when it came to this. I remember one time watching the movie "David and Bathsheba". I was so impressed with the scene where King David was bringing the Ark of the Covenant into Jerusalem. It was an impressive scene with David dancing before the ark; musicians; priests carrying palm branches and the Levite priests carrying the Ark itself up the hill. I was so impressed and dragged my brother out of his room to see it. His response was: "What's so special about that ? It's just a grubby bunch of superstitious Jews dragging a box up a hill." I was floored. I couldn't imagine how he could treat such a special moment with such utter disregard and disrespect. But that's where we were different. He really didn't believe in much of anything other than human determination and self-reliance and I was willing to believe just about anything without requiring any credentials or proof at all; just blind faith. But you see, that's how I got myself into trouble in the first place.

Back when my Mom was sick and I was making all those deals with God and believing all of those Bible promises that if we asked anything in His name, it would be granted, I just set myself up for a big fall. But the fact is that God never told me that if I asked anything in His name he would grant it. God never told me, personally, that he would heal my Mom or bring his Kingdom to earth or any of it. I was just believing what I was told or had read in religious books claiming to be the Word of God. And then, when none of it came true, I saw God as a liar and grew to hate Him as I'm sure that many other poor retches have likewise. Poor old God. How many words have we put in His mouth over the centuries ? You see, this is the problem with organized, institutional religions. They each, individually claim that their BOOK is the Word of God, to the exclusion of any possibility that the others could possibly be the Word of God. If they all do, in deed, have the actual Word of God, then why do they all contradict one another and why have they all been persecuting one another and slaughtering one another for centuries? I thought that God was Love. It just didn't make any sense to me.

Since, to my young mind, Christianity had done me no great favors and having a natural spirit of rebelliousness toward authority, I decided that I would now investigate all of the ancient and pagan religions which both the Watchtower Society and the Church forbade it's members from practicing. I wondered exactly what it was that those religious authorities didn't want us to know. Was it that those ancient religions were the real sources of truth and faith and that Judeo-Christianity based religions were the upstarts and heretics? I had a fleeting interest in Hinduism and Eastern thought as a result of my contact with my young Hindu monk, but at this point in my life, I wasn't ready for anything as humble and accepting of fate as Hinduism appeared. I wanted something that would make me feel empowered; something that would make me feel as though I had some control over my life and fate.

As I just happened to be strolling down Chapel St. in New Haven, CT. one afternoon, I stumbled across a little shop dealing in occult and Witchcraft supplies. Hmmm. The owner, Tom, was a very nice man who turned out to be what is known as a solitary Witch; in other words, he didn't have a group or coven. But he was very nice and proceeded to explain all of the tenets of the "Old Religion" or Wicca as it is called and I found it all very interesting. We're not talking about Satanism here. That's an entirely different issue. That's not a religion, it's more of an anti-religion and therefore negative. But Wicca was just a primitive early earth religion, the religion of our pre-Christian ancestors; nothing negative about it at all and it sounded like fun. The Witnesses had always warned us never to talk to anyone involved in the occult because they said that we could become possessed and fall under their control. Well hell, isn't that what THEY had just done to me for ten years; hadn't I been under their control ? How could I be in any worse danger with these new people? They weren't proselytizing me, I was seeking out them; besides, what greater revenge than to rush into the arms that were forbidden me by my previous master? So I decided to join a coven. Tom gave me the telephone number of a local priestess in Bridgeport who had a group or coven; the rest was up to me.

I must admit that I was a little uneasy doing this, but all my fears and apprehensions were absolutely unfounded. This was, in deed, one of the nicest groups of people I had met up to that point. They came from all different backgrounds; all ages, sexes, races, sexual orientations and they were delightful, lovely nature loving people. There were no human or animal sacrifices; they loved animals. Nor were there any dark mysterious incantations or connections to the devil. They worshipped God in the form of a female Goddess as opposed to worshipping a male deity. They believed that fate or the future could be altered through the practice of intricate spells and herbal magic, coupled with powerfully directed will and positive thinking. They were sort of the precursors of the New Age movement. The Priestess, Rose, was a middle aged hereditary Witch and college graduate with great psychic skills. The skills of the others varied by degree. But Rose was very gifted and was often used by the police department to help locate missing individuals. She was a very light-hearted soul and very open minded. She knew that I was gay the moment she set eyes on me and welcomed me into the group anyway. We became great friends and she broke me of the habit of feeling that there is only one way of seeing things.

Rose taught me that all religions were merely spokes on the same wheel and that the center was God however you conceive Him or Her to be. She did not teach us to follow only the teachings of Wicca, but encouraged us to explore the vast sources of spirituality available and take what was best from each and incorporate it into my life. What a radical difference from the kind of rigidity and conformity that I had been used to. It was truly refreshing. She taught me that setting up finite sets of beliefs and practices and rigidly enforcing them cuts one off from any possibility of finally experiencing the Infinite Reality and that it was also the root source of most of the human suffering in the world. It was an act of incredible pride and arrogance to think that either you or your group have been specifically chosen by God to the exclusion of all other peoples.

If there is in fact an anthropomorphic Deity who created the universe and man, could a deity of such intelligence have been so insensitive and shortsighted as to have set the families of man at odds with each other by singling out only one group as his Chosen People to the detriment of all others? And worse yet, would he then have given them land already belonging to other peoples and authorize them to go in and slaughter the indigenous peoples and take the land for themselves? Would he give them as one of their ten commandments "thou shalt not kill" and then authorize them to slaughter thousands? I think not. Why have Jews and Christians alike, set themselves up for centuries as somehow superior to the rest of mankind and sanctified by God Almighty to dominate and show the rest of us poor, fallen, ignorant people the path to God? Who gave them the right to destroy ancient cultures; to decimate and slaughter the Central, Mezzo and South American Indians? Was that God's will for mankind?

Wouldn't a loving intelligent deity rather raise up mystics, prophets, mullas, Buddhas and rishis in all of the various human families and in every generation, so that truth would always be available to the family of man in their own languages and cultures and so that all of mankind could feel equally loved and blessed by Him?

So this was the beginning of a wonderful and more expansive spiritual education than I had previously known and it paved the way for greater spiritual growth in the future. I met some wonderful individuals who, even though I am no longer actively involved in Wicca, are still in my life and, unlike Jehovah's Witnesses, are not forbidden to speak to me or associate with me simply because I have embraced other forms of spirituality other than Wicca.

Now as I mentioned earlier, due to the open mindedness of most Wiccans, people of all backgrounds are attracted. One such individual, a young man, H----d had joined our little group. By this time, I had advanced and was considered High Priest of the group; of course subservient to the Priestess, but High Priest none the less. "H" was new to the group and asked if he could talk to me in private some time because he had something weighing on his mind that he felt might prevent him from continuing with our group. I told him that I would be glad to listen to him.

Once at my place, I assured him that there was very little that he could confide in me that would shock me or prevent him from remaining with us, but that I would be glad to hear him and help him unburden himself. "H" was about 8 years my junior. He hesitated and hesitated and I wondered what kind of trouble he might be in until he finally blurted out: "I'm gay." Well, at that point I just started laughing and laughing which upset him even more until I told him: "I'm not laughing at you, I'm laughing with you because I'm gay too. Hell, is that what you were worried about"? Well he was so relieved. I told him that most of the other covens that I had run across were likewise, pretty evenly integrated with straight and gay practitioners so he had nothing to fear or be uncomfortable about. "H" had looked up to me from the beginning; maybe because I was a big brother image or maybe because he thought that I had special mystical powers I don't really know why. But for whatever reason, the next words out of his mouth were: "Do you have a lover?" Well, it took me by surprise. I mean I was celibate for 10 years and had only recently "come out". My new found freedom had allowed me to start going to local gay bars and I had experienced one or two brief encounters, but certainly nothing serious.

I really hadn't had the chance yet to "sow my wild oats" yet, but I answered "No, why do you ask?" to which he inquired, "Would you like me to be your lover? Well, that was sudden! I really didn't know what to say, I was really looking for someone closer to my age, but he was adorable and I couldn't resist his pleading, brown, puppy-dog eyes, so I said "Yes" that I would certainly be willing to give it a try and see where it goes. He was very much like the young man that I had first loved in both appearance and personality so it was easy to fall for him and fall I did.

In almost no time, I had fallen madly in love with him and what made it easier yet was that his parents and brother knew and accepted it and liked me very much. They didn't mind the age difference at all and in fact felt that I would be a much better influence on him that some of his younger friends of which they did not approve. By this time, I had finally put all my old flunkie jobs behind me and had finally landed a good and secure job with the telephone company as a customer service representative. Oddly enough, my future "father-in-law", the father of "H" worked for the same company and I guess considered me a good catch for his son. It was absolutely amazing how accepting they were of it all. So the way was paved, or so I thought. Of course the time was going to come when I would have to explain all of this to MY family. I only hoped and prayed that they would be as accepting as my future in-laws.

So now I finally had a great new job and was making new friends at work; was seeing my Dad and brother with more frequency and loving it. Participating in holidays and birthdays and I had a delightful, handsome young lover. God was in His Heaven and all was well with the world. I surprised myself in that I found that my love for "H" was even more intense than the love I had felt for my other young men in the past. But then I suppose that was partly because "H" and I could finally go "all the way"; we could express our love physically and verbally. To be honest, the sexual part of our relationship was not all that good. "H" was young and a little limited, but I really didn't mind or care. It was like Christmas morning just to hold him in my arms or to touch him; it was simply magic. He was not super romantic though, and rarely liked to kiss; I got the impression on occasions that he was holding back and afraid that he had gotten in too deep, but I reassured myself that it couldn't be the case, I mean he was the one who asked me to be his lover; I hadn't initiated it. There were even occasions when we were making love that he would stop me and tell me that he didn't want to climax. Then he would go wash up and say that he had to go home. I couldn't figure out why anyone who want to go right to the brink of ecstasy and then stop. But I found out why afterward.

"H" finally admitted that he had a "thing" for younger guys and that while he did have feelings for me, he couldn't control his physical desire for younger men. He saw nothing wrong in having an "open relationship" and having sex with other men. On all of those occasions when he stopped me short, it was because he was going to be seeing someone else later that same afternoon and wanted to be in full form for them. Of course it didn't matter to him that I was getting short changed because he was "saving it" for someone else. I was very upset. I really didn't want to say anything to his parents because I didn't want them to think that there son was a tramp; hell, I didn't even want to think it myself; I loved him and always thought highly of him.

I decided that if I wanted to keep him, I was just going to have to be patient and tolerant. Maybe an open relationship wasn't the worse thing in the world. But then, I didn't really want to be with anyone else other than him so what was I supposed to do? I figured that so long as he made time for me and that his wanderings weren't too frequent, that I could live with it. But my giving him free rein didn't seem to win any appreciation; he just became more and more neglectful. I decided that I needed to do something to change all this and I was a practicing Witch wasn't I? The last time he had slept over I had taken a clipping of his hair while he slept. In desperation, I decided to use that hair in a clay doll image that I had made of him to be used in a prescribed ritual. I performed the ritual with gusto and believe it or not, it worked. While he still had not actually changed his mind about having an open relationship; he found it impossible to get to his "other appointments".

He confided in me that he couldn't figure out what was wrong with his car. Every time he tried to go into the "cruise" area in downtown New Haven, something would go wrong with the car; either the headlights would go out or the car wouldn't start or he would have a flat tire; whatever. On other occasions his dates would not show up or he would be headed to New Haven; here "our song" on the radio and feel compelled to make a U turn and come to me. He found it all just a little too coincidental and asked me point blank if I had "done anything". I couldn't lie to him so I confessed that I loved him so much and didn't want to lose him. He asked me a very wise question for such a young man. He asked me did I want him to love me from his heart or simply love me like some kind of robot who had no choice? I told him that he was right. I wanted genuine love, not servitude. I promised to undo the spell and I did, but that was my undoing. It wasn't long after that when he packed up and left for Atlantic City to become a male stripper and escort in a club down there.

I was totally shattered, as were his parents; but there was nothing that could be done about it. I didn't think that I could survive. I wept continually for days, didn't want to see anyone and actually experienced physical pain; a sort of leaden ache deep down in my chest. Every time I would open my picture album and see pictures of him I would break down all over again. But survive I would and survive I did, and I learned that this would neither be the first nor the last time that I would suffer such pain and loss.

About six months later, "H" was back in Connecticut again, but this fact was unknown to me until his mom called me to beg me to go see him in the hospital psych ward where he had been temporarily committed due to a suicide attempt. As much as he had hurt me, I still loved him and perhaps selfishly thought that under the circumstances, I just might be able to get him back. His mother assured me that despite everything, I was the only one who had ever made him happy, and she felt that I might be able to pull him out of his depression. So I went to see him and ask him exactly what was so terrible that had driven him to such drastic measures.

"H" was really glad to see me and gave me a big hug. He confided in me that he had been desperately lonely even with all of the attention that he had been getting because he found that his life had become very superficial and shallow. He recognized that people were just using him for their gratification and didn't give a damn about him; he felt cheap and used and unloved. He conceded that my belief system had been right all along and all he wanted out of life now was to love one man and be loved in return. Well, my heart lept at that prospect, but I didn't want to appear over anxious so I simply agreed that we would put all of this behind us and never mention it again and that as soon as he was released from the hospital that we would try to recapture what we had, but slowly and cautiously.

One week after he was released, I invited him out to dinner to celebrate his homecoming and to try to pick up the pieces. When he arrived at my door I was shocked and all aghast. He was wearing a three piece suit and his lovely brown hair was all styled; he was just so much more mature and handsome than I had ever seen him before. Maybe he had learned something from his experience. He certainly seemed to be trying to impress me and putting his best foot forward. He was much more respectful to me and attentive than he had ever been before. We had a lovely dinner and then went back to my place. I felt certain that this was the beginning of a renewed and even better relationship than we had experienced before and that we would consummate it that evening.

He confided in me that while in Atlantic City, he had fallen in love with a young man who merely used him and cheated on him, so now he fully understood the difference between liking someone and being in love with someone. He also understood how deeply he had hurt me because now, he had experienced the same pain. He apologized profusely and then uttered these words: "Remember when I told you that all I want out of life now is one man to love and to be loved by?" I said: "Yes, yes" and held my breath waiting for and anticipating his next words, but then he said: "Well, that's true, but now that I know what love is, I have to say that as much as I deeply respect you and love you on a certain level; I am not "in love" with you and it would be very cruel for me to play with your emotions or lead you to a wrong conclusion".

I guess I should have appreciated his candor and honesty because he really could have used me and "taken me to the cleaners" since there wouldn't have been anything that I wouldn't have given him or done for him. But at the time, all that I could feel was intense emotional pain and disappointment. For an instant in time, I had felt that life was just beginning all over and then my hopes were suddenly dashed to pieces. I didn't let on how terribly hurt that I was; I kept it all inside. We had one last caring embrace and then he left. Once I heard his car start and heard him drive away, I simply slid down my front door onto the floor weeping and sobbing uncontrollably.

Much later, I learned to love him and respect him for what he had done that night; he had at least loved me enough to be honest with me and spare me any false hopes. Years later, we actually did live together as friends and I was actually instrumental in fixing him up and helping him to settle down with the man that was to be his true love partner. But for the time being, all that I could do was to mourn the loss. I ultimately decided that I needed some distraction, so at that point, I totally threw myself into the gay bar scene.

CHAPTER 2
IN SEARCH OF MR. RIGHT

Although I had been gay all of my life; I had little experience behind me. There had been those brief encounters in Junior High and High School followed by ten years of celibacy. My relationship with "H" had centered principally on cuddling, foreplay and some mutual gratification, but nothing really heavy, so I was pretty naïve about the gay counter culture and what would be expected from me by other gay men. So it was with great anxiety and uncertainty that I approached the situation.

First of all, I had no idea that gay bars in those days were often the target of sudden police raids and that I could be carted off to jail just for making the wrong move or approaching the wrong person, like asking a plain clothes officer to go home with me. Entrapment you say? Certainly, but that's the way it was. I also didn't know that I might be set upon and beaten by local youths in the parking lot for being seen coming out of a gay bar. Neither did I suspect that men who I invited home might just rob me or threaten to blackmail me or tell me that they were underage and would report me to the police unless I gave them money. Nor had I given any thought as to picking up sexually transmitted diseases. All this was unknown to me and had to be learned by trial and error.

Of course, as a result of being constantly under threat of danger or imprisonment, many gay men became very talented and skilled at extricating themselves from impending troublesome situations. One such gay man, who had just invited the excessively virile and handsome young man next to him home for the night suddenly had the object of his affection flash a large police shield at him, to which he replied: "Oh God, what a tacky broach!", he then vaulted over the bar, through the kitchen and out the back door. Well of course this all took the undercover agent so much by surprise that he never caught the man. Another gay man at an outdoor patio, after a lengthy conversation with the object of his attraction, gently leaned his head on the man's shoulder at which point the man inquired: "Exactly what do you think you're doing?" To which the gay man replied: "I'm just resting"., followed by the agent retorting, that's nice, and I'm just ARRESTING" at which point he pulled out a set of handcuffs. At that point, the gay man leaped onto a picnic table near the stockade fence, yelled to the officer: "Oh no, you won't take a Queen", and jumped over the fence to safety.

When I entered a gay bar, I thought that I had somehow entered a "safety zone" where everyone was just like me; sincere and seeking either new friendships or meaningful, monogamous permanent relationships......wrong, wrong, wrong. Of course some were just like me, but others there because they saw the gay community as a lucrative environment to victimize. They assumed that we were all sissies who wouldn't fight back and knew that we dare not go to the police since we would more than likely be the ones arrested. Our assailants would simply say that they were fighting off our unwanted advances; they would go free and we would go to jail. But we never made any unwanted advances to strangers. These young men, known as hustlers, always approached us and peddled their wares with great skill and sensuality. They knew exactly what they were doing. They led us to believe that they were uncontrollably attracted to us when all that they really wanted was our wallets. And we felt safe to go with them because we met them on our own turf and therefore assumed them to be gay; we also assumed them to be of legal age otherwise they wouldn't have been admitted to the bar in the first place.

But none of these assumptions were correct. Many gay men went to prison as a result of entrapment by minors; many were blackmailed; many lost their jobs and still more were beaten or murdered by these young thugs whom society sympathized with and said that THEY were the victims of our unwanted solicitation. So you see, the gay bar was not the safe haven that one would think, but it was certainly a necessary evil for networking because where else could gay men and women meet one another? , Certainly not at church or on the job.

Heterosexuals have all kinds of options as to where they can meet prospective spouses: at churches, at social clubs, in the workplace, through family and relatives, etc. but gay men and women have no such resources; hell, we can't even tell any of the above that we are gay. Even if our "gaydar" (gay-radar) cuts in and we have reason to believe that someone in our church or at work is gay, we can't just go right up to them and ask them. If we are wrong, they will tell everyone else at church or work that we propositioned them. And even if they actually are gay, they may deny it for fear that you might slip up and tell someone else and then they would lose their job or their standing in their church or social group.

Consequently, unknown to me at the time, most gay men in the bars were NOT looking for permanent, long-term relationships because they feared exposure. All that most of them were looking for was brief, uncommitted, anonymous sex, which was exactly what I didn't want. But what else could they do? If they lived at home, they couldn't bring a lover home. And even if they had their own place, in time, their landlord would figure it all out and they would be evicted. You couldn't take your lover to company parties or church on a regular basis because you would be discovered and ostracized or even worse, fired from your job.

So most gay men and women during the 1960's and 70's were either forced to enter into unhappy marriages and lead double lives or remain single and settle for shallow, meaningless, anonymous sexual encounters in public places. And how Society and the Church loved to and continues loving to comment on the alarming promiscuity of homosexuals and the alarming amount drug and alcohol addiction found among gay men, yet is it any wonder? Given the shallow, degrading and meaningless situations that we were forced into by that same Society and the Church how could one expect anything else? Gay people aren't any more promiscuous or susceptible to drug or alcohol abuse than anyone else. These things don't occur as a result of simply being gay, but they are created by being made to feel like worthless degenerates and second rate citizens by the Church and Society.

So this is the environment that I and all those who I was attempting to meet, entered into; an environment of fear, self-loathing, suspicion and hopelessness. Even if you could find one stable, well adjusted individual out of the hundreds you encountered, the chances of building a stable, long term relationship without being discovered; mocked, and ostracized by Church, family and community was next to nil. And how were you to find anyone stable while moving among the "walking wounded"? Some gave up and tried sexual reorientation type therapy, which resulted in very short term results at best. Others subjected themselves or were subjected by their families to therapies as drastic as electro-shock therapy and ended up with a large part of their memory and education gone, but still irretrievably gay. What a tragedy. Still others, like myself, decided to face the "Mount Everest" of obstacles and scale it with varying degrees of success.

Some of the men who I met during those years, while not turning out to be the "man of my dreams", did at least become true and loyal friends, many of whom I have to this day; so the networking was partially successful to that extent. You have to remember that after I left Jehovah's Witnesses, I had lost all of my friends. I had gained some new ones in the workplace, some of whom I was able to share the more private aspect of my life with, and I had gained some friends in the occult circle, but I really needed to expand my circle of gay friends. I finally met a wonderful new friend, K-n, during that period. He was so handsome, with thick, jet black hair and a wonderful moustache, button-down white sailor pants and other "nice qualities". He looked like Omar Sharif or Doctor Zhivago. We took an immediate liking to one another and I hoped that maybe we could have a relationship since he was much more open and fearless than the others who I had met. Unfortunately, K-n preferred to play the field rather than settling down, but at least he was honest and up front with me so no one got hurt and we became great friends.

K-n knew many gay men and women from all over so he was able to help me expand my circle of acquaintances. He used to throw unimaginable weekend parties which resembled Bacchanalian Feasts; the following mornings however, more closely resembled the "Last Days of Pompeii". One would find clothing and naked males strewn all over the apartment; many still clutching the same martini glass they had been holding when they drifted off into oblivion. A little excessive one might say, but then we had to blow off steam occasionally.

I made a big mistake at one of those parties; it was a New Year's Eve party. K-n had a supposedly straight roommate renting a room from him who did not have any date for that evening and was going to be present. He was pretty open minded and had no objection or problem with any of K-ns gay friends. He was a young biker type with long hair and full beard and moustache and I was rather attracted to him, but K-n advised me: "Don't even think it", so I pretty much stayed away from him that evening. But suddenly, out of the clear blue, he came to me, champagne bottle in hand and asked if I would like to share a New Year's toast with him in his room, so I gladly obliged. I must admit, I am such a pushover when it comes to getting attention from a handsome virile man and especially a straight man. Well, in no time at all, the next thing I knew was that he had gently reached across the table, took my jaw in his hand and gently directed my lips to his. He was a wonderful, passionate kisser and the next thing that I knew was that clothes were flying and that he was suddenly wrapped around me like a pretzel. Things were getting pretty intense and he asked me if I had any lubricant. Well, it wasn't my house and I was a little tipsy and didn't know exactly where K-n kept all of those kinds of items, but I left my partner briefly and ran to the bathroom to see what I could find. I returned with a tube of something which resembled K-Y or lubricant and the rest is history. How could I not surrender to this hunky, stud who so obviously "wanted me"?

Well, the next morning we awoke, still wrapped around each other in an eternal embrace, but experiencing extreme itching and burning in our private areas. We wondered what the problem could be. I immediately decided to examine the tube which I had taken from the bathroom and discovered that it was Amway furniture polish and restorative. Well! I'm quite certain that cured the poor guy of any further bi-sexual encounters for quite some time to come, but we did have a good laugh out of it and I must admit that I have never suffered from termites nor wood rot in the groins ever since.

Now after this roommate moved out, K-n got another renter in, but this one was a newly emerging young gay man; his name was R-ck. He was a very attractive, tall and lean young man with wavy brown hair, a trim beard and moustache, beautiful, dreamy blue eyes and a wonderful sense of humor. We took an immediate liking to one another. It was a sultry June evening and K-n had decided to throw a birthday party for me. After most of the guests had left, K-n presented me with a large, six foot tall dracaena plant which he had grown for me after remembering how often I had commented on the ones he had in his apartment. He advised me that since I certainly couldn't carry it to the car myself and would have difficulty unloading it at the other end, that he was sending R-ck along with it as part of my birthday present. I asked him if this was his idea or that of R-ck, to which he replied: "both". So I felt comfortable with the idea.

Well, R-ck and I had a wonderful night together. Everything just fell into place naturally. And the nice part was that it wasn't just a sexual thing; he was very loving, romantic and tender and loved just staying in bed cuddling and stroking my hair and talking. It was great and truly refreshing; not like some of my prior experiences where the men were up and dressed and out the door within record breaking moments following their climax. No, R-ck genuinely enjoyed being with me and I with him. We continued seeing one another for several weeks, going to coffee houses together and dancing together. He even accompanied me to a gay bar as my escort at a Halloween party. I had decided to compete in a female impersonator drag contest.

I was at K-ns place with a friend of mine doing my hair and applying makeup. When I finally emerged from the bathroom in a floor length, dark green velvet evening gown, replete with evening gloves, chandelier earrings and tiara, R-ck thought that I was just too stunning to go without an escort so he volunteered his services. He ran into his room and changed into a dark brown three piece suit. He looked stunning and I was just so proud to be seen with him. I had never seen him dressed this way before. We made quite a hit as we entered the bar, my gloved hand on his arm and he, towering above me, even in my heels.

We danced the night away; mostly slow dances and of course, he led; it could not be otherwise. It was amazing. As I leaned my head upon his shoulder or clasped my hands behind his neck and gazed into his eyes, I felt like a young girl at her High School prom. It was absolutely wonderful and I wasn't ashamed of my feelings. Oddly enough, neither was he embarrassed about my being dressed as a woman, nor the way that I was responding to him as many other gay men might have been. How often you would hear gay men saying: "I want a man; I don't want no damn sissy drag Queen." But R-ck was fine with it all, probably because he was a real man with no hang-ups and secure in his own masculinity. He was my ideal man, but I let him slip away. Why?

It wouldn't have taken much effort on my part to fall in love with him, in fact, I was beginning to fall in love with him, but after my tragic situation with my prior lover who was younger than me, I feared that the same thing might happen again. R-ck was about 8 years younger than me and new to the gay scene. I reasoned in my mind that he had really not had the chance yet to "play the field" and date other people and I didn't think it wise for him to just settle on the first man he met. Also I felt that perhaps the age difference was too great; that he should be with someone his own age so I didn't pursue him any further. I guess R-ck took that as sort of a rejection or at least a lack of serious interest in settling down so he began dating other people.

I really was not aware of the kind of people he might be attracted to; we had never really discussed that. So I had the shock of my life when one day he walked into K-n's apartment and introduced us to his new lover, a man 20 years older than him. I could have fallen on the floor. I couldn't believe it and asked K-n what was going on? Ken replied: "Didn't you know that R-ck is attracted to older men"? I could have kicked myself then and even now when I think of what I lost. He was everything that I ever wanted in a man: handsome and mature, and yet boyish and playful, affectionate, intelligent, and caring, a good lover, gainfully employed, accepted me just as I was, even if a bit feminine; almost too good to be true wouldn't you say?

Now oftentimes, young gay men will seek out older men because they are looking for a sugar daddy or a free ride, but R-ck wasn't like that at all. And the worst of it is that the man he settled down with was boring, domineering, demanding, possessive, and a cheater. Certainly R-ck deserved better than that and so did I. After he settled down with his new Beau we never saw much of R-ck again. His partner didn't want him seeing his old friends. On occasion I would see the two of them together on the patio of a gay bar in New Haven. R-ck would always run over to me and give me a big bear hug, at which point his partner would take him by the hand and say: "Sorry, but we were just leaving" and proceed to lead him out of the bar. Losing R-ck was a great loss, even if only as a friend, but much more as a lover.

This period of my life became very difficult. I wanted so desperately to be settled down with one special person, but this was the 70's remember?, sex, drugs and rock and roll and the sooner that I arose to the occasion, the better. It was a time to simply play until you dropped and not to be concerned about love or feelings. But that just wasn't me. So in order to enable myself to be like the rest, I resorted to a lot of alcohol, poppers, grass and coffee to keep myself going; gallons of coffee and sometimes amphetamines. When inebriated or stoned, I became more aggressive and secure enough to pursue the objects of my desire and entrap them, or so I thought. What was actually happening was that wiser men than I or anyone that might have truly been available for a relationship, more than likely saw me in the bar acting foolishly and aggressively and reasoned that I was a tramp and entirely unsuitable; while still others thought: "That drunk Queen over there in the corner might be good for a quick roll in the hay, but that's all she's good for". And so many just took advantage of me and used me, or perhaps we mutually just used each other. Whichever the case, it all led to self-hatred and alcoholism and drug abuse on my part and on the part of many others of my brothers, and sisters. Sad isn't it?

During this period I continued to experiment with dressing in drag. A friend of mine suggested that I should compete in an upcoming contest at a New Haven gay bar, Ricardo's Copa. Now I had been to a bar before in drag but only for a Halloween party, not actually competing against other Drag Queens, so this was going to be a stretch. But I figured that since most Drag Queens usually over dress with boas, fox stoles and such to the extent that they are not believable, then I would dress down a bit and go dressed as a real woman would. So I did. This time, I had as my escort a gay neighbor of mine who I had become friends with. P—l, was about 5 years older than me; he was a massive, rugged weight lifter and Vietnam vet who held the Purple Heart and many other medals for bravery; a real man here, certainly no sissy. He thought that I looked really good as a woman, in fact, far better than I looked as a man. As a man I was just OK, just average, but I made a truly striking woman. P—l felt that I would have no problem at all winning the contest because I was beautiful and believable so he agreed to escort me in full military uniform. We made quite a couple when we entered the bar; we were like something out of a Hollywood movie and I did become "Miss Copa 1975".

I wasn't in love with P—l, he had some serious drinking problems worse than mine, plus he was attracted to younger more masculine men, but we were good friends. But again, as we slow danced under the glittering disco ball, I, firmly held in the arms of an extremely masculine, uniformed man with pecks to die for, knew for a fleeting moment the magic and passion that every woman must feel at her prom or wedding; a magic that I guess I was fortunate to have felt even if only once or twice in my life. I just wish that I could feel it again just once more before it is time for me to "shuffle off this mortal coil".

You know, it's tough being expected to be the man all of the time. There is a wonderful feeling in sometimes being passive and vulnerable; sometimes being the so-called weaker vessel. I often envy women who have that available to them all of the time and yet so often don't seem to appreciate it or would rather be in the male role or dominate their husbands. I'm tired of always having to be the aggressor and initiate everything. Just once, I would like to have a strong, passionate, take-charge man in my life,who would overpower me and make all of the first moves without later downing me and making fun of me for being passive or feminine or a "bottom" as the term goes. But unfortunately, in the gay world, that's a rare possibility. Everyone is expected to be overtly masculine and butch all of the time and if you weaken and show any signs of passivity or domesticity, you will be dumped as a "femme". But who does anyone think they are kidding? Part of the reason that we are gay males is precisely because there is that female part of us that wants to be "taken" or mastered by a man. There needs to be more give and take in the gay community; we need to be more versatile and be able to play both the male and the female roll from time to time so that both partner's inner needs get met.

We simply cannot expect gay male relationships to work if we keep everything on a male-male basis and ignore our feminine sides. The male side is primarily the hunter, the progenitor, the aggressor and that is good, but the female side is the nurturer, the homemaker, and the fidelity side and we should not and must not ignore those facts. Remember, as in the case of magnets, opposite polls attract, while like poles repel. Nor should we lock ourselves into a straight mode where one is always the husband and the other is the wife; that simply won't work either.

Sometimes we gay men are our own worst enemies. Many gay men reject other gay men and prefer to exclusively date only straight men. In our constant search for ultimate masculinity we somehow see other gay men as somehow flawed or not quite masculine enough. I am always amazed at many of the gay personals adds that I see on the internet which read something like this: "Looking for 19-22 year old masculine, uniformed men to serve and worship. Fats, femmes and gays need not apply". Now, honestly, who exactly does that little fag slave think he is rejecting but other gays just like himself. Yes, I often think that we are our own worst enemies and that we do a far better job of rejecting each other than even Society does to us. But "don't cry for me, Argentina", I did survive this period and will continue to survive with a little help from my friends and I finally did meet my second lover, T-m.

CHAPTER 3
ON THE LIGHTER SIDE

I thought that at this point you probably needed a little comic relief from the "Perils of Pauline"; it ain't easy being gay, let me tell you. Anyone who says that it is a "chosen lifestyle" certainly hasn't "been there" and doesn't know what they are talking about. But there are some funny moments too, so I want to reward you for your patience by telling you one of the funniest things that ever happened to me, or in deed, to anyone. This is a very delicate area and I don't want to be vulgar so I may use some euphemisms to ease the shock. If you are not prepared for some truly intimate and personal information, skip over this chapter. Also please be certain that there is no one under 18 peering over your shoulder. Actually it's not really all that bad and it's certainly been a hit at any party where I have been asked to repeat it because it is a true story; my story.

You will remember the trouble that I got myself into back at my friend's New Year's Eve party when confusing Amway furniture polish for K-Y lubricant. Well this is far worse with far deeper (no pun intended) ramifications. Shortly after that debacle, perhaps only weeks later, I got myself into a far worse situation.

On a boring, gray, winter, Saturday afternoon, "the winter of my discontent", my ex-lover, "H" called to acquaint me with a new discovery that he had made. He asked me if I had ever used a vibrator or other similar "toys" like. Well, I was shocked to say the least. I mean weren't vibrators strictly for women? "H" said, "No, not at all". In fact he had many male friends who used them with great results. What results?, I thought to myself. "H" then began to explain to me that if you "hit the right spot" with them, you can have a climax. Really? I questioned. "Yep", he responded, "they're really great". Well, I must admit that I was rather impressed and inspired by his little infomercial and with no hot date lined up for this dreary evening, decided to rush out and get one. So I went to a local adult bookstore to see what they had available. This was a bit embarrassing, but I could always tell the clerk that I was getting it for my girlfriend; RIGHT. I looked through their inventory and finally found what I wanted.

Now, I postulated that if the little 4 inch vibrator which "H" was using with AAA batteries was doing the trick, then certainly the 8 inch anal torpedo which I had in my hands, which ran on 3 "D" cells should certainly do the job. The clerk kindly installed the batteries; hit the switch and the vibrator jumped out of his hands and onto the counter. We both laughed and he said: "I think this should do the trick"; I readily agreed and purchased it. I rushed home like a child to play with my new toy. I took a shower, jumped into bed and "fired up the rocket".

Of course this was all uncharted highway for me so I wasn't sure how far to insert it; there were no lengthy directions on the box other than the words "for a relaxing massage". So I inserted it half way. It was relaxing and tingling and gave me all kinds of new sensations, but it wasn't doing what "H" said it would do so I called him on the phone. I explained to him that it was very nice and very relaxing but then it wasn't doing what he said that it would. Of course I failed to give him a full description of my new instrument so he was about to give me advice with only the partial information that I had given him. He told me: "Push it in further". I thanked him, hung up the phone and resumed my experimentations. I used my middle finger to push my torpedo further up the tube when all of a sudden WHOOSH ! It just disappeared. Where could it have gone?

I jumped out of bed and threw back all the blankets and it was nowhere to be found! It was just gone! But where? I could still hear the buzzing noise, slightly muffled, but I could still here it and as I bent over the bed to examine the bedding I would notice the sound getting louder, then softer, then louder then softer as I bent over and then straightened up; zzzzzzzZZZZZZ, zzzzzzzZZZZZZZ. Oh my God! It was inside of me...way inside of me; what do I do now? Don't panic, I told myself, just go to the bathroom, sit on the toilet and it will certainly fall out. So I went to the bathroom, sat on the toilet and it DIDN'T fall out. I strained and strained and it still wouldn't come out. Oh my God! What do I do now? I tried to compose myself and call one of my friends who lived nearby, but what would I tell him? How could I explain this? Well, after telling him my grizzly story he asked me: "Well, what do you expect me to do"? I told him that I couldn't reach it myself and thought that perhaps with a pair of robber gloves, he would be able to get a hold on it and pull it out. He agreed and told me that he would be right over.

When he arrived, I answered the door in my bathrobe, at which point he asked me what that strange buzzing noise was. I just looked at him with a look of disgust and said : "What do you think it is"? He laughed and laughed and affirmed that this was the absolutely most stupid thing that I had ever done. I gave him the rubber gloves and bent over, but try as he would, there was just no getting it out; it was just in to far and lodged against some part of my anatomy. He asked me what I was going to do now. I said: "Hell, I guess I have to go to the hospital". He asked me if I was in pain, to which I responded "No", other than the vibrations and buzzing noise, I wasn't in any kind of discomfort, but it had to be removed; I couldn't just leave it in there. Once he was assured that I was in no pain, he asked me if I thought that I could drive in that condition. Well, I could comfortably sit down so I assumed that I could also drive. At that point he said: "I'm out of here. I am NOT going to the hospital with you in that condition, but bend over again and let me see if I can at least turn the damn thing off so you don't go buzzing into the hospital". He was successfully able to turn off the switch with a long handled wooden spoon. Guess I can't use that one anymore for stirring sauce. My friend left me to mull this one over by myself.

I sat there at the kitchen table trying to figure out what to do. Since I normally had much more courage and could just come right out and say things when drunk, I figured that the best solution was to chug down a pint of vodka, which I did and then proceeded to drive to the hospital so that I could safely get there before the booze cut in.

Upon arrival at the emergency room desk, I was greeted by a large Jamaican nurse who asked me what I was there for. I told her that I didn't want to discuss this with her, but could she please just get me a doctor. Now I don't exactly know why I felt more comfortable making this bizarre revelation to a male doctor than to a female nurse, but I just did. She replied: "I'm sorry sir, but I cannot get you an appropriate doctor until I know the exact nature of your ailment; you appear to be in good health". I repeated : "Please, just get me a doctor, any doctor and let him figure it out". Again she replied: "No sir, I cannot admit you to this hospital until you tell me what is wrong". By now the booze was starting to cut in and the adrenalin was starting to surge and I blurted out : "So, you really want to know do you? OK then; I have an 8 inch vibrator stuck in my rectum, now are you going to get me a doctor or not"? The nurse then immediately got an orderly to wheel me into one of the emergency rooms, strip me and place me in a bed with my legs in stirrups, much like a woman about to give birth or have her gynecologist examine her. What humiliation!

Several doctors entered the room and each in turn attempted to remove the vibrator; all to no avail. The second doctor accidentally hit the switch on the vibrator and turned it on, scaring the hell out of himself; he hadn't known that it was an electrical device, he just thought that he was dealing with a dildo. Then a nurse approached my bed with a phone on a mile long extension chord and asked me if I wanted to call my father. "Are you out of your mind"?

I replied. "No thanks". Finally an Indian doctor got me out of bed and instructed me to hold onto the bars on the bed, squat over a bedpan and bite down on a rubber implement which he placed in my mouth. One of the other doctors entered the room and asked him what on earth he was doing to which he replied: " I saw this done in a movie "Man In The Wilderness", it was the way Navajo women gave birth and I thought that it might work". My God! I thought, now I am at the mercy of Indian movie buffs. When the hell, are they going to get this thing out of me; they're supposed to be doctors?

The head doctor on duty finally came in to tell me that they would not be able to remove it that evening, but that they would schedule me for surgery first thing Sunday morning. SURGERY! Oh my God, wasn't there any other way? The doctor explained that while he didn't believe that they would have to cut anything, that my muscles and body at this point was too tight, but that in the operating room they would be able to put me out and give me relaxants and use forceps to open me up. I signed all of the necessary forms and was then taken to X-ray so that they could determine exactly how it was lodged.

Now of course X-ray technicians are not always told what they are taking pictures of in advance, they are simply told to take an abdominal X-ray. Then they wheel you out into the hallway where you wait until they develop the X-ray, put it on the screen and make sure that it is not blurred or defective. So they took the X-rays, wheeled me out into the hallway and I lie there in bed waiting for the bomb to fall. I knew that when they saw the X-rays that they would go crazy and they did. I heard a roar of laughter go up in the X-ray room; technicians screaming and laughing and peeking out the door at the star patient. It was just too much, but I must admit that I even laughed myself. Then they finally wheeled me up to my room for the night.

The night nurse, another Jamaican lady, but much more pleasant than the admitting nurse, picked up my chart and started laughing. She then apologized and said to me: "Oh sir, I am so sorry for laughing, but how on earth did you do it"? I told her that it was a long, difficult story. She comforted me by assuring me that there had been other patients in the past with foreign objects stuck in them, but it was usually carrots, cucumbers, corncobs or something easier to remove. I had really done it big time.

The next morning they prepped me and began rolling me down to the O.R. They began administering anesthesia on the way and I was out cold before we ever got to the room. Next I knew, I was in a recovery room with the surgeon telling me that the operation was a success. I asked him what happened to the vibrator to which he replied: "Surely you didn't want it back did you"? "I thought you wanted me to remove it; not just replace the batteries." He assured me that no damage had been done and gave me high powered suppositories to shrink everything back to normal. I asked him what they were going to put on the report since I feared that my insurance wouldn't cover it. He kindly replied that they were simply going to put "removal of a foreign object from the digestive tract". Good ! I left the hospital around noon, but since it was Sunday, the offices were closed and I was unable to retrieve any of my personal belongings like my wallet. I would have to return the next day for that. I had somehow managed to retain my car keys. So it doesn't end here folks, wait until you see what happened next.

On Monday morning I went to work as usual, but I didn't have my wallet and my ID card to show the guard, so I had to have my supervisor sign me in and I had to think up an excuse to tell her as to why I did not have my ID. So I told her that I had been hospitalized over the weekend with a chicken bone stuck in my digestive tract which had to be removed. Word spread fast that I had been hospitalized and everyone was very sympathetic. I asked my supervisor if I could take a little longer than usual lunch to go to the hospital and retrieve my personal papers; she agreed. So I went to the hospital and got my wallet back.

Upon returning, one of the girls who I worked with from the front office came up to my desk with tears streaming down her face, just laughing and laughing. They all knew that I was gay and had no problem with it, so any of them would feel free to tell me gay related jokes or whatever. So now, this girl tells me: "Bob, I have a story for you that is so funny that you will pee your pants. I responded that I always enjoy a funny story, so she proceeded to say: "My sister is an X-ray technician at Bridgeport Hospital and this weekend some faggot was in the hospital with an enormous vibrator stuck up his ass". She caught me off guard and rather than laugh, my face must have gone white as a ghost and my eyes filled with terror at which point she said: "Oh my God! You didn't choke on a chicken bone, it was you! It was you!

I then tried to quiet her down and told, her for God's sake, don't repeat this to anyone, but it was already too late and others had come to the same conclusion. For the next three weeks I was receiving magazine clippings of vibrators through the inter-company mail; as I walked down the street on lunch hours the guys in our building across the street were hanging out the window blowing kisses; it was terrible, but funny all at the same time. I didn't think that I would ever live this down, but that's one good life lesson that I learned. Everything has a lifespan and if you wait long enough, eventually people will forget and life goes on. So there is absolutely no reason to believe that you will never survive a loss or never outlive an embarrassing moment. The human psyche is bigger than all that and has unfathomable resiliency and ability to survive and move on. So never give up; "Where there's life, there's hope. Needless to say, I have never used a vibrator again since.

Now let me explain something that I mentioned a little earlier, namely that everyone knew that I was gay; how that came about and why, because there is a very good reason for it. Back then, I wasn't some kind of activist who just felt that I had to force my lifestyle on everyone. I was pretty laid back and not a "screamer" at all. When I first started working there, no one was aware that I was gay at all, in fact, quite the opposite. I was the first male customer service representative hired in that department due to the Equal Rights Amendment that had just gone into effect, so I was the only male in the department and I was roughly the same age as most of the girls that I worked with. I was an immediate hit and all of the girls were continually inviting me out with their group to discos and singles dances and dinner. I wasn't totally comfortable with it all, but they were nice girls, I needed new friends and I didn't want to blow my cover at that point because I wasn't too certain of how it might affect my job. So I went along with it all.

One of the girls, a very pretty young lady with layer upon layer of beautiful ringlets of blond hair and lovely large blue eyes took a special liking for me. She started inviting me over for dinner and taking me over her parent's house for dinner and inviting me to go to the movies with her. One time I noticed all of the apples that had fallen off a tree in front of her apartment and suggested that we make applesauce and apple cake together. E----n was thrilled. She wasn't that much of a cook and didn't have much in the way of kitchen utensils so I went out and got her some baking pans and such. We had a wonderful afternoon making applesauce and baking apple cake and it turned out really good; she surprised herself. I enjoyed myself too, it was like having the sister that I had never had. But I know that she was seeing it differently and I was worried about that.

Finally, one evening she invited me over to dinner and during dinner it began snowing heavily. She suggested that I stay over rather than drive in the snow, but on other occasions when it was only raining she had suggested that I stay over too and I was starting to get worried. Had she thought up to this point that I was simply a gentleman and that's why I didn't stay over? Or was she starting to wonder if there was something wrong with her? Why wasn't I co-operating? I mean, she was a beautiful girl and any normal red-blooded man would have been happy to stay the night with her. I didn't want to make the same mistake that I had made before. I didn't want to hurt her like I had hurt that other young girl from Norwich; I had to tell her. The only way to stop this fast rolling avalanche would be to melt it in the "sun of honesty". I was taking a big chance. I had never "come out" to anyone straight before. How would she take it? Would she be angry? Worse yet, would she find it disgusting and not want my friendship anymore? I couldn't bear that; I enjoyed our friendship immensely. But I had to tell her for her own sake, even if it meant pain and loss for me so I took a chance and told her.

I began: "E----n, first off, I want to thank you for the months of friendship which you have shared with me. You really made my first months at a new job happy and I have really enjoyed all of the great times we have spent together. You are a loving, kind and sincere person and you have probably wondered by now why our relationship has not become more intimate. You are a beautiful young woman and any man in his right mind would have certainly shown you more affection and intimacy by now. Perhaps you thought that I was just being a gentleman or perhaps you thought that I just didn't find you attractive, but nothing could be further from the truth. The fact is, E----n, that I'm gay". There, I said it; I actually said it, now cover my ears and hit the floor. No need for that. E----n smiled kindly and took it all in stride. She confided that she had, in fact, wondered what was up, or rather wasn't up. We both laughed and became the best of friends. She accepted me just the way I was and our friendship never skipped a beat, in fact it grew because she felt that I must certainly love her and trust her in my own limited way enough to share something that personal with her. And she was right, I loved her in the only way that I knew, as a sister.

It's sad that so many of my gay brothers and sisters are too frightened to take that kind of chance and "come out" to their straight friends. Instead they choose to live a lie and feign relationships with the opposite sex, which always end in tragedy one way or the other. I do believe that honesty is the best policy. I certainly can't live my life as a lie or live a double life. And if your friends are halfway decent people; if they are compassionate and caring, it won't make any difference to them. You are the same friend now as you always were before you told them, so why should it make any difference? Whereas on the other hand, if they find out from someone else, they will always wonder why you didn't love them enough or trust them enough to let them into that more intimate part of your life. If they reject you, then that's their loss; they were only superficial fair weather friends who only befriended because they didn't know who you truly were. Had they known, they wouldn't have befriended you in the first place. Can you call people true friends who don't even really know you or if they really did, wouldn't like you at all?

The best part of "coming out" is that it is freeing. I would never again have to play those silly dating games; never risk hurting another sensitive soul; never have to fear being blackmailed and I could just be myself. Plus, it broadens your networking. All of my straight friends are continually looking for perspective husbands for me among their other gay friends and their friends' friends and God knows, I need all the help that I can get. Not only that, but it helps broaden their minds too.

Many of my heterosexual friends have thanked me over the years for my honesty and revelations because they said that it was a real education for them and gave them a whole new attitude toward gay men and women that they might never have known had it not been for my willingness to be honest with them. They said that before me, they had never known anyone gay and it has helped them to see that we are not freaks and degenerates, but genuine people with genuine needs and family values just like them. Now they are comfortable if their son or nephew "comes out" to them; it has made life easier for them. They are more comfortable with their gay neighbors and gay issues in general because they have interacted with a real person rather than getting their information from some TV talk show or worse yet, from the Christian Right Movement. This, in turn will make it easier for future generations of gay people.

I think that so much of the time, the reason that we were in the closet so long isn't so much because someone straight locked us in, but because we locked the door behind ourselves. We lacked the faith; faith in our own ability to rise above stereotypes and we also lacked faith and trust in the ability of our friends, neighbors, and loved-ones to be able to accept us and love us unconditionally as we do them.

Now, enough seriousness, here are a few more anecdotes from this period that I am sure will brighten your day.

When I was working in the public office of the telephone company I would wait on customers face to face, but of course if they later called in, they would reach someone entirely different over the phone and so would often ask to speak with me. One such elderly customer kept calling in asking to speak with the lovely young lady in the Phone Store named Bobbi. When the rep advised him that there was no young lady in the Phone Store named Bobbi; he was adamant and said: "There certainly is, I just spoke with her earlier today. She's the pretty young rep with curly blonde hair and the blue and white polka-dot blouse." You see, I had just had a permanent wave only days earlier which left me looking like "Little Orphan Annie" and the poor elderly man thought that I was a woman and when I had told him that my name was Bob, he kept saying, "no, isn't it Bobbi"? and of course I had never corrected him. The customer is always right !

On another occasion, during my "party hardy" period, I had been out all night carousing at the bars and came staggering into work late. The girl across the desk from me kept going PSSSST, PSSSST "I think you better go to the men's room. I couldn't imagine what she meant by that. So I asked her "What are you trying to say"? She just continued, "Go to the men's room", so I asked her again, to which she replied: "I don't want to yell this out, but you apparently didn't look in the mirror this morning before coming to work. You went a little heavy on the eye shadow and blush my dear".

Then there was that first Christmas Eve when my youngest nephew first began speaking. At that point he could only say short phrases like "Mewwy Twistmas Dwanpa", which translates into "Merry Christmas Grandpa. And so that was his holiday greeting to his grandfather as Dad and I walked through the front door on Christmas Eve. But to my shock and astonishment, he had a greeting for me too and it was distinctly, "Mewwy Twistmas, Aunty Bob." They say, out of the mouths of babes comes wisdom.

Then there was the time when Dad and my Step-Mom had stopped by unexpectedly and I had not had a change to "De-Fag" the apartment. That's when we hide away things in our home that might be a dead giveaway to relatives or strangers. I had this lovely 5x7 framed picture of myself in drag on the coffee table, replete with floor length gown, evening gloves and chandelier earrings. My Dad, who was always eagerly awaiting any possible announcement of my pending engagement to some lovely lady, noticed it first and inquired: "Who's the pretty girl"? When I realized what he was looking at I panicked and had to think really fast. "Oh, that's a lady friend of mine, Vicky, do you like her"? I said. My Step-Mom then took the picture and said: "Well she certainly is very pretty, but she looks a little on the wild side". To which I responded: "She is, she is, but she's only a friend, nothing serious".

I felt bad deceiving them, but my Dad had such high hopes for me. Why was it so easy for me to come out at work, but so hard to tell my family? I guess it was because if worse came to worse, I could always find new friends, but how could I find a new family? Plus, it always seemed to me that nothing that I had ever done in my life had ever pleased my Dad, so how could I imagine that telling him of my gay nature, would please him ?

CHAPTER 4
STRANGERS IN THE NIGHT

It was a night like any other night, except that this time, I put my best foot forward to kick the eye makeup and platform shoes and try to be a little more butch; with the exception of retaining my little diamond earring in my right ear; which was an open confession to all that I was gay; straight boys and those who don't want to give themselves away, normally wear it in the left ear. Well, as I gazed across the dance floor, I noticed an attractive, Mediterranean looking man who appeared to be making his way toward me. Now usually when this kind of thing happened and I thought that someone was interested and about to approach me, it invariably turned out that they were looking at someone near me or trying to get to the cigarette machine that I was standing in front of. But this time it was for real! The young man, T-m, introduced himself and said that he couldn't help but notice my earring reflecting the disco lights and the continual flashing attracted his attention. So you see, diamonds REALLY ARE a girl's best friend.

You must understand that back then, the dances were much more personal than now; usually slow dances; cheek to cheek; body to body; not the kind of calisthenics and impersonal dances done today which are usually danced miles apart and intended to attract someone other than who you are with. So T-m asked me to dance; not once; not twice, but continually. So I did. We danced cheek to cheek; crotch to crotch until we had endured all of the stimulation that we could handle without immediately heading for a motel. T-m was more reserved than I and decided that we should cool down a bit by leaving the dance floor and meeting his friends whom he had come with. I thought to myself, just the fact that he has taken the time in his life to make friends is a positive quality; this may be a very nice young man. So I met his friends and they were all delightful. He then invited me to join his group at the diner next door for coffee, so I could clearly see that nothing was going to be "consummated" this evening, but that was OK with me. I clearly liked him and wanted to get to know him better and felt that he was worth waiting for. We had a great time at the diner and made an arrangement to meet again for a date the following week.

I thought about him all week. He was a very attractive young man; average build, but solid with thick, wavy black hair, dark intense eyes, a deep tan; all together very Mediterranean looking and for good reason; he was Italian-American and about 5 years younger than me. He called me mid week and talked and talked and confided that he was counting the hours until we could meet again. Counting the hours? Wow, I thought, I really stumbled onto a live one this time. But we mutually agreed to take it slow and get to know each other first before moving on to the next stage. And we did take it slow; really slow for my taste, but again, I felt that he was worth waiting for.

Well, as fate would have it, one fine Sunday afternoon we finally consummated the relationship and boy, was it worth the waiting! I think that we were in my boudoir for six hours rather than the usual three minutes of foreplay, five minutes of heavy duty and then a rapid exit. No, this was a wonderful experience with a lot of tenderness and of course passion too. This was certainly a wonderful and new experience for me.

We did have our differences though. You must remember that at this point in my life, I had little use for the Institutional Church as a practicing Witch or Wiccan, while T-m was a devout Roman Catholic and very involved in politics, both of which kept him firmly "in the closet" with the exception that, oddly enough, he was "out" with his family and they accepted his homosexuality. He clung to numerous straight relationships both male and female, which I felt were very superficial and would only end tragically once they found out that he had been deceiving them all along. You see, he had not made any attempt to fend off the advances of his straight lady friends and allowed them to think that he was in fact available, so they continued to pursue him. To my thinking he was merely using them so that he would have someone to be seen with at political and religious functions; someone to hide behind to back up his disguise of heterosexuality. And so we had many arguments about this.

But he was younger than me and perhaps I was wrong to have expected him to have attained to the same level of "outness" and growth to which I had attained. It wasn't entirely that he lacked courage; I mean he had "come out" to his family, which was more than I had done, I think that he just didn't want to lose his friends and public standing. We just didn't see eye to eye on a lot of issues, but we did try to compromise. One of the areas of compromise was in religion. T-m felt that I was entirely too bitter toward Christianity and was uncomfortable with my practicing Wicca. He reasoned with me that just because Jehovah's Witnesses had done a number on my head, that this was no reason for me to "throw the baby out with the bathwater" and reject all denominations of Christianity. At that time, with the

Roman Catholic Church becoming increasingly hostile toward homosexuals, we both decided to investigate the Episcopal Church.

It was around Christmas time and T-m saw an ad in the newspaper announcing that a local Episcopal Church was hosting a medieval Boar's Head Christmas Dinner, replete with minstrels and other entertainment; so we went. And what to my surprise, as we sat chatting at one of the tables, two male parishioners approached us and said: "Why aren't you two girls dancing"? We were shocked, but couldn't help but laugh. Their "gaydar" must have been on in full force, because they wanted to let us know that we were on friendly turf. They explained to us that the church was very gay friendly; that in fact, the priest, organist and half of the choir were all gay and that they regularly hosted marvelous musical events, concerts, cocktail parties and such. Well, we had found a home at last.

I felt a little awkward moving away from my Wiccan association, but then it wasn't as if I was leaving them behind entirely. Rose had told me to go out and investigate and that was all that I was doing. I had enjoyed nature worship, but it was a little impersonal. Wiccans did not really have what could be called a close, personal relationship with their deities; it was more of a manipulative relationship in which you attempted to bribe or force nature to do your will. Then too, I always questioned one of our seasonal chants which went like this: "Queen of the Moon, Queen of the Stars, bring to us the Child of Promise. For it is the Great Mother who gives birth to Him; it is the Lord of Life who is born again…", and so on. I always pondered: "Who is the Great Mother and who is this Child of Promise spoken of in those ancient pre-Christian chants? Had the ancients been prophetic and foreseen the coming of Christ? Was Mary the Great Mother? I had to find the answers to those questions so I began my journey of faith in the Episcopal Church.

T-m was relieved that I was moving away from the occult, but he was still vacillating and trying to play both sides. He was still very actively involved in the Roman Catholic Church, while at the same time having a breath of fresh air at social events held in the Episcopal Church. I couldn't understand that. I mean the Roman Church had become increasingly hostile toward us. For a short time, compassionate and well meaning priests had a form of ministry for gay people and had created an organization known as "Gay Dignity". They would hold monthly masses in various Roman churches, expressly for homosexuals, followed by pot luck suppers, discussion and often a dance. They were very refreshing and although separate from mainstream Catholicism, still, a step in the right direction. But it wasn't long before

Rome put the torch to Dignity and said that these meetings could no longer be held on or in Church property.

During that period, I was privileged to hear a lecture by a wonderful and enlightened man, Father John J. McNeill, who at that time was still a Roman Catholic priest and who had written a book "The Catholic Church and Homosexuality". Prior to his lecture, he had passed out little folded flyers entitled: "What did Jesus Say About Homosexuality"? Of course when you opened the flyer, it was absolutely blank inside which said a lot. If God considered homosexuality such a great social ill, then why did Jesus never address the subject? He certainly had a lot to say about the hypocrisy of the religious leaders of his day and other issues, yet there was not one word about homosexuality.

Father McNeill in both his book and lecture exposed all of the traditional seeming references to homosexuality as misinterpretations and poor translations from the ancient languages. He explained that the "Sin Of Sodom" was simply a sin against hospitality, which was very important to Semites. If the men of Sodom had really been homosexual and seeking relations with Lot's male guests, then why would Lot have offered them his daughters? No, the men of Sodom simply wanted to rob and rape Lot's guests. Father McNeill also explained that most of the prohibitions of men being with men in the epistles of the New Testament were in reference to men sleeping with male prostitutes, which was frowned upon even by the Ancient Greeks. He also strongly questioned the sanity and logic of the Church in routinely granting forgiveness or absolution to gays who came to confession week after week confessing gross acts of promiscuity with countless numbers of anonymous partners, while yet refusing forgiveness and refusing the sacraments of the Church to any two homosexuals who were living in a monogamous, loving relationship because they said that was deliberate and premeditated sin as opposed to acts of passion, which were not necessarily premeditated. Father McNeill said: "So while the Church can readily forgive repeated acts of promiscuity and degradation; it cannot and will not forgive the "sin" of love". Does this make any sense at all? Father McNeill was ultimately repaid for his compassion toward homosexuals by being defrocked and ultimately excommunicated from the Roman Church when he refused to stop speaking out on these issues.

Other authors and specialists in studies on ancient religions and the early years of the Christian community would later corroborate Father McNeill's statements; one in particular, Yale professor, John Boswell, wrote a fine work with impressive documentation from historical archives: "Christianity, Social Tolerance and Homosexuality: Gay People in Western Europe from the Beginning of the Christian Era to the Fourteenth Century" in which he documented that homosexuality was accepted in the early Church and that there were even prescribed ceremonies for same-sex unions. So what went wrong? And why does the Church today, feel that they have greater wisdom than that of the early Church Fathers?

So T-m still had one foot in the church which I considered to be one of our greatest persecutors and I couldn't understand why. The amount of time that he was spending serving the needs of the Church, coupled with his political meetings and family duties was beginning to detract from the time that we needed to spend together nurturing our new relationship. Apparently he was starting to get "cold feet" and was having second thoughts as to whether he really wanted to put it all on the line and settle down. I, on the other hand, was spending more and more time alone, eagerly waiting for him to squeeze me in somewhere in his busy schedule. Finally, he put the cork in the bottle entirely by announcing to me that he was very sorry, but that he had decided to become a Franciscan Brother and that our intimacies would have to desist.

Of course, he never did become a Franciscan and some time later, I saw him in the same gay bar where we had met, in the arms of another man, so I knew that the monastery had lost out. But I overlooked it due to his age and newness to the gay counter culture and we remain friends to this day. In fact I did one of the scriptural readings at his wedding in a Unitarian Church some years later and we still keep in touch. Fortunately for me, the relationship had never quite grown to the point where I found myself "in love" with him, so while I was certainly disappointed, yet I was not crushed. I do owe him a great debt of gratitude because it was through T-m that I met other gay men who, like him, were to become lifetime friends. While Lesbian and Feminist bumper stickers back then read: "A woman without a man is like a fish without a bicycle", hell, I'll be the first to admit that I needed a man in my life.

My bumper sticker would have read: "A gay man without a lover is like a boat without a rudder". The reason that I felt this way may be partially because I lacked self-esteem and tended only feel worthwhile when I had achieved the love of another man. I then pour myself, heart and soul into the relationship, waiting on my man hand and foot and finding personal fulfillment through loving him. I am happiest when in love, but it's a bitter-sweet thing; a mixed bag of joy and ecstasy, but mingled with possessiveness and the constant fear of losing him either to natural causes or to another man.

I was now without a man again so what did I do? I became more promiscuous, more inebriated and more cynical about life. During that phase, one of K-n's friends, we'll call him

"C" asked me if I had ever thought of renting out my extra room since by this time I had purchased a two bedroom condo in town. I had never thought about it, but I said: "sure" and let him move in. He really wasn't my type; but he seemed nice enough, and I figured that it wouldn't hurt to have company and share some of the expenses. "C" had spent most of his life living with one man after another and had always found fault with each one and had ended up either leaving on his own or being asked to leave. But he was pretty street-wise and seemed to know all of the places where we could find men, so we began hanging out together; partially because he didn't drive nor have a car.

"C" was 5 years my senior, but acted much younger; he hadn't really had much of an education and didn't have a job. He had been on SSI for years due to childhood illnesses which his mother claimed left him a bit "slow" and totally dependent on SSI and her or other people. But as my Dad once said a few years later: "He can't be too dumb if he has managed to travel the world and live like a king without ever working." "C" did know how to manipulate people. In any event, we became "girlfriends" and spent most of our spare time hunting down eligible bachelors, but without any great success. All who we met were the usual assemblage of largely bi-sexual and married men who had infiltrated the gay scene simply to "knock off a piece": it was simply one loser after another. Of course none of them ever told you up front that they were married, you only found that out months later by some slip up on their part.

During this period, my ex, T-m also found that he was largely just meeting one loser after another and decided that he wanted me back. I figured that now that he had seen that there wasn't all that much out there, that he would appreciate me now. He must have thought that something was going on between "C" and I because this time he wasn't content just to date me; no this time he moved in with me, lock, stock and barrel. Even though "C" has his own room and we hadn't been going with each other; he became jealous of the lost attention and resented T-m sleeping in my bed with me so he got huffy and moved out leaving T-m and I to our domestic bliss.

Now during our temporary separation, T-m had met a very emotional and possessive Latino boy whom he dated for several months and then gave the same walking papers that he had given me, telling the boy that he wanted to pursue his calling to the monastic life. Only this kid did not take it as well as I had and wanted revenge so he called the Bishop and exposed T-m as a homosexual. Poor T-m was immediately removed of all of his church duties and it was strongly urged that he not even attend that church any longer. He was crushed, but knew where he could find a home, so he too finally joined the Episcopal Church that

I was attending. But then several months after that, he had another relapse into "monastic obsession" and decided that he now wanted to join the Episcopal Franciscans. What could I do? I had to let him go, but I'll tell you, this was not improving my relationship with God very much. I mean He had already taken my mother, and now he was taking my lover. I had to think this one out.

CHAPTER 5
WEDDING BELLS

Once that "C" found out that T-m and I were no longer an item, he moved in for the kill. He called me and asked me to marry him. Well, this was so sudden and I didn't know what to say; he totally caught me by surprise. I wasn't even aware that he had any kind of feelings for me and while I liked him, I certainly wasn't in love with him; he really wasn't my type. But he went on and on about how much he loved me and that he was so hurt when T-m moved in that was why he left because he couldn't bare to see me with another man. I told him that I was very flattered, but just needed a little time to think it all through, to which he said: "NO", either say yes, right now or I never want to see you again.

I couldn't help but think of the many disappointments that we both had suffered over the years and how very miserable and promiscuous I get when I feel rejected. I knew how desperately I wanted to be settled down with one man in a nice respectable relationship and thought: "Hell, this may be the one and only time in my life that anyone ever asks me to marry them; I better go for it. Surely in time I can learn to love him and we can make a go of it, I mean we're half way there, he already loves me." So after a brief pause, I said "yes". So we began making our wedding arrangements.

While of course, we couldn't get any kind of marriage license from the State, still, the priest at my church agreed to perform a ceremony at the church, to which we could invite friends and relatives. It was to be possibly the first of its kind in an actual church in Connecticut so we were pioneers in this. Father H took it all very seriously and sat us down and discussed with us the importance of a monogamous relationship and the duties that we owed one another. He kindly offered his services as a counselor, should we run into deep water along the way and promised us his blessing. We then set about getting rings, sending out invitations and all of the usual arrangements. I must admit that the girls at the telephone company were wonderful. I don't know how it leaked out, but ultimately they threw me a wedding shower and some of them asked if they could attend the service.

Of course our upcoming wedding brought me to the edge of a very dangerous precipice which I would either have to jump or remain forever behind. C's mom already knew that he was gay, so there was no problem there other than would she attend our wedding or not? But my Dad and Step-Mom were not aware of the situation and I wouldn't be able to hide my new husband from them indefinitely. What was I to do? I mean I couldn't just blurt out to them: "It's not like you're losing a son, you're gaining a son-in-law". Up to this point in life, I had never had any really lasting relationships worthy of bringing to the attention of my father, but now this was something which I thought would be real and permanent, so naturally, it was something that I would now want to share with my family. Plus, I felt really bad always lying to my Dad and giving him false hopes that I might someday marry and give him grandchildren. My brother had already done that so why should he need any more grandchildren from me?

So off I went to tell Dad and my Step-Mom. I premised it all by telling them that I had not been entirely truthful with them over the past years by leading them to believe that I had all of these girlfriends and potential wives and that I was truly sorry for misleading them, but that it was what I though that they wanted to hear. I explained to them that I loved them both too much to keep up the charade and that there never was going to be a wife in my life, but that I had found happiness with another man and wanted to at least share that happiness with them, just as I had accepted and celebrated their marriage and happiness.

The room went silent and then after a long pause my Dad began a mild tirade stating that I had disappointed him all of his life; that I had disappointed him when I joined Jehovah's Witnesses; I had disappointed him when I left home; I had disappointed him when I refused to go to college and that I was now dumping on him the final and biggest disappointment that he would have to take to his grave with him. Fortunately, and oddly enough, my Step-Mom jumped in and said: "It's not really all that bad, honey, my daughter has gay neighbors that are a couple and they have a good life together". Well thank you Mom! You saved the day.

My Dad finally calmed down and assured me that despite everything, I was still his son and that it was my life to live and that I had to do what was right for me. He further said that he felt that maybe it was just a passing phase, to which I assured him that I had been this way now since puberty and doubted very much that it was a passing phase, but that of course anything is possible. I told Dad how hard I had been fighting it all of my life; how that even the seminary experience was not able to overcome it. I told him that I had been to a therapist, which I had, who pronounced me one of the most well adjusted homosexuals that he had ever met. I explained to him that the therapist told me that any course of treatment to try to make me heterosexual would only lead to loss of identity and undue mental stress with absolutely no guarantee of long term benefits. He said that statistics proved that even those who responded favorably to sexual preference change therapy usually revert back to homosexuality in time leaving broken marriages and broken families behind.

So Dad took it all in stride, but suggested that I might not want to share any of this with my brother and his wife. He felt that having three young sons, she might not be comfortable with it, not wanting it to unduly influence the development of her children. So I did wait for many years until my nephews were grown and also only told my brother when it became absolutely necessary. So, I had now reached and passed another great milestone in my life. So in October of 1975, "C" and I had a lovely church wedding accompanied by many friends and co-workers and even my two ex-lovers, H and T-m, but unfortunately the parents of the groom and groom were conspicuously absent; neither of them were able to handle it, but wished us well. So "Sadie, Sadie, married lady" ran off to Niagara Falls with her new husband for her first week of marital bliss. Hopefully this was the beginning of "…and they lived happily ever after…" but since life is not a fairy tale (no pun intended), that was not to be the case.

CHAPTER 6
MARITAL BLISS

Since Niagara Falls is some distance from southern Connecticut, I had decided to break up the journey by stopping to visit and stay overnight with an ex-Witness friend of mine and her husband in Rochester, NY. P---y had always been a nice person and now no longer under the constrictions of the Witnesses, she had become even more compassionate and broad minded. I advised her of my new life style and new husband and she and her husband welcomed us both with open arms. I was very touched by this.

"C" had never been a very talkative person or great conversationalist, but his lack of exchange with P---y and her husband struck me as borderline rude. Had I not been so naïve, this might have clued me into the intense and incessant jealousy that "C" was later to exhibit toward all of my friends. We finally bade P---y and her husband farewell and took off for the Falls. We spent the day happily on the Maid of the Mist, shopping and dining out. I had looked forward to a romantic honeymoon in our beautiful room with balcony overlooking the falls, but that was not to be. "C" had a "headache" and wasn't in an overly amorous mood, so rather than push the issue, I spent the evening watching TV turned down low while "C" turned in early. However at 4 AM, he must have gotten a second wind, not for romance, but to move on. He was bored, and kept nagging me to get up so that we could pack, check out and get an early start going somewhere else. I asked him what would be wrong with staying in Niagara a little longer; the hotel was already paid for and we really hasn't investigated all that was there. But he wouldn't hear it, so off we went for Montreal.

But basically the same thing happened there. He neither liked French gourmet food, French cigarettes, nor the language and resented me speaking French to waiters and service people, so now we headed south through New York state to Howe Caverns. He did enjoy the caverns, but still, simply seemed to want to get back home to familiar surroundings. I loved traveling and had traveled extensively to England, France, Germany, and Switzerland and had assumed that he would enjoy travel too, but he just wanted to be near home.

Once back home, it was only a matter of time before he was bored again and, perhaps, not without reason because he didn't work. I, at least, kept my mind active all day at work and interacted with other people. But he did not work nor drive and there are only so many soap operas that one can watch. So I tried to at least make things nice for him in the evening. He wasn't happy entertaining friends at home, even though I did all of the preparations, cooking and cleanup afterward. He would say that I was just being ostentatious and "piss-elegant" with my dinner parties and that it was all my friends anyway, but it wasn't my fault that he didn't have any friends other than our mutual friend, "K". And I wasn't just showing off for friends because I often made lovely elegant candlelight dinners for just the two of us, but he didn't seen to like that either and would always blow out the candles and turn up the lights claiming he couldn't see the food.

I couldn't help but wonder why "C" didn't have any friends. He maintained that it was because gay people are all superficial fakes who like to "put on the dog", wine and dine, and generally act elegant and that if you don't have the money to keep up with them they'll just drop you by the wayside. Now while that may have been at least partly true, it certainly wasn't the rule. I had met many down to earth, genuine gay men and women over the years. Interestingly enough, "C", himself didn't seem to have much use for anyone who didn't have a good job, at least some money and a place for him to live so who's "calling the kettle black"? "C" had, in fact, spent the last 15 years prior to knowing me, living the life of a gypsy, moving from one man's house to another. I was naïve enough to feel sorry for him and think that he had simply been given a raw deal by a number of promiscuous gay men with short attention spans who had simply used him and then tossed him out when he stopped "putting out." But I soon realized that was not the case. "C" simply found fault with everything and everyone and nagged and moaned constantly until people couldn't take it anymore and asked him to leave.

But I kept exercising patience and continued giving and trying to make up for all of the bad experiences that he had suffered in the past. I tried to expose him to the finer things in life: operas, ballets, concerts; all of the things that I and my friends loved, and of course, at my expense, but he wouldn't have any of it. All that he seemed to enjoy doing was hanging out in gay bars from 6PM until closing night after night. I didn't see much point in that since we had each other. It might have been different if he liked dancing and we went to the bars so that we could dance together. But he never danced with me. I couldn't figure out what was going on. The relationship had deteriorated into the same relationship that my Mom and Dad had. He was constantly pushing me away; rationing out his affection and watching TV until 3AM every day so as to avoid having to "give me any". Two years later after I had put on some weight as married people often do, he confided that the reason he wouldn't dance with me was because he was embarrassed to be seen with me. But that certainly wasn't the case in the beginning so what was his excuse then?

Too many times to count, I would come home after a hard day's work to a home cooked meal? No; to a loving embrace? No, just a note on the kitchen table that he had taken the train to New Haven to go to the bars and that I should come to pick him up in New Haven at such and such a bar. In stead of helping me a bit with our monthly expenses, he was blowing his entire disability check monthly on booze and cigarettes. He finally became somewhat friendly with my friend and neighbor "P", the alcoholic Vietnam vet and weightlifter. I doubt that they were "doing" anything with each other, but "P" would take him to the beach or whatever and at least it got him out of the house for a while when I was at work.

But oddly enough if "P" came over during the evening and gave me a hug or whatever in front of "C", he would become livid, go storming upstairs and would later threaten that if I let that man in our house again, that he would pack up and leave me. He maintained that "P" was a drunk and degenerate and that he did not want him, or for that matter any gay people in our house. Yet he was the one who was inviting "P" over daily while I was at work. "C" hated gay people, and whenever I reminded him that we were gay he would become hostile.

It had pretty much become ritual for me to take "C" over to his mother's or his sisters at least once a week for a visit. I felt that it was important to keep up family ties. His mother liked me very much and appreciated all that I was doing for him, but repeatedly cautioned me that "C" was helpless and dependent and that he would never be able to make anything of himself and so I shouldn't expect much. I felt that she was simply overbearing and that this was a classic case of co-dependency where she had wanted to keep "her baby" to herself for all of those years or even forever and then all of these men had come along, including myself and had messed it all up. But then again, maybe she knew something that I didn't. Anyhow, week after week we visited with his family and I enjoyed it well enough. Yet he refused to visit with my family, even if they were coming all the way down to us rather than we having to go to them.

In June of 1976, my brother and his wife decided to come down and celebrate my birthday. My sister-in-law had baked a nice cake for the occasion and was bringing some take-out food; they were coming all the way from New Milford at least an hour's drive. Do you think that "C" would put on coffee for them or help me clean up the condo? Oh, No. "C" called for a taxi to take him to the train and went to the gay bars in New Haven for the day. And do you think that he had any kind of birthday present for me after I later picked him up in New Haven and brought him home? Of course not; no card, no present; and certainly no present of a more personal and intimate manner, which wouldn't have cost him anything other than giving of himself. So you see, it was a one-way relationship; HIS WAY.

Then one day, out of a clear blue sky, my "I don't need sex" hubby suggests that maybe we could spice up our relationship by having threesomes with another person as some acquaintances of his were doing; they had "open relationships". I reminded "C" that wasn't what we had committed to when we were married; to the contrary, we had promised fidelity to one another, which doesn't allow for a third party. "C" said that I was narrow-minded and that it was what all of the gay couples were doing and so should we. Well, the reason that he was so insistent on doing this was because he had already been "having a thing" going with a neighbor's friend while I was working and wanted to drag me into it to sooth his own conscience. Oddly enough on the evening of this scheduled tryst, the new guy, P-t and I seemed to hit it off and be much more compatible in bed that either he and "C" or "C" with me, so "C" left the bedroom all in a huff and went storming off to his room.

Later that evening after P-t had left, I had to hear over and over how that I preferred P-t sexually to him and that he knew it would only be a matter of time before I threw him out and replaced him with P-t. I told him that was ridiculous and that if he remembered correctly, the whole thing had been his idea. I also explained to him that was precisely why I was against threesomes, because someone always ends up feeling left out and you do run the risk of one of you becoming involved with the third party and ruining your relationship.

After that, "C" began advancing ultimatums and telling me that I would have to banish P-t from our home and also a lot of my friends because he insisted: "your friends hate me and are trying to break us up." The fact was that my friends did not hate him and tried to make him feel accepted, but he shunned them and avoided them. It seemed to me that "C" was doing a marvelous job of breaking us up far better than any of my friends could ever have done.

Finally, it all came to a head when I accepted a dinner invitation from a straight co-worker with whom I had been car-pooling to work for a few months. R----t was a strikingly handsome Italian-American who was living with a divorced woman and her 25 year old son not far from where we lived. Since she worked the night shift, she did not make breakfast, or for that matter any meals for him, he and I had started having breakfast together at a local IHOP on the way to work. He had a lot of problems in the relationship, as did I in mine, so we cried on each other's shoulders each day and became friends. He didn't have a problem with my being gay and was amazed at how similar our problems were.

One evening he asked if I would like to go out to dinner with him because he was getting tired of take-out suppers. I thanked him, but declined because I always came home and made dinner for myself and "C". But when I got home, I found a note that "C" was off to New Haven again at the gay bars and that I should come there to pick him up . Since "C" never wanted to leave before closing, there was plenty of time and I didn't like hanging out in the bars all night so I called R----t and told him that yes, I would like to go out to dinner. We had a nice dinner together and then I told him that we would have to go our several ways since I had to go to New Haven to pick up "C".

When I arrived in New Haven around 10 PM "C" wanted to know what had taken me so long so I told him that not liking to go to the bars on an empty stomach, that I had gone out to dinner with "R----t first. Well, "C" flew into a rage. He told me that he just "knew" that I had been having an affair with this married man, that the car-pool was just a cover-up and that he had just about enough of my abuse and neglect and was leaving me. The next day he moved in with our mutual friend K-n back in Milford since he had no where else to go. He left me a note demanding half of everything in my condo, which was a bit bizarre because none of it was his, nor had he contributed towards anything. I should have seen this coming because for months prior to this, "C" had been moaning and arguing that the condo should be half in his name, etc.

But I had explained to him that his own case worker had told us that he couldn't remain on SSI Disability and have anything in his name or he would lose all of his benefits. And I explained to him that I couldn't put him on my company insurance because companies back then did not offer "domestic partner benefits". So it wasn't that I flat out didn't want his name on the condo. All along I had been trying to get him into some kind of training program so that he could get a simple job and get off of SSI. That way I could have put his name on the condo or left it to him in the event of my demise. But he wasn't very co-operative and neither was the State. All of the counselors that I spoke with told me that I was out of my mind and should mind my own business. They said that if they got him training and then a job and he failed at it, that they would not be able to get him back onto SSI at a later time.

"C" reasoned that he was self-supporting and self-sufficient due to his monthly SSI checks. But between lottery tickets; entire days spent in gay bars, cigarettes, taxis, trains and donations to TV evangelists, his check was always spent by mid month and I had to carry him for the rest of the month to say nothing of our living expenses which I had to handle on my own. But it wasn't just the financial area where I was lacking in support; neither was I getting any emotional support from him nor having any of my physical needs met. For emotional support I had to turn to my other friends. For companionship at ballets or concerts or visits to museums or art galleries, I had to turn to my friends; "C" would have none of it. For my physical needs, I had to turn to myself, if you get the drift.

Many months later, the priest who had married us gave me a piece of really good advice which I would like to share with you. It may sound snobbish initially, but hear it through because it does make sense. He had been worried about our compatibility from the start and advised me: "Bob, never seek out a mate who is markedly inferior to you either financially or mentally because they will ultimately be jealous of you and your successes or they will pull you down to their level. Only seek out those who you consider equal, or better yet, slightly superior because then you will strive to be like them and improve yourself. If you take on someone beneath you, it will more than likely be out of compassion rather than true love and based upon the false assumption that you will somehow be able to transform this little "Liza Doolittle" into a princess. Well, sad as it may be, swans do not turn into princesses and frogs do not turn into princes in the real world.

Father H was right, I never did fall in love with "C", I merely felt sorry for him. But after two years spent trying to instill confidence and trust in him, the end result was nothing but mistrust, jealousy and hostility. Of course there are two sides to every story. "C" claimed that I wasn't romantic enough; he wanted me to constantly use terms of endearment like, "sweetheart", "honey", "darling" and the like, but I had difficulty assigning terms that I felt were intended for a woman, to a man. I had no problem saying:"I love you", but apparently that wasn't enough. I wanted a mature male to male relationship, not something that resembled the "Donna Reed Show" or "Leave It To Beaver" with me going to work; taking out the garbage; mowing the lawn, etc. and "C" sitting home all day watching soaps and imagining infidelities on my part.

For one thing, I had no time for infidelities between work, grocery shopping, cooking, cleaning and taxi driving Miss. Daisy everywhere. But this is what can happen when a gay couple starts roll playing and imitating rolls held in the straight world by a husband and wife. So "C" left me for the second time, but even then, I felt obligated to help him get an apartment and give him many of my things to furnish it.

Well, as the saying goes, when one door closes, another opens and that's exactly what happened. Now, if you will remember; four or five years prior to this I had been madly in love with my first lover, H----d, who left me to become a stripper in Atlantic City. I had wanted desperately for him to move in with me and share life together, but he wasn't ready. Well, now he was; not for a love relationship, but ready to live with me as friends. I had gotten over the initial hurt by now and figured, "what the heck"; he needs an apartment and can't afford it alone; and I could use the company and some rent. So Howard moved in with me and we got along famously. Isn't that odd? As lovers, we killed each other, but got along great as friends. He even helped me around the condo and shared the expenses and utilities. Evenings, we would go out to the bars together in search of that one special man for each of us. When we didn't score, we would come home and trade stories over all the duds we had met, so it was a nice working relationship.

All the while, H----d had an older sugar daddy, which he treated horribly. The poor old guy would give him anything he wanted; money; expensive gifts; pay his rent; whatever; and H----d just teased and tormented the poor guy and rarely gave anything in return. I talked to H----d about that to which he replied: "You can't spoil these guys; if you give them too much, they take you for granted." Well, I was just glad that he hadn't done this to me; I guess he did respect me and care for me after all.

One evening as a surprise for me, H----d brought home a friend of his for me; he thought that we might hit it off and by now he knew my taste in men. On the surface, everything seemed great; he was just my type; a rugged, masculine ex-marine, construction worker with a handsome face and great steel girder forearms and biceps. Plus he was really sweet too, but bi-sexual, not gay. He would take me for moonlight walks on the beach and make out for hours, but unfortunately it was always accompanied by what I felt were excessive amounts of beer and or drugs of one kind or another. He still functioned well, but I felt that perhaps he wasn't really comfortable with all of this and that was why he needed alcohol or drugs to "go all the way".

I did the noble thing and suggested to him that maybe this was uncomfortable for him and that he may need to give some more time to his straight side before making any serious decisions. It was sad to lose him; I had always wanted a "real man", but I learned from this that a "real man is probably better defined by how comfortable a man is with himself and how confident, rather than how masculine he appears or how buff his body is.

Finally H----d, himself, met a wonderful young man; an attractive; lean; dark-eyed Italian-American beauty with a solid career and his own home, his name was T—y. They seemed to hit it off pretty well, however T—y was professional, aggressive and success oriented while H----d was not, in fact H----d had never finished High School. H----d was falling in love with T—y, but slightly resented T—y making demands on him to finish school and get a career. H----d lacked confidence as to whether he would be able to meet up to T—y's expectations. I advised H----d that T—y only wanted what was best for him and that he should take his advice and stick with him because he might never have this opportunity again.

Separately, I went to T—y and advised him how much H----d loved him and assured him that H----d would do anything possible to try to please him and live up to expectations; T—y would simply need to be firm, but patient and give H----d credit and encouragement for even small accomplishments and progress. I also reminded him that "love" doesn't knock often and that he really shouldn't pass up this opportunity. So they both took my advice and embarked on a life together. Would that I had been so fortunate; but I was glad to have had a share in helping someone that I had loved so very much to find happiness in life. But now my little friend was gone and the room was empty? Who would occupy it next?

CHAPTER 7
MR. RIGHT MOVES IN

One morning, over breakfast at IHOP, my carpooling friend, R----t, advised me that things were coming to a head in his household. Hostilities between he and his future step-son were reaching a climax and that he was going to give his woman an ultimatum; she was going to have to choose between her son and him. Well, I told R----t right then and there that I could tell him what the answer would be. No mother is going to give up the son that she carried for nine months and raised to adulthood. He asked me what I was doing with my spare room and if he could rent it if things didn't work out for him back home. I reminded him of my lifestyle and asked if that would be a problem? I reminded him that I would be entertaining men from time to time and asked if that would make him uncomfortable? He said, "no", that he had other gay friends and that it would not be a problem. I advised him that of course he would be free to entertain young ladies too should he choose.

I was right about his woman's response to the ultimatum and R----t ended up moving in with me. I helped him move a number of items and finally retired around 11 PM. At around 12 PM, I heard a timid knock on my bedroom door. I assumed that he didn't know where the extra towels were or something similar and asked what he needed. Well, I was shocked when he said that he didn't need anything but wondered if I would like company in my big bed? He said it was too large for only one person. I couldn't believe what I was hearing. I had always been attracted to him, but never dreamed that anything like this might be possible, so I didn't hesitate. He who hesitates is lost. Of course he who doesn't hesitate can get lost too, which fact I hadn't thought of. But I just couldn't resist him. I mean we were already friends and he was so handsome; taller than me, around 5'11", thick black hair, moustache, my favorite 5'o clock shadow and a mildly hairy chest.

When I knew that he was moving in, I had resigned myself to the limitation of only being able to admire him from a distance, but now here he was in my bed; I was traumatized to say the least. And the next day he did not follow it up with a typical "boy was I drunk last night" excuse, but invited me to go to dinner with him. I had no idea where this was all headed, but I decided to just enjoy it one day at a time. I was just so proud to be seen with him; he was so handsome and distinguished looking and finally someone on my own level. Not a boy; not an alcoholic; not a financial burden; just a "real man"; he was everything that I had been looking for. Of course I overlooked one very important thing that he WASN'T. He wasn't gay; he was bi-sexual and I had been through that before hadn't I?

Years ago, after H----d left me, I wondered if I would ever love anyone that much again? I kept meeting people after that and even establishing relationships of sorts yet I could never again feel the depth of love and devotion for them that I had felt for H----d. I reasoned that perhaps your first love is always the most intense and after that you may love again, but not quite as fully. Well, I was wrong. The feelings that were welling up within me for R----t were getting stronger and stronger, surpassing even what I had felt for little H----d. And then, one night over dinner, when he clasped my hand in his, looked me in the eyes and said: "Do you have any idea how much I have grown to love you"? I was an absolute goner. I had to suppress the tears of joy that were welling up inside of me. I couldn't believe the intensity of what I was feeling; all kinds of crazy feelings; and tingling; feelings that I would explode with joy; feelings of complete vulnerability and losing control. I had never felt like this before and it was glorious and wondrous to say the least.

And we did all of the things that I had always wanted to do with a lover; theater, ballet, concerts, opera, fine dining; we had so much in common. Occasionally we would go to a gay bar simply to dance. He was a little shy at first, but would sometimes give in to my whims and dance with me. Of course he would lead, but that was only rightly so. It was magic being held in his arms and I would just melt, gazing into his beautiful blue eyes. But then he would always go and spoil it by saying something stupid like: "Don't get too used to this because you know that I am straight and may someday leave you for a woman." Well, that was ridiculous! It was too late for him to tell me this now, I was already hooked; so I ignored his words and just pulled him closer to me. But after a while, I had to admit to myself that something was wrong.

One evening as we were having dinner in a club in New Haven with live entertainment, he was unusually attentive to me; holding hands; kissing my knuckles; gazing into my eyes and telling me how much he loved me. Then, suddenly, he invited the female vocalist to our table and began telling her how beautiful she was and how much she reminded him of his wife and crap like that. He was making a complete fool of himself. I mean the vocalist wasn't blind, she saw him smooching with me all evening and then to lie to her and tell her that she was beautiful like his wife; what wife? He wasn't even married to the woman who threw him out. I asked him why he was doing this and he just became very abrupt and cool towards me.

It wasn't long before the physical favors and affection began tapering off. He began spending more time away from home; sometimes spending entire weekends at his parents helping them with yard sales, or so I thought. Then he began complaining that I was trying to make him gay, when I knew very well when he moved in that he was straight. He said that I had no right to "cramp his hetero lifestyle". But he wasn't living a hetero lifestyle. He made absolutely no attempt to meet or date any women whatsoever and seemed very interested and attracted not only to me, but to all of my male friends. I caught him on several occasions being very flirtatious with some of my friends and then found out that he had a fling with one of my acquaintances. He suggested that I should continue to meet other people and not depend so much on him. I decided to give us some space and took off for a five day vacation in Provincetown for my birthday.

Provincetown is, of course, a gay haven and a lot of fun, but it's better if you're there with a lover or circle of friends because unless you are 19-22 and a gym rat, you will spend a lot of time alone. Unfortunately, gay male culture is predominantly youth oriented and extreme beauty oriented; average is just not good enough. Of course so many of these men who will only date rare beauty and youth, haven't looked in the mirror within the last 30 years; they think that they are still 19 themselves. And let me tell you, there's nothing more ridiculous than a 55-65 year old man, shirtless with pierced nipples, leathery skin from over exposure to the sun, tattoos, a ponytail (with what's left of his hair), headband and Speedos; revealing skinny legs with so many blue varicose veins that they resemble a road map. They would do far better to dress maturely and act their age, but they seem to think that they are hot and will reject anyone their own age or slightly younger.

So this was what I was faced with going to Provincetown on my own and I was only 35 at the time. I got off to a slightly bumpy start on my first evening. Gay men tend to be attracted to illusion and image and I had found over the years that if I went to a bar just as plain old me, I got no results. But if I went to a bar or cruise area in full leather gear with motorcycle cap; chest harness; motorcycle jacket, etc, I had great results. This time I decided to go to the bar in Western gear; cowboy hat, vest, boots and spurs. I thought that would certainly attract attention and it did as my spurs got hung up on the front steps of my guesthouse porch and I fell down the stairs and into the street. Needless to say, I decided to dispense with the spurs.

Well, the costume didn't work; probably because 35, is just too old in the gay world. After the bars closed, I decided to go to the beach area where one could usually find some stray men "in need" at that time of night. And I did find this big muscle number who beckoned me over to him. We made out for a while and then he navigated me to my knees and made what he wanted from me very obvious. Well, he was extremely handsome and seemed nice so I obliged and was in the process of pleasuring him when someone just a little younger and prettier than I came walking down the beach near us. At that point, the "object of my affection" just wrenched himself away from me and took off after the other guy. Now if that isn't the epitome of crudeness and lack of appreciation. I was pretty angry and depressed at that point; I mean this was my birthday.

Suddenly out of the shadows, emerged a handsome young man about six years younger than me who approached and said: "I saw what that guy just did to you; that was really low. Let me make things better for you." I introduced myself and explained to him that I was a bit down both because it was my birthday and I wasn't getting any younger and because of being alone on my birthday. My new acquaintance advised me that I was not alone any longer and that he would be my birthday present for the evening. Well, I could hardly pass that one up so we went back to my guesthouse together for the remainder of the evening and into the next day. He was so handsome and so sweet and affectionate and we spent a wonderful time together. He was from upstate Maine so we knew that the chances of seeing each other on a regular basis was out of the question, but still it was a beautiful evening of mutual respect and mutual caring and genuine affection; not just "wham bam". So at least that saved my birthday and vacation, but I still kept thinking of R----t back home and wanted to get back so I left for home the following day.

Now when partners, straight or gay, start saying things to each other like: "I think we need some time apart' or "I think that WE should meet other people, why can't they just be honest and say: "I'm bored and I want to meet other people"? Why lead the other person on by pretending that there's still something there when there isn't? They should just let the other person go, rather than "beat a dead horse" and prolong the agony to the point where they end up hostile and hating each other. But they never do; they just go on lying and cheating and making life unbearable. I didn't want to meet other people, I wanted R----t. He was the one who wanted to meet other people and did and it wasn't women either. How do I know? Let me tell you an interesting story.

One Saturday evening I met a very nice man a little older than myself at one of the New Haven clubs, his name was Tom. We talked for quite some time and I was honest and acquainted him with my disturbed domestic situation and told him a little about myself and my partner. He invited me home for the night and being that R----t was supposed to be away for the weekend again; I didn't see much reason for returning to an empty condo so I agreed. We spent a very nice time together and he invited me to stay over so he could make me breakfast in the morning; again, I obliged.

At breakfast something was playing on his mind and he said to me: "You say that you both work together at the telephone company", I responded "yes". He continued: "And your lover originally comes from my area"? , I responded "yes". He continued: "By any chance is your lover's name R----t "So-and-so"? I responded "yes". To which he replied: "Oh my God, we've been seeing the same man." And then he related to me how he had been seeing my lover for six years, all during the time when he had claimed to be straight and living with that married woman. Not only that, but all of those weekends when he was supposed to be helping his parents with garage sales, were spent with Tom. And yet my lover was accusing ME of making him gay? I'd say that he was doing a pretty good job all on his own and didn't need me to influence him.

When I returned home Sunday afternoon, low and behold, R----t was home; he had not gone to his parents after all. Or perhaps he had tried calling Tom and hadn't gotten an answer and that's why he was home. He taunted me about the fact that I was out all night and asked if I had met anyone that he would approve of? I assured him that he would approve of this man because his name was Tom and that he had been dating him now for six years. R----t turned white as a ghost and didn't know what to do. I mean, let's face it, the chances of my meeting "the other man" were pretty slim, but it had happened none the less. I asked him: "Is this the way that you are pursuing your heterosexual side"? "And I'm the one who is making YOU gay"? "Apparently you've been this way for some time". Well, he refused to discuss it at all and retreated to his room and I went to visit my Dad.

My Dad had never liked him any more than he liked my prior lover; simply because he felt that all of these guys were taking advantage of my kindness. But R----t had gone one step further in alienating my father by making it a point to embarrass me in front of him. There were several times when my Dad had popped over around supper time when I had gotten home a little late from grocery shopping and R----t would make it a point to bellow out: "Where's my supper? I'm hungry and you're late". My dad called him King Farouk and questioned why

I put up with it? Well that's what you do when you're in love with someone, but the love was beginning to wane. I had reminded R----t on those occasions that his "wife" had never cooked for him at all and the reason that I did was not out of any inherent obligation but because I loved him and that if he was going to "take it and me for granted" that I wouldn't do it at all. I had begun feeling like a typical neglected housewife.

Several days later he packed up and moved out, getting an apartment by himself, and still protesting that he was straight and that I expected too much from him and that he wanted to explore his heterosexual side. But within only a few months, he had embarked on another male-male relationship with one of our co-workers from the same office; so much for his pursuit of his heterosexual side. Well, this was just all too much for me. I had the loss of R----t on one hand, coupled with problems at work and caring for my Dad who was finally abandoned by his wife and was suffering from grief and one heart attack after another. The stress was just too much for me, so once more I turned to alcohol. I began missing time from work; was arrested for driving while intoxicated; and was continually victimized and mugged by cheap street hustlers who looked good to me when I was drunk. The ultimate was when one hustler robbed me at gunpoint in the bathroom of a downtown Bridgeport gay bar and then proceeded to buy me a drink at the bar with my own money. Can you believe it?

My life had completely fallen apart and even though I had become very involved in the Episcopal Church several years earlier; most of my friends in that church were gay and going through similar problems. Also, most of the theology of the church was not terribly helpful. It was all based around man's sinfulness and fallen state and how the only way that God could forgive mankind was through a human sacrifice and the spilling of blood; namely the blood of Jesus. Somehow that all struck me as barbaric; human sacrifices, and what amounted to a form of spiritual cannibalism? Even the pagan rites of Isis accepted grain and vegetable offerings and the Hindu deities required offerings of flowers and incense, but the Judeo-Christian deity demanded blood; He said so in his "Word". In Hebrews 9:22 it states that unless blood is poured out, no forgiveness can take place.

We remember the example in Genesis 4:3-7 where God was pleased with the animal sacrifices of Abel, but refused to accept the grain offering of Cain, thereby causing enmity between the two brothers which led to Cain killing his brother Abel. After that, God decided to destroy the entire human race and even the animal kingdom in the "Flood" because apparently His experiment with creation was now totally out of control and he had chosen to destroy it rather than fix it; saving only vestiges of the human race and two of every species of animals, or at least that's what one biblical account states in Genesis 6:19. Later in Genesis 7:2 it states 7 of every clean animal and only 2 of every unclean animal. A contradiction you say? The Bible abounds in contradictions. And what would cause the animals to be determined as "clean" or "unclean"? Presumably all of God's animal creation would be clean, I mean He had created them and unlike man, THEY had not betrayed him by eating the forbidden fruit.

Now God had punished Cain for the murder of his brother Abel and was later to establish "Thou shalt not kill" as his 6th Commandment in Exodus 20:13. Yet he commanded that Abraham sacrifice his only son as a burnt offering to God. Now admittedly theologians say that this was only to test Abraham's loyalty to God, but why would an omniscient deity who can read the innermost thoughts of the hearts of men (Jeremiah 17:10) need to test anyone's loyalty by having them violate their own conscience and commit murder? Other theologians stated that this was merely a metaphor for God offering up his only son as a sacrifice for mankind, but why was even that necessary? Could not God just forgive mankind without any blood offering? I mean He was God and made the rules.

None of this made any sense to me and the week to week readings in church simply reminded me of my failings and inadequacies. In fact, for me to even imagine that I might be OK and not in need of anyone to die as a blood sacrifice on my behalf would have been an affront to God who said that ALL had fallen short of the glory of God and were deserving of death (Romans 5:12). My church was not helping me, but I knew that I needed help; I had to get off of this merry-go-round, so I called AA.

Attending the 12 step program offered by Alcoholics Anonymous was very helpful. The counselors did encourage all of us to, first of all, admit that our lives were out of control and that we were, in fact, alcoholics, but they didn't attach any stigma to that and didn't belabor our "sinfulness" or "fallen state". They simply admonished us to take "one day at a time". I will be forever indebted to them for my recovery and the beginning of looking at myself in a different way. Their meetings, to me, were far more spiritual than those at church. I made far greater strides at self-acceptance and spiritual growth at AA than I had ever made within the ranks of institutional Christianity. It seemed to me that the religious institutions had spent far more time instructing followers as to what they "shouldn't do" than at what they "should do" to live full and rich lives. The Old Testament in particular is mostly bent on what "thou shalt not" do, while I do concede that Jesus, in the New Testament does focus on what "thou shalt" do; "Thou shalt love the Lord thy God…and Thou shalt love thy neighbor as thyself" (Matt 22:37).

One can't help but wonder why the religious institutions of today prefer to choose the Old Testament teachings of blood sacrifice, vengeance, and hundreds of laws which held the death penalty, over and above the compassionate teachings of Jesus who never said one word about homosexuality. Now, granted, the Apostle Paul had a lot of negative things to say in condemnation of anything from temple prostitutes to eating food sacrificed to idols. He also put women in a decidedly inferior position, but then he was not even one of the original apostles and preached long after Jesus' crucifixion, when Jesus was not physically present to chastise him.

Perhaps we choose our form of spirituality based more upon who WE are rather than on who God is; we choose to create God in "Our Own Image". Perhaps vengeful, judicial and bigoted individuals choose to worship a paternal, patriarchal god who is judgmental, avenging and xenophobic just like they are; while forgiving, compassionate and loving people are attracted to an unconditionally loving and compassionate deity like Jesus or Buddha. Perhaps one can tell a lot about an individual just by what form of spirituality he or she chooses.

All that I know was that I was singularly blessed by my association with AA and would highly recommend it to anyone who knows that they have hit bottom. Suicide or continuing drug and alcohol addiction is not the answer; a good 12 step program is. Twice in my life already, my religious persuasions and the negativity which I had imbibed from them had almost led to my self-destruction. I thank God that He somehow prompted me to continue searching for the light at the end of the tunnel. But now, again, I still had a vacuum that needed to be filled. Traditional, institutional Christianity no longer filled the void in my life and while AA was very helpful, still, I had questions that remained unanswered: Why was I here? Where was I going? Was there really some kind of divine plan or was the universe simply all randomness? How could I harmonize my spirituality with my homosexuality if all of the religions of man universally condemned homosexuality?

The final straw which broke my umbilical to Christianity came to me when I finally found out how individual parishioners in my church felt about people like me. Under the previous regime with a gay priest officiating, the true feelings of the parishioners was somewhat sublimated. Oh, they all knew what was going on, even the Bishop knew, but it just wasn't discussed. Then when our gay priest retired and was replaced by a new married priest, I wasn't exactly sure of what my standing would be under the new regime. Up to this point I had enjoyed great freedom and position in the local church; I was on the board of elders, served as sub-deacon and Eucharistic minister and enjoyed great respect. Perhaps that was partly because I wasn't all that obvious and partly because of my longtime friendship with another parishioner, my dear friend Linda, who I had met earlier on in the Wicca Coven, but who had now followed me into this church.

I believed that I needed to get to know the new priest and I believed that honesty was the best policy if we were going to be working closely together so I decided to go to confession. We had a face to face confession, not hiding safely behind a wall, but I was honest and up front and told Father R everything and then held my breath and waited for the lightning to strike. Well, there was no lightning; Father R was wonderful; he was sort of a New Age thinker; very compassionate and very wise. He explained that most promiscuity is aggravated by a lack of love; that most people confuse sex with love. He explained to me that all he would ever expect of me was the same honorable conduct that he would expect of any single heterosexual parishioner; and then he concluded by giving me a wonderful bear hug and advising me that his act of Christian love should be able to "hold me" for at least a while without the need for excessive sexuality. We both laughed.

Father R was a great humanitarian and progressive and believed that we should use our church buildings to the greatest advantage of all when not using them for our own immediate needs. We were already using our church hall for weekly suppers for the homeless and jobless; for women's abuse groups and now for AA meetings. At a meeting of the elders, he suggested that we further open our doors to an Episcopal sponsored organization known then as "Integrity". He proceeded to explain that Integrity was a spiritual group which held masses specially geared towards the needs of gay Episcopalians, followed by a social group meeting and discussions.

Well, you had to hear the reactions! Some said that they didn't want filth like that in their church. Others said that the term "homosexual Episcopalian" was a misnomer because one simply couldn't be gay and still be a Christian. Still others said that while they had tolerated this kind of behavior under the leadership of their prior rector, that they were glad to be rid of him and his friends.

Father R was appalled and horrified for me, but hardly speechless. He asked them all what kind of Gospel they had all been reading because it obviously wasn't the same one that he had read and studied? He concluded the meeting and once they had all left, apologized profusely to me, at which I asserted that there was no need for him to apologize for their behavior and that

I knew that he was supportive of me. But I explained to him that it would now be impossible for me to continue serving the needs of that church knowing how they felt about people like me. So off I went in search of a form of spirituality that I would be able to live with.

On the lighter side, I must admit that during the "old regime", I and Linda and my ex- "T" had had some fun times and some really funny moments. I remember one funeral service that "T" and I were assisting at, which was oddly enough funny although a funeral. As "T" proceeded down the long nave, carrying the processional cross, his long sleeved surplice got hooked on a wheelchair just off the aisle. He made it halfway to the altar dragging the wheelchair behind him before a thoughtful parishioner was able to free him from it.

On another occasion while processing to the baptismal font, one of the younger servers, carrying a tall candlestick got just a little too close to the girl in front who tended to use excessive amounts of hair spray. All of a sudden there was this bright flash and a WHOOSH noise and her hair was on fire! We quickly extinguished the flames and no one was hurt, but the horrible scent of burn hair lingered in the air, slightly covered up by incense.

On another occasion, a parish cocktail party in honor of the Bishop, Father H's feet were aching after a long service which preceded it; plus his cassock was slightly constricting. So Father H, who had already downed a few cocktails said to the Bishop: "If you'll excuse me for a moment, let me just go change into something a little more comfortable and get out of these "opera pumps". Also hanging in the kitchen, the rector and organist had matching aprons labeled accordingly "Mrs. Bridges" and "Rose", alluding to the two female maids in the channel 13 series "Upstairs, Downstairs". They were both a lot of fun and I missed them terribly when they left. And oddly enough, during their regime, the church actually had much better attendance and was much more active than now, so how distracting and destructive could their gay presence have been?

Father H had a friend, a fellow priest, who was also gay and had a large gay following in his parish in Norwalk, CT. That church too was very effective and had a special ministry to the Hispanic peoples of Norwalk, with their own priest and masses in Spanish. The church was approximately 60% English and 40% Hispanic and everyone got along beautifully; which again attests to the gay priest's lack of xenophobia and his ability to harmonize diverse groups of people.

The average churchgoer or temple attendee would be shocked if they knew the full extent of the percentage of gay priests, ministers, nuns, monks, rabbis and Bishops serving them in their religious institutions; perhaps numbering as high as 20-30%. So if people are afraid of gays in the pews, maybe they had better wonder about the men and women at the altar. Or maybe better yet, they should appreciate the debt they owe the gay community for their service and for the beautiful church art and music created oftentimes by gay artists and composers.

CHAPTER 8
THE PRODIGAL SON RETURNS

As I mentioned earlier, for reasons unknown, my step-mother flipped out and abandoned my dad and went to be with her mother in Florida; a short while later, a sheriff was at the door serving him divorce papers. My Dad, who was always the pillar of morality and propriety, was both crushed and humiliated at being divorced and went into deep grieving and depression. My brother lived an hour away and was often on job assignments as far away as Massachusetts or New Jersey, so the responsibility of looking in on Dad and helping him with heavy chores, went to me. But I didn't mind it; this was a nice way for making up for all the time that we had lost together when I was growing up. I always called him twice a day to make sure that he was all right and visited several times during the week. I was also the one who he would call rather than 911 when he felt odd or was experiencing chest pains. Consequently, I felt that I needed to be more available to him at this time so I curtailed my "husband hunting" activities. In many ways I had gotten just a little tired of being abused by insincere people anyway while undergoing my recovery from alcohol abuse and thought it best to spend more time at home.

One thing that helped immensely was the purchase of a new and really loyal little friend for me, in deed, the only woman in my life, my little Yorkshire terrier, Lady Anne. My ex-"T", had allowed me to use his Visa card to get her since all of my cards were "maxed-out". She really was the joy of my life and continued to be for many years. She loved me unconditionally. I didn't have to look my best or be witty and charming every moment and she was much more attuned to my moods and lulls than any human ever was. So Lady Anne gave me a reason to stay home more, if for no other reason than to keep my carpet dry if you catch my drift.

I noticed at that time that once I stopped drinking and drugging and chasing men, that I had much more time to investigate more meaningful pursuits. I began going to operas and ballets and the theater again. I also began taking more walks and noticing the first buds of spring and the seasonal changes and all of the beautiful little things in life that had previously gone unnoticed. I was finally beginning to see and enjoy life as it was meant to be enjoyed, through the eyes of a human rather than those of a satyr or nymphomaniac. I also noticed that as my relationship with Dad grew steadily, that with that growth, my need for other men in my life sharply diminished. I do not here allude to any possibility that I was becoming less homosexual, but merely I believe that much of my obsessive-compulsive attitude toward men and sex sprang from an incomplete relationship with my Dad and that now that the relationship was growing and those emotional needs were being met, I had far less need for sex.

Dad began to mellow quite a bit after his divorce and began to question less, my homosexuality, in fact on several occasions, due to his disillusionment with my Step-Mom, he said that he could now begin to understand some of the underlying foundations of my homosexuality. He acknowledged to me that the image of my own Mom's relationship with him was not one that any young man would hope to recreate in his own life. He also realized that the risks of a failed marriage, a broken family, alimony and child-support were also not risks that a gay man had to deal with; at most, one could lose one's partner. So he reasoned that maybe it wasn't such a bad lifestyle after all; not that he wanted to engage in it, but at least he could understand why I did. Of course I explained to him that despite the "perks", it was never a lifestyle that I had consciously chosen, but after fighting my impulses for years, had simply resigned myself to, in compliance with my new found self-acceptance.

I reminded him that even my gay relationships had not been without pain and loss so that neither gays nor straights had any advantages one way or the other. These were human problems that he and I were jointly dealing with; problems of fidelity; problems of commitment; and they were no respecters of lifestyle. But I admired my Dad's ability to assess other's personalities; let's face it; he had been right about my last two lovers being "users". Being often blinded by love, I needed the advice of someone who could be impartial and just see others as they truly are, so I looked forward to his advice in the future.

Though I wasn't actively pursuing any more relationships at that time, I did meet a very nice young gay man at work who I became good friends with although not lovers. His name was Tom and he was from New Haven and a new employee. I couldn't recall ever having seen him in any of the clubs in New Haven, but that was probably because he spent a lot of time in New York. But there was something decidedly different about him and my "gaydar" went into full alert. But Tom kept a very low profile and was very cautious about letting on to anyone. But there was no need to hide in that office. Most of the straight people were either divorced; unwed mothers or were dating gangsters, so no one could exactly "call the kettle black" or "throw stones" in their glass houses and no one was judgmental. There were also two lesbians in our office that also felt that Tom was probably gay and confided that in me.

So we decided to take him to lunch with us and drag him "out of the closet". Over lunch, we simply asked him which gay bars he went to because none of us had ever run across him in our travels. He was shocked at our abruptness and asked: "Is it that obvious"? To which we replied: "No, but it takes one to know one". We all became great friends after that and Tom felt so much more at ease in the office, so we had done him a real service. Tom and I grew very fond of one another over the succeeding years and did much together. I wanted to take it a step further, but due to both of our tastes in men, he would always remind me that we were just "sisters" and couldn't violate that boundary. But it's a shame that we didn't. Tom was one of my best friends and we might have had a good life together had I been able to pull him out of the "fast lane" in time. But as fate would have it; he continued running with the crowd in New York having multiple anonymous sex partners until he succumbed to Aids in the spring of 1985; the first of my friends to succumb to such a fate.

Now my Dad, who was already a heart patient, began having a series of mild heart attacks and mini strokes. Each time, of course, he would call me to tell me that he couldn't breath or was having chest pains and each time I would call 911 for him and then rush over to his place to be with him until the EMT's arrived. Then I would usually end up in the hospital with him until the wee hours of the morning until he was through the crisis. I would just sit next to his hospital bed and hold his hand. He had asked me to do that; he said that somehow when I was holding his hand it made him feel more secure, like everything would be all right and no harm could befall him so long as I was holding his hand. I must admit, that I never thought the day would come when I would be holding hands with Dad and that he would be accepting my love with gratitude rather than squeamishness.

But I was just glad to be there and to be able to muster the courage to tell him that I loved him without his thinking that it was a "gay thing". No, the love that we shared those last years and days was a wholesome father and son love that I feel blessed to have experienced and shared. I urge all men not to wait until their dads are dead to express their love in a eulogy; no, express that love NOW while you still can, so that there may not be any regrets later.

I remember one incident during all of those emergency visits to the hospital that totally threw me in a different way. I was going out for the evening, but everything kept going wrong. I would leave the house but forget my wallet. Then I would retrieve the wallet but forget the car keys and so on. During one of those returns to my condo to retrieve something, the phone rang; it was Dad. He said that he didn't feel right, had difficulty breathing and was dizzy. I rushed right over and found him staggering around the living room and very nervous. I asked him if he wanted me to take him to the hospital to which he replied: "No". He said that he was sick of the hospitals and their heroics and wasn't sure that he wanted to go on anymore.

I explained to him that if he wasn't hospitalized that he would possibly die that night, but that was his choice. I further explained that while I would miss him terribly, that he had raised me well and that I would survive and didn't want him to continue suffering on my account. I promised that should he decide to stay home and pass quietly in his sleep that I would stay by his bedside that night and watch and wait with him and that I would not leave him to die alone. He appreciated that, but then decided that maybe he would give the hospital one more chance. At that point, he was staggering so badly that I could not get him out of the apartment and so I called 911. After the EMT's arrived, they told me that it was very serious and rushed him to the hospital, with me following closely behind the ambulance in my car.

After about two hours in the hospital, the staff advised me that he probably would not survive that he was unconscious and would probably not survive the night and that I should contact my brother, which I did. I explained to my brother that had I not been there, Dad would probably have died then and there, to which my brother oddly responded: "Maybe you should have left well enough alone" and not interfere with the process. He also added that it was pointless for him to travel all of the way down to the hospital if Dad was unconscious and probably would not regain consciousness; he would rather remember him the way he was in better days. He told me to keep him posted. I hung up the phone more alone than I had ever felt in my life. I couldn't believe that my brother felt that I should have just let him die and that now he wouldn't even come to the hospital to see him one last time. I believe, as many doctors, that although unconscious, a patient can hear what people are saying and is aware of the presence of loved-ones and that sometimes that's all that it takes to pull them through a crisis.

Maybe my brother was just being pragmatic, but it hurt deeply at the time and it bought up a lot of submerged hostility in me because it seemed to me that my brother had somehow always escaped all of the ugliness of life and that I had to continually witness it all up close and by myself. It reminded me of the days of my mother's seizures which I had to contend with alone. And it reminded me of all of the prior races to the hospital with my Dad which I had to go through alone, without the support of any living being. It also frightened me to wonder who would be there for me someday when my turn comes. At least my Dad had me, but who will be there for me? I was tempted to start drinking again, for now I was all alone; I was now the orphan, just like my brother had told me all of those years ago, that I would someday be. But by the Grace of God, I fortunately, realized that drinking wouldn't solve anything and someone had to be strong for Dad and it all fell upon me.

Dad did survive that bout, but only for a few days; during which time my brother did get to visit him. But Dad was severely depressed and didn't want to go on anymore, so he shrewdly got well enough to be taken out of the ICU unit and close monitoring and advised his doctor that should it happen again, he didn't want any medical heroics this time. I believe that on a higher, subconscious level, dying people know that they are dying and want to make a final statement, possibly to make amends. On the evening before my Mom died, and I forgot to mention this before, she confessed to my Dad and his mother that she had loved him all along, but had been too stubborn and proud to admit it. She further confessed that she had envied the love and strong family ties that her mother-in-law had always displayed and wished that her own mother had been more like that. This was the reason that she had always been cold to her mother-in-law. She asked for everyone's forgiveness. Unfortunately, she still died a very unhappy woman unable to fulfill any of her dreams.

Dad, on the other hand, had a different legacy for me. Lovingly he divulged to me that despite some of the disappointments which I had showered upon him, that I truly had been the true son and had been there for him in his hour of need. But then he began reminiscing about his life and how that life itself had been an abysmal disappointment. He spoke of the years that he had worked ten to twelve hours a day on the farm and had gotten nothing for it; not even an acre of land. My grandmother's last will and testament left everything to him, but there was nothing left. He then spoke of the thirty years that he had spent at the United Illuminating Company toiling in 100 degree temperatures with perspiration dripping off of him and breathing in coal dust which had contributed to his demise, and had never gotten a promotion in all of those years. He spoke of losing his only daughter, Jeannie; followed by the mental turmoil and estrangement of Mom and due to that, estrangement from his own family. He spoke of finally finding some joy in his later years with his new wife; only to have that wrenched away by divorce. His summation of his entire life was "zero to zero" and felt that it had all been a waste with far more suffering than joy and that he was a failure.

I reminded Dad not of his losses, but of all of the things that he had been; that he had been a loving and faithful husband despite all of the problems. I reminded him that he had been a responsible father and a good provider and that the only reason that he had never received a promotion at work was because he was such a good mechanic and trouble shooter that they needed him on the floor and not behind a desk. I further reminded him that part of the reason that he failed to be promoted was because he wasn't a "butt kisser" and wasn't ruthless enough to be in a managerial position but had integrity and was highly respected by anyone who worked with him. I told him how much I admired and respected him for being able to live such a difficult life without succumbing to alcohol or drugs as I had. I'm sure that some of it sunk in; he seemed a little changed by what I said, but apparently not enough to go on.

In the early hours of the morning of October 13, 1986, Dad "snuck away" without even the nurses noticing immediately. At 3 AM my phone rang; it was his doctor who was clumsy with this at best. He advised me that Dad had suffered another heart attack and he thought that I would want to know. When I enquired, "Well, how is he now; is there any residual damage"? His response was: "Well yes, he's dead". I hung up the phone, flooded with conflicting emotions. Part of me was relieved that his suffering was over; part of me felt guilty for feeling relieved; part of me felt as though I had just lost a limb; part of me realized the terrible finality of what had just happened. And another part of me recognized my new status as an orphan and now with no generational buffer between me and Death.

And of course, there was no one there for me to share this with, save my dear little terrier, Lady Anne, who began to perform every cute trick in her repertoire to stop my tears and she was successful. I saw no point in calling my brother at 3 AM; there was nothing that could be done about it now, it was over. There would be time enough later on to call him and begin making funeral arrangements. They say that time heals all wounds and it does partially. But the feeling of emptiness and isolation does not seem to dissipate. It's difficult enough losing one parent, but when you lose the second parent it is accompanied by a strange sense of the severing of the umbilical and being set adrift in space. It also brings one face to face with one's own mortality. However, that does generate within you a greater appreciation for each day of life and a resolve to make each day count and leave nothing of importance undone or unresolved. Still, there is the nagging reminder of your own eventual demise. I am glad that I was able to have "been there" for my Dad, sober and not in an "altered mental state", to make his last days more comfortable and let him know that he was loved and respected.

Now in order to add insult to injury, the institutional churches of Christendom chose this final opportunity to deal Dad and I a final blow. I contacted the Russian Orthodox Church where my Dad had been baptized and which all of his family had been buried from; to say nothing of the fact that they had been some of the early co-founders of that church. But the priest in charge advised me that since Dad hadn't attended nor financially supported the church recently, that he would not be able to have a funeral at that church.

Well, what was I to do now. My Dad's dying wish was to have a Russian Orthodox funeral and now that was not possible. So I called the priest, who had always been very ecumenical, at my former Episcopal Church and asked if the Russian Orthodox priest could come to his church and co-conduct a funeral service there since the Russian church was unavailable. Father R said that he would call the Bishop and get back to me. Well, Father R called me back and advised me that the Bishop forbade it. In turn, the Orthodox priest called me back to advise me that under no circumstances would he co-conduct a funeral with an Episcopal priest. Whatever happened to ecumenism? I might just as well have been living in the 1500's. Was the entire Ecumenical Council nothing but a farce; so much for Christian brotherhood and tolerance. So now what would I do? Get a justice of the peace, for God's sake?

I should have seen this coming because a few years back when my brother's godfather died, who was Protestant, but whose wife was a Roman Catholic and very zealous and active in the Church; she had gone through this same circus. Her priest refused to bury her husband and was overheard by a relative saying to someone else that he would rather bury a dog than a Protestant. So I should have seen this coming, but try to treat each situation as it arises and had somehow thought that the Church had matured since then. Well it hadn't. But finally, the Orthodox priest consented to perform the full Russian Orthodox funeral rites, but at the funeral parlor instead, so my brother and I agreed. At least this way, Dad would get the rites that he wanted, albeit without the pealing of the Tsar's great bells or the gaze of the icons of Saints Nicholas and Alexandra from the high altar.

Oddly enough, the only people outside of my small immediate family who attended his funeral were my small circle of friends; all of Dad's friends having preceded him to the "other shore". I did appreciate that support from my friends, even though there's not much that anyone can do for you at a time like that other than just "be there" for you. We didn't even have enough strong healthy people to act as pall bearers so my brother and I served in that capacity and helped lower our Dad into the earth. I must admit that it was much more personal and I know that Dad would have liked that extra touch. So we laid him to rest along side of our Mom and his beloved daughter Jeannie.

This refusal of Christendom to co-operate with me in any way, shape or form, coupled with the previous words of hatred and intolerance toward homosexuals which I had to endure at the

Episcopal Church vestry meeting prior to this all culminated in my complete alienation and ultimate exodus from it's ranks. In my earlier days, a religious institution had excommunicated me unjustly. Now it was my turn to excommunicate the Church only for just cause. It had been useless to me and destructive of my spirituality.

Oddly enough, this time I did not become an agnostic again as I had following my Mom's death. I reasoned that truth and spiritual emancipation must exist somewhere. If there was a conscious, and anthropomorphic deity out there somewhere who really did have a plan for not only the universe, but for me as an individual, he surely must have provided for us somehow. He couldn't be just leaving us at the mercy and machinations of these false shepherds, wolves in sheep's' clothing.

The fact that all I had found up to this point was hypocrisy, spiritual slavery and patriarchal despotism didn't mean that there was no truth or compassion or unconditional love to be found anywhere on earth; I just needed to seek it out; "Seek and ye shall find, knock and it shall be opened unto you"; hadn't Jesus said these words in Matthew 7:7? Oh, to be sure, I could have remained within the safe confines of Holy Church had I been willing to remain in the closet and lead a life of quiet abstinence with no love or romance; no life partner to share with; merely to draw strength and sustenance from the assurance that God would overlook my degeneracy and unworthiness if I only abdicated my right to love and happiness and wholeness to live a singular life and desist from "pocket pool".

So what is a gay man or woman who is spiritually inclined supposed to do given these circumstances? Should we grovel under Church authority or should we demand equal rights in churches where 20-30% of the clergy who are gay are already enjoying the lifestyle we seek with no ramifications whatsoever while they persecute us. Or should we live nebulous lives devoid of all spirituality and simply embrace materialism and humanism? But better yet, wouldn't it be far wiser to seek out a spiritual path which is already enlightened enough and broad enough to embrace all humankind unconditionally regardless of our individual backgrounds or sexual preferences? Those paths DO exist and I spent the next seven years of my life seeking them out.

You need not accept my viewpoints per se; you can check these paths out for yourself. I only offer them to let you know that there are other avenues available to you. I want you to know that you need not live your life in a spiritual void simply because one or more religious institutions has hurt you or let you down. You need not "go it alone". There are far more positive paths available to you should you need a path to help you in dealing with life's daily struggles and transitions; with loneliness, aging, self-acceptance, self-integration, HIV and loss. And so I invite you to follow me in my search. Hopefully there will be something there to assist you on your path through this often confusing wilderness we call life.

CHAPTER 9
GO EAST YOUNG MAN, GO EAST

Now that I was devoid of any religious institution, I was left with an enormous void and a deep seated fear that these negative forms of spirituality were all that existed. And what if they were, in fact, true? Would I be condemned to an eternity in some hell fire? My life on earth hadn't exactly been "paradisaical", would God then follow that up with an eternity of torment? Well, for one, the Jehovah's Witness's prophesies had proven false; the world had not ended in 1974; hell, it was now 1986. So maybe all of these other religious interpretations were wrong too. My inner self couldn't believe that God could be that cruel, so I kept my eyes and ears open. I also prayed about my search, hoping that some kind cosmic ear would hear me and direct my quest.

One day while traveling home from New York City on the train, I noticed that the young girl next to be was totally enthralled and absorbed in a book that she was reading: "Autobiography Of A Yogi". I excused myself and interrupted her reading to ask her what it was that had her so engrossed and made her appear so happy and aglow. She explained to me that it was an autobiography of a great Hindu spiritual teacher who had made it his life's work to bring Eastern spirituality and enlightenment to the West; the teacher's name, or rather spiritual name rather than birth name, was Paramahansa Yogananda. She explained to me that it wasn't so much that Yogananda felt that Western spirituality was devoid of any value or lacking in meaning, but that it had been so many years since Jesus walked this earth and we were so far removed from his original teachings that the West was perhaps out of touch with the underlying great spiritual truths and principles which could really unite all of the world religions if people simply took the time to study them. The original teachings of Jesus had been buried under centuries of ecclesiastical authority, dogma and other spiritual rubble which clouded and obscured the original teachings.

She explained to me that Yogananda believed in the great Hindu truth found in the Vedas, their holy books: "Truth is one, though the paths are many". But what was that "Truth" that underlies all spiritual teaching and could unite all of mankind? I would have to find that out for myself. All I knew right then was that the young lady next to me displayed the same serenity and self-assurance that I had seen years ago in the young Hindu monk that I had met during my preaching tours with Jehovah's Witnesses; the same monk who had told me that someday I would understand what he was saying and that someday I would know the nature of reality for myself. Needless to say, as soon as I arrived home in Bridgeport, I ran to the nearest bookstore and purchased "Autobiography of a Yogi". I read it from cover to cover in a very short while. I soaked up it's words like a dry sponge and although a lot of the concepts were a little foreign to me (I don't pretend to have comprehended it all at that point in time) still, I tried to read it with an open mind.

I tried to empty my mind of all previous religious teachings so as to rate it based upon its own merits and not judge the information based upon how well it corroborated

my preconceived notions or personal opinions. I remembered how the monk had told me the story of a great teacher who had filled his student's tea cup until it overflowed and then explained that you cannot pour tea into an already full cup. Hence, I knew that I had to empty my mind of old thought and old belief systems while embarking on my spiritual search to allow space for new ways of thinking and new concepts. And so that's what I did, I mean really, what did I have to lose but a lot of destructive concepts and negativity?

One thing that I immediately noticed about Eastern teaching, which is 180 degrees opposite to Western teaching is their entire basic concept for why the world is as we find it today, complete with suffering, cruelty, poverty, starvation, etc. How could this be if the universe was created by an all loving; all powerful God who had a definite plan and goal in mind when he created it and pronounced it all to be "good" on the seventh day of His creation? Well of course Western theologians will explain this apparent disparity by explaining that it was all perfect then when God created it, but that since Adam and Eve sinned in the Garden of Eden, that creation was condemned along with them and thrown into confusion. But in the light of modern science, that is absolutely ridiculous.

We know for a fact that the universe has been in existence for billions of years and our own earth for at least millions. We know that man is in fact the newest species to evolve of all existing animal life and that our earth was plagued with comet strikes and upheavals of momentous proportions causing extinction of large numbers of species long before man ever stuck his head out of the primordial mud. So how do theologians account for that? If all of this chaos is due to Adam and Eve, and of course SATAN, we mustn't forget him; then how do we account for the chaos and random disasters of colliding planets and imploding stars along with their solar systems all throughout the universe? Well of course any self-respecting priest will tell you: "It's all just a mystery. We poor fallen children of Eve can't possibly hope to comprehend the ways of God." Well, I'm sorry, that's not an answer; that's simply uninformed and meaningless rhetoric.

Now don't get me wrong, Eastern thought does not have answers as to why planets collide or why suns implode either, but at least they don't blame it all on a man, a woman and a talking snake. You and I have been led to believe by ministers, priests and theologians that God created man to live eternally in the paradise of Eden where there would have been no aging; no pain during child-bearing, or for that matter at all, no sickness and no death. Well, that's absolutely ludicrous. Aging, pain, suffering and death already existed in the animal kingdoms for millions of years, what plausible reason is there to believe that it would have been any different for mankind? The entire theorem is faulty. To believe that death is strictly the punishment for sin is absurd. What sins did the animals commit? But that's all right; blame everything on man and of course, the other scapegoat, Satan. Make man feel even more unworthy than he is; tell him that he was "born in sin and shaped in iniquity" and deserving only of death, but that God, in His mercy has made provision for man's salvation, which of course is only receivable at the

hands of his chosen people or chosen priesthood. This of course turns mankind in general into the surfs and vassals of said priesthood that will then ration out and dispense their blessings or curses depending upon how obedient the surfs and vassals are to the will of the priesthood. No, sorry, I'm not buying into it, although I did for many years.

Eastern theology or rather cosmology begins on an entirely different premise and even though its genesis is far older than that of Judaism or Christianity it is far closer to modern science in that it postulates the creation of the universe very much in the same mode as the "Big Bang" theory. The ancient Hindu holy books, the Vedas postulate that the "formless" undifferentiated energy and matter which have always existed; basically willed themselves into material form in an explosive act of creation. Consequently since all energy and matter came from God, then God exists in all energy and matter and there is no atom or molecule or sub particle that is not part and parcel of God. Now while God in his cosmic, formless and changeless state is in fact perfect and eternal, God in the form of matter and energy is found to be in a lesser state and not perfect nor eternal and is always subject to change and hence suffering if the created becomes obsessed with the desire to maintain his material form and material identity indefinitely.

The entire of creation or the material worlds is termed in the Vedas as both, Maya, or illusion, and as God's Lila or God's Play. It was simply God's desire to manifest outside of Himself. And it was His will to create a universe, peopled with beings like Him, and see how they would inter react and what feats they could perform together and separately. Therefore, the creation was never intended to be perfect because, by its' very nature of change and evolution, it could never be perfect or eternal. It was only intended as a playground and school wherein the soul could grow through experience. The writers of the Vedas, had no concept of "original sin"; nor did they blame the often abysmal state of things in the world on an Adam and Eve or on a rebellious spirit son of God, Satan. The universe to them was simply as it is and still evolving, and wherever possible, it is our responsibility as sentient Sons of God to make life better not only for mankind but for our animal brothers and sisters as well and for plant life and mother earth. We were to respect all life because all life is part of God. No one ever gave us license to abuse other life forms.

The Vedas are far closer to modern science in that they not only fit in with evolution, but even postulate parallel spiritual evolution; so that as each soul grows and matures, it earns a more evolved and higher body in its' next life or incarnation. They also teach that self-realization, direct experience of God, or enlightenment is the birthright of every living being and is not dependent upon blind faith, nor on the whims of a priestly class who can dole it out to obedient surfs or withhold it from those not in their favor. Enlightenment is achieved by self-effort in the practice of certain tried and proven methods of meditation which channel energies and innate knowledge which we already possess as sons of God to a point where we can experience a direct connection with the Almighty. These are in fact the same procedures and methods which enabled great

spiritual teachers and leaders of the past like Moses, Buddha and Jesus to be the great souls that they were. Every one of them went into the dessert or forests and practiced meditation for great lengths of time prior to their emergence as Holy Men. Likewise, all of the great mystics in the Church, Saint Francis of Assisi, Saint John of the Cross, Saint Theresa of Avila and others, all practiced forms of meditation which elevated them to the heights that they ascended. None of them reached those advanced levels simply by attending church on Sundays and going to confession, in deed they reached those levels despite the guilt trips and constrictions of the churches that they belonged to by bypassing the priesthood and going directly to God. In prayer we speak to God, but in meditation, we listen for God to speak to us. There must be two way communication; not a monologue.

This is why even Dr. Carl Jung spoke highly of yoga and meditation. In one of Self Realization Fellowship's booklets (SRF was founded by Paramahansa Yogananda), Jung is quoted as saying: "Quite apart from the charm of the new and the fascination of the half-understood, there is good cause for Yoga to have many adherents. It offers the possibility of controllable experience and thus satisfies the scientific need for facts; and besides this, by reason of its breadth and depth, its venerable age, its doctrine and method, which include every phase of life, it promises undreamed-of possibilities".

To quote a great Indian spiritual teacher at the turn of the century, Ramakrishna, the Ramakrishna Order in their tract, "What Is Vedanta?" quotes him stating: "Vedanta is a philosophy taught by the Vedas, the most ancient scriptures of India. Its basic teaching is that our real nature is divine. God, the underlying reality, exists in every being. Religion is therefore a search for self-knowledge, a search for the God within . We should not think of ourselves as needing to be SAVED. We are never LOST. At worst, we are living in ignorance of our true nature. Find God. That is the only purpose in life".

So rather than a deity who stands apart from his creation and has the right to destroy it all if it doesn't suit him, Vedanta proposes a deity who is both transcendental on the one hand and yet always imminent and personally present in every atom of the material universe on the other hand. It proposes a universe and planet which is not alien and frightening, but rather one in which everything and everyone is divine, related and has value; certainly a theory which if carried to its logical end would truly unite all of the families of mankind and even animal life; as opposed to some of the theories we espouse today which destine some for high purposes and others worthy only of exploitation and death.

Since the ONE became many, then we might say that we are in effect all reflections or clones of that original one reality that many call God. Fifty years ago, this kind of thinking may have sounded odd. But now with science practicing cloning and genetic engineering, such thinking is not so far fetched. Of course more highly spiritualized individuals far more accurately reflect that divinity than does a homeless person lying in

the gutter, but God is present there too. This is why when the apostles asked Jesus to show them the Father, he responded, "He who has seen me has seen the father". It is, likewise why he later said that if someone gave his followers so much as a cup of water he would bless them because "He that did it to one of the least of these my brothers, has done it unto me". So according to Vedanta, the purpose of each and every one of us is to find within ourselves our own divinity, help others to find theirs and mold the world in such a way as to help even those lower on the evolutionary ladder to move up and eventually find their divinity until at last all are free.

This is simply a far more positive approach to life and a loftier goal than believing that "The End Is At Hand" and longing for the destruction of the wicked. And it represents a far more compassionate deity than one whose only answer to rebelliousness and ignorance is to destroy everything and start over. Then too, teachers of Vedanta and meditation do not expect or ask you to accept these theories with blind credulity, but simply ask you to go into the laboratory of your own soul, try the methods they have used for centuries and see if you don't have the same experience of reality and transcendence which the Great Masters like Jesus, Buddha, Moses, Ramakrishna and Yogananda had. This is a living and evolving path.

It isn't just something that happened two thousand years ago once for all time. In John 14:12 Jesus asked his followers why they wondered at the things that he did and inspired them by saying that they would do even greater things. One wonders based upon that why there have not been so many "greater things" done in the Church over the last 2,000 years; while in the East, thousands of such miracles have occurred right down to this day. Of course the Church will label such miracles wrought by Eastern teachers as demonic or staged by the devil to mimic the miracles of Christ, but they exist none the less.

Now admittedly, not all Christian denominations are living in the 15th century with its fire and brimstone ravings. Some like the Unitarians, Quakers, and Unity churches are also on the higher path toward self-realization and would also make fine homes for gay men and women or for that matter anyone who feels that they are stagnating where they are. I personally, was simply attracted to Vedanta and Buddhism because I still had a very bad taste in my mouth for anything with the name Christian attached to it. But the aforementioned basically non-sectarian churches would also be fine choices. Some people might feel uncomfortable with Eastern thought because they feel that it runs contrary to Western thought but that is not entirely true. We had great Transcendentalists in this country like Emerson and Thoreau in the 19th century who certainly would not be considered foreign, although certainly not main stream.

While they were writing about transcendentalism, southern white Christians were twisting Bible verses to justify their right to keep slaves and abuse their women and children. Hell, even members of the Ku Klux Klan claim to be Christian and will try to justify themselves and their behavior based on some vague Bible reference, yet I can hardly imagine Jesus donning a hood and lynching people.

How much longer will the Christian Right and some major denominations of Christianity and even some sects of Judaism continue to persecute God's gay children based upon their clever cataloguing of obscure Old Testament texts, improperly translated from ancient Hebrew and Greek which "appear" to argue against homosexuality? Many of those same texts authorize the death penalty for unwed mothers and sex outside of wedlock, but I don't hear too many preachers daring to open that "Pandora's Box"; they might lose too many members and too many votes that way. They rave on and on about abortion, but can't explain what happened to the fetuses in the wombs of those unwed Judean mothers who were stoned to death under the Mosaic Law. I don't recall anywhere in scripture where the mothers were allowed to live until after they gave birth and then stoned to death afterward. So apparently killing the fetus along with the mother is OK in God's eyes. Hmmm; strange religion I would say. Inspired by God? I strongly question that.

I have to admit that part of our plight is our own fault. These religionists attack us with impunity because we are seen as such a minority and why? Because, too many of us lack the courage to "come out of the closet". The thousands who march in San Francisco and New York yearly during Gay Pride Weeks represent only the tip of the iceberg, but our enemies don't know that unless we show them. But let me tell you something; there is NO SAFETY IN THE CLOSET. If you are a cleric and think that you can hide by refusing communion to openly gay men and women, look again. If you are a public official or legislator and think that you can cover your tracks by voting against all gay-friendly legislation, look again. The Mayor of Spokane thought that he could do that and it caught up with him didn't it? Probably most people wouldn't have cared whether he was a homosexual or not had he not involved a wife and children in his cover up, but now they also see him as a liar, an adulterer and a hypocrite, not to be trusted; its public domain; I'm not telling you anything that you don't already know.

Probably the best and loudest statement that gay people could make would be to exit the religious institutions that persecute us "en masse", so that they can see our numbers and see the talent and devotion that they have lost through their bigotry and myopic vision. Suddenly the churches would be left with few organists, few teachers, few musical directors and even fewer ministers and priests. I hope that someday I may be able to draw a truce between myself and the Judeo-Christian empire, but until that day, I would have to be crazy to lend them one dime or one ounce of support so that they can take my hard-earned money which I had intended to help support the destitute and needy and use it against me to buy votes and congressmen to further their twisted political, not spiritual agendas.

Well, enough of that. I just wanted to explain why it was not possible for me to take my new found belief in the divinity and oneness of all mankind back with me into one of the major institutional churches and work for the good of mankind from there. Even Jesus said in Matthew 9:7 "…neither do people put new wine into old wineskins. If they do,

the wineskins will burst". So it simply was not feasible for me to work from within the confines of an institutional church.

During my studies under a wide variety of Hindu and even Sikh Masters, I have not found any contradiction nor disparity between their teachings, and this is certainly what one would expect from self-realized Masters teaching Truth. I have found great freedom within Vedanta; not childish concepts of freedom. I most certainly am not free to harm creation or free to exploit others. No, along with freedom comes responsibility to try to touch others lives and to try to make the world a better place, not just pray for it to be better and leave the hard work of transformation to others. Yes, Vedanta or Sanatan Dharma, as it is also known, is a religion or philosophy which tends to physical and spiritual emancipation, but coupled with a healthy sense of that which is ethical and right. I feel that it, along with Buddhism, Unitarianism, Quakerism and some others could help gay men and women jettison all of that old fundamentalist baggage of unworthiness and poor self-image.

But I don't want to get too preachy; you each need to find your own path, a path that works for you. I just wanted those who don't know where to turn to know that there are other options out there for you rather than staying put and keeping a low profile. As the old story goes, some people see the glass as half empty; other more positive people see it as half full. I would say that Judeo Christianity and Islam represent the half full approach; a glass half full, evaporating and fit only for God's destruction with the exception of course of a handful of the faithful. While Eastern thought represents the glass which is not yet full, but will become full of divine waters as soon as a critical mass of humans realizes their divinity and oneness with God and begins acting upon it.

CHAPTER 10
LOOKING FOR A SHORT CUT

As enthralled as I was with Vedanta and Eastern philosophy, and still am, I tended to be an impatient creature and reasoned that if I combined my meditation with many or all of the New Age practices that were then coming into vogue, that I might be able to accelerate my spiritual metamorphosis. So I investigated every new method and concept as they presented themselves to me. One such opportunity presented itself right after Shirley McClain's book and movie, "Out On A Limb" came into vogue. A friend of mine told me of a group of spiritual seekers that was traveling to Peru to be present at the ancient spiritual site known as Machu Pichu. They were planning on their trip coinciding with a metaphysical even known as "Harmonic Convergence." It was and is believed by many that there are certain "power centers" scattered all over the world. They believe that the natural energy, coupled with the high spiritual vibrations which worshippers have contributed to those centers can aid one in accelerating their spiritual development. So after much soul searching and wallet searching, I decided to take advantage of this opportunity.

I was very concerned about going, however, because for one thing, I suffer from periodic anxiety attacks and didn't know how I would handle the thin air in high altitudes in the Andes. But my traveling companions, a group of about 30 young men and women assured me that this was no coincidence; that we were in fact, meant to be there; that we had been "chosen" and that nothing bad could befall us. So I prepared myself for that great moment. One thing that the facilitators of this pilgrimage urged all of us to do prior to making the journey, was to clear our minds and souls of any unfinished business so that we could begin, as it were, a new life from that point forward with no mental or spiritual baggage left from our old life. Well, the only unfinished business that I had left was the job of advising my brother of my homosexual status. Now that my nephews were pretty much grown, there would be no fear that Uncle Bob was "fiddling about" with the children. It seemed the prime time. However each time that I went to my brother's either the opportunity didn't present itself or conversations of a decidedly anti-gay nature were already in progress which angered me but weakened my resolve.

Finally the day came when my brother and some of his friends hit the wrong nerve. Somehow on that day the conversation wandered into the dangerous area of AIDS. When I commented on how I felt that the medical profession had been lax to the point of criminal in their failure to immediately alert people back in the early 80's as to the immediate danger that it posed; they responded that it didn't much matter "since AIDS only killed low life and faggots and they're better off dead anyway". Well, as you can well see, that wasn't the prime time to flash my "fairy ID card" so I simply excused myself from the picnic and drove home livid, hurt, and angry; you name it. I mean, I had just lost several close friends to AIDS; my friend Tom who I worked with and another dear friend, Armando and several other acquaintances. Not only couldn't I share my grief with my family, but had to be subjugated to listening to their friends saying that these people were low life and faggots and were better off dead.

Something had to be done but what? I couldn't continue visiting with my family and having to sit quietly listening to all of this and I didn't know if and when the opportunity would present itself for me to sit them all down and speak privately about this. I mean maybe they didn't understand the issue. Maybe they didn't personally know anyone gay and therefore were simply speaking out of ignorance, not knowing who these people really were that they were saying deserved death or were better off dead. So I decided that it would probably be best to tell him my story uninterrupted, by letter and wait for his response.

Well, it all turned out for the best and it really put the ball in my court because my brother was so embarrassed about the statements that he and his guests had made that he called me immediately, very apologetic and set up a lunch date during which we could talk about it. At that lunch, I was finally able to explain my lifestyle to him without interruption or attack. That certainly lifted a great weight from me and ended the possibility of either being discovered as being gay or simply continually having to endure the unintentional insults. I took a risk; my brother might have rejected me all together. But I just couldn't believe that he really meant the things that he had said; I mean, I had always known him to be a generally kind and decent person. That's why I felt that if he really knew the mental suffering that gay men and women go through, coupled now with the dread of AIDS, he surely wouldn't continue to feel or speak that way.

Just as people can mistrust a new neighbor of a different race or ethnicity unless they already have a friend of the same race or ethnicity, people tend to be wary and uncomfortable about gays if they don't personally know one. So again, it really falls to us to reveal ourselves and let people know that someone who they already love and respect is also gay and that they should not view the entire Gay Community as a group of sick, degenerate, mincing little fairies. So all was well now the last hurdle had been jumped and I hadn't fallen on my face and I could now set off on my spiritual quest with no old baggage.

The group that I traveled with was quite a microcosm; men, women, straight, gay, Christian, Buddhist, Hindu, Jewish, doctors, students, activists, authors, etc. They were all a lovely group of sincere spiritual seekers; some a little extreme and incredulous; others more cautious and skeptical like myself, but all seeking some kind of spiritual completion for ourselves only, but for the entire world.

The journey did present us with many opportunities for growth and maturing; we had to learn to live closely and co-operatively and be able to depend on one another in a very short period of time. Lack of co-operation could cost someone their life because we were dealing with mule trains, high cliffs and the like and were in more danger that some would admit to or than others even contemplated.

Peru, itself, is a very beautiful country replete with jungles, mountains, interesting and mysterious ruins, charming villages and wonderful relaxing natural hot springs and mineral baths. Unfortunately, it appeared to have been governed by a handful of elite, wealthy Peruvians of purely Spanish ancestry who lived in excessive luxury while the rest of the mostly Indian populace either lived quiet, simple lives in the rural areas or suffered a desperate and squalid existence in the large cities, huddled into abandoned buildings and surviving by prostitution and criminal activities. There were heavily armed police and soldiers everywhere in the large cities like Lima. Their uniforms were complete with machine guns and bandoliers. Lima seemed like a city about to explode into violence at any moment and I was glad that we did not have to stay there for long; we immediately moved on to Cusco which was much nicer. There were a few camera thieves there, but the city was pleasant and one did not sense the overpowering violence and negativity and desperation that one felt in Lima. Most of the time, we traveled into the countryside where the people were poor, but not starving and desperate. In fact, they were very charming and generous with what little they had.

When we gathered at the ancient sacred spots; ruins of temples, etc. I must admit that my companions and I did experience many strange and cathartic sensations and emotions. Some began spontaneous weeping or going into trance-like states, while others were able to work out childhood traumas which they had been trying to work out for years under the supervision of professional therapists, yet with no resolution until now. Others experienced a powerful sense of "deja vu" to the point of seeming to recognize some of the sites and knowing where certain buildings were. Was this a proof of reincarnation? Who can be sure? I only know that the experiences, real or imagined did, in deed, have an emotional healing effect on many. I might have felt that this was all a big act had these experiences been manifested only by the "facilitators", those close to me were having similar experiences as was I, myself.

One very strange experience which I had when we were chanting and drumming at one of the sacred sites was that I felt an incredible surge of electrical energy pulsating through my arms and hands as though I had just grabbed two "hot wires". I immediately dropped my partner's hands because I thought that it was coming from them, but then I became aware that it was just the opposite; it was coming from me. I felt drawn to the center of the circle and felt the need to lie down; I felt as if I was losing consciousness. I could still hear the drumming and the voices of my friends in the background, but what I was experiencing with closed eyes, was a vision of bright blue sky with brilliant bolts of lightning shooting upward from earth to heaven, and not just from the earth but from my own hands. While in that state, I somehow felt that I had all of this incredible energy at my disposal which I could use for good, but I had to think really fast what I wanted to do with it before it dissipated. So I concentrated on an elderly lady friend of mine back home with some serious health problems. I endeavored to send her that healing energy which I felt that I then had access to.

Oddly enough, several weeks later when I got back home from Peru, I called her to see how she was doing. I did not describe anything that had happened while in Peru. She said that she was doing much better. She said that there had been an unusually powerful electrical storm in her town while I was away with bright lightning bolts ascending from earth to heaven rather than from the clouds to earth and that she had begun feeling much better after that storm. Her crones' disorder which she had been suffering from began stabilizing from that point forward. Well, you can believe it or disbelieve it; I don't quite know what to make of it myself, but I just wanted to relate a firsthand personal experience from our mystical journey to one of these ancient power centers.

One less psychic and far more harrowing experience which I had on this pilgrimage was a day trip up a mountain to an ancient ruin. We ascended a very narrow and treacherous path which wound around the mountain all the way to the summit. Initially, we were on donkeys, but even though I had chosen the largest, strongest looking donkey which I could find, still, I am 250 pounds and the poor thing was loosing his footing and both I and the attendants feared that we would fall off the trail and plummet hundreds of feet down. I also feared that the mule might be frightened by something and throw me off, so I proceeded up the mountain trail as best I could on foot, holding onto the donkey for support. The air is very thin at those heights and with my weight, it was a serious struggle; I feared having a heart attack.

By the time we arrived at the top; I was soaked with perspiration and my legs felt as if they would buckle under me, but I was so proud and thankful to have accomplished it that I kissed my companion, the donkey at which point everyone laughed. Then, to my astonishment I noticed in the clearing, some twelve little Peruvian ladies selling Coca Cola by the case. I was stunned and asked them: "How did you get here"? To which they responded: "on the bus senior." Well, I was livid to think that I had endured that horrendous two hour trek of unspeakable terror and pain, clutching onto that mule for dear life only to find out that I could have taken a bus. The facilitators advised me that the pain which I experienced and overcoming my fears was part of what this pilgrimage was all about. I needed to develop courage and trust that the universe would always sustain me and keep me safe. Well, at the time, I wasn't all that pleased with the answer, but in retrospect I can see the wisdom behind it.

Part of the reason that I was not pleased about the concept that "the universe will always sustain me and keep me safe" was because I had grown very cynical over the years. And to my thinking, the world was a very uncertain and scary place which did not sustain anyone or keep them safe. I mean what about the thousands who starve to death daily and millions who are victims of earthquakes, tsunamis and other natural disasters? Did the universe or any deity watch over them? I had always been amazed when a jet liner went down with 250 passengers who all died except, maybe one small child. People would always say: "Wasn't it a miracle that God saved that child"? But to my reasoning I wondered why He felt that the other 249 were unfit to live?

Well, now that I had learned my cosmic lesson that I have more courage and determination than I had previously thought, I decided that I would take the bus next time. Seriously though, after that, I always made sure that I had all of the detail first before embarking on dangerous adventures and if I felt that the group was taking unnecessary risks, I felt free to abstain, as did two or three others of my friends. But you see, that was growth too because up to this point, I had always been a "yes person" and now I was finally able to say "no" without hesitation or the fear of displeasing someone. Consequently the remainder of our quest went well because I now felt that I had more control over my own life. I was certainly cordial and co-operative, but just knowing that ultimately, I was in control of my own life and choices made me feel proud and content.

Machu Pichu, itself, was an incredible place to see. High in the mountains and so remote that it must have been the best kept secret for centuries, it had an air of mystery and magic. What went on there and what suddenly happened that erased the entire culture from that mountain peak five hundred years ago? Perhaps we will never know. All of the buildings were perfectly in tact; no signs of an invasion or war. So what happened? The indigenous peoples in those rural areas of Peru believe that those ancient cultures were the design and creation of alien beings from other worlds. They believe that when those beings left earth to return home, that the cultures disappeared because the designers had not educated the Indians to such a point that they would be able to continue and improve on those cultures. That is entirely possible.

I remember once watching a public television special where a camera crew went back to many of the old British colonies in Africa only thirty years after they had been given their freedom and home rule. What they found was that many of those areas had returned to stone-age living. No one knew how to run or maintain a tractor or any of the other items of mechanized farm equipment or even buildings, so thousands of tractors stood rusting in the open fields while the natives plowed with oxen and returned to living in grass huts. So apparently, it doesn't take very long for people who have not been educated or trained to return to primitive ways. At any rate, the Peruvians of today certainly do not have the skills of their ancient ancestors to build pyramids or create maps of the universe and elaborate calendars purportedly spanning eons of time. You see, the ancient Peruvians, or Inca, much like the ancient Hindu Rishis, believed that both the earth and the universe had gone through and will continue to go through countless cycles of creation and dissolution; and that civilizations have been developed and destroyed over and over again an infinite number of times. This is certainly something to ponder.

Now, we had hoped to make contact with alien beings or at least mystical beings as Shirley McClain had in her adventure. We did not experience any UFO sightings which are supposed to abound in that area, but all in all, my adventure in Peru was certainly an interesting and rewarding growth experience. We didn't return fully enlightened as saviors of mankind, but I think that we did return a little wiser and a little better prepared to be responsible citizens in our little world and planet.

We most definitely became acquainted with the reality that most of the world's population does not live as we do nor have access to the comforts, education and wealth of knowledge that we have available to us. What a shame that we take it all for granted, and squander our resources, opportunities and lives by wasting them on the pursuit of wealth, power, "drugs, sex and rock and roll." And yet I can't help to wonder if excessive "civilization" and materialism doesn't have a negative effect on the possessors or those who want to possess such things. I noticed during our travels that the same Peruvian children who got along so well, were so happy and sharing prior to our visits often became quite violent and aggressive whenever we passed out dolls or stuffed animals as gifts to them and there weren't quite enough to go around. Perhaps the third world peoples are better off without our baubles. What always makes us think that our way of life is the best and that everyone else should live like us? Granted, all of mankind needs shelter, good nutrition, clean water, healthcare, etc. But what makes Corporate America think that it is the destiny of every family on earth to have three gas guzzling autos, a large screen TV, 2 VCR's, 2 DVD's, 3 cell phones; 3 beepers and a TV and DVD in their SUV ?

The fact of the matter is that the planet cannot support such a world picture; all of the natural resources and energy which exists would not be sufficient to support such a world or at least not for long and not without causing permanent detrimental effects to our air, water and the earth in general. So obviously, someone is going to have to go without or we are going to have to make a concerted effort to stabilize or reduce world population growth. Of course again, Corporate America doesn't care about such trivialities, in their incessant greed and avarice, they are bringing the enticement of such luxuries to the third world countries and they are moving all of their manufacturing to said countries where they can victimize and exploit the poor and ignorant and pollute air and waters as much as they please. And what is taking place is a great shift.

As I write, the middle class in China is growing in leaps and bounds while the middle class in the United States is being decimated. Millions of Americans are losing their jobs and being reduced to poverty and left with no health insurance as their jobs are either being moved overseas or farmed out to third world countries. Even those who thought that they could retire securely are losing their pensions and could end up losing their social security or receive a reduced amount. Ultimately I see the U.S. as a third world country, only still with the highest taxes and cost of living in the world.

CHAPER 11
OUT OF EGYPT I CALLED MY SON

My Peru experience had taught me that I had greater courage and more spiritual reserve than I had previously realized. It had also taught me that I had the right to say "no" to people and to voice my own opinions. It did leave me, however, a little disappointed because just as the Witnesses had promised a New World in 1974, which had come and gone; now the New Age practitioners had given me reason to believe that August of 1987 would begin a New Age of vastly greater spirituality and even measurable energy and that geographical world changes and phenomena would occur. So what were the end results? Absolutely nothing. Each of us went our several ways with all of our crystals and souvenirs, back to our boring mundane jobs and monotonous routines and the world at large remained unchanged. Some of us made an effort to keep up the lines of communication and we did have a few sparsely attended reunions, but they didn't amount to much. None of us had become great New Age Spiritual Leaders; none of us had made much of an impact on the world around us; most of us just got swallowed up in the struggle for survival in today's competitive "dog eat dog" world. So another "bubble of mine", the desire for an instantaneously changed New World had burst.

But just as I implored my readers earlier in this work, not to "throw the baby out with the bath water", I now had to struggle with myself, not to throw in the towel. Still in the center of my soul was this deep sense that all was not lost; that there was still hope for the planet and the human family, but perhaps, not according to my time scheme nor as the result of some external force. Perhaps God did have an overall "will" for mankind but perhaps he created us as extensions of himself to be his arms and legs. Perhaps it was for us to implement his will and make our world a better place rather than sit here helpless and moaning waiting for some great Cosmic Fairy Godmother to make it all better.

Of course we do have to remain alert to those inner communications and cosmic inspirations, because left to our own devices, we could easily implement changes in the world to the detriment rather than edification of all life like the Nazis did in World War II. Obviously not all of the German People of that time could have been intensely evil people led by a desire to enslave mankind. Most of them simply had no belief systems of their own; they had been failed by their churches; failed by their political systems and we all know how a vacuum needs to be filled. So they easily became pawns of sinister leaders who convinced them that genocide and world domination were God's Will for mankind and that the Third Reich was His Instrument. Ergo, we see the value and necessity of having your own values and spirituality to protect you from being an unwilling dupe and victim of others with their so called "spiritual agendas". Remember, that the Nazis, at first, came across as protectors of Family Values and used the Bible to support their claims that the 1,000 year reign of Christ was to be in the form of the Third Reich. They justified their practice of genocide by citing scripture that the Jews were Christ killers.

This is how all people become victims. Had I been more knowledgeable in comparative religion at the time the Witnesses approached me, I would not have been impressed nor swayed by what they said. But they filled the vacuum in my soul and intellect. Likewise many young people fall victim to cults and questionable political movements because they have no knowledge or informed opinions of their own and feel so helpless and powerless in the world around them. Then along comes some questionable spiritual or political movement which offers them a sense of belonging to something bigger than themselves; it gives them a sense of pride and empowerment and suddenly they are snagged and become victims and dupes of the very organization that promised them freedom and liberation. So while it has been said that "a little knowledge is a dangerous thing", expansive knowledge in politics and religion is a safeguard against being enslaved. People say, "I never talk about religion and politics"; maybe they should; and especially these days when there appears to be an ever growing and looming specter of religion "using politics" to regain the power it once had to enslave mankind.

After my pilgrimage to Peru, I continued in my Eastern, Western and New Age studies to see how I might glean the best from all three and come up with a workable spirituality for myself. I continued visiting and imbibing wisdom at the feet of great Indian Gurus whenever one would pass through Connecticut or New York on their teaching tours. I continued to be impressed by the universality and wisdom of their teachings and by the kindness, serenity and unconditional love which they radiated. Also I was impressed with the fact that they do not proselytize; probably due to their belief that "when the disciple is ready, the teacher will appear". They believe that once the human soul has reached a certain level of development, it will automatically seek out the teacher who can help them to progress to the next level and at that point, the compatible and appropriate teacher will be connected with the disciple; there are no accidents. Conversely, it would be manifestly incorrect for a teacher or Guru to pursue, proselytize or force his or her opinions and teachings on a soul that was not yet ready for those teachings.

So quite opposite many cults and religions which pretty much force their teachings on the naïve and disenfranchised of society, often producing little more than "rice Christians" or those who become believers only out of gratitude for food and shelter, Gurus simply make themselves available and one usually finds them by word of mouth or by handbills circulated by loving disciples. I guess that pretty much reflects even Jesus' teaching: "Seek and ye shall find". The only difficulty with this is that most of us would prefer to have a permanently "fixed" teacher and community that we could visit with on a regular basis, but that is not the case and perhaps for good reason. Even Jesus, when he was about to leave his disciples explained that unless he physically left them, the Holy Spirit could not come to them; See John 16:7. Undoubtedly Jesus recognized as do the Indian Masters, that so long as a disciple stays affixed to his or her teacher, she will never venture into the laboratory of his or her own soul to find the God-Within. He will remain so dependent on the physical manifestation of God before him that he will fail to venture and become one with the God/Goddess that lies within, which mystical union the great Hindu teachers call Yoga or Self-Realization; and which Buddhists call Nirvana and Zen teachers call Satori.

So perhaps I betrayed my spiritual adolescence by longing for external gurus and temples, but I was a creature seeking quick fixes and immediate gratification rather than following a consistent daily practice of going within to seek that which is always available to me and not dependent on physical teachers or temples. So my next great pilgrimage was to take me all the way to Egypt, which I believed to be possibly the cradle of all mystical teaching and spirituality.

From a very early age, say ten, when all of my little friends were playing cowboys and Indians; I was totally enthralled and mesmerized by anything Egyptian: photos, statues and movies, anything connected to Egypt. I remember sitting alone in my bedroom with a carefully folded bath towel over my head in the form of the ancient Nemys headpiece of a pharaoh with arms folded across my chest and holding two crossed dowels and repeating the formulae: "I am Pharaoh, living God of Egypt" I remember when I first saw "The Ten Commandments" by Cecil B. DeMille, that I was much more drawn to the Egyptian priests and their way of life than to the Israelites. I somehow felt that the latter had been deported and driven out of Egypt rather than freed or released and I didn't know why.

Since then, I have found several contemporary works, by several archeologists, who corroborate my theory, but how could I have known that when I was ten? One very gifted psychic and friend of mine did assure me that I had a prior life as a priest in ancient Egypt and that if I journeyed there I would meet an old friend and a lot of memories would come back to me. So off I went to Egypt with a dear lady friend of mine, Linda who I had been close to ever since we met years back in my Wicca days and who had joined the Episcopal Church with me. Linda, likewise, was obsessed with Egypt, so we made great travel companions.

It was a very long flight, but the weather was clear and the rewards inexpressible when our pilot told out to look out over the right wing of our jet liner for a panoramic view of the Giza plains and the pyramids. Linda and I were as ecstatic as little children on Christmas morning. Seeing the pyramids from the air and all of Egypt stretched out before us was overwhelming. Egypt, like Peru, is a multidimensional land; beyond time. Present, past and future exist simultaneously. As our rickety tai transported us from the Cairo Airport, we passed luxury high-rises, mud-brick two story dwellings, limos, camels, motorcycles, donkeys, cable TV dishes and women washing laundry on the banks of the Nile. It was an incredible sight to behold.

We were not at all prepared for what was to follow when we arrived at our luxury hotel, the Mena House. A very cordial, and I might add, extremely handsome young bellhop escorted us and our luggage to our room. Once inside, he asked if we would like the drapes opened since they are usually closed during the day to keep the sun out, but it was now getting toward sunset. We responded "yes", at which point the drapes went back much like the proscenium curtain in some great theater, revealing an incredible panoramic view of all three of the great Giza pyramids. Not only that, but they were silhouetted against the stunning backdrop of a rose colored horizon and a brilliant crimson solar disc which was now beginning to set. It was not unlike those beautiful depictions in the masterfully done tomb paintings which one sees in history books and travel brochures. I think that we will remember that moment as long as we live.

The next day, Linda and I went to the wonderful Cairo Bazaar and immediately donned traditional, Egyptian robes known as galabyas and deposited our dull and uninteresting Western garb in storage. Egyptian clothing is so comfortable with nice full cuts and good air-flow. The long sleeves and full length rather than being hot, protects one from the direct scorching effect of the hot Egyptian noonday sun. Most of our touring companions in their shorts and halter tops were burnt to a crisp the first day, not only by the sun, but by the eyes of Moslem onlookers who find too much skin offensive. But Linda and I were happy, cool and comfortable and well-liked by the native Egyptians.

Our first visit was to the Cairo Museum, which, while the repository of inestimable treasures of antiquity, houses and displays it all very poorly with disregard for the artifact's continued longevity. Most of the display case lids don't meet the sides, so they are certainly not air tight or climate controlled like those at the Metropolitan in New York. Also, the guards, being very poor and mercenary, offer tourists the opportunity to photograph rare textiles and papyri which should under no circumstances be exposed to the bright flashes of light from flash camera devices. But they do it for money or baksheesh as they term it with little concern for their national treasures. But aside from that, it was wonderful to view the incredible treasures of King Tut and other great pharaohs. One cannot view the actual unwrapped mummies any longer; only the sarcophagi and funerary equipment. The late President of Egypt, Anwar Sadat had all of the mummies removed from general viewing by the public because he felt it disrespectful to the ancient dead and rightly so. It is bad enough that their bodies were desecrated thousands of years ago by tomb robbers, but there is no need for tourists to pass by and gawk at them now, continuing that desecration.

The sheer vastness of the funerary texts and the skill of those ancient artisans, unmatched by today's technology made one wonder exactly what those ancients knew and where the knowledge came from. When one reads passages from the "Book of the Dead", one is baffled by the seemingly endless superstition and ritualism. The ancients seemed to believe that they could somehow bribe and trick their gods and goddesses into granting them a comfortable afterlife; not unlike Christians during the Middle Ages who bought Papal indulgences to buy their loved-ones way into heaven. But the impressive structures which they built, the medical procedures they developed, the cosmology they pictured all point to much more intelligence than is revealed in their mythology and rituals and therein lies the enigma. Did the priesthood know infinitely more than they let on and simply enshroud all those truths in ritual to keep that knowledge from the vulgar, the laity; the uninitiated? And if so, how do we now decode and decipher it?

Then, there is the other postulate that most of the architecture, medical science, civil engineering and even written language, was brought to Egypt by either a far older civilization like the elusive Atlanta or by Aliens from a distant planet. If that were the case, then the ancient priests and scribes would have simply recorded what they saw and heard without really understanding the underlying truths and over time, those truths would have become obscured and degenerated into centuries of blind ritual, superstition, tradition and myths; not unlike what can be found in parts of Christendom and even Buddhism and Hinduism today.

I can't help but think of a story I once heard from a Master about a great Guru and his disciples. It appears that whenever they sat to meditate, the cat which lived with them would create all kinds of disturbances and break their concentration. So the Guru told them to tie the cat to a pole whenever they meditated to solve the problem. Years later, the Guru had passed on and the original disciples had passed on and the cat had passed on, but the center was still operating under newer monks. A young student at the center asked the monks why they always tied a cat to a pole prior to meditation, to which the teacher advised her: "Didn't you know? One must always tie a cat to a pole during meditation in order to achieve maximum results"?

There are those today who believe that the three Giza pyramids and the Sphinx are far older than four thousand years; possibly going back ten thousand years and prior to Egyptian civilization. Some of the basis of their theories is connected with the amount and type of erosion found on those monuments which could have only taken place during a period of vastly different climate which scientists pinpoint as having been ten thousand years ago. Likewise, some scholars base it on the line up of these monuments in relationship to certain stellar alignments which also existed ten thousand years ago. There are equal numbers of historians and Egyptologists who feel otherwise, so who is to know? But if the former are correct, then there probably remain vast stores of information still buried in Egypt, which if found, would tell of previous civilizations which had peaked, and then collapsed and reduced humanity to primitiveness all over again. If found, that information could totally rewrite history; and yet, this is what the ancient Indian seers or Rishis taught; namely, that there have been countless civilizations and Ages or Yugas, prior to the one in which we now live. It really humbles one to think of that possibility.

The next morning, we arose early to travel to the Cairo Airport to embark on a flight to Luxor, where we would begin our Upper Nile trip by boat. We were up, dressed, had eaten and were outside awaiting our bus by 6AM. We witnessed once more that same brilliant solar disc ascending this time in the eastern sky, and we were chilled by the wonderful and hauntingly mysterious chants emanating from minarets all over Cairo to awaken the Moslem Community to prayer. It was a thrilling and peak experience. Unfortunately, that beautiful serenity was soon to be shaken to the foundation at the airport.

All of our traveling companions on that trip were either Australian or German; Linda and I were the only U.S. citizens. All of our tour had already passed through customs and had proceeded to our flight, but as Linda and I approached the desk, we were halted and basically taken into custody and our passports were taken from us. No one spoke English and we had no idea what was going on. Two guards with assault weapons were standing in front of us with their weapons held out in front of them horizontally and barring our way to the flight. We remained in that posture for what seemed like an eternity, but which was actually about 30 minutes. We didn't know what to do, but memories of American hostages in the news fueled our fears and kept pumping adrenaline through our bodies. Finally an airport staff person handed back our passports and told us to go with the guards.

We boarded a shuttle bus with the two guards and other passengers who were not from our tour group, but we felt at least some relief to be on the bus and on our way to our flight. When the bus finally pulled up to a large Air Egypt jet liner, the guards allowed everyone off the shuttle except Linda and I and again barred our way with their assault weapons. Now we were beginning to get really concerned; we were the only ones left on the shuttle as it pulled away from the jet liner. Why? Where were they taking us? Why were we not let off the shuttle and allowed onto our flight? Now the adrenaline was surging and our hearts were pounding; we were certain that we were being taken hostage or worse, possibly to be taken behind a hangar somewhere and shot or mutilated. We didn't know what to do; we had visions of Terry Wait and other victims of abduction.

But, alas, low and behold, to our surprise and great relief, the shuttle stopped about fifteen hundred feet further down the runway at a second jet liner, which we hadn't noticed before and which was our flight. The guards told us "go, go" and pushed us out of the shuttle with their weapons. Well, if you wanted to see two heavy-set Americans move faster than the speed of light, you should have been there. We ran to our plane, not even knowing where our luggage was or caring. Once inside the plane, we were met with cheering and applause, but it still took us about an hour to really calm down. I must admit that it really was a learning experience. One can read about hostages and only imagine what they go through, but cannot truly appreciate the absolute terror of feeling totally helpless and thinking that one's very existence is at the mercy of expressionless, emotionless, assault weapon-wielding guards. God bless Terry Wait and others like him who endured that for years on end.

The experience gave us a renewed zest for life and a greater sense of how little control we actually have over our own survival. Now you may say, but things like that don't happen here? Well, maybe not, but other things certainly do. Can you actually say with any certainty when you go to sleep at night that you will wake up the next morning? Can you actually say with any certainty that when you leave for work in the morning that you will definitely return home safely later in the day? The victims of 911 found the answer to those questions. So these are sobering experiences which, rather than depressing us, should motivate us to make good use of each and every moment of our lives; leaving no task undone; no kind words unsaid; no rifts extant and no dreams unrealized. Yes it was wonderful to be alive! Even with graying hair and aches and pains, it was still wonderful to be alive! Carpe Diem! Seize the Day.

Our mental anguish was totally vanquished by the mental reward we received at our first glimpse of the marvelous Temple of Amun Ra at Karnak. Linda and I had longed in excess of 30 years to set foot in those temple precincts. I know that you will think me crazy, but by this point, I think that fact has been pretty well established; but before I entered the Temple, I felt obliged to remove my sandals. To me, this was Holy Ground and not to be trod on lightly or without reverence. Also, I did enjoy the intimacy of experiencing the Temple through all of my senses; sight, smell, touch, etc. It was an incredible experience.

Our guide showed us all of the sacred sites and wall murals; some seemingly less sacred than others due to our Western point of view which seems to separate the sacred portions of our lives from the more mundane; we never speak of God and sex in the same breath. But to the ancients, all life was sacred and interrelated. The particular engraving of which I speak, located in the Holy of Holies, was an ithyphallic form of the Supreme God, Amun (known as Min) which sported an enormous erect penis. We all got a good laugh out of it, but it was interesting to see how the ancients integrated sexuality and fertility into their spirituality with no shame or embarrassment whatsoever. This was not unlike the ancient Hindu sage Vyassa, who is considered to have written the "Kama Sutra" which is considered an inspired religious text intended to teach men and women how to achieve incredible heights of ecstasy and even God-Union or Yoga through sexuality.

On a more metaphysical level, the guide explained to us the layout of the Temple, beginning with the spacious and very tall hypostyle hall with it's massive lotus topped columns and followed by each succeeding chamber becoming increasingly less spacious and less well lit; all the way down to the smallest and darkest chamber of all, the Holy of Holies, as it were, in which dwelt the small gilded image of the Deity, usually set inside the cabin of a sacred ark or solar boat, which was carried in procession on feast days. Even the great lotus topped pillars in the outer courts were architecturally designed to become shorter and shorter as one moved away from the central isle which represented the Nile itself.

Now the intentional symbolism behind all of this is very interesting and coincides with later Eastern teachings, so I think that the Egyptian priests preserved for all time some basic spiritual truths in their temple architecture. First off, the outer courts with their massive and once brilliantly painted columns, symbolized the physical world of man with all of its sights, sounds, scents and physical experiences. This is where temple musicians and choristers would be playing and chanting offerings to the god. The knave or central isle running down the center represented the Nile, the link to God, sustenance, fertility and preservation. Therefore the further the columns were from the center, the smaller they were to symbolize that distance from "source" or God, limits growth and vitality.

The fact that no one in the outer courts could at any time see the god, represented his invisibility to man in general. They could glean ideas and concepts of the god from the representations on the temple walls, and they could indirectly worship him and see him in the person of Pharaoh and the priesthood, but they did not have direct experience of the deity itself. No, for one to have direct experience of God, one had to be dedicated, trained, initiated and ready for such an experience. One had to delve deeply, chamber by chamber into the innermost recesses of one's heart and soul to that place where God dwells in all men.

The fact that, as one proceeded toward the Holy of Holies, each chamber became smaller and darker, symbolized that in order to reach God, one must go deeper and deeper within oneself and become separated from the sights and sounds and distractions which keep one from becoming focused and centered on God. The final chamber, the Holy of Holies, contained only you and God. Even though the god was invisible to all outside; yet He from within his shrine, could look outward as it were and clearly see everything and everyone with completely unfettered vision. So this symbolized that God is omniscient and omnipresent and sees us, even though we may not be able to see Him.

Not unlike the situation in the Temple of Solomon, built much later, only one person had access to the Holy of Holies, but in this case, it wasn't even the High Priest as in Israel, but only Pharaoh, who was both Priest and King and Son of God, in fact, the physical manifestation of God, or God-Incarnate. What this symbolized was not that only one man had the right to experience God directly; that is the birthright of every living soul, but rather that only those who seek training and initiation and who persevere at "going within" until they truly recognize their "son ship" and divinity are gifted with a direct experience of God.

One wonders how many metaphors in stone, the Egyptian priesthood memorialized for all time, which would be obvious to seekers, but totally overlooked by the vulgar or those with only a limited and materialistic interest in spirituality. Were the ancients trying to tell us that God can only be experienced once the seeker has removed himself from all outside distractions, even the distractions and mind chatter of his own thinking? Were they trying to tell us that God can only be known to us if we are willing to focus deeper and deeper into our own interior temple and plunge ourselves into the darkness of self exploration?

Were they hinting at the knowledge that once we reach the place where God is, that we will no longer know limitation, but rather be flooded with light where we can see and experience all things as God sees them, simultaneously past, present and future and truly know the Will of God? Were they saying that the only ones who could stand in the presence of God were those who truly acknowledged their own son ship and identified more with Him than with their own physical bodies? If that is the case, then so long as we continue to consider ourselves poor, fallen Children of Eve; born in sin and shaped in iniquity, we will always continue to wander aimlessly in those outer courtyards with a deceptive sense of freedom and salvation, yet in reality with only limited vision and blind to the greater freedom and light that is our birthright.

That evening, we were given the opportunity of going back to The Temple of Amun Ra at Karnak for what they called a "light and sound show". Basically they have a recorded narration of the history of the temple precincts with some recreations of the sounds and experiences which a worshipper at Karnak would have experienced. As they describe each area, lights focus on that area. I remember especially their recreation of the Festival of Apet, a festival during which the sanctuary stood open and empty awaiting the arrival of Amun by boat from the Temple of Luxor. They described how a marvelous procession would make its way from the docking point into the temple precincts. It would be led by maidens strewing flowers and priests and priestesses bearing incense, followed by musicians with trumpets, sistra, drums and stringed instruments. Next, would follow priests carrying the sacred Solar Bark or boat, which housed the gilded cabin or shrine, containing the golden image of Amun Ra. Lastly, the bark would be followed by the High Priests and Pharaoh himself, who would proceed through the hypostyle hall into the inner chapels and finally arrive at the sanctuary. There he would incense the Deity and anoint it with precious unguents and perfumes and robe it in ceremonial vestments and then he would begin his communication with Amun.

Well, the very realistic recording began with the sounds of the trumpets, sistra, drums and the chanting of litanies or prayers in ancient Egyptian. As I listened, tears and emotions welled up inside of me which I had never felt before. I suddenly just "lost it". I began weeping and weeping uncontrollably; great sighs and tears. I ran off into a distant corner of the great hypostyle hall and just held onto one of the great columns and wept. I was filled with sadness and anger all at the same time. My friend, Linda ran after me and asked what was wrong, but on a conscious level, I really didn't know and couldn't tell her. All that I knew was that in a very real sense, I missed the glory and beauty and sanctity of those days and that I was enraged at the presence of all of these "uninitiated" tourists who I felt had no business being there and were defiling sacred ground by their very presence. I was genuinely angry and wanted them all out of there; I felt very protective of the temple precincts and resented their presence. Now was this vivid experience a proof of reincarnation memories, or just the ravings of a vivid imagination?

I leave that for you to decide, but one thing was certain, no one else was weeping over the "defilement of the Temple". After I regained some composure, I was suddenly struck with the reality of how truly transitory we and all of our accomplishments are and how fruitless it is to try to hold onto anything or preserve anything against the assault of time. In my own mind's eye, I saw Washington D.C. and my own home in ruins with archeologists pouring over the remains trying to discern how we lived and what we believed in 1989. I saw them pouring through my artifacts and trying to determine who and what I was. At first they found my bronze Shiva Nataraj and assumed me to be Hindu. But later they found all of my Egyptian statuary and wondered if I was Egyptian. Then they found both male and female clothing in my closets and assumed me to have been married, but where was the skeleton of my wife? I was a real enigma to them.

All of this troubled me greatly. If nothing can stand the test and ravages of time, then what is eternal, I wondered? It was almost enough to push me over the edge. Just like many starlit evenings when I venture out of doors and gaze up into the night sky and ask: "Where does it all end"? "What is infinity"? "Why is it all there and where are we going"? It is dizzying and I often have to stop myself and feel like Scarlet O'Hara in "Gone With the Wind" when she said: "I can't think about this; if I think about this I shall go mad".

But at least for that one evening, Linda and I were alive again and at "home", and The Temple of Amun Ra reverberated with hymns to the old gods; all was as it should be. It was a cool, moonlit evening with light breezes playing with my hair and the Arab head cloth which I imagined to be my Pharoahonic Nemys and my long flowing galabaya to be my robes of state. Yes, that evening as Linda and I were escorted to the front row and foremost spot in the viewing stand which overlooked the sacred bathing lake, we were Pharaoh and Consort, Isis and Osiris once more after many centuries of deprivation and degradation. I will always remember that moment in time with the sounds of the past and the Nile breezes gently caressing us and playing with our garments and hair like a loving mother, playing with her children's tresses.

The next day we visited the Temple of Horus at Edfu, where I had another unusual experience. Remember how my psychic friend told me that I would meet an old friend or associate from a prior life if I ever went to Egypt? Well, as we were touring the temple with our guide, one of the local keepers of the sight singled me out from the rest of the tour group and beckoned me to come with him. I was a little worried because I had no idea what he was up to. I reasoned that he was either going to try to sell me contraband or some fake relic or worse yet, just rob me; yet I felt strongly attracted to follow him. He gave me a big hug and took me into parts of the temple which are usually off limit about four spots in all. In each of those chambers he directed my attention to bas-reliefs depicting the travels of the great solar bark with the god, Horus in his sanctuary. Horus was the ancient equivalent to Jesus; he was also the only-begotten Son of the God Osiris, begotten of a virgin mother, Isis miraculously and long after the death of his father Osiris.

In each of these chambers he bade me kneel and he pressed my forehead up against the relief of the solar bark while he placed his hands on my shoulders and chanted what seemed like ancient Egyptian incantations over me. Of course I can't be sure, not knowing ancient Egyptian. He then repeated this procedure in each of the chambers and then took me to the Holy of Holies to show me an actual Solar Bark which was preserved there. After we had completed the circuit; he gave me a warm loving hug and smiled at me with a kind of "knowing smile". Now was this some kind of renewed initiation or just plain craziness? And how did he know that I, out of all of those people would be accepting of it? Also, most Moslems, although they may work around these ancient sites to support themselves and their families have absolutely no reverence for them because they consider the temples remnants of pagan, polytheistic, and infidel worshippers. Over the centuries Christians and Moslems alike had defaced many of the images of the gods on these temples. So it is odd that this man would have escorted me on this journey of initiation. My friend, Linda, was not party to any of this; she wondered where I had wandered off to.

The rest of our trip up the Nile was also edifying and wonderful. The tour guides, however, were a little overly protective of us so we didn't have much freedom to do things on our own. It was only once we came to the end of the line at Aswan, that we were allowed the afternoon and evening at leisure. So Linda and I made off to the marketplaces which we loved so much. They were incredible; visiting them was like being part of a National Geographic special or better yet, going back in time. The Aswan marketplace, with the exception of Arabic music coming from tape players, might just as well have been Egypt or Bethlehem in 30 AD. It was full of baskets full of fresh produce and herbs and spices and camels and donkeys and pottery of every kind. The sounds, colors and the scents were so profuse and alluring that one could suffer from sensory overload. But it was all wonderful to me.

Most of the city sat high on a hillside overlooking the Nile below and beautiful botanical gardens. It was heaven to sit on that hillside and watch the white sails of the hundreds of small boats or falukas, as they were called, sailing listlessly and serenely down the river past date palms papyrus plants and sacred white ibises resting on the shoreline. And it was wonderful to witness again, that gorgeous red solar disc cooling itself by immersion into the restorative waters of the Nile until all that remained was a faint rose glow silhouetting the palm trees and minarets. I think that I could easily wile away the remainder of my days in a place like Aswan, but there wasn't time now; the next day we had to travel back by train to Cairo because, as of yet, we had not yet received the final initiation in the Great Pyramid at Giza.

I am glad that we went to Egypt when we did because who knows when I could ever do this again. Since our relationship with the Moslem world and with Middle Eastern countries has become strained, Americans are at risk in those areas. What a shame that religious fundamentalists have to ruin it for everyone; even their own people. Because of their violence and hatred they have ruined the tourist trade that their own people are so dependent upon. It's sad that fundamentalists of whatever religion cause so much suffering. They are a disgrace to their own individual religions and they dishonor God by creating rifts between His children of different faiths; rather than striving to unite all of God's Human Family.

To me, fundamentalism belies true faith and rather demonstrates a severe lack of faith. If you are threatened by the fact that others see things differently than you and need to convert everyone to your belief system either through coercion or by the sword, then how strong is your faith? Does the fact that others believe differently call your own faith into question? If it does, then perhaps your own faith or lack of it is not founded upon your own examination of the facts, but is a faith merely handed down to you or part of your ethnic tradition. If this is so, then rather than attack those of other faiths, one would do well to examine the teachings of those faiths and based upon that knowledge, come to an intelligent decision as an adult, rather than blindly accept a faith that was decided for you by parents and grandparents, but never really your own intelligent choice.

The following morning we left early so as to avoid the sun getting too hot; one does not want to visit pyramids at high noon. While we normally think of stone structures as being cool and shielding one from the heat; when that structure is situated in the dessert and is subjected to heat most of the time, it becomes like an oven and can be unbearably hot with no good air flow circulating in it. We went first to Saqquara, the site of the earliest successful pyramids in Egypt. While the great Step Pyramid of Djoser, designed by Im Hotep, was off limits, we were able to visit many of the lesser underground tombs and mastabas, which were very pleasant and reveal a much more optimistic attitude toward death than our culture. Our tombs, crypts and cemeteries are usually morbid and decorated wither with skulls, suffering saints, or melancholy scriptures and poems, but theirs were bright, cheerful and hopeful, depicting only life.

Finally, the great moment came when we arrived at the Great Pyramid of Cheops back on the Giza plain. I must admit that I was a little nervous. As I mentioned earlier on, I am subject to periodic and unanticipated anxiety attacks and am not wild about tight, enclosed places. The fact also that I noticed some large, hulking Teutonic males emerging from within, drenched in tears and perspiration and visibly upset; only exacerbated my concerns. But again, just as in Peru, I needed to conquer my fears and press on to get the continued experience and training which I needed. So Linda and I entered the Great Pyramid. I comforted myself and prepared our way by reciting out loud an ancient Egyptian prayer which I had stumbled across years back and had taken a liking to. Linda got a kick out of it. Most of the way, we proceeded in a stooping posture, but the last stretch to the King's Chamber had to be negotiated on your hands and knees.

Once through that passage, however, you found yourself in a rather large, tall, cubicle chamber with nothing but an open sarcophagus. There were no inscriptions, no hieroglyphs, no artwork or decoration of any kind, which is in direct contrast to all other tombs and which has led some scholars and Egyptologists to believe that this was not a tomb at all, but rather a hall of initiation.

Some believe that initiates would be led into this chamber by mentor priests, who would then leave them there, possibly lying in the sarcophagus in total darkness so that they might "go within", totally undistracted and find that all pervasive and transcendental Light. In the darkness of the sarcophagus, they could contemplate their own physical mortality, but even more so, their own spiritual divinity and eternal life. They could undergo metanoia, or a transformation of mind and spirit, much as the caterpillar undergoes metamorphosis while in the chrysalis and emerges as a new creature, a butterfly. Therefore there would be no need for beautiful decorations or inscriptions in this chamber because it was never to be viewed in bright light. There were, interestingly enough distinct air shafts, which would be unnecessary in a tomb also and those shafts were not just air shafts intended for the workmen who built the pyramid because they would have been sealed afterward. Not only that, but they were astronomically aligned with specific constellations. Does this allude to where man originally came from? Who knows?

At any rate, it was a special moment for Linda and I and rather than unnerving us, filled us with a sense of tranquility and wonderment. I wondered how many men just like myself, had experienced enlightenment in that chamber. How many initiates had found there in that chamber, what I had been seeking all of my life? Would I find it myself? But of course, again, there are no quick fixes. Those initiates in the past, even if not here, but in temples elsewhere, didn't enter these chambers for twenty minutes with no advance preparation. No, they had studied and meditated and purified themselves prior to this moment. Every facet of their lives had been geared to this special moment. I, however, although sincere, had not spent my life in prayer and meditation and had not purified myself; I was by no means celibate or chaste. So the results were commensurate. I was not immediately enlightened, but I do feel that the experience helped me and perhaps left me with some seeds of enlightenment which in time will bear fruit.

I did, in deed, receive a small token gift from the Great Pyramid to assure me that I had its blessing. On emerging from the pyramid and for some time after that, I experienced something not uncommon to many psychics, but certainly not to me. At first I thought that I was experiencing blurred vision, possibly from the heat or from my eyes trying to adjust from intense darkness to the bright light of the outdoors. But it persisted. And then as I focused in on objects I noticed that it wasn't blurred vision so much as it was that I saw a halo of light around all living things or an aura as psychics would call it. I noticed that when I focused my attention on inorganic matter, that my vision was perfectly clear. I felt elated at the experience and took it as a loving gesture from the powers beyond, that although a slow learner and not the purest of the pure, still God was blessing my efforts and beckoning me home. It whetted my spiritual appetite and made me realize that any future spiritual growth from this point on would be directly proportionate to the effort and discipline that I put into it.

Spiritual teachers and holy sites would of course always have a positive influence on me, but could only take me so far. The rest would be up to me. But it was comforting to know that there was a loving and patient Cosmic hand out there reaching out to me and saying: "Come on, take another step, I will not let you fall; please come home to me, I have been waiting for your return for millennia". That is no small lesson to have learned. It is probably the crux of all higher spiritual attainment and I found it in Egypt. So our pilgrimage was not in vain by any means. Linda and I finally bade farewell to our ancient homeland Egypt or Tamara as it was known before the coming of Alexander the Great; amidst tears and sadness at leaving Her. We would now have to reintegrate ourselves into our usual monotonous jobs and mundane life, but always holding dear to our hearts these wonderful memories and aspirations of some day returning.

I'm glad that Linda and I had that special time together; not that we hadn't traveled together before; we had been to England together also, but this was something very special between us. You must understand that Linda had fallen in love with me way back in the early 1970's when we had first met at High Priestess Rose's home. She was well aware that I was gay, but somehow fell in love with me anyway. She followed me through all of my broken romances and offered to enter into a totally platonic marriage and allow me my men on weekends, but I didn't feel that would be a wise move. I loved and respected Linda too much to use her as a cover and then move some man into our home who I really loved in a romantic sense. I felt that would be devastating to her.

But this was the first time that Linda and I had been away together without friends tagging along; sharing the same bed and appearing to all as a genuine husband and wife team. Linda suggested that we wear wedding bands so as not to offend the Moslems. We didn't tell anyone that we were married; it was just assumed and I know that Linda enjoyed at least living that fantasy for two weeks. Life and nature can play very cruel tricks on us. I think that Linda may possibly be the only person who has ever truly loved me, yet due to my chemistry, I was unable to respond to that love. Yet Linda never fluffed me off; she was always there for me to comfort me and help me pick up the pieces when the men who didn't love me walked out of my life. She was most certainly a dear and precious soul and I hope that as she looks down on me from the "Summerland", that she knows that in my own imperfect way, I did and still do love her.

You see, my dear friend passed away on May 20, 2004; another victim of "outsourcing." She had worked for years at Remington Shaver here in Bridgeport; it was the only job she had ever known and when the company moved to China she was devastated; she was in her early 60's and had never had any other job; she had also recently lost her mother. Linda tried desperately to find jobs in other factories, but most of the factories which used to be in Bridgeport are all gone now. She had extreme difficulty adjusting to new jobs and skills and invariably got laid off or fired from every job that she tried. When she finally reached dead end and no one had even responded to her applications in over nine months, she gave up. She went into a deep depression that no one was able to pull her out of; not even her pets this time; and she simply died. I am sure that she simply willed herself to die and she did.

Her passing hurt me in a way that I had never expected or anticipated. I was absolutely devastated. Her sister asked me to join the family in all of the funeral proceedings because she said that I was Linda's closest friend and the closest thing to a husband that she had ever experienced. I apologized to her sister that I was never able to be what Linda wanted me to be, but her sister stopped me and reminded me that I had opened a whole world to Linda that she would never have experienced without me; a world of concerts and plays and travel and friends. Linda was a very quiet person and somewhat of a loner and would never have done all of these things on her own. I wept and grieved for several weeks; longer than I had grieved for my Dad. At her funeral I felt like the grieving "husband", so I guess I did love her after all far more than I had realized. I wonder if some man will ever weep at my gravesite and miss me the way that I miss Linda. Somehow at this late stage in life, I tend to doubt it. I remember one New Year's Eve, a drag queen performer singing this little song and strewing glitter all over everyone in the audience. The lyrics were: "Nobody loves a fairy when she's 40". Well, I'm over 50 now so I guess it's entirely out of the question.

CHAPTER 12
INTEGRATION AND DISILLUSIONMENT

No, I'm not talking about integration of the public school system nor of suburban neighborhoods, but rather how was I now to take all of these experiences up to this point and build them into one cohesive spiritual system that I could live by? What had I, in fact, learned from my Eastern teachers, Christian teachers, New Age Teachers; Gay Life experiences, pilgrimages and of course, last but not least " The School of Hard Knocks"?

Allow me now to share with you the original belief system with which I began life ; undoubtedly instilled within me partly by my parents and educators; partly by blind credulity; and see how it stands up to the litmus test which we call LIFE. You may recognize some of these belief systems in your own life.

As a child, I believed that Mom and Dad loved me and would always be there for me. I believed that all other children, adults and animals were innately good and could not possibly do me any harm. I believed that there was an all loving omnipresent God who watched over me and would never allow any harm to come to me. I believed that my parents and friends would always be there for me. I believed that all churches and synagogues were houses of God and I believed that ministers, rabbis, and priests somehow had some kind of direct link to God, which of course, I did not; so their word was TRUTH and GOSPEL.

I believed that eventually, love would find me and that I would meet someone and fall in love, perhaps raise a family, and live happily ever after. As I grew a little older and went to school I believed in equality and freedom and justice for all and that the U.S. government was the sole repository and guardian of such a state and such values. I believed that if I was honest and responsible and worked hard, that there would be nothing unattainable for me; hell, that was the American Dream.

I believed that teachers, doctors, lawyers and authority figures in general always knew best and had my best interests in mind in all of their dealings; I could trust them because they would never steer me wrong. Then, at last, I believed that after a long life a honest, hard work and integrity, that I would be rewarded; that I would ease into a well earned, well deserved retirement with the security of a good pension and social security and healthcare. Maybe I would travel a bit with the wife or visit with the grandchildren; whatever. Eventually I would just slip off one night into heaven, to the tunes of harps and angelic songs, sorely missed and lovingly remembered.

Now let's see how well those beliefs have served me and played out in reality. We'll examine them one by one and see what the Laboratory of life has taught me.

Premise #1: First off, Mom and Dad plan for a child and wanted a child, but they wanted a girl; not me. Hence, they loved me as best they could, but basically, I was a disappointment to them. As far as them always being there for me, Mom, through no fault of her own, died too young to be there for me through most of the important moments of my life. Dad and I were estranged until perhaps the last few years of his life. Fortunately we made up for it then, but right after that; he was gone.

Premise # 2: "All children, adults and animals are innately good." Are you kidding? From an early age I found that many children were quite cruel; greedy and violent; in fact, just like their parents. Children love to stick their fingers in your eyes, pull your hair; torture small animals and other children who they feel they can safely overpower. School wasn't fun for me as it was for many other children. All through my schooldays I was made fun of and rejected and bore the brunt of name calling and physical abuse. No, I don't have any fond schoolboy memories. Oh, I did manage over the years to attract one or two friends, who were also considered some kind of misfits like me, but I certainly never became head of the Student Union or Prom King or Queen for that matter. Even the educators, who I thought would be sympathetic or at least empathetic were very cold and cruel with me and simply told me that if I was going to survive that I would have to learn how to fight and be tough.

Premise # 3: "God is an all loving omnipresent Being who has numbered the hairs on my head and notices the fall of a sparrow." Well, he may notice the fall of a sparrow, perhaps right into a cat's mouth, but he certainly doesn't do anything about it; so where is the security in that mode of thinking? I mean where was God in Auschwitz? Or for that matter where was God in Hiroshima or Nagasaki? Where was God at 911? What ? Does He only do cameo appearances every two thousand years like some kind of divine David Copperfield or Houdini? In between appearances of God mankind just has to hoof it as best he can.

In my own personal experiences, I had found that none of my prayers or pleadings or deals with God had brought any results whatsoever. To my mind, God was either non-existent or uninvolved. In either case, he was of no help to me. And as far as those religious institutions which supposedly had a hot line to Him; they were just as ambiguous and aloof. Hell, they were directly responsible for much of the human suffering on this planet. They authorized the slaughter of every man, woman, child and beast throughout the land of Canaan and Jericho; they authorized all of the Inquisitions and Holy Wars; they authorized the burning of thousands of witches and homosexuals all over Europe in the Middle Ages. In fact, the period of history when the Church held supreme power was appropriately know as the "Dark Ages". During the late Middle Ages and Renaissance, people began to take the Church "with a grain of salt". They no longer actually believed Her teachings; they merely used her as a means to wealth.

No, I found that clergymen had neither "hot line" nor any direct contact with God; they merely repeated beliefs and statements of those who came before them "parrot-like" and without ever having investigated any of those beliefs or claims. They had simply become as a great Indian teacher termed them "book worshippers" not worshippers of God. They violate their own commandments against idolatry because they worship their books; their Bibles, their Korans, their Talmud and Torah above all. If God Almighty were sitting with them and talking with them, they would first have to check what he was saying to see if it was in their BOOK. So they are idolaters, they are in effect book worshippers. You cannot reach these people based on reason or rationality because their minds are closed; and they are neither reasonable nor rational.

I am amazed that 21st century, supposedly educated people continue to entrust their spiritual lives and often finances, unquestionably, to institutions which are basically practicing a slightly more sophisticated form of three thousand year old shamanism; believing in virgin births; changing wine into blood; participating in spiritual cannibalism; casting out demons; instructing starving, impoverished millions of their adherents to abstain from birth control. This is all madness. But maybe I could have swallowed their bitter pill if I had at least found the love and acceptance which Jesus had said would be the mark of his disciples. But I did not find that either. All that I found was bigotry, intolerance and hypocrisy. I found "do as I say, not as I do" theology. And is it any wonder? I could hardly imagine that the same church which only 1600 years after its founding had deteriorated to the point where it could use scripture to justify human slavery, would be open-minded on the question of homosexuality. No, the same institutions which had sponsored the Crusades; Witch trials and executions; the slaughter of the Huguenots in France and Protestants in England; and the same infallible leadership which excommunicated Haley's Comet, could hardly be expected to be compassionate with homosexuals.

Premise # 4 I believed in equality and freedom and justice for all and that the U.S. government was the sole repository and guardian of such a state and such values. I believed that if I was honest and responsible and worked hard, that there would be nothing unattainable for me. Wrong, wrong, wrong.

All men are created equal and are entitled to life, liberty and the pursuit of happiness provided that they are white, heterosexual males. This is the way our institution was set up from its very inception. There was certainly no freedom or equality for women, children, blacks or for that matter non-landowners and there would continue to be none for over one hundred years. This sort of makes one question the real intents of the founding fathers and how genuinely they believed in freedom and justice for all after all. I mean they didn't set the example by freeing any of their slaves did they? Somehow our educators failed to acquaint us with all of those minor details and just left us with Betsy Ross, Paul Revere and other quaint stories.

Now don't get me wrong; we have made some progress. Slaves were eventually freed in the 1860's but somehow still couldn't vote without reprisals until the 1960's. Eventually black men were allowed more honorable positions in the military and allowed to even become officers. Then women began to gain more acceptances in the military and become officers. Of course gays, either men or women, are simply out of the question.

But then what reason would I have to expect justice and equality from a government which conducted witch hunts of their own during the McCarthy "Reign of Terror" or which put Japanese-Americans into concentration camps as a "threat to security" while leaving German-Americans at large; interesting how we can pick and choose. And what reason would I have to expect justice from a system in which it is increasingly evident that money buys justice. And how can I believe in the integrity of congressmen who tell me to tighten my belt and who freeze my wages and social security while voting exorbitant pay raises and health benefits for themselves?

How can I justify in my mind, the sacrifices of millions of U.S. soldiers who died in Korea, Vietnam and Cambodia fighting the same Communist Chinese that our government and Corporate America are now kissing up to and handing our jobs over to? Did those millions die so that China could be the leading power and manufacturer in the world while the U.S. is reduced to third world status? While it may be true that U.S. businesses may be benefiting from these trade arrangements and U.S. CEO's may be lining their pockets; the average U.S. citizen is losing his job, his pension, and his healthcare as a result.

And how can I support the U.S. military actions against supposed hostile powers when, invariably, you find out twenty years down the line that the CIA artificially created the situations just to entice these powers into a conflict because as we all know, war is good for the economy. And then when our young men come back in body bags, we discover that they were killed by weapons and bombs and germ warfare made in U.S.A. and peddled to hostile nations by mercenary American gun-runners. How do you think that we had such an accurate knowledge of Saddam Hussein's arsenals? We knew what he had because WE SOLD IT TO HIM.

See, we believe in human rights so deeply, that we had no problem selling Saddam Hussein germ warfare and lethal gasses, so long as he used them on Iranians. We never anticipated that someday he might use them on us. We are hypocrites of the lowest level because at least these dictators will tell you up front that they have no regard for human life and will do whatever it takes to remain in power. But we are the ones who CLAIM to believe in human rights while supporting dictators and Communists all over the world and why? for money of course. Somehow "Old Glory" is looking just a little more Red to me lately; it's hard to find the white and the blue.

Yes, it would appear that the wheel has come full circle. While we no longer have actual slavery in this country, the middle class is being rapidly reduced to a state of indentured servitude to exorbitant taxes, auto insurance gougers, medical and pharmaceutical extortionists; gouging, grasping oil companies and crooked lawyers. While the cost of living continues to rise, our wages, in essence, continue to plummet due to employer take backs; actual reductions in wages; added expenses for health insurance, etc. We are forced to work 60-80 hours per week split between two different employers at two different locations; not to get ahead, but merely to survive, and that's if you are lucky enough to find a job at all. Oh sure, you can always get a job at a fast food restaurant since the turnover is so high. But I'd love to see how one of these loud mouth right- wingers would be able to survive on $300. per week when they feel that anyone earning under $150,000 per year is basically poor and shouldn't have to pay additional income taxes. Yet these same hypocrites feel that it would be wrong to raise the minimum wage to anything over $7.15 per hour.

This is hardly the American Dream; and hardly progress; in fact it is a retrograde back to pre FDR days when people were working over 60 hours a week with no weekends off or any time to be with their families. They keep telling us to "buy American", but even that doesn't help American workers because the products are all produced overseas and Chinese and Mexican workers are being employed; not U.S. citizens. The only Americans benefiting by any of this are your usual voracious CEO's and Boards of Directors. When their companies prosper, they don't raise wages, hell no; they vote themselves multi million dollar bonuses and lay off a few people to increase profit margin even more. And if the business fails; no problem; you see the CEO's and Board of Director's retirement funds are safely stashed away in some Swiss bank, but the rank and file employees will not only lose their jobs, but their pensions as well, and with the blessing of Washington D.C. because although these pensions are supposed to be fully funded up front; no one is monitoring these companies or making them comply; hell no, that might lose some congressman votes.

Now Ford and General Motors and companies like them say that the American auto workers are just too greedy and that they can't afford to hire them. Well first off, is it that American workers are greedy or wouldn't it perhaps be more accurate to say that they are needier than their foreign counterparts? Their equivalent workers in China do not pay $1200 a month rent, $800 a month health insurance $200 a month auto insurance, $300 a month in energy related needs; to say nothing of incidentals like food and clothing. So of course Chinese and Mexican workers can accept lower wages. Yet I find it interesting that foreign companies like Toyota and Nissan seem to be able to higher American auto workers and yet still pay out dividends to their stock holders. Could that possibly be because they do not demand a 400% profit margin? Nor do they pay their CEO's 50 Million dollars a year.

Premise #5 "Love would somehow find me". Well of course, that one blew up in my face too. Once I recognized who I actually was, all hopes of a wedding or raising a family, or having children to be a comfort to me in my old age, were dashed to pieces. All hopes of carrying on my family name or giving my parents grandchildren…dashed to pieces. The only thing that I could hope for would be a lover and possibly some surrogate kind of family that we could create. But I was wrong there too. All that I was finding were multitudinous frightened, wounded, hiding little people who were too full of self-loathing and self-hatred to love anyone else; hell they needed to learn to love themselves first.

I had thought that at least among other gay men and women, I could find acceptance and community and a sense of belonging, but I was wrong there too. The gay women for the most part, weren't all that comfortable around gay men. The gay men, on the other hand, considered each other a threat and preferred to be with straight lady friends, commonly known as "fag hags". The fag hags, ultimately fell in love with the gay men and felt that they could somehow change them, but that didn't work either and they ended up estranged from one another in time. What a disaster this was ! No one really wanted to have a permanent long term relationship because that would expose them to persecution and ridicule. Most were more than content to simply have anonymous sex in motels and parks and swear undying love and loyalty all the while hiding their marital status and true identities.

Of course now it was starting to get a bit risky because now there was AIDS. Many had already died; how many more would succumb? I mean if you were tested and found yourself positive with HIV, you weren't even in a position where you could at least call your sex partners and warn them to go get tested because they had all given you fake names and fake telephone numbers. And if you were tested and found yourself OK, there was almost a sense of "survivor's guilt" that afflicted many gay men. We wondered why we had been spared when so many of our dear brothers had already shuffled off their mortal coils and not too prettily either; their bodies ravaged by disease.

My dear friend, Tom with whom I worked, met such a fate. He developed that terrible wasting syndrome where he closely resembled someone from a concentration camp at the end. But he was so loving and so patient. He still loved God and said that he was responsible for his own condition and should have been more careful. He only hoped that his suffering might frighten his friends to the point where they would be careful and avoid suffering the same fate. What a truly loving friend he was. Likewise another dear friend, Armando met the same fate after a long illness. I have memorialized both of them by making quilts for them which are now part of the National Aids Quilt. I am very glad to have been able to do that much for them.

The AIDS epidemic did scare me; and watching my friend's sufferings did frighten me into celibacy for a least a while; probably for 9 or so years. But then I just couldn't stand it any more. Just like the character in the movie and play "Jeffrey", who refused to love anyone or be sexual with anyone out of fear of catching HIV; and then on his way home one night was mugged and almost killed by gay bashers. After he survived the ordeal he realized that no one is getting out of here alive and that there were countless other things that could happen to him that could lead to his death. He realized that it was pointless to put his life on hold and deny himself and others love just to "stay alive" and lead a bland, meaningless, loveless half-life. So he took a risk and decided to love a man with AIDS. I began taking risks again, myself, but calculated risks; I at least tried to "play safe" and minimize the risk factors.

Premise# 6 " I believed that after a long life of honest, hard work and integrity, that I would be rewarded; that I would ease into a well earned, well deserved retirement with the security of a good pension and social security and healthcare". Well, that was blown out of the water when after only 22 years at SNET; they decided to downsize, like so many other large companies. They said that they needed 1,500 people to voluntarily leave and accept the company's "early out offer". Otherwise they would need to begin laying off employees by inverse seniority. What they were actually preparing for was to make the company "lean and mean" so that they could sell it to SBC Communications. So as a result of this, I got cheated out of 17 years of work at maximum pay which would certainly have added to my pension fund and ultimately made my pension payments higher. It would also have added to my social security funds and made those payments higher.

In stead, I was put on pension immediately at a much lower rate than I would have gotten had I worked the other 17 years. The pension was not adequate to live on, and I was not old enough to receive social security, so I was forced to work all manner of menial jobs with unreasonable schedules and hours to make up the funds that I need to live on. At the rate that things are going in Connecticut with ever increasing taxes, oil, gas, etc. and low wages; I would imagine that I will never be able to retire and will ultimately be hauled out of some horrible job at Home Depot or Wal-Mart in a body bag or casket. I wouldn't be at all surprised if SBC renegs on our pension and health plan at some point down the road since we are only "grand fathered" under SBC as SNET retirees. Who can stop them; the government? That's a laugh. We all know that Congress is little more than a "rubber stamp" for Corporate America."

So what has that dear little boy, Bobby, with all his trust and hopes and dreams learned in 57 years? Well, he has learned that just about everything that he was taught as a child, either through ignorance or deliberate deception, was and is absolute rubbish and lies. Everything that he held sacred has been violated and exposed as the worst possible deception and he has suddenly realized that unless he very rapidly adjusts to the brave New World that he now finds himself in, he will soon become just another dinosaur mired in the tar pits of this world.

No, one doesn't survive in today's world by having values, loyalty or ethics. One survives by "dressing for success"; exposing the errors of his co-workers; stealing ideas; stepping on people's faces on the way up the corporate ladder; through blackmail and deceit and steeling from one's employer. We've come full circle now and we're back to survival of the fittest, or I should say survival of the most ruthless; so much for human progress.

But then you see; this is what happens when man lives by a Cosmology, in which he sees himself as the center of the universe, and views everything and everyone else as existing solely for his own enjoyment and exploitation. This is the Cosmology which the Roman Church promoted for years; and excommunicated Galileo for exposing it when he proved that the sun was the center of our solar system and not the earth. This is the kind of Cosmology produced over the last 500 years by religious and political leaders to justify their imperialism; cruelty and exploitation and now we will all pay for it.

Unfortunately, one even sees this attitude spilling over into interpersonal relationships. Now that I am constantly between jobs and have the opportunity to watch daytime TV; I am horrified at what I see. You must remember that I left off watching daytime TV back in the 1960's with Mr. Mrs. Cleaver and family values. Back then an unwed mother would immediately be rushed to a convent where she would be confined for life. There simply was no such thing as divorce; men supported their families; children who graduated from High School could read and write; Liberace, Danny Kaye and Pinky Lee were not gay, they were simply overly refined, polite and elegant.

But the daytime TV that I see now shows me a world of little more than predators. I see men who father 5 children by 5 different women and have no intention of acknowledging or caring for any those children. If you ask them they will reply: "If women want to be stupid, they deserve to be taken advantage of. Hell, I was just having fun." If you then ask the 5 women, their response will more than likely be: "Men will just be men; there isn't anything that you can do about it". Half of our children are born out of wedlock and have no father in their life.

Then you turn to the next channel and hear serial killers who show absolutely no remorse for their crimes and tell the interviewers that they would do it again and enjoy hearing the screams. This is then followed up by a scene outside the prison where 15 morons with candles are pleading for the serial killer's life. Then you get poor little Matthew Shepherd, beaten to death and left to die on a fence for the crime of "daring to look at" or "talk to" fag basher who he met in a gay bar.

We have ten and eleven year olds robbing and mutilating their grandparents and killing people either for drug money or just because they thought that it might be "fun" to set someone on fire or whatever. We have parents acting like pimps and selling off their adolescent children to sexual predators to get drug money. We have criminal medical clinics in China and elsewhere that will lure the ignorant and poor into their facilities, offering a free check up and will then anesthetize them and remove body organs so that they can sell them on the black market. We have unscrupulous business sharks stealing the retirement funds of the elderly; and who will never see a day in prison for that crime.

And amidst all of this horror which neither religious leaders nor political leaders are even addressing; out rides "The Christian Right" to the rescue to do battle against such serious issues as the "Rainbow Curriculum" in the public schools and the possibility of Gay Marriage. Hell, most of the straight couples aren't bothering to get married at all, even though they can; apparently they like living in sin and have done a marvelous job of making a mockery of marriage already. It is said that 50% of all marriages end in divorce within the first 5 years and as for the other 50%; the husbands are more than likely cheating on their wives anyway. I can't see anything that we could do that would degrade marriage any more than it has been degraded already.

Now I know that this sounds like a pretty sad litany, but it's true and you know that it is true. But despite the fact that everything that I have ever believed in or hoped for as a young man has been proven to be lies or at least false hopes; my entire life hasn't been wasted. I have learned some very valuable life lessons that you never learn in college or anywhere but in the "School of Hard Knocks". If I can pass them on to you and you can benefit from them without actually having to go through these experiences for yourselves, then I have done my job and my life will not have been in vain. So let me share these observations with you to the end that you may escape the "Wheel of Karma" and not end up reaping what you sow.

Just to lighten up a bit; let me relate one funny incident which occurred when I was slaving away at one of my flunky jobs behind the concession stand in a movie theater. I had just come back from break and put on what I thought was my approved bib style apron, when the girl working with me said: "I think you're wearing the wrong apron." I couldn't imagine what she meant; all the aprons were the same, so I ignored her. Then she repeated again: "I think you're wearing the wrong apron", to which I replied? "How can I be wearing the wrong apron; they're all the same?" At which point she asked me: "Is your name Mary?" Well, when she said that,

I just started laughing and laughing; I hadn't noticed the big name tag on the apron, so there I stood waiting on customers with this big name tag which read "Mary". That, coupled with the fact that "Mary" is a slang term for an effeminate homosexual man, kept me intermittently laughing for a good half hour every time I thought about it. I finally jokingly told the girl who I was working with that I am only Mary on weekends.

CHAPTER 13
HOW TO BEAT THE SYSTEM

One of the major reasons that most of us become enslaved by Corporate America and its partner in crime, the International Banking Systems, is because we are so poorly educated, deliberately misinformed and because we fail to "read the fine print". If something seems "too good to be true", then rest assured that it IS TOO GOOD TO BE TRUE and that it is a trap. We buy into all the big business rhetoric without ever investigating the claims to see if they are indeed true. We also have the chronic problem of our inability to distinguish between actual "needs" as opposed to our "wants". Of course part of that problem arises due to Corporate America constantly bombarding us and brainwashing us with commercial advertising which leads us to believe that we are somehow deprived of life, liberty and the pursuit of happiness unless we own all of the endless array of products which they offer us. However they fail to mention that working two jobs and never seeing your family; hiding from bill collectors and suffering through foreclosures and repossessions, can hardly be termed as either life, liberty or the pursuit of happiness.

A wonderful book which should be required reading in high school for all young people is "Your Money Or Your Life" by Joe Dominguez and Vicki Robin, first published by Penguin Books in 1992. People are constantly making statements such as: "It's only money", "You can't take it with you", etc. etc. But in their book, Joe and Vicki put money into its true perspective by stating that "money = life energy". We all basically sell a portion of our life and life energy to our employers in exchange for money. Since our lives are finite, we need to recognize that we are selling a portion of our lives and life energy, which once gone, can never be replaced. This is why Joe and Vicki state in their book: "Now that you know that money is something you trade life energy for, you have the opportunity to set new priorities for your use of that valuable commodity. After all, is there any "thing" more vital to you than your life energy?"

Their book goes on to show readers a path to financial independence with far less time spent in the workplace; a way to conserve your life energy for other more meaningful pursuits and goals. The book is a real eye opener. Why DO we need to buy hundreds of books, CD's, videos, etc. when we could just as easily borrow them at the local public library? Do we really need to spend $100 per month on cablevision programming when we are too busy working to pay for it and have no free time to watch the programs after all? Is there any point in a mother working at all if her entire paycheck is only going to be handed over to a daycare facility at the end of the week for mediocre care given to her children? Wouldn't she do far better to raise her children herself? And what about all of these wonderful sales in major stores offering 10% or 25% off? First of all, it's only a savings if you actually need the product. Second, it is only a savings if you are paying cash. Otherwise if you think that you are saving 10% when you are putting the items on an 18% or 20% credit card, then you are sadly mistaken.

This brings me to another insidious topic; namely the banking institutions. How do I know? because I work in the MasterCard department of an international bank. Now of course, the banks will tell you that they give full disclosure on all transactions and that it is the customer's responsibility to read their contract carefully. And while this is true, still, the contracts are written in such complicated terminology that I as a bank employee can barely comprehend them, much less a poor confused customer with minimal education. A vast number of my customers barely know the difference between their ATM card and their credit card and they are in no way prepared to comprehend the subtleties of their credit card disclosure.

One common "come on" which all banks use is offering a promotional rate of 0% for one year to new customers on balance transfers, while establishing a purchase rate of perhaps 15%. So of course many customers see this as a great way to consolidate other debts and pay them all off at 0% rather than at the higher rates which they are already paying. But what they are not stopping to consider is that if they transfer say $15,000 of debt to their new credit card, there is no way in hell that they will be able to pay off that debt in one year's time and the 0% will default to 15% on their one year anniversary. They will be billed minimum payments of 1% or $150 per month; after one year they will have paid of $1800, leaving a balance of $13,200. That new balance will then be billed at 15% resulting in a new minimum monthly payment of $297 per month of which $132. will go toward the principal and $167. to the finance charge which is compounding daily.

What's worse, there is usually a 3% up front balance transfer fee which is charged to the account and billed at the purchase rate of 15% even though the amount borrowed may be at 0% for one year. Now 3% of $15,000 = $450 @ 15% this equals $5.62 per month which gets added onto the original $450 and compounds daily. If in addition to that $450 which is being billed at 15%, the customer makes any purchases on the card, they will also be added to that $450 balance and billed at 15%.

Now here comes the clincher! When you are making payments on your card, you cannot choose how the payments are allocated. In other words, you cannot choose to pay off the higher interest rate items first to get rid of them. No, in fact, the bank will always apply your full payment to the lowest interest items first until they are paid in full and then work up to the higher interest items. Now while you are paying off what was originally a 0% item, the balance transfer fee of $450 plus any purchases are just sitting on your account earning 15% interest. And of course if you do not pay the original 0% balance in full within one year, it also will default to the 15% rate.

Another thing that the consumer needs to be wise to is the fact that if their payment is late, they will lose that 0% promotional rate and immediately default to the higher rate, plus they will be billed a substantial late fee of $35-$39. One method that the banks use to assure that the customer will be late and default is by confusing the customer with due dates which change monthly or which fall on a weekend or holiday. Say the customer has set up with his banking institution to pay the credit card bill each month on the 15th, based upon their first bill which had a 15th due date. Well, next month the due date may be the 14th or it may fall on a weekend when no banking transactions can be posted. Even if the customer goes onto the bank website to make a payment on the weekend due date, a message will advise the customer that his payment will not post until the following Monday. Now how can a bank get away with establishing a due date that cannot possibly be met unless the customer pays on an earlier date? Then the due date is actually the Friday before the due date isn't it? So why wouldn't the bank just make the Friday date the due date instead of confusing the customer with a weekend or holiday due date? Obviously the banks make millions off of these late charges and default rates. Yes, some customers will call in and dispute the charge or default rate, but millions are too busy to even notice and will just pay the late fee and the higher interest rate without ever even noticing.

Another trick the banks use is to mail out "convenience checks" with that 0% offer to established customers who already have high balances on their accounts at perhaps 12-15% interest. They do this in the hope that those customers who are unaware that their payments will be allocated to the lowest interest item first, will use those checks and get themselves deeper in debt by putting their high interest, high balance loans on the back burner for a year or two or three while paying off the new 0% loans. You see the bank disclosure only says that the bank "MAY allocate your full payment to the lowest interest items first"; it does not state that they definitely WILL, yet that is what they do.

So my advice is, avoid banks at all cost and beware of "special offers"; they're not so special after all. I think a common equation might run something like this: If you take out a car loan from a bank and make just the minimum monthly payments, you will be purchasing one auto for yourself and two for the bank. Likewise, if you take out a mortgage and make only the minimum monthly payments, you will be purchasing one home for yourself and two for the bank.

That being the case, one might even question the common belief that it is cheaper to buy a home than to rent. Is that just another part of our common belief system foisted upon us by the banking industry and real estate sharks? People will tell you: "I bought my home for $100,000 25 years ago and now I can sell it for $300,000; that's a $200,000 profit! No it isn't. If over a 25 year period you paid the bank $300,000 to say nothing of property taxes which could easily be $125,000, not mentioning repairs, insurance and maintenance, then you spent well over $ 425,000 on your home which you can now sell for $300,000. And if you sell the property without buying something more expensive, you will pay exorbitant capitol gains taxes.

A friend of mine thought that paying $800 a month rent was just a waste so he bought a condo, as a result of which he now pays $1,600 per month plus over $200 per month in commons charges. Now since he can apparently afford this, he might just have easily have been able to set aside $1,000 per month into high interest CD's or an IGA account and have eventually had enough money to buy a condo in cash and not end up buying one for himself and two for the bank. These are things that we all need to think about because too many of us have ruined our lives and have become trapped by the banks with debts that can never be paid off. People say, "But it's nice to own your own place" and yes it is. But the question remains? Do you ever really own it? Skip a few payments and you will soon find out who owns your home. Skip a few tax payments and you will soon find out who owns your home. And once either the mortgage holder or the City forecloses on you and sells your property, they are not obligated to sell it for an amount that would assure you of getting your equity back. So as the old adage goes: "Don't bite off more than you can chew". Plus if both you and your wife have to work two jobs to pay for this home and no one is enjoying it other than your dog, then you are making a big mistake. Remember "money = life energy". Maybe a little smaller home with a few less conveniences and more time to spend together living life would be a better equation.

So you too can beat the system by taking more time to analyze your needs as opposed to your wants. You can beat the system by paying cash whenever possible or simply postponing "wants" until you have saved enough to pay cash. You can beat the system by paying bills and taxes on time rather than paying unnecessary late fees and interests charges which only make the banking institutions and government grow richer. You can beat the system by reading all contracts and disclosures carefully before signing for anything. Watch out for weekend due dates and penalty clauses. And remember that if something is "too good to be true", it IS JUST THAT, too good to be true.

CHAPTER 14
VALUES & CONCEPTS
WORTH KEEPING

COMPASSION

I find it interesting that one of the many representations in art and literature that one finds in reference to Buddha is that of the "Compassionate Buddha" or Avalokiteshvara. I find this interesting because one never seems to hear mention of a "Compassionate Moses" or a "Compassionate Mohammed". But that's neither here nor there. The point is that as a result of being gay, and as a result of NOT being an Ivy League College graduate; and as a result of being a spiritual seeker rather than a locked-in Fundamentalist, I have been thrown in with every sort and every level of mankind; male and female; rich and poor; educated and uneducated; straight, gay; bisexual, transsexual, black, white, Hispanic, Oriental; married with children; unwed with children; prostitutes; druggies, and thieves; Christian, Moslem, Jewish, Hindu, Sikh, Buddhist; Mormon; agnostic. You name it. I have not READ about these people, I have LIVED amongst them. I have worked and struggled side by side with these people; eaten with them; slept with them; suffered with them; loved them and watched them die, as part of me died with them. If I have learned one thing, I have learned compassion.

Being a gay male; has put me into a unique situation and this is a situation that my straight friends have attributed to me, not I to myself. My straight friends have told me that apparently due to my unusual genetic makeup, I seem to be able to fully understand what a male feels and experiences in life; but equally what a woman feels and experiences. Married couples love me; they say that I would have made an excellent marriage counselor or minister or priest because, they say that I have the ability to see both sides, totally unfettered and I am able to tell the man what he needs to do to improve his relationship with his wife. Conversely, In am also able to tell the woman what she needs to do to improve her relationship with her husband. And there's a lot of truth to their observation. There are times, when I feel very aggressive and protective and very much a man; but there are other times when I feel very passive; very vulnerable; very nurturing; very "mothering" and feel exactly as I would imagine a woman feels.

Consequently, I no longer sit in judgment, as so many self-righteous individuals do on unwed mothers, mixed marriages, failure to use birth control, divorce, abortion, etc. because I have been where those women are coming from. I have loved without the benefit of marriage; ergo have "loved and lived in sin". I have loved outside of my own race. I have refused to use condoms whenever I wanted to be especially close to someone that I was beginning to love, and would therefore have been an unwed mother myself many times over if I had ovaries. And I can now fully understand why a young woman in love might want to have the child of the man that she loves; even if she has no commitment from him or he's on his way off to prison; at least this way she will always have a part of him near her. I'm not saying that I approve of these situations, because they aren't good for the children, all I am saying is that I can understand why and how they could happen and be compassionate rather than condemnatory.

And what about all of these young people selling drugs and stealing and all, how can you justify this? Well, again, let me tell you what I have had to do to survive over the last 57 years. I have cleaned gas station toilets; I have sold Amway products; I have worked behind candy counters in movie theaters; I have worked in clothing stores; been a room service waiter; worked in catering joints; ran cash registers; answered phones; mowed lawns; and worked in hot kitchens with the perspiration running off of me. I have taken abuse from bosses and customers alike all of my life and haven't had one job that I either enjoyed or found any kind of meaning or mental satisfaction from. I have hated every moment of it. Isn't that sad; to be miserably unhappy five out of seven days each week of your life?

And at least, for the most part, I was better off than most. I have worked with unwed mothers working two jobs who could not even afford an automobile. I have worked with others who were working two jobs and taking taxis between jobs and yet lived in squalor and poverty despite being hard working people. I have worked with people who can barely afford lunch or any kind of minimal nutrition. I have worked with those who are ill and coming to work anyway because they can't afford to see a doctor.

Children aren't blind. They see their Mom or Dad struggling day after day, year after year with no way out; and no improvement in their lives. Hell, faced with a life of low income housing, roaches and rats and spending 40-60 hours a week working for minimum wage plus all of the abuse one can take at a Burger King or a Wal-Mart, I think that I would turn to both using drugs and selling them myself. In fact I almost feel that way right now.

I'm so sick and tired of hearing TV and radio conservatives harping about how this is the land of opportunity and how all of these people on minimum wage should have thought about that when they were in school and applied themselves better. Don't give me that crap; I have nephews who graduated from good colleges with honors, who can't get good jobs unless they are willing to become highly degreed migrant workers, following the "buffalo" all over the country or even out of the country in search of work. It wasn't bad enough before when corporations were forcing you to sell your family home and relocate to another state; now they expect you to relocate to another country.

And I am sick of hearing how all of the men and women losing their jobs to overseas outsourcing should have anticipated that and gotten training for new careers, and so it's their own fault that they are now jobless. Well, you know, maybe it's just a little easier to anticipate and plan for the future when it's your own rich cronies and friends who are creating and manipulating the market trends and can let you know ahead of time which way things are going. You see, that's the only real advantage of college, and in particular Ivy League Colleges. It's not what you learn there that will make you successful, but who you can meet there and network with. It's not "what you know" it's "who you know" and who owes you favors for whatever reason. And maybe if we all earned $150,000 or more per year we could all afford IRA's and slush funds for further education. But as it is; all of the time of average Americans is consumed in just trying to keep up with property taxes, auto insurance, and medical expenses.

And even if we could get additional career training, tell me, exactly which careers CAN'T be outsourced to India or China or Mexico so that we could feel safe in choosing such a career. The most recent rumor I have heard is that McDonalds is contemplating outsourcing the drive-up window position. When you pull up and speak into the microphone, you will be speaking with someone in New Delhi, who will then hit the appropriate keys at their end to print up an order and a bill at whichever McDonalds you are parked at. Yes, that's right folks; let's just eliminate all the jobs we can. Of course, the powers that be, fail to realize that the person in New Delhi will not be paying U.S. income tax; nor contributing into the social security system; nor will they likely buy any burgers since they don't eat beef and more than likely won't be paid enough to afford a Big Mack anyway.

You see, this is where old Henry Ford was far more of a visionary and brilliant industrialist than any of these short sighted clowns that they call CEO's today. These men are for the most part not the founders of the corporations which they lead, but merely highly overpaid wheelers and dealers who got where they are by some hostile takeover or a friend in Washington D.C.

They do not care about their employees; hell they don't even care about the future of the business which they just procured in the sense that they would want to make it successful. No, they just want to trim it down; make it lean and mean; sell it to the next bidder; make an overnight profit; line their pockets and move on. But, Henry Ford had a vision; he wasn't just in it for immediate financial gratification.

He realized that if he paid his workers decent wages and manufactured automobiles which were affordable, that his best and most dependable customers would, more than likely, be his own employees. And you know what? He was right. He built a business that was to last almost a century; a business, that in his day benefited not just him, but the stockholders and employees and suppliers and the economy as well.

But businesses today do not function on that level. The only goal today is instant profitability by whatever means, with no concern or culpability for the plight of employees and suppliers, nor communities and cities that will be devastated when these large businesses pull up stakes and move away. This is capitalism at is most evil and rapacious extreme.

And they are not doing any favors to these third world countries which they are victimizing either. They are merely exploiting these people; and giving them false hopes of a bright and secure future which will never be. These false hopes will cause them to take chances. They will have more children, they will have to get bigger homes to house those children and they will have to buy on credit because they certainly won't be earning enough from their parsimonious U.S. corporate employers. They will then over consume and buy things with money that they do not have, but have been promised will have down the line. These poor souls will ultimately dig their own graves and forge their own chains of servitude by becoming indebted to credit card and loan corporations and banks charging ridiculous interest rates.

Now before these poor people can ever pay off these debts, the "International Corporate Rapists" who hired them and promised them a bright future, will find other slaves in other host countries who will produce their poor quality garbage at even cheaper costs and allow them to pollute and destroy with even more freedom. And so, like any good "rapist"; they will pull out leaving in their wake, millions of unemployed, starving, homeless and indebted people. Then the corporate bosses' friends and cronies in the banking business will be able to foreclose on all of these people, confiscating their property and selling it at a profit. What fun!!!

Actually, this is the way that the banking industry has already prospered here in the U.S. with Congress approving of all of their rapacious tactics and policies. But now they would like to carry that destruction and pillaging to other countries. Don't take my word for it. Two wonderful books that you would do well to check out are: "Merchants of Misery or How Corporate America Profits From Poverty" by Michael Hudson and similarly "Nickeled and Dimed, On Not Getting By In America" by Barbara Ehrenreich.

LOVE AND FRIENDSHIP

While compassion is one of the greatest things that I have learned in life; I must not and cannot overlook the value of love and friendship. Partly because of the demands made upon our time in this modern world by employers; partly due to the ugly reality of having to work more than one job to merely survive; people just aren't making friends and forging tight knit circles like our parents once had and I find this very sad.

When I was young and growing up, my folks, had many friends, all of whom I was taught to address as "Uncle So-and-so" or "Aunty So-and-so", which basically alluded to the fact that these were not just casual acquaintances; these were like family members. And they really were. Usually, the only thing that removed one of these individuals from their "family" status was death; that's how strong the ties were. Now of course I am by no means saying that all of these people were perfect. Of course they weren't. It required patience and good communication and honesty; and knowing when not to speak, to keep all of these various relationships working smoothly. But I believe that it was worth the effort. All of our friends were a great comfort to my Dad after Mom died and they were a help throughout his life. Having seen such a good example of this; I picked up the tradition for myself. I followed suit and endeavored to build my own little circle of friends over the years; many of whom I have known for over 35 years. I have found that while "lovers come and lovers go; my friends have been consistently here for me all along to help me pick up the pieces.

What concerns me, is that I don't see younger people today; either straight or gay doing this. As I mentioned earlier, part of the problem may be the lack of extra time, which oddly enough we used to have back in the days BEFORE all of today's labor saving devices. Now we have all of these labor saving devices, but are working two jobs to pay for them and so still have less free time than our parents did. It's ludicrous isn't it? But another more negative reason for this phenomenon seems to be that most people in our fast paced world want instant everything. They don't want to spend the time or effort required to build relationships or friendships; plus they are very selfish and only want relationships where there is "something to gain"; never once thinking of what they can "give" or "bring" to a relationship themselves.

Consequently in today's world; people don't make friendships; they "network"; and that's about as personal and intimate as it gets. Even sex isn't intimate any more; hell it's as perfunctory as having a bowel movement or urinating and brings about the same degree of satisfaction and why? Again, it's poor quality because no one is willing to put forth any effort; they just want to "get off" and get it over with. I think that to a great degree, the internet is adding to this problem. While it is true that it enables one to communicate all over the world; the question is: are we "communicating" or simply disseminating information?

Let's face it; most people go into chat rooms because they lack the social graces or the desire to learn those social graces to be able to actually meet anyone. So without having to take a shower or brush their teeth or comb their hair or make any effort whatsoever to be presentable; they can just sit in front of a computer and present a total deception to the person on the other end who thinks that they are talking to a handsome, well groomed young man or young lady who is genuinely interested in them. The person on the other end does not know that they're just talking to some dirty pervert who isn't listening to a word that they are saying , but is merely playing with himself and will drop off line as soon as they climax. This is dreadful and inexcusable behavior.

Ever wonder why you keep meeting people from Arizona and California in the Connecticut Chat Rooms? That's easy enough to explain: because anyone who lives in Connecticut is in the Alaska or Oregon Chat Room. Why is this? Because No one really wants to meet someone on line who could actually show up at their door someday; of course not. For one thing; they know that they have lied to the other person about their age, weight and God knows what else. They have emailed that other person a picture of either a model or a friend of theirs who looks reasonably good; or possibly a picture of themselves but from twenty years ago. So now they cannot run the risk of their internet lover actually meeting them and finding out that it was all lies and deception. They have no desire to make the effort required to actually meet and court a real person who lives nearby, but neither do they want to feel alone. So they "court" this imaginary lover via the internet; sometimes for years. My God, I thought only little children had imaginary friends! All that these people are doing is wasting their own and everyone else's time. I guess the only unintentional good that they may be doing is providing jobs for all the internet staffs involved in these internet dating sites; but what a waste of time and human life.

Now, undoubtedly, a lot of these people will use the classic cop out of "I don't want to be hurt again." Well, honey, to that I say: "No pain, no gain." Those who try to live life "safely", don't ever live it fully or richly; they merely exist. It's comparable to having sex while pumped full of Novocain; oh it won't hurt that way, but neither will you feel any pleasure. I love the words of Kahlil Gibran, in his wonderful work, "The Prophet". When his character, Almitra asks the Prophet to speak of love, the Prophet says:...But if your fear you would seek only love's peace and love's pleasure, then it is better for you that you cover your nakedness and pass out of loves's threshing floor, into the seasonless world where you shall laugh, but not all of your laughter, and weep, but not all of your tears."

And yet this is exactly what the majority of people both straight and gay are doing; but in particular, gay males. They are filling the voids in their lives with brief, momentary, fleeting anonymous encounters which do not even sexually satisfy them or they wouldn't need to fly from one partner to the next within the space of two hours. And not only aren't they making any effort to find a permanent partner, but they don't even want to make the effort to have friends. I am both amazed and horrified at the number of young men that I encounter who are anywhere from 35 years old and older who have NO FRIENDS; I may be their only friend. I can't figure out how anyone could have spent 35 years on this planet interacting with other people throughout high school, college, church, fraternities, etc. and have no friends. But you see, to have a friend, you need to "be a friend" and that is just too costly for some.

Oh no. "Do you mean that I actually have to bring something to your party other than my appetite? Oh, no, that's just asking too much; I don't want to have to go out of my way to stop by the grocery store or bakery on my way over. The fact that you spent one day grocery shopping and another cooking all day for this occasion is your own fault, no one asked you to do it and don't expect me to do the same". "Oh, thank you for the lovely birthday card and present; I hope that you're not expecting one in return and if you are, you're just "too high maintenance for me."

What it all seems to boil down to is a general attitude of: "You must be there for me and be available at all times whenever I should need your attention or assistance. But don't expect me to be there for you. I really don't want to hear about your petty problems and only want to be with you when you are funny and can cheer me up. I will see you when I feel like it; which may very well be when I have nothing better to do and don't expect anything from me because I just may not be in the giving mood." Well friendship is a two way street; just as marriage is a two way street and I think many people have forgotten that, which accounts for the lack of lasting marriages and even friendships.

What are these gay men going to do once they grow older and can no longer turn a trick? I have no idea. They won't have a lover to grow old with; they certainly won't have any children to visit with them at home or in a hospital and if they don't have any friends either, what will their advancing years be like? Of course they are not thinking of that now because they are young and hedonistic and invulnerable. They're the kind who routinely put in their ads: "If you're over 30, don't even think of writing me". Well, sweetheart, I hope that once you are over 30(and it will come sooner than you think), that you will kindly remove yourself and your profiles from the internet and slither off into oblivion yourself since you had no compassion for anyone older than yourself and should now expect none either.

I suppose they will still be able to "buy love", but when they look into the eyes of their "rent boys" they will not see two loving eyes looking back at them, all they will see will be dollar signs or worse yet, possibly the muzzle of a revolver. I find it odd that those who are fearful to take a "risk on love" are more than glad to risk their lives for no love at all.

Now, I will say this much. If you simply cannot bring yourself to love another person, at least promise me this. Don't let your entire life be without any purpose other than making money; LOVE SOMETHING; love an animal. Animal friends require so little and give so unconditionally in return. It's a proven medical fact that they add to your longevity because they give you a reason to live. We will speak more of this shortly.

So along with developing a healthy sense of compassion, one needs to develop the gift of love; love for family and friends and love for one special person or even pet. And lastly, one needs some form of spirituality. We're not talking religion here; we're merely talking spirituality.

SPIRITUALITY

"Devotion to spiritual rather than worldly things", is the way that one dictionary defines "spirituality". Perhaps another definition might be "devotion to the non-material things of life rather than to the physical things of life". Of course we fully acknowledge the necessity of certain physical needs like sunlight, heat, water, air, food, oxygen; growth, and reproduction. All of these things are necessary for continued existence on this space craft that we call Mother Earth. But to live only for survival is a "half-life" and best. We need to address the non-physical realities of man and yes, even the non-physical realities of our animal friends and plants because these things do have a measurable affect on us either to our advantage or to our detriment.

So when we speak about spirituality, we are simply addressing those issues which are not of a purely physical nature; we are talking about thoughts, feelings, belief systems and relationships and not necessarily about religion as such. Religion is described as "belief in or worship of God or gods". The word's etymology means to "bind fast again" or fasten again, which almost implies being bound, which could have a positive or negative connotation depending entirely upon if one likes to be bound or has volunteered to be bound. So the word religion almost has a negative connotation to the free spirit and free thinker, while the word spirituality does not.

One great Indian Guru, Ramakrishna described religion as being the "distillation of the teachings of a Great Master by his disciples, finally put into writing years after the actual events occurred and with questionable accuracy." That's why the Indian Masters and teachers of meditation always tell you: "Do not believe this because I said that it was true or because you read it in some book. No, go into the laboratory of your own soul and test it out and see if it is in fact true.

So while one does not necessarily need "religion" in order to mentally survive and lead a balanced life; I do believe that one does need some form of spirituality which one has the right to create for oneself; something that is uniquely "you" and works for you. You need some kind of plan to live by; some kind of parameters and some kind of expectations or at least partial answers to such heavy questions as: "Why am I here?" "Where am I going?" "What is my ultimate fate?". Now of course, anyone who tells you that they have the absolute answers to these questions is an absolute liar because these are all strictly faith issues and can only be empirically proven at best. So simply choose a path that makes sense to you and is workable for you. But do choose one or create one if you have to; don't go without. There will be many obstacles and crises along the way that will require inner strength and conviction to overcome or survive and you don't need to be trying to create a belief system then, while in the middle of a major crisis.

My newfound spirituality, which works for me, is a little bit of Hinduism; a touch of Buddhism; a little of the best of Christianity (the things that Jesus said; not others); some New Age philosophy and some common sense. I guess my beliefs are not unlike those immortal words of "Desiderata" by Max Ehrman; in particular the section which says: "You are a child of the universe, no less than the trees and the stars; you have a right to be here. And whether or not it is clear to you, no doubt the universe is unfolding as it should. Therefore be at peace with God, whatever you conceive him to be..."

Part of the core of my spirituality also centers around another set of immortal words; those words of advice by Polonius to his son Laertes in Shakespeare's "Hamlet": "To thine own self be true, and it must follow as the night, the day; thou canst not then be false to any man."

Let's face it. If you can't even be honest and true to yourself; then of what use can you possibly be to anyone else? Too many people are living totally false, disingenuous, double lives and as a result are bringing great pain and suffering not only to themselves but to others. So BE YOURSELF; love YOURSELF; "come out , come out, wherever you are. Yes there is a price for such freedom, but the price for staying in the closet is far higher and it's not fair that others should have to pay that price along with you.

Ultimately, time and sickness can take my friends and loved-ones away from me; the City or the banks can take my home away from me; my employer can take my job away from me and possibly even my pension; old age and health can rob me of my sight and sanity, but NO ONE and NO THING can rob me of my integrity and the record of how I treated my fellow creatures while I walked this earth. That's why, to my thinking, the only three things that matter are: compassion, love and spirituality.

CHAPTER 15
MY FURRY FRIENDS

This will be a refreshing little departure into a lighter side to my life during all of these years, which has been coexisting all along with the tragedies and misfortunes, but I wanted to give it full attention and treat it separately. It is a part of my life that has helped me maintain some kind of balance amidst turmoil; and a reason to go on when life was at its bleakest.

A little while back, I advised you the reader, of the following; that if you couldn't rise to the occasion of risking love with another human being, that you should at least love an animal or have a pet. You see, the wonderful thing about pets is that there is no risk at all; for the most part, they will simply love you unconditionally.

My first pet, mentioned earlier on, was a wonderful little female Yorkshire terrier, which I purchased around July of 1982 and subsequently named Lady Anne Galters after the woodlands which surround the City of York in England where her grandparents lived. Lady Anne was just such a dear little soul, so full of life and love and so attuned to all of my moods and needs. She just gave of herself to everyone. She loved everyone and made no bones about expressing it too, whether they appreciated it or not. As soon as anyone entered my home and sat down, she would just leap into their lap and cover them with kisses; there was absolutely no stopping her. And she had such a vast reparatory of cute little things that she would do to make you laugh.

Of course she slept with me each night and would be so considerate as to not awaken me in the morning unless she saw at least one eye open. So she was shrewd. She would nuzzle up to my face with her cold, wet little nose pressed against mine and peer into my closed eyelids until one of them opened. As soon as I cracked an eyelid, she would fly into action; she would grab the blankets and start pulling them off of me down the length of the bed. Now if that wasn't enough to get me up, then she would proceed by running down the length of the bed, standing erect on her hind legs, flailing her front paws at me in the air and growling; something like a Grizzly Bear about to attack. I would then always start laughing and laughing; it was so cute, one couldn't help but laugh.

Lady Anne hated baths or any kind of grooming for that matter. As soon as she heard me filling up the bathroom sink, she would start running and hiding and yet there were other times when she tried to jump into the bathtub with me; maybe she just didn't like to be bathed alone, but she seemed to hate it; and she hated the blow dryer even more and would growl at it when you tried to dry her. Once clean and smelling pleasant and nicely combed out; she would immediately want to go outside, where she would then proceed to roll on her back in the dust or a patch of leaves and twigs until she once more looked like a bedraggled homeless pet from the animal shelter. But that was the way she was; she was not feminine at all like a friend of mine's little Yorkie who was always impeccably groomed and covered with little satin bows. No, Lady Anne would not wear satin bows.

But she was such a love. Sometimes we would sit for hours in the evening on the sofa; she on the arm and I on the seat. She would just sit there looking in my eyes and wagging her tail so fast that it was just a blur. Actually, she did not just wag her tail; she wagged her entire hind quarters. Then she would run up the arm to my face and cover me with kisses and then leap off the arm of the sofa sort of sideways and backwards so as to throw herself into my lap on her back where she would then roll and wriggle around kicking her legs in delight while I scratched her belly. Once done, she would then make her way back up to the arm of the sofa, stare into my eyes; cover my face with kisses once more and then repeat the procedure again by throwing herself into my lap again. It was amazing. The relationship that I had with her was not like a dog and her master; it was more like a soul to soul relationship. The eye contact that we made repeatedly communicated something far beyond our physical senses and I know for a certainty that there is some kind of soul link between us.

One could learn a lot from Lady Anne. Nothing could daunt her; not rain, snow, hail; pain, sickness or aging. She simply ignored inconveniences and found all life absolutely intoxicating and wonderful. Even the day before she died as a result of congestive heart failure, she dragged me out of bed and went bounding down the stairs like a puppy to go outside; she simply loved the outdoors; no matter how cold or inclement. The poor little thing couldn't have felt well, but she would never let on; life was just too much of a celebration for her. But that's probably why she lived so long; she was almost sixteen when she crossed over, which is pretty old for a dog.

Now a year after I had gotten Lady Anne, I felt that it was wrong to leave her alone while I went to work, so I wanted to get her a little friend to keep her company. I friend of mine's mother cat had just had kittens, so she gave me the choice of the litter. I chose an adorable little pure white male kitten with just a stump left of a tail. For whatever reason, his mother had bitten his tail off. I felt that no one would want him, so I chose him, plus he was very sweet and affectionate.

Well, when I brought the kitten home, I thought that Lady Anne would be pleased to have a new friend that she could raise, but it was just the opposite. Lady Anne went berserk: her eyes were rolling back into her head and she was foaming at the mouth; I didn't know what to do. I called the vet and he explained to me that terriers are a one man dog and are insanely jealous and that this was a jealous reaction. He advised me not to leave the dog and kitten alone, because he felt that the dog would definitely kill the kitten out of jealousy unless I could reassure her that she was the "beloved" and the kitten only secondary. So that's what I had to do and it worked. But I felt sorry for Siegfried, the poor little kitten because I felt that he was getting short changed.

But as time went by, Lady Anne grew to love the kitten and care for him and they got along famously. The only time she would be nasty to him was if he came up on the sofa and attempted to sit in my lap for any amount of time. Then she would always come up on the sofa and force him off. But she really did grow to love him almost as intensely as she loved me. I remember at one point, when I was taking the garbage out, Siegfried snuck out the door and ran off. He used to sit in the window for hours watching other cats and birds and I guess you couldn't blame him for wanting some adventure. But apparently; never having been outside before and all of the condos looking alike; he didn't seem to be able to find his way home. I scoured the neighborhood, but couldn't find him. Possibly some well meaning neighbor took him in because he was gone for 4 days, during which poor little Lady Anne refused to eat and just sat in the window gazing out and whimpering for four days. She was inconsolable at the loss of her little friend.

Finally one evening I heard this loud cat howl out front and went to the outer front door of my condo to find Siegfried pawing the outer door and looking very bedraggled and irritable. Well, I picked him up and yelled to Lady Anne: "Wait until you see the surprise I have for you". I carried Siegfried inside and put him down on the floor. Lady Anne came running to him and literally pounded on him and licked him from head to foot for at least ten minutes; over and over and over. She would kiss him, then me; then him , then me. She was absolutely beside herself. It was a happy moment for all three of us. Now no cold, calculating scientist is going to tell me that what I experienced was nothing but blind instinct or survival behavior. Siegfried contributed nothing toward Lady Anne's survival; nor was he her mate who had fathered puppies with her; there was absolutely no other motive for her behavior than pure love.

Eventually, after 13 years together, poor little Siegfried was to leave us. He was a really hearty eater and had overdone it; he was enormous and had developed diabetes as a result. We had it under control for about 3 years with me giving him needles daily, which he accepted very passively and without retaliation. But eventually the vet just couldn't seem to get the amount of insulin right and he would keep going into shock one way or the other. One could learn a lot from Siegfried too. He was only willing to accept so many indignities and so many trips to the hospital and he ultimately decided his own fate. He stopped eating. There was nothing that I could do to make him eat. I would open his mouth and try to spoon feed his most favorite foods into him, but he would just spit them out. In his own little soul, he had determined that this body could no longer serve him and had decided to "drop the body" and be free.

He went into shock and I of course took him to the emergency animal hospital. They, also could not get any kind of balance with the insulin and called me the next day to advise me that now he was blind and still going into shock periodically. I knew what Siegfried wanted and knew what had to be done. So I went to the hospital to see him one final time. He couldn't see me and stumbled all over, but he knew that it was me. He clutched onto me and then went into another shock. The vet advised me that this would just continue happening over and over for perhaps weeks until he ultimately died. I knew that Siegfried wouldn't tolerate blindness and didn't want to suffer, so I told the vet to "get the needle".

I told Siegfried that his little body was no longer serviceable and that there was nothing left that we could do but free his spirit. I told him to "go to the light" as the vet administered the needle. Even before the needle was administered, Siegfried simply laid his head on my chest and closed his eyes as if to say "I'm ready; let's go." It was the most beautiful and peaceful passing and I knew that I had done the right thing. Of course, I knew there would be a lot of explaining to do back home.

I brought his little body home for burial or cremation; I had to decide which. I felt the best way to handle the homecoming was head on and that little Lady Anne would need "closure". So I lay Siegfried's body on a pillow on the floor at first, so that Lady Anne could see him.

Oddly, in some strange way, she understood death, much better than she had understood separation. When Siegfried had been lost for four days, she grieved and grieved. But now that he was dead, she slowly approached the body; sniffed it; gave him one lick on the face; then shook her head and walked away with total acceptance. No grieving this time; nor was there to be any in subsequent days. Now isn't that odd? It was almost as if she knew that her little friend was no longer in that body, so she gave the body minimal respect but that was all; no emotions; no kissing and pouncing like on the prior occasion when he had come back to her.

After that, I waited a respectable amount of time, but felt that Lady Anne again needed a companion. This time I adopted a little black kitten from the animal shelter; or I should say that he adopted me. Actually I was all ready to take home a kitten who looked just like Sylvester the Cat, in fact I was going to call him Sylvester, when a little kitten in the cage below kept reaching out and grabbing me. I couldn't ignore the incessant grabbing so I looked down to see who it was and I saw this adorable little solid black kitten. I then put kitty number one back and took kitty number two out of the cage; and he was just so loving and sweet that I couldn't resist. I called him Seti, after an Egyptian pharaoh. Well, Lady Anne did not go cannibal this time; she accepted the new kitten, but he was a bit much for her; she was now a little over 16 years old. Seti loved her though and would follow her everywhere; whereas, she just sort of tolerated him. I'm sure that they would have been great friends had she been younger, but she was just too old for this.

On Christmas Day of 1997, after I returned from celebrating the holiday with my brother and his family, I came home only to notice that Lady Anne was flat out in the kitchen and couldn't seem to stand up. I thought that maybe something was wrong with her legs. I picked her up and she was visibly shaken and upset and was breathing extremely rapidly as she might on a hot summer day, but this was winter. She didn't seem to be able to catch her breath. So I decided to take her to the emergency animal hospital. As I put her little coat on, Seti gave her one last big hug and then I took her to the hospital. They diagnosed her as having congestive heart failure and didn't hold out much hope, but they offered to keep her overnight; put her on Lasix, to remove the fluid from her lungs and see what might happen. I went to see her before leaving her overnight. I opened the door of the oxygen chamber and leaned into the chamber.

She gave me a very sad and tearful kiss as if she somehow knew that this wasn't going to work and was afraid that she would pass without my being there; I think she thought this was the last time we would see each other. I didn't know what to think. I went to my car and just cried and cried until I could pull myself together and safely drive home. Well, we waited almost 24 hours, but the vet advised me that it wasn't working and that she could not survive outside of an oxygen chamber. So again, I knew what had to be done, but I wanted to be with her. A friend of mine, A—n, drove me to the hospital and we both proceeded into the holding room.

A nurse brought Lady Anne out for the final time; she was so happy to see me and kissed me all over and urinated all over me, but I didn't exactly care about that at that particular moment. I told her that I loved her with all my heart and would always love her, but that her little body was shot and that she would have to go on ahead of me and wait for me. I told her to look for Siegfried and go to him. They put the needle into the same fixture in her little paw which had held her "IV" prior to that. It didn't take effect immediately; she sort of jumped up a little startled; looked around the room at me, then at my friend and then she collapsed on my chest with a big sigh. I felt really bad. It wasn't as peaceful a passing as I had experienced with Siegfried. It seemed that he was ready to go, but that she wasn't. Somehow she still wanted to hang on; even though she couldn't breathe and would have had no quality of life. She was a stubborn little soul.

Likewise, I brought her little body home so that Seti could have closure and likewise, he looked at her, sniffed her, kissed her and then walked away with full acceptance. I had both Siegfried and Lady Anne cremated and kept their remains together in a small shrine in my living room.

Seti was a wonderful little cat; he went out of his way to entertain me and try to cheer me up; and he was very successful. I'm sure that my grieving for Lady Anne would have gone on far longer than it did had not Seti been there for me. He really was a big help. Every day when I came home from work, he would be waiting for me in the window. As soon as I opened the door he would be there weaving in and out of my legs as I walked to the kitchen to hand up my keys. He would sit on my lap for hours; just purring away and loving me. He was wonderful. Again, I did not want him to be alone while I was at work and my neighbors advised me that a neighborhood mother cat had just given birth a few weeks ago and they wondered if I would take at least one kitten. I went over and inspected the litter. The kittens were barely weaned, but the mother cat was basically a feral cat and they didn't want her to raise the kittens; they wanted the kittens to be socialized and ultimately they were going to have the mother neutered. So I chose a lovely little orange ball of love with white paws and belly and I called him Ramses, since he was to now become the son of Seti.

Now this was an odd turn of events; Seti did not roll his eyes back into his head and go nuts when I brought Ramses into our shared home. He accepted Ramses totally as a kitten and decided to raise him as his own. But he was pissed at me and hissed and growled at me initially. I was concerned that I might have lost his friendship, but my fears were without foundation. Within forty-eight hours, all was back to normal again and we were a normal family once more. Seti was such a good parent and really taught Ramses to be loving and caring. Seti like Lady Anne before him, loved everyone; he was unusually friendly and gregarious for a cat. Most people find cats sneaky and aloof, but not Seti; he was a real love.

Unfortunately, I was not destined to have him long. One early October evening in 2000 when I came home from work, I found it unusual that Seti did not greet me as usual, but I was preoccupied with a lot of problems at work and just figured that he was with Ramses somewhere. Ramses was acting sort of strange and funny, but as I say, I was tired and went to bed. When I awoke on Saturday morning and Seti was not in my bed, as was his habit, I got worried. I began searching all of the closets and under the bed and such and couldn't find him anywhere.

I knew that he had not slipped past me when I came home because my front door does not directly lead outside; it opens into a hallway or foyer leading to the outer door. So even if he had slipped by me, he would be in the hallway and he wasn't there either. Finally I crawled on my hands and knees everywhere, only to find poor little Seti cold as stone lying behind a bookcase. He had been dead for several hours, but did not smell and had oddly enough not urinated when he died. That being the case, the vet felt that he had died of urinary blockage, which apparently is not uncommon for male cats. I missed him terribly; Ramses, accepted it and what could we do but get on with our lives. So Seti is now "interred" in the living room also.

Now I needed a companion for Ramses, so off I went to the animal shelter again; this time returning with, not a kitten, but a semi adult female cat which I named Isis. She was a shrewd kitty in the animal shelter and came onto me all kinds of sweet and domestic; with that "please save me" kind of decorum. But after I brought her home, she would not bother with me at all and went into hiding for a week. She did finally warm up to Ramses though, and he was the one that I had gotten her for anyway so the experiment was relatively successful. I would have been just as content with Ramses alone, but I wanted him to have a buddy. After about 2 years, she finally began warming up to me, but that's all right, so long as I had Ramses love; and what a love he was.

Again, my orange tabby, Ramses, was just a dear soul very much like my dog, Lady Anne. Ramses just loved everyone intensely and everyone loved him. He would lie on my chest and just gaze into my eyes with his big expressive yellow eyes and he would stroke my cheek with his paws. He, like Lady Anne, would also sleep on my pillow and lie in wait for my first eyelid to open; then he would stroke my cheeks or bite my nose to get me up. He was an absolute love. One time when I had company over and was busy in the kitchen making snacks, one of my guests alerted me to the fact that there was something wrong with Ramses. I asked what they meant and they said that he was running around the living room smoking. Well, I ran to the living room to see what was going on and sure enough; Ramses had been sitting quite casually with his tail over a votive candle and while his tail hadn't actually ignited, still he was running around the living room leaving a trail of smoke from his smoldering tail. We all laughed ourselves to tears. It looked so funny. Fortunately no harm was done.

I never thought that I would ever love another pet again as much as I had loved Lady Anne, but little Ramses did steal my heart, I guess partly because of his habit of looking in my eyes and stroking my cheeks; and partly because he was just so loving and accepting of everyone. While I loved all of my pets in one way or another; Ramses taught me that I had not, in deed, become hardened, but that I could really love another animal again in the same way which I had loved Lady Anne.

Unfortunately, fate was unkind to us again. I had taken a July weekday off in 2003 because I just couldn't stand how congested and cluttered my condo had gotten, so I decided to do some sorting and move some things to the dumpster and others to storage in the basement. Of course Ramses found this all exciting and was always looking for opportunities to sneak out of the kitchen door which lead directly to the outside world. As I kept taking things out that door I had to repeatedly push Ramses back and tell him to stay away from the door. I was just coming in for the fourth time when Ramses began running toward me and suddenly flipped over on his side and looked as though he was having some kind of seizure. I had recognized this kind of behavior from when Siegfried had his diabetic seizures, but Ramses wasn't diabetic to my knowledge, but I thought that might be the problem so I took some carob syrup which I used to use on Siegfried and tried to administer that, but he went all limp. I ran to the desk and grabbed a stethoscope but couldn't detect any heartbeat. I began blowing in his nostrils and massaging his little chest, but it was no good; he was gone and there was no getting him back.

I called the vet and explained all of this. He felt that it was either a heart attack or again, a urinary tract problem since again; little Ramses did not let loose when he died. This time my reaction was strange, I was more angry than sad; angry at God, angry at Ramses. I remember holding his little body and screaming: "How could you do this to me ? I was just beginning to love you and now you have abandoned me". And I remember railing at God saying: "What more can you take from me? You've taken everything and everyone that I ever loved. Is this your life lesson for me; never to love anything ever again?" Somehow the anger was good for me though; at least it seemed somehow to lessen the grieving, but it was still painful none the less.

So now it was just me and my hateful, cold as ice female cat, Isis; alone and against the world together. I have to admit that I am guilty of wishing that it were she that had died instead of Ramses, but she didn't and we would have to make the best of it. Oddly enough, after Ramses' passing, Isis actually became very sweet and warm toward me. It was almost as if she wanted to ease my pain and her own. I appreciated her little attempts to comfort me and we became good buddies.

After that on a cold February day when I was on my way to lunch from my work place, a scruffy, emaciated little male cat found me. He came right up to me in the parking lot and began meowing and rubbing up against me to take him home. My workplace was nowhere near a residential area so apparently the poor little guy had been dumped there or had gotten lost. I took a chance and took him home. I put him in the bathroom to keep him isolated from Isis until I could clean him up, take him to a vet for a checkup and shots and make sure that he did not have any communicable diseases. He let me wash him in the bathroom sink without any biting or scratching so I felt that was a good sign as to his temperament. I later took him to my vet and everything checked out OK, so I kept him and named him Sudi, which is Egyptian for "lucky".

He immediately bonded with Isis and me and became a wonderful addition to "my family". He has proven to be a very appreciative and loving little guy; actually much more loving to me than even Isis and I am so glad to have him in my life. Animals seem to instinctively know that you have saved them and show true love and appreciation. He is no longer the scruffy little creature that I met in the parking lot. With tender loving care he now has a "fuller figure" and beautiful silky shiny fur and bright, loving green eyes.

Little Isis eventually learned to come out of her shell and became a very loving partner to Sudi and myself. It is just unfortunate that just as her little soul was blossoming, she suddenly became ill with some weird kind of hepatitis and she left us. Sudi and I both miss her very much.

Now what is the lesson behind all of this? First of all, when you choose to love anything, human or animal, you are in fact running a risk. With a human, you are running the risk that the love may not be returned. At least with an animal, no such risk exists; an animal will almost always return your love ten-fold. So there is nothing to worry about there. But in both cases, animal or human; there is the risk of losing them to sickness and death. I guess you just have to weigh the costs alongside the benefits. All I can say is that you are never quite so alive, happy and fulfilled as when you are in a state of love. All of life becomes illumined by your love and you blossom as a human being. So grab any chance that you can at love; even if it's simply the act of loving an animal, so that you may experience love and see how different you yourself are as a result of loving. The rewards far outweigh the cost.

And if you do choose to love an animal; either by itself or possibly in addition to a human; please, do yourself a favor. DON'T go to the Westminster Dog Show or some prestigious kennel club. Those animals will do just fine without you. DO GO TO THE LOCAL ANIMAL SHELTER. There you will find a true friend who without your help, will lose his or her life, and on some strange psychic level, they seem to know that. If you adopt them; they will love you and appreciate you forever; they will "know" what you have done for them.

I will tell you right now, that the reason that I am still alive today is because of my "furry friends". When lovers had failed me and personal losses had whittled me down to the point where I no longer had any desire to live; the concern of "what will become of my pets?" kept me going and made me want to live on to be there for them. I think that especially for single people without a significant other in their lives, pets are absolutely necessary to your mental and physical well being. Do yourself and them a favor and adopt a pet. But do so soberly, realizing that there is responsibility and commitment involved. Maybe this will be good practice for you and teach you how to commit to a human. Just remember, as the movie character, Forest Gump said: "Life's like a box of chocolates", but you can't just put one back after you've already bitten into it and especially if It's a "soft center".

PART III
MOVING ON

CHAPTER 1
WHERE DO WE GO FROM HERE?

So where do we go from here? Where can any of us go in this sort of twilight of the gods? I guess we need first to determine where we are right now and then formulate a plan to proceed from there. I find where gay people are right now in time and where I am , personally, in my own mid-life situation similar and equally confusing. Any transitional period is always difficult because you find yourself neither here nor there.

For example, an adolescent is physically able to procreate and to go to war and die for his country, but cannot vote or marry without parental consent nor is he respected as a man. So the poor young thing is neither really a child nor an adult and that is an extremely difficult situation to be in. This undoubtedly accounts for the difficulty which most parents have trying to understand and work with adolescents.

Likewise, when one reaches mid-life, one is too old to land the best jobs and opportunities due to our youth-oriented society coupled with the concerns of greedy health care providers who are fearful that too many claims will be filed by older workers. Yet at the same time, one isn't old enough to actually retire and enjoy the harvest, the fruit of all of his or her years of work. So once again, we are faced with this sort of nebulous, indefinable period of life; almost a second adolescence as our beauty fades and our sexual prowess diminishes. What to do?

I find the Gay Community as a whole, faced with a similar confusing transitional existence. Our situation as a whole seems much more open these days and our lifestyle is getting much more exposure both on TV and in the movies; yet still, I strongly question where we are in the stream of time? This apparent growing acceptance or at least tolerance for us can be misleading. It disarms many and leads them to believe that they can be complacent when this is not the time for complacency. As I write these words, many large corporations which formerly granted domestic partnership benefits to gay couples are already beginning to renege and reverse their decisions on those benefits. Many state legislatures which seemed "gay friendly" in the past are now turning 180 degrees opposite in their attitudes toward gay rights.

And then there is the ever looming Christian Right specter made up of some very strange bed fellows, who prior to this, all hated each other, but who are now united in their hatred of gay rights and even women's rights. Even though evangelicals have not been shy in the past about naming the Roman Catholic Church and the Pope as the "Whore of Babylon" and the "Antichrist", yet now they seem more than willing to sleep with her if there is any hope of their "holy coalition" crushing the advancement of women's and gay rights. I think that they want to "test the waters" first by reversing and destroying any gay rights that may have been achieved over the last few decades. Then, if they are successful; they will proceed to reverse Rowe Versus Wade and destroy all women's rights also. Odd, isn't it that the same people who seem so obsessed with saving the fetus are adamantly against any form of child welfare or child healthcare and support the death penalty and the use of weapons of mass destruction and chemical warfare so long as the nation under attack is not a "Christian nation".

So again, I entreat all gay men and lesbian women to continue to participate in Gay Pride events and continue to keep an eye on the news and contact your congressmen whenever necessary. The battle for equal rights and that is all that we want, is hardly over, and unless we remain forever vigilant and proactive, we will most certainly lose ground.

I, for one, want to celebrate the lives of gay brothers and sisters like Oscar Wilde, Quentin Crisp, Walt Whitman, Gertrude Stein, Harvey Milk, Cole Porter and others too numerous to mention, who have contributed much to society through their art, activism and writing. And I also want to celebrate and honor whenever possible, that courageous little band of drag queens, who back in 1969, stood their ground and fought the police who were persecuting and harassing them in the Stonewall Bar in NYC; while their more macho brothers, fled the bar. That little band of "sisters" touched off the entire Gay Rights Movement and the Gay Community certainly owes them a debt of gratitude.

Now there's another much larger group of gay men who, hopefully, future generations of straight and gay people together will remember and honor for their service to mankind both voluntarily and involuntarily and that is the band of brothers in the 80's who fell victim to a lax and unfeeling country and medical establishment which either withheld or simply failed to be responsible and publish early warnings of the threat of AIDS. Early warnings would have saved thousands of lives. Those poor early victims of HIV and AIDS had no idea that the virus existed at all and so couldn't possibly practice safe sex or abstinence.

Rather than being regarded as simply wanton, promiscuous individuals who "got what they deserved" as many evangelists said back then, describing AIDS as God's punishment of gays; these individuals lives and deaths were instrumental and indispensable in the medical institution's research and progress in the treatment of a virus which could easily decimate the human race. Their willingness to serve as "human guinea pigs" may ultimately save millions of lives. And the monetary and fund raising efforts of the Gay Community in the battle against AIDS will ultimately save millions of lives; not only of gay men, but of heterosexual men, women and children both here and in many third world countries which are already being ravaged by AIDS.

The straight community, for the most part ignored the threat of AIDS labeling it as a gay disease from which they were somehow immune. But the fact my friends is that AIDS originated in the straight communities in third world countries and continues to flourish in those areas because their cultures encourage sex with multiple partners while discouraging the use of any kind of "protection". Here again is an area in which the Church has exhibited totally irresponsible behavior by telling people "NOT TO USE CONDOMS". Apparently the Church feels that having babies born with HIV infection is preferable to using birth control or protection.

So I try to honor our fallen brothers and sisters whenever possible by contributing panels to the AIDS QUILT and financial aid to both the QUILT and AIDS research. I never cease to be amazed when many of my gay brothers and sisters methodically avoid attending either public displays of the QUILT or Gay Rights parades. Many seem to be "part-time gays" who are gay only when in the process of engaging in a sexual act, but "straight" for the remainder of their lives. They are like the typical man who when asked if he is gay responds: "Hell no, I'm simply a heterosexual man who prefers sex with other men."

So you see these individuals do not want to be seen associating with gays even though they themselves are gay; and especially if the gay men in question are even moderately effeminate. Oftentimes some of these men will go so far as to even persecute the Gay Community themselves by either legal means or outright fag baiting and bashing; just to obfuscate those who may be getting just too close to the fact of their homosexuality. Of course drag is out of the question. And yet isn't it odd that no one questions the masculinity of straight men who dress in drag at Mardi-Gras in New Orleans or "Carnival" in Rio?

They ask absolutely stupid questions like: "Why does so-and-so have to act so effeminate; can't he tone it down"? It never seems to dawn on them that so-and-so acts effeminate because he IS EFFEMINATE! And why should he have to "tone it down" for anyone? Just because YOU are traveling "incognito" and YOU are ashamed of who YOU are and want to deceive others into thinking that you are the same as them so as to gain their acceptance, doesn't mean that the rest of us have to live your lie.

The fact of the matter is that there are many effeminate men in the world who aren't even gay. And there are many male cross-dressers who love to wear women's clothes, but who are not even gay. And there are many women who want to work at jobs that were once traditionally male-orientated jobs and want to wear men's clothing but who are not necessarily lesbians. When the Gay Community fights for rights, it isn't only for themselves, but for these straight people also, who are often mistaken for us and consequently persecuted or beaten to death.

I have heard many gay men say that they might be willing to participate in a Pride Parade or rally if they could be assured that there would be no drag queens, leather men, or overtly masculine lesbians in the parade. Well isn't that "special?" What should we do then? Should we have all males in the parade clad in oxford button down shirts and chinos and all women wearing cocktail dresses and heels? That's NOT who we are. We are a diverse group of human beings ranging over a broad spectrum from bisexual to overtly gay; from very masculine to very feminine. Unless we represent all levels of that spectrum, we are not accurately depicting our diversity, but merely presenting a watered-down image that we feel might be more palatable to the heterosexual community. Well, damn if even straight men can be effeminate or cross-dressers, why can't gay men? And if straight women can be marines; firefighters and police, then what's wrong with a lesbian in leather attire on a motorcycle? If overtly masculine lesbians and overtly feminine gay men cannot gain acceptance even in the Gay Community, then I ask you where are they to turn?

If gay men and women can't even respect each other's broad spectrum of diversity, then how on earth can we honestly expect heterosexuals to accept us? Of course we need not "air all of our dirty laundry" in front of straight people, but neither should we be deceitful and present them with an image that we are a community of mostly overtly masculine men and overtly feminine women "just like them"; that we are mostly asexual and will keep a low profile if they will only accept us and allow us into their social clubs and institutions. No, the time for begging and groveling for acceptance is long overdue.

Maybe I'm just different from many of my peers, but for me, being gay is more, much more than just my sexual preference; it's my entire life. It involves much more than simply having sex with a same sex partner; even heterosexuals can do that under the right conditions. No, to me, being gay is an entire mindset. I remember loving and being in love with men long before becoming genital or physical with them. And I remember being well acquainted with the feminine side of my nature long before ever hearing the word "gay". Perhaps my definition of a gay person would be a man who is totally at ease and at peace with his feminine nature and a woman who is totally at ease and at peace with her masculine nature.

I feel that too many gay men make the same mistake as their straight counterparts in refusing to acknowledge any female aspect in their nature whatsoever; thereby remaining fractured and disoriented rather than being a fully integrated human being. Whether you choose to accept it and work with it or not; every man does in fact have a feminine side, just as every woman has a masculine side that's simply the way we were born. Now we can choose to ignore it if we want, but how much better to learn to understand it in ourselves and in others.

Those men who refuse to acknowledge the feminine aspects within themselves, usually end up becoming wife beaters and fag bashers; the two seem to go together. You see in actuality they don't love women, they hate women and only want to use them sexually and dump them when they're done. They really prefer to be with other men; hunting, fishing, wrestling, weight lifting, fighting; almost sounds like thinly veiled homosexuality doesn't it? Maybe that's why they bash fags because fags only remind them of what they really are, but unlike the fags, these men lack the courage to be themselves and be free and that's what makes them angry and hostile.

I think that it is high time that we begin accepting one another unconditionally and marching for each other's rights. We can make a difference if we stand together. As one of the Founding Fathers stated in contemplating the American Revolution "…if we don't hang together, we shall surely all hang separately…" We need to develop more of a sense of community and solidarity or all will be lost and we must not allow that to happen. We owe it to gay youth of today and to all who will come after us. And ultimately this new freedom and equal rights will even benefit the straight community because there will be no fear of "hidden agendas"; and no one will be marrying their daughters and sisters only to hide their homosexuality. The gay suicides and bashings will cease as mutual respect for both communities grows.

I can't help but think of a poster that I saw years ago. It read: "When they came for the Jews, I said nothing. And when they came for the gypsies and gays, I said nothing. Now they are coming for me and there is no one left to speak up for me." Something for us all to think about; wouldn't you agree?

CHAPTER 2
THE GAY AGENDA

Most people are universally frightened by the unknown, so let's allay those fears right now. The Christian Right extremists love to bandy the term : "gay agenda" because they know that it strikes terror to the hearts of genuinely concerned folks with high family values, but who are simply uninformed or deliberately misinformed by others who DO HAVE AN AGENDA. And make no mistake about it, The Christian Right most definitely does have its own agenda. And that agenda is to ignore the rights of gays, straights, Buddhists, Moslems, Hindus, Taoists, atheists, humanists and others and turn the U.S. government into a Judeo-Christian Theocracy with them calling all the shots.

Is the purpose of the "gay agenda" to convert the entire world to homosexuality thereby bringing an end to human reproduction and the demise of the human race? I think not. And is it to lobby legislators to pass laws so that we can prance around in the streets in wedding gowns and corrupt young people? I think not. And is it to lobby for the right to adopt children so that we can have a constant supply of young people to violate and molest? I think not.

First of all, no sane homosexual would encourage everyone to be like him or her for two reasons. First, it would mean the ultimate demise of the human race. And second, we would have too much competition then, just like straight people have today. As far as adoption is concerned; many gay couples who have been able to adopt have usually adopted opposite sex children and have done a great job at raising them. The vast majority of gay men and women are attracted to ADULT same sex partners. Oddly enough, most children who are victims of molestation or any kind of abuse suffer at the hands of their own parents (presumably straight), relatives or trusted clergy; not the hairdressers down the street.

One of my co-workers when I was working at the telephone company a few years back asked me one day: "What do you people want? You're always marching and picketing; what is it that you want?" I responded "the same things that you already have". In a nutshell, we want equality and acceptance; real equality and real acceptance; not mere tolerance. We're tired of being merely tolerated and pacified with the crumbs from religious and political tables. We want full citizenship rights and responsibilities in the nations in which we reside. Full citizenship does not consist of being excluded from military service, political office and government security positions.

I saw a fascinating show on public television which demonstrated that while the official U.S. military position toward enlisted men engaging the services of prostitutes is negative; yet for years the government has "unofficially" worked with local communities to make sure that such elicit services were available to servicemen because officers concluded that such services were necessary to the mental well being and moral of the troops. And yet these same officers insist that if gays are allowed in the military at all on a "don't ask, don't tell basis" that such enlistees must remain celibate throughout their military career. Now how can that be considered as equal treatment?

Likewise, most of the institutional churches take the same attitude. A homosexual can only be allowed to participate in the activities and sacraments of the Church if he or she agrees to remain single and celibate and not "act on his homosexual urges". So we are not entitled to either marriage or the love and intimacy which is the right of every other church member. No, we must agree to a bland, non-sexual, loveless existence in order to be condescendingly accepted within the Church. Well, I'm sorry, but that is not equality and it is not acceptance and it is simply unacceptable.

Now, don't get me wrong. I respect the right of any church or religious institution to lay down requirements for membership whether I agree with those requirements or not; that is their right; I don't have to join their church. So I respect the right of any religious institution to full autonomy even though I may not agree with their thinking. And neither I nor my brothers and sisters would ever interfere with or try to abate the state or constitutional rights of a religious organization. So we are in no way any kind of a threat to religious institutions. But we do expect the same mutual respect in return.

On a political level; the above rules do not apply. Unlike a church or social institution, a state or federal government which is supposed to represent the needs of all of its citizens does not have the option to pick and choose which citizens it will support and which citizens it will deny freedoms to. If it fails to treat all citizens equally under the law, then its promise of freedom and justice and equality for all is simply a lie.

I might also ask the question that since there is no scientific proof anywhere that homosexuals make inferior soldiers or are security risks any more than heterosexual soldiers, then what is the prohibition based upon? If it is based on Judeo-Christian ethics, then it is in violation of the U.S. Constitution which promotes separation of Church and State. If it is based upon simply rules of conduct and some commonly held civil belief that sex outside of marriage is detrimental and could lead to health hazards, then the military should strictly enforce celibacy from ALL of it's single, enlisted men and women; not just from gay men and women.

In a nation which does not provide health insurance for its citizens and where most employers do not either; and in a nation where single people pay a disproportionate amount of the taxes, then if I am fortunate enough to be employed by a company that does offer health coverage, I want my significant other on that coverage too. And why not? Heterosexuals by paying a small premium can put their entire family on their health plan, so why may not I, put my "family" on my health plan?

Also the general public does not understand other issues at stake which could be remedied by the state governments at least providing for civil unions if not outright marriage certificates. If I had a monogamous relationship with a lover for 30 years and that individual was rushed to the hospital as a result of a heart attack or auto accident, do you realize that I would be refused access to him because I am not a blood relative or a spouse? And even if he has no living relatives, then he would be put into the custodial care of a total stranger before being given into my care. And if he died, I would not be able to collect any kind of survivor's pension or benefits. If he lived, he could be declared mentally unstable by his relatives; taken from me; put into an institution and I would be evicted from our home which would be liquidated to pay the hospital bills. You see these are all important issues which have already been taken care of for heterosexuals, but which remain serious problems for us. Now I ask you in all honesty; is this equality?

And yes, not all, but many gay men and women would like the right to adopt children and why not? If heterosexuals have the right to sire and gestate children while on drugs and then either abandon them later in life or worse yet abuse them and "pimp" them off to predators to finance their drug habits, then why may not I adopt, nurture, love and raise that unwanted child? Now I know that the argument can be made that a child needs a mommy and a daddy and I agree with that 100%, but a mommy and daddy are not always what the child gets, not even in the heterosexual world where most children are being raised by one parent in a broken family.

In all of the studies that have been done to date relating to either two gay men or two gay women raising children, none were in any way detrimentally affected or unduly influenced to pursue a gay lifestyle themselves, in fact most remain straight. Let's face it gang. ALL gay children were raised by STRAIGHT PARENTS in a predominantly straight world. So if all of that straight influence was not able to make us straight, then I highly doubt that being parented by gay parents would make anyone gay. You simply are what you are and no amount of influence or exposure is going to change that. And then too, what about children in foster homes, who may have already identified themselves as being gay? Wouldn't they be better off adopted by gay parents who could be role models?

Why should young people be left to pine away in group homes simply because the "system" has not been able to match them up with "Ozzie and Harriet" parents, when there are loving, prospective gay couples out there who would be happy to adopt them? I have always found it odd that there are so many restrictions and requirements for even heterosexual adoptive parents, while there are no qualifications or restrictions placed upon biological parents. Biological parents need not be married, drug-free, disease-free, mentally balanced, working, have a home to take the child to, or be of the same race as the child. Yet adoptive parents have to fulfill all of the above?

Why are biological parents, not held responsible for their actions? Why are they not required to take courses in parenting and required to secure a license before having children? If the real issue is protecting children from harm, then the requirements for biological parenting and adoptive parenting should be the same. The State should not be waiting until the child is abused or killed before stepping into the situation. If the State chooses to bar me from having anything to do with children, then maybe I should be entitled to some kind of large tax break since I do not have any children in the school systems. Why should I be paying enormous taxes to educate the children of "dead beat dads"? And why should I be paying toward education systems which do not include as part of their curriculum at least the basics of social tolerance so that I do not end up being the victim of a hate crime committed against me by the very children whose education I finance through my taxes? How many more Matthew Shepard's must die before the hate crimes cease all together?

So that's the Gay Agenda, "in a nutshell", friends. Is it still scary? I hope not. Is it looking for special rights? No. Is it looking for preferential treatment? No. Separate, but equal? No. We seek equal rights, but also equal responsibilities. Surely, that is fair enough.

CHAPTER 3
STONEWALL REVISITED

I mentioned the 1969 Stonewall uprising earlier on, but I just want to take this opportunity to explain it in a little more detail since it is a critical point in Gay History and also since I had the honor of hearing the story first hand from a survivor of Stonewall and great soul, Ivan Valentin, who I met a few years ago on the 27th anniversary of Stonewall.

Back in the 1960's, in addition to the possibility of being beaten and harassed in the streets by "gay bashers", one was not even safe in the confines of a designated gay bar or club. The police themselves would routinely come into gay clubs and either entrap gays or arrest them. Or they would simply go into a rampage; order everyone out of the bar and begin beating those slow to respond with Billy clubs. Well, one hot, uncomfortable June evening in 1969, the police made one of those routine shakedowns on a gay bar in Greenwich Village called the "Stonewall", only this time the patrons were not in the mood to be hassled again. They had finally had it. They were not welcome in the straight clubs; they were not safe on city str5eets; their only oasis was the gay clubs and now even that was being threatened. Well, when you push someone against the wall, there's no longer any choice but to fight for your survival; so they did, but not all. I was told that the more macho of the gay men in the bar fled when the police began swinging. Isn't that interesting?

To quote Ivan, a prominent Stonewall veteran: "We had had it; we weren't going to be beaten or taken to jail again." Those with good jobs and positions ran out of the bar and fled, but the remainder; largely drag queens, minorities and the unemployed stood their ground. Since it was too late to lock the police out, someone decided to lock them in. One of the patrons barred the door and in self defense the drag queens began fighting the police with bottles, high heels or anything else they could find. The police injured many of them; Ivan still had scars from that evening, but over all, the gays won and the police managed to unlock the door and escape into the street.

By then many gays who had fled the bar earlier had managed to enlist the aid of other gays who lived in the immediate area. Before long, drag queens were overturning police cars in the streets and setting fires. Thus began a five day uprising which was to be the birth of the modern gay liberation movement. Now, due to the courage of that small band of drag queens some 34 years ago, gay police officers now are allowed to march in uniform down Fifth Ave. in New York City along with thousands of gay clergy, firemen, educators, military, politicians, entertainers, etc. None of this could ever have been if not for the courage of that small "band of brothers" at the Stonewall Bar; and it could never have been so long as gays remained invisible.

That year, 1996 which was the 27th anniversary of the Stonewall Riot, I decided to go into New York to celebrate. Following the parade down Fifth Avenue, I decided to make my pilgrimage over to the Stonewall Bar to sit in the bar and reflect on what took place some 27 years before, when to my surprise, I noticed two elegantly dressed drag queens toward the rear of the bar who looked very much like the Stonewall Veterans which I had seen on the float in the parade. I made my way to the rear of the bar and approached one of the two, who did , in fact, turn out to be Ivan Valentin, an original Stonewall Veteran with two of his friends, China and Stephan, also a Stonewall Veteran. Ivan told me that they were just sitting there reflecting and wondering how and why they were privileged to have had a share in it. That meeting was certainly the pinnacle of my Pride Weekend and an honor which I will always treasure; but it didn't end there because Ivan was gracious enough to give me his phone number and invite me to visit him at a later date.

After the Vets left the bar, I decided to go outside and just sit on one of the park benches and get some fresh air; it was sort of stuffy back in the bar. Now, while I wasn't in total drag, in the spirit of the festivities, I was wearing a sort of 1950's looking black hat with a veil and a black feather boa, but with a shirt and slacks. Before I knew it, a fairly attractive Arabic man asked if anyone was sitting in the seat next to me, to which I responded "no" and invited him to sit down. It was beginning to get dark at that point, but still it was a pretty public spot. All of a sudden, this guy started kissing me on the lips. Well, I didn't stop him because it had been a long time since anyone had shown me that much attention so I was not about to stop him. Well, it didn't stop there. The next thing I know, this guy had carefully pulled his "member" out and was now humping my leg and tongue kissing me all at the same time. I didn't know what to do at that point, I was sure that we would be arrested for some form of public indecency, but fortunately, he "popped" and it was over.

Now, oddly enough, he did stick around to engage in polite conversation. He told me that he was from Egypt and worked one of the food carts that one sees up around midtown Manhattan. He wanted to see me again, I thought it odd, but we exchanged telephone numbers. The following Monday morning he called me and started attempting phone sex with me. He was telling me all about how aroused he was and how "big" he was at that point and then asked me if my "pussy" was getting worked up. I responded by telling him that I think that he may have made a mistake that day in the park because I didn't have a "pussy", but that his conversation was giving me an erection.

Well, he went wild! He was totally shocked and insulted and insisted that he didn't know that I was a man or he would never have humped my leg or kissed me. Well, I took the opportunity to assure him that he was very lucky to have humped a gay man because a real woman would have either kicked him in the nuts or called the police. Aren't people amazing? I have been to Egypt, as you well remember, and I know for a fact that you just don't walk up to an Egyptian woman sitting on a park bench and hump her leg. Why did he think that he right to do that in this country? And yet he was the one offended that I turned out to be another man. Too bad !

CHAPTER 4
MY VISIT WITH IVAN

A few weeks later, I called Ivan on the phone and asked if I could come down and see him; he lived on the lower east side of Manhattan. Unlike so many who give out their phone numbers with no intention of ever seeing you again; Ivan was genuine and gave me his address and directions. I really didn't know what to expect; I didn't even know if I would recognize him at this next meeting because I had only seen him once in his two-foot high platinum blonde hairdo and rainbow flapper dress. But he was watching out for me so that helped. When the door opened, I was faced with the diminutive frame of a middle-aged; "five o'clock shadowed" little Hispanic man in a brightly colored tropical shirt and shorts; not at all the larger than life Yvonne who had towered over me at the Stonewall only weeks earlier in her platform shoes.

Yet in the long run, Ivan was more majestic than Yvonne and turned out also to be larger than life. I had made it a point over the years in my continuing spiritual quest to study people and to seek out the company of those whom I considered to be great spiritual men and women. I wanted to find what it was that made them so incredibly different from most other people. I have met gurus, monks, mystics of all denominations and they all possessed a certain commonality. They all manifested a kind of humility and quiet poise; a contagious kindness; a spirit of sharing and a charisma which made everyone feel welcome. They also lacked any sense of hostility or vengefulness toward those who had wronged them in the past. This I witnessed in all of the great teachers who I had met and these same qualities I witnessed in Ivan. It may seem strange to equate this dear little gay activist and drag queen with a great spiritual master, yet out of the depth of my soul, I was forced to acknowledge that the same advanced and evolved Spirit which drove those masters, was present also in Ivan. God works in strange ways.

Ivan had spent his entire life; selflessly working toward public understanding and compassion for gay people with no pay and no reward other than the reward of helping many to find a deep sense of self respect and meaning in their lives. His mission began at the Stonewall, but it didn't end there. He was the primary fighter in my own state, Connecticut in overturning ridiculous puritanical laws banning female impersonators from entertaining in bars and clubs in Connecticut. He picketed the State House in Hartford on many occasions and continued as an activist throughout his life; despite poor health and even poorer finances. He went on many speaking tours in an attempt to try to build bridges of understanding between the gay and heterosexual communities.

At home in the East side of Manhattan in his very humble apartment; he shared what little he had with all. He tried to be like a "mother" and a "father" to young gay men who had been tossed out of their family homes as a result of their "coming out" to their parents. His door was always open and he made himself available to those in emotional need and turmoil. His kind, soft words seemed to sooth everyone better than any psychiatrist or counselor because he could empathize; he had "been there".

In his Pride day speech which he had given in 1996, Ivan related that in all of his trials and tribulations, that the one thing which he had never felt was "fragile". He declared how many straight men consider us fragile and weak, but then he went on to use the metaphor of the snowflake, which while delicate and fragile can bring the strongest machines known to man to a screeching halt when "snowflakes stick together". He urged the Gay Community to do the same because he said that "our strength lies not in our ability to assimilate, hide and become absorbed, but in our ability despite our great diversity to stick together and continue to fight for the rights of all men and women to be different and diverse and live their lives in dignity and freedom according to their own life choices.

Ivan was too good for this world, and went to his reward in 1997. I only knew him for so short a while, yet he touched my life as he touched the lives of countless others. I feel deeply grateful and honored to have met such a great soul, masquerading in the guise of a little Puerto Rican Drag Queen.

CHAPTER 5
WHAT IS NATURAL?

The major argument which the Judeo-Christian Community and even Islam has for centuries used against us and which the Christian Right currently uses to condemn homosexuality is that it is "not natural" and that the Bible condemns "unnatural acts". That being the case, then it behooves us to define "natural" before proceeding any further.

nat.u.ral

ADJECTIVE:

1. Present in or produced by nature: a natural pearl.

2. Of, relating to, or concerning nature: a natural environment.

3. Conforming to the usual or ordinary course of nature: a natural death.

4. Not acquired; inherent.

5. Having a particular character by nature.

6. Characterized by spontaneity and freedom from artificiality, affection, or inhibitions.

7. Not altered, treated or disguised.

Now, as to the first definition; "produced by nature", scientists and biologists have found that homosexuality exists quite naturally in the animal kingdom in more that 450 species of animals which would represent approximately 20% of the animal kingdom and with apparently no harm done to either the species themselves or any immediate dangers of extinction since not all of the animals in these species are homosexual. In a Time Magazine article of April 26, 1999. Vol. 153, No. 16, pg. 70. the author, Jeffrey Kluger states: "What humans share with so many other animals, it now appears, is freewheeling homosexuality. For centuries, opponents of gay rights have seen same-gender sex as a uniquely human phenomenon…but nature's morality, it seems, may be remarkably flexible...what's more, same-sex partners don't meet merely for brief encounters, but many form long-term bonds, sometimes mating for years or even life."

Cognitive scientist, Bruce Bagemihl, in his new book "Biological Exuberance" by St. Martin's Press, explains that the homosexuality in many of these species goes way beyond mere sexual gratification. He explains that Humboldt penguins may have homosexual relationships lasting six or more years and that male graylag geese may stay paired for fifteen years or more, which is the entire lifespan of a goose. He goes on to say that even bears and other mammals in same sex unions will raise their young together just as they would with an opposite sex partner. Many male penguins in the Central Park Zoo and in the wild have been seen to steal fertilized eggs from an unsuspecting female's nest and then proceed to take turns sitting on and hatching the eggs. Once hatched, the two male penguins will then raise the young together. A male pair of chinstrap penguins in the Central Park Zoo in New York City were partnered and even successfully hatched a female chick from an egg. Other penguins in New York have also been reported to be forming same-sex pairs. Roy and Silo, two male chinstrap penguins at the Central Park Zoo have been inseparable for years and show classic pair bonding behavior; mutual preening; entwining of their necks; flipper flapping and such. They also have sex together, ignoring any potential female partners.

Some black swans of Australia form sexually active male-male mated pairs and steal nests, or form temporary threesomes with females to obtain eggs, driving away the female after she lays the eggs. More of their cygnets survive to adulthood than those of different-sex pairs possibly due to their superior ability to defend large portions of land. In nature, one also finds male ostriches which only court their own gender; mate, build nests and even raise foster chicks.

Zoos in Japan and Germany have also reported gay male penguin couples. The couples have been shown to build nests together and use a stone to replace an egg in the nest. Researchers at Rikkyo University in Tokyo, found 20 gay pairs at 16 major aquariums and zoos in Japan. Bremerhaven Zoo in Germany attempted to break up the gay male couples by importing female penguins from Sweden and seperating the male couples, they were unsuccessful. The zoo director stated the relationships were too strong between the gay couples.

So how does one explain all of this? If homosexuality is so "unnatural" then why does it exist in roughly the same percentages in the animal kingdom (or Nature) as in humans and not only that, but oftentimes producing positive results as in the case of the cygnets which are better equipped to protect the young than their female counterparts? Now unless some evangelist is going to try to tell us that homosexuality didn't exist in the animal kingdom until after Adam and Eve sinned or until "after the flood of Noah" which would be a real "fairy tale", then what is their explanation for this phenomenom? According to the Bible, on the "sixth day" God declared all of his creation as "good".

Now the fourth definition of the word, "natural" was that it was: "Not acquired; inherent". And of course this is entirely true. I know that in my own case, I have been attracted to my own sex since age four, even before I even knew what sex was. I did not suddenly wake up one morning and say: "Gees, those guys on "Queer Eye For The Straight Guy" make good money and seem to have a lot of fun; I'd like to be gay too. Let me check the Pink Pages to see where I can take some courses in becoming Gay." No, quite the opposite; I didn't even know what "gay "was; I had never even heard the term. All that I knew as I was growing up was that I was naturally attracted to men and NOT to WOMEN. I liked women well enough; had a lot in common with them too; but mostly saw them all as mothers and sisters.

The sixth definition of "natural" is a good one too: "Characterized by spontaneity and freedom from artificiality, affection, or inhibitions". Again, I am spontaneously gay and without any inhibitions and always have been. Conversely, I had to pretend to be straight because that did not come naturally nor spontaneously to me. I had to watch the actions of heterosexuals and try to copy them as closely as possible so as not to be discovered as not being one of them. My whole courtship and dating period in high school was nothing but a cleverly pulled off act. While my homosexual activities during that period were totally natural and spontaneous and did not have to be thought out in advance or rehearsed.

It rather reminds me of a TV show which I once saw where an adoption agency counselor was interviewing a young gay man who was applying to adopt a child. The counselor questioned him asking: "Are you a practicing homosexual"? To which the young man replied: "No, I don't need to practice, it comes naturally and I'm very good at it".

Now I love the seventh definition of "natural": "Not altered, treated or disguised". This one is crucial folks because it forms the whole basis of the Christian Rights recent "sexual reorientation" programs in which they are claiming to be able to change gay people from gay to straight. Wouldn't that be considered as "TREATMENT" or better yet, disguise?

They are not treating anyone, they are just brainwashing unbalanced, unhinged homosexuals who are so consumed with fear and terror of being discovered that they will resort to anything to hide the reality of who they are. Having prior to this, more than likely considered suicide as a real possibility; the offer of "treatment" sounds appealing to them. Not only that, but they have ready-made victims who will be more than glad to marry them to "make them straight" and score points with God. So of course it is an option, but not a wise one.

Statistics prove that their cure may last a few years at best until the novelty wears off and then they will be out on the street again looking for men. People love attention. The wedding; the dreaded honeymoon and the first child will give them the attention and acceptance that they are seeking. It will make them feel like "REAL MEN". I mean doesn't a wife and child PROOVE that I'm a real man and normal? Nope; not a bit; it merely proves that you're a good actor and wanted to be "normal" so badly that you were willing to ruin the lives of a compassionate woman; and any children that might result from that union; while sacrificing your own genuineness and integrity. It also proves that it's not beneath you to lie to everyone in your life and choose a double life of sneaking and cheating on both the woman and the men in your life rather than be true to the nature God gave you at birth.

One of the most outrageous and laughable instances of this that I saw for myself on TV was on the gay related show "In the Life" which airs on public television monthly. Apparently two of the early founders of one of these Christian Right therapy schools for sexual reorientation of gays were being interviewed on the show because while working together to heal gays in these programs; the two male founders fell in love with each other; left the organization and the church and have lived happily ever after sharing life together as a gay male couple ever since. So much for the efficiency of their therapy and the Church's ability to "transform lives". You see, it's not "nice to fool Mother Nature" and you will never win; so don't even think it.

Yes, Cole Porter (one of "ours") was certainly right when he wrote those eternal words: "Birds do it, bees do it; even educated fleas do it. Let's do it; let's fall in love." Although back then, when he was writing, I don't think that he knew how close to the truth he had come. Back then the illusion was simply to the fact that birds and bees have sex, but now due to modern studies in biology, we know that they also love and that in some cases, the nature of their love is gay love. You tell them, Cole; you go girl !

CHAPTER 6
ESCAPE FROM THE
PRISON OF EDEN

Being that the basis of all of the negative theology which modern day fundamentalists use to condemn not only homosexuals, but man himself as being "born in sin and shaped in iniquity originates in the Genesis account of Adam and Eve, I think that we should examine that account carefully. The first thing that one notices in reading Genesis is that there is more than one account of creation, apparently written by several different authors at different points in time and then meticulously pieced together in an attempt to make it look as though written by one author. But the attempt is anything but "seamless" and riddled with contradictions. Modern day linguists and historians know for a fact that there were at least two distinct sources for Genesis; they call them "E" for Elohist sources, "J" for Yahwist sources and possibly more. The Elohist renderings of Genesis and creation appear to be the more positive of the two while the Yahwist versions of the same events are far more negative and punitive.

Just to give you some examples, the Elohist version of creation found in the first chapter of Genesis describes all animal life created as male and female at the time of their creation, including man and woman. And God gives dominion to both man and woman over all of the other animals and tells them that he has given them "EVERY PLANT BEARING SEED UPON THE FACE OF THE EARTH AND EVERY TREE…" Gen 1:29. God closes chapter one by declaring : "Then God saw everything that He had made, and indeed it was very good." Gen 1:31.

But then the second chapter of Genesis begins the Yahwist version which rearranges all that and God starts doing some "take backs" and reorganization of pecking order in his creation. In the second chapter of Genesis, Adam is not created simultaneously along with Eve; no, in the second chapter of Genesis God parades all of the animals past Adam and has him name them and when no suitable partner is found for him, as an after-thought, God creates Eve from Adam's rib; thereby aluding to the fact that she should be dependent upon him and subservient to him.

Also God now changes his mind and tells them that one of the trees that HE planted in the garden is deadly and that they should not even touch it lest they die. A deadly tree in the midst of a perfect garden which God Himself had declared "good" only one chapter before? Also God had given man and woman "dominion" or control over all animal life in Genesis 1:28, so how is it that one of these creatures over which Adam had dominion at this point (no fall from grace yet) was able to trick him and decieve him? And if this talking serpant was in fact the Devil as Church writers and theologians would lead us to believe, then where in deed did that "evil" come from since God had created everything? How or why would God even allow this? Jesus taught us in Matt 7:17,18 that "Every good tree bears good fruit, but a bad tree bears bad fruit. A good tree cannot bear bad fruit, nor can a bad tree bear good fruit." So if that's the case? Then where did the Devil or this talking serpant come from? This seems a little odd to me. But don't take my word for it, read it for yourselves.

There is an answer to all of this, but it's going to be a real "Mrs. Marple twistaroo" that you would never have guessed in 6,000 years. And now are you ready for this? For $6,000,000 dollars, eternal mental and intellectual freedom, freedom from guilt and hangups and hell fire; do you want to know the answer? Do you want to see what's behind door number 2 ? Or would you rather play it safe with your cozy god; hold onto your scapulars; confess to the world and to your brothers and sisters that you are a worthless, fallen child of Eve; worthy only of death and eternal fire unless some compassionate angel should show you mercy by urinating on you to cool the flames.

Well, whether you want it or not, here's the answer: THE ONLY ONE TELLING THE TRUTH IN GENESIS IS THE SERPENT, and I will explain to you why I believe this to be the case. Am I not glad that I put this toward the end of my book? If I had put it in the beginning, you would never have read this far. Seriously, though, allow me to advance my theory and it is only a theory, but one which I feel explains the radical difference between Eastern and Western thought and spirituality.

A few years ago I went to the movies to see a wonderful film entitled "The Little Buddha", starring a hearthrob of mine, Keanu Reeves as Prince Siddartha, who was ultimately to become the Buddha. Now I had read the book, "Siddartha" by Herman Hesse and had read Buddhist teachings regarding the evolution of the Buddha from secular Prince to the "Enlightened One", but had never given much thought as to the similarities in the Buddhist and Judaic metaphors, while starkly different, yet describing the same events in both the history of man and the history and evolution of every soul. But somehow as I watched the story of Siddartha unfold on the silver screen, I was struck as though by a lightning bolt of revellation, an epiphany if you will. The impression was so overwhelming that I ran to my car and wrote it down in sort of short hand because I didn't want to lose the moment. I knew I had stumbled onto something of immense reality and truth.

Now the story behind Prince Siddartha is basically this. He is the son of a very powerful, but obviously mentally insecure King who basically has enslaved all of his people and doesn't want to make his son an exception. So he keeps his son, Siddartha, in extreme and lavish luxury in a beautiful palace where he is only attended by handsome, young and beautiful companions. The King keeps his son in blissful ignorance of any and all realities of life. He is totally unaware of aging, sickness, death, poverty or anything unpleasant whatsoever. And all those around him are under strict order under pain of death to make absolutely certain that Siddartha never finds out the truth of things. But Prince Siddartha has an inquiring mind and wonders what lay outside those palace walls and decides that he wants to venture out. Well, the King is furious, and doesn't know what to do, but he allows it, once more commanding that his servants whereever possible, not allow Siddartha to "see anything" along the way that might shed any light on reality.

Well, of course, the best made plans of man fail and Siddartha accidently sees an old man or whatever, I can't remember now, but that prompts him to command his bearers to put his litter down on the ground because he wants to walk among his subjects. When he does so, the jig is up. He discovers aging, death, suffering, pain, poverty and all human suffering and he is livid that his father had lied to him and withheld this vital information from him. He recognizes that it wasn't love that prompted his father to hide this from him but fear and possessiveness and the desire to control his son and make his son totally dependent upon him and grateful to him. But the King wasn't doing Siddartha any favors, because someday he would find out the truth of things, but then it might be too late to do anything about it. Prince Siddartha then left his father's palace and his own wife and newborn child and went off into the forests as a monk in search of the causes of human suffering and how they might be alleviated. He ultimately became the Buddha or "Enlightened One" when he found the source and remedy for all human suffering.

Now as I watched this I was suddenly struck with the similarity between this story and the story of Adam and Eve in the beautiful Paradise of Eden where there was to be no sickeness, no death, no pain; abundant beauty of flora and fauna; and plenty for everyone. Well, it was obvious to me that this was the same story of a jealous and insecure "father" who lied to his children and told them that they would live forever in a paradise where there would be no aging, suffering or death SO LONG AS THEY OBEYED HIM; when he knew very well that the animals had been aging, suffering and dying and decomposing for countless centuries. I'm not sure exactly how long this deity thought that he could fool them before they found out the truth, but apparently he thought that it would work long enough for him to control them and subjugate them and make them dependent upon him.

Now had Siddartha stayed in the palace and never ventured out to find out the truth; I guess his life would have been nice, but he would have been complacent and would never have been forced to grapple with the question of human suffering, which he would ultimately have to deal with at some point anyway. But he would have had to deal with suffering without any answers as to the nature of reality; the causes of suffering and how to end human suffering. He would have spent his life living in the shadow and under the good will of his father in blind obedience and servitude and ultimately suffered and died just like his father He would never have become the Buddha; never have become free and never have been in a position to help others find freedom.

So the writers of Genesis, betrayed themselves by their concepts; they "Created God In Their Own Image", not the reverse. They created a deity that was exactly like them; not one who encouraged exploration of the mind and intellect; not a diety that would have been proud of man's accomplishments, not a " God of Unconditional Love", but an insecure and domineering father who offered only conditional love; "obey me or die" and who would "take all of his toys back" if his children didn't play according to his rules. They created a vengeful and punitive god, whose only answer to difficulties was to destroy the world rather than help it to evolve. The god that the scribes created in Genesis drives Man out of the garden; destroys all life on earth in the Flood; topples the Tower of Babel; confuses the languages of the peoples so as to stifle their progress and establishes blood sacrifices as the only means to assuage his hostility toward his children. Not a pretty picture here.

And this is why I maintain that the only one telling the truth in Genesis is in fact the serpent; which oddly enough in Hindu lore is a symbol of divine wisdom and Shakti energy which eventually leads to human enlightenment and spiritual freedom. You see; priesthoods and clergy over the centuries have never truly wanted man to experience spiritual freedom because it's FREE; it wouldn't net them any profits in the Temple coffers or in the vaults at the Vatican. They much preferred systems of religion which required expensive offerings and sacrifices which were basically bribes offered up to god by his special priesthood. How convenient; convenient for them that is; not for mankind in general who often had to endure terrible hardships and travel miles over dangerous terrain to make their annual pilgrimages and bring their tithes to God, who although God of the Universe, could somehow only be contacted in one geographical location. Somehow this doesn't seem to say much for an omnipresent God.

And apparently, I am not the only one who sees it this way; in fact, I am rather a late bloomer since a truly great writer and philosopher of the 18th century saw it all exactly as I do. Thomas Paine wrote:

"Whenever we read the obscene stories, the voluptuous debaucheries, the cruel and torturous executions, the unrelenting vindictiveness, with which more than half the Bible is filled, it would be more consistent that we called it the word of a demon, than the word of God. It is a history of wickedness, that has served to corrupt and brutalize mankind". (Thomas Paine, The Age of Reason, 1794-1795).

And we don't have to stop with Thomas Paine. We can go back much further. I hate to admit that I am not the first to come up with this theory that the god of Genesis is in reality an enemy of mankind, but after further research since I had this epiphany, I have come to find that others like the Essenes, the Gnostics of Jesus time and later the Cathars of 11th, 12th and 13th century France also espoused similar beliefs, which is why the Cathars were tortured, killed and eradicated by the Roman Catholic Church in the 13th century.

THE CATHARS AS DEFINED BY WIKEPEDIA:

General

"Catharism was a name given to a gnostic religious sect that appeared in the Languedoc region of France in the 11th Century and flourished in the 12th and 13th Centuries. Catharism had its roots in manichaean and dualist beliefs. It held that the physical world was evil and created by Satan, who was taken to be identical with the God of the Old Testament; and that men underwent a series of reincarnations before reaching the pure realm of spirit, the presence of the God of Love described in the New Testament and his messenger Jesus. The Roman Catholic Church regarded the sect as heretical; faced with the rapid spread of the movement across the Languedoc and the failure of peaceful attempts at conversion, the Church launched the Albigensian Crusade and suppressed the Cathars with the help of nobility from northern France.

Cathars in general formed an anti-sacerdotal party in opposition to the Catholic Church, and raised a continued protest against the claimed moral, spiritual and political corruption of the Catholic Church. They claimed an Apostolic Connection to the early founders of Christianity and saw Rome as having betrayed and corrupted the original purity of the message. Cathar Elders, called *Perfecti* or *Parfaits* as in *Perfect* or *Complete* Heretics by the Catholic Church and known to themselves, their followers and their co-citizens as "*Bons Hommes*" and "*Bonnes Femmes*" or "*Bons Chrétiens*", literally "Good Men/Women" or "Good Christians", were few in number; the mass of Believers (*Credentes*) were not initiated into the deeper doctrines and were not expected to adopt the ascetic lifestyles practiced by the Elders.

The human condition

The Cathars claimed there existed within mankind a spark of divine light. This light, or spirit, had fallen into captivity within a realm of corruption — identified with the physical body and world. This was a distinct feature of classical Gnosticism, of Manichaeism and of the theology of the Bogomils. This concept of the human condition within Catharism was most probably due to direct and indirect historical influences from these older (and sometimes also violently suppressed) Gnostic movements. According to the Cathars, the world had been created by a lesser deity, much like the figure known in classical Gnostic myth as the Demiurge. This creative force was identified with the Old Testament God and was not the "True God", though he claimed for himself the title of the "one and only God". The Cathars identified this lesser deity, the Demiurge, with Satan. (Most forms of classical Gnosticism had not made this explicit link between the Demiurge and Satan). Essentially, the Cathars believed that the Old Testament God of Jews and Christians was an imposter, and His worship was a corrupt abomination infused by the failings of the material realm. Spirit — the vital essence of humanity — was thus trapped in a polluted world created by a usurper God and ruled by his corrupt minions.

Theology

The Catharist concept of Jesus might be called docetistic - theologically speaking it resembled Modalistic Monarchism in the West and Adoptionism in the East. Simply put, most Cathars believed that Jesus had been a manifestation of spirit unbounded by the limitations of matter — a sort of divine phantom and not a real human being. They embraced the *Gospel of John* as their most sacred text, and completely rejected the Old Testament — indeed, most of them proclaimed that the God of the Old Testament was, really, the devil. They proclaimed that there was a higher God — the True God — and Jesus was his messenger. While many in the West who adhered to a modalistic theology proclaimed He was True God himself. These are views similar to those of Marcion. The God found in the Old Testament had nothing to do with the God of Love known to Cathars. He had created the world as a prison, and demanded from the "prisoners" fearful obedience and worship. This false god was in reality — claimed the Cathari — a blind usurper who under the most false pretexts, tormented and murdered those whom he called all too possessively "his children". (This exegesis upon the Old Testament was not unique to the Cathars: it echoes views found in earlier Gnostic movements and foreshadows later critical voices.) The dogma of the Trinity and the sacrament of the Eucharist, among others, were rejected as abominations. Belief in metempsychosis, or the transmigration of souls, resulted in the rejection of hell and purgatory, which were and are dogmas of the Roman Catholic Faith. For the Cathars, this world was the only hell - there was nothing worse to fear after death, save perhaps a return visit to this world.

While this is the understanding of Cathar theology related by the Catholic Church, crucial to the study of the Cathars is their fundamental disagreement over the meaning of 'resurrection'. In the book *Massacre at Montsegur* (a book widely regarded by medievalists as having a pro-Cathar bias) the Cathars are referred to as "Western Buddhists" because of their belief in 're-incarnation' and non-violence.[1] Such were the disagreements that eventually led to the extermination of the sect." Such was the fate of the Cathars according to Wikepedia and other historical sources.

Yes, the serpent told the truth when it said: "You will not surely die. For God knows that in the day you eat of it your eyes will be opened and you will be like God..." Genesis 3:4,5. You see, the "deity" of Genesis was going to hold mankind hostage by always holding over them the possibility of the death penalty for disobedience. But the serpent was basically telling them that they would not really die in the sense that apparent bodily death is not the end of existence, but merely a transformation from one life to the next. But the serpant was alluding to the fact that if the couple ventured out from the security of their paradise and the complacency that it would generate and ventured both outward and "inward", that they would become like God, or eventually discover their own divinity and sonship with the real Creator of the Universe and not merely this local "garden god".

And this is true. It has been said that "neccessity is the mother of invention" and it is. Most human progress over the centuries has been directly linked not to creature comforts and complacency, but to suffering and adversity. It is illness that fuels medical science; it is violence that creates the need for self defense; it is suffering which can lead to compassion and starvation which can lead to better and more efficient production of food. All of these pairs of opposites are part and parcel of physical life in this realm of forms and physical manifestation.

There was never any "Fall of Man" and there was never any ageless, deathless paradise. It was all a very comforting and lovely myth, but simply a lie; and worse yet, a lie deliberately crafted to enslave mankind and rob them of their birthright as natural born sons and daughters of God. If you want to read a really great book which beautifully exposes endless inconsistancies in the Bible, be sure to read "Steve Allen on the Bible, Religion, & Morality" by Prometheus Books. It is very insightful. Also check out the works of famous professor and writer, Elaine Pagels such as her work "Adam, Eve and the Serpent" and also her works relating to the Gnostic Gospels and the Nag Hamadi Library. There are works like these too numerous to list.

CHAPTER 7
INTELLIGENT DESIGN?

The fact of the matter, my friends, is that the earth and the universe never was and never will be "perfect". Stars were imploding and celestial bodies colliding and the earth was being struck by enormous meteors destroying most life and plunging the planet into Ice Ages for eons before Adam and Eve ever ate the apple. Vast species of animal and plant life have become extinct repeatedly and the Earth has suffered through global warming and global freezing long before man ever appeared. So one may very well question the fundamentalist proponents of "Intelligent Design", which is merely a euphamism for "Creationism" and which they want to force on the education system. One may ask them how a personal deity who designed everything with intent and purpose and perfection allowed it all to go awry? Obviously it was never perfect but more an exercise of trial and error and didn't just cease being perfect after the "Fall of Man".

Intelligent design is the claim that "certain features of the universe and of living things are best explained by an intelligent cause, not an undirected process such as is a modern form of the traditional teleological argument for the existence of God, modified to avoid specifying the nature or identity of the designer. Its primary proponents, all of whom are associated with the Discovery Institute, believe the designer to be God. Intelligent design's advocates claim it is a scientific theory, and seek to fundamentally redefine science to accept supernatural explanations.

The unequivocal consensus in the scientific community is that intelligent design is not science. The U.S. National Academy of Sciences has stated that "intelligent design, and other claims of supernatural intervention in the origin of life" are not science because they cannot be tested by experiment, do not generate any predictions, and propose no new hypotheses of their own. The National Science Teachers Association and the American Association for the Advancement of Science have termed it pseudoscience. Others have concurred, and some have called it junk science.

Argument for poor design

From Wikipedia, the free encyclopedia

The **argument from poor design** or **dysteleological argument** is an argument against the existence of God, specifically against the existence of a creator God (in the sense of a God that directly created all species of life). It is based on the following premise:

1. An omnipotent, omniscient, omnibenevolent creator God would create organisms that have optimal design.

2. Organisms have features that are suboptimal.

3. Therefore, God either did not create these organisms or is not omnipotent, omniscient and omnibenevolent.

4. **Examples of poor design**

Examples of "poor design" cited include:

- In the African locust, nerve cells start in the abdomen but connect to the wing. This leads to unnecessary use of materials.

- An artist's representation of an ectopic pregnancy. Critics cite such common biological occurrences as contradictory to the 'Watchmaker Analogy'.

Poor design of the human reproductive system include the following:

- In the human female, a fertilized egg can implant into the fallopian tube, cervix or ovary rather than the uterus causing an ectopic pregnancy. The existence of a cavity between the ovary and the fallopian tube could indicate a flawed design in the female reproductive system. Prior to modern surgery, ectopic pregnancy invariably caused the deaths of both mother and baby. Even in modern times, in almost all cases, the pregnancy must be aborted to save the life of the mother.

- In the human female, the birth canal passes through the pelvis. The prenatal skull will deform to a surprising extent. However, if the baby's head is significantly larger than the pelvic opening, the baby cannot be born naturally. Prior to the development of modern surgery (caesarean section), such a complication would lead to the death of the mother, the baby or both. Other birthing complications such as breech birth are worsened by this position of the birth canal. Birth would hypothetically be easier if the birth canal passed through the front of the abdomen.[citation needed]

- In the human male, testes develop initially within the abdomen. Later during gestation, they migrate through the abdominal wall into the scrotum. This causes two weak points in the abdominal wall where hernias can later form. Prior to modern surgical techniques, complications from hernias including intestinal blockage, gangrene, etc., usually resulted in death.

- Other arguments:

- Barely used nerves and muscles (e.g. plantaris muscle) that are missing in part of the human population and are routinely harvested as spare parts if needed during operations.

- Intricate reproductive devices in orchids, apparently constructed from components commonly used for different purposes in other flowers.

- The use by pandas of their enlarged radial sesamoid bones in a manner similar to how other creatures use thumbs.

- The pointless existence of the appendix in humans, also the corresponding potentially fatal condition of appendicitis. The appendix, which is highly developed in herbivores, is meant to aid in the bacterial digestion of cellulose. Since people use fire and heat to cook now the appendix has become useless. (It has also been proposed that the appendix is involved in development of the immune system within the first year after birth, but subsequently has no function. However some people have congenital absence of their appendix without any reports of impaired immune system function.)

- The existence of unnecessary wings in flightless birds, e.g. ostriches.

- The route of the recurrent laryngeal nerve is such that it travels from the brain to the larynx by looping around the aortic arch. This same configuration holds true for many animals, in the case of the giraffe this results in about twenty feet of extra nerve.

- Portions of DNA — termed "junk" DNA — that do not appear to serve any purpose.

- The dystrophin gene is the largest ever found in nature — 2.4 millions of DNA base pairs; or 0.1 percent of the human genome. Its only known function is to inhibit muscular dystrophy; and such a large gene is highly susceptible to harmful mutations.

- The prevalence of congenital diseases and genetic disorders such as Huntington's Disease, and the inability for DNA to self-repair, leading to poor genetic performance, hereditable malformation and eventual death.

- The common malformation of the human spinal column, leading to scoliosis, sciatica and congenital misalignment of the vertebrae (vertebral subluxation)

- Photosynthetic plants that reflect green light, even though the sun's peak output is at this wavelength. A more optimal system of photosynthesis would use the entire solar spectrum, thus resulting in black plants.

- The existence of the pharynx, a passage used for both ingestion and respiration, with the consequent drastic increase in the risk of choking.

- The structure of humans' (as well as all mammals') eyes. The retina is 'inside out'. The nerves and blood vessels lie on the *surface* of the retina instead of behind it as is the case in many invertebrate species. This arrangement forces a number of complex adaptations and gives mammals a blind spot. (See Evolution of the eye). Six muscles move the eye when three would suffice.

- Crowded teeth and poor sinus drainage, as human faces are significantly flatter than those of other primates and humans share the same tooth set. This results in a number of problems, most notably with wisdom teeth.

- Almost all animals and plants synthesize their own vitamin C, but humans cannot because the gene for this enzyme is defective (Pseudogene ☒GULO). Lack of vitamin C results in scurvy and eventually death. Defective vitamin synthesis pathways are a hallmark of "higher" animals — of which many are predators — because the prey accumulates vitamins that stems either from the eaten plants or are self-synthesized in the captured individual. Thus, higher animals are mostly unable to return to a purely "vegetarian" lifestyle; while conservation of such pathway genes is of no apparent cost to the animal.

- If rodents do not regularly wear down their incisors, which self-sharpen by chewing on wood, such upper and bottom teeth curl toward the rodents' skull and drill into their brain.

- Other critics argue that if these design failures are the deliberate products of an intelligent designer, then the designer must be either inept or sadistic. Or possibly there was a committee of designers, as in the old joke that "a camel is a horse designed by a committee".

Natural selection is expected to push fitness to a peak, but that peak often is not the highest.

"Poor design" is consistent with the predictions of the scientific theory of evolution by means of natural selection. This predicts that features that were evolved for certain uses, are then reused or co-opted for different uses, or abandoned altogether; and that suboptimal state is due to the inability of the hereditary mechanism to eliminate the particular vestiges of the evolutionary process.

In terms of a fitness landscape, natural selection will always push "up the hill", but a species cannot normally get from a lower peak to a higher peak without first going through a valley, a method known in computer science circles as "naïve hill climber".

The argument from poor design is one of the arguments that was used by Charles Darwin; modern proponents have included Stephen Jay Gould and Richard Dawkins. They argue that such features can be explained as a consequence of the gradual, cumulative nature of the evolutionary process. Theistic Evolutionists generally reject the argument from design, but do not necessarily reject the existence of God.

Intelligent Design of Tumors

Defenders of Intelligent Design, other forms of creationism, and the "argument to design" (as a proof of the existence of God) commonly point to the complexity of life as evidence that it didn't develop by natural means alone. According to them, anything with such complexity as the eye couldn't have worked if only half-way developed, therefore it had to be "created" fully-formed. Curiously, they never cite as an example of such complexity the basic tumor. Why is that?

Carl Zimmer writes:

Cancer cells grow at astonishing speeds, defying the many safeguards that are supposed to keep cells obedient to the needs of the body. And in order to grow so fast, they have to get lots of fuel, which they do by diverting blood vessels towards themselves and nurturing new vessels to sprout from old ones. They fight off a hostile immune system with all manner of camouflage and manipulation, and many cancer cells have strategies for fending off toxic chemotherapy drugs. When tumors get mature, they can send off colonizers to invade new tissues. These pioneers can release enzymes that dissolve collagen blocking their path; when they reach a new organ, they can secrete other proteins that let them anchor themselves to neighboring cells. While oncologists are a long way from fully understanding how cancer cells manage all this, it's now clear that the answer can be found in their genes. Their genes differ from those of normal cells in many big and little ways, working together to produce a unique network of proteins exquisitely suited for the tumor's success.

All in all, it sounds like a splendid example of complexity produced by design. The chances that random natural processes could have altered all the genes required for a cell function as a cancer cell must be tiny--too tiny, some might argue, to be believed. And surely the only way that a cell could become cancerous naturally would be for all the genes to change at once. After all, what good is it for a cell to be able to increase blood flow towards itself if it can't grow quickly? Getting so many genes to change at once makes an impossibility an absurdity. By this sort of reasoning, you'd conclude that cancer is the work of a supernatural designer.

This matters because creationists want to be treated like scientists, but creationist writers have never offered an explanation for tumor - evolutionary biologists, however, have done just that:

Martin Nowak of Harvard University ... and his co-authors argue that you can't understand cancer unless you recognize it as an evolutionary process. As cells divide, they mutate on rare occasion (roughly one out every 10 billion cell divisions). Most of these mutations will kill a cell, so that the genomes in most of the new cells in your body are identical to the old ones. But a few of these mutations can allow a cell to divide more quickly than its neighbors. They begin to outcompete the ordinary cells for resources, becoming even more common. These cancer cells continue to mutate, so that there's lots of genetic variation in a growing tumor. In a few cases, these mutations make cells better adapted to a cancerous existence, and the offspring of these cells come to dominate the tumor. As the tumor matures, new kinds mutations may be favored--ones that let it metastatize, for example, or withstand the abuse of chemotherapy.

I'm sure that tumors aren't cited as examples of "intelligent" design because cancer doesn't sound very "intelligent" - after all, we're not *really* talking about some vague "designer," we're talking about **God**. Until defenders of creationism and Intelligent Design can incorporate things like tumors into their "science," they don't really have much to offer either the scientific or the education community.

Collisions of Stars

Background

Like human beings, stars evolve and change their appearance substantially during their lifetime. They are born from the collapse of huge galactic gas clouds and contract under the influence of gravity until they become hot enough for nuclear reactions to ignite their interior. Stars spend most of their life burning their nuclear fuel quietly. A good example of a typical star, a so-called **Main Sequence Star**, is our sun that is currently burning hydrogen into helium. Once their nuclear fuel is exhausted, stars die. Depending on their mass they either blow up tremendously first, then eject their envelopes and finally leave behind a cold and very dense remnant, a so-called **White Dwarf**, or they end their lives in a spectacular explosion, a **Supernova**. Such a Supernova leaves behind the most exotic objects in the universe: either a **Neutron Star**, something like a giant atomic nucleus of about 10 km radius, or a **Black Hole**.

Collisions between stellar objects do occur quite frequently in the universe, either in places with a high density of stars like in a **Globular Cluster** or in binary systems, that emit according to Einstein's Theory of General Relativity **Gravitational Waves** and finally coalesce. **Collisions** between a Black Hole of a few solar masses and stars like our sun occur quite frequently in Globular Clusters.

The Five Worst Extinctions in Earth's History

Here are details of the five worst mass extinctions in Earths history and their possible causes, according to paleobiologist Doug Erwin of the Smithsonian Institutions National Museum of Natural History. Erwin said estimates of extinction rates are from the late John J. Sepkoski at the University of Chicago:

Cretaceous-Tertiary extinction, about 65 million years ago, probably caused or aggravated by impact of several-mile-wide asteroid that created the Chicxulub crater now hidden on the Yucatan Peninsula and beneath the Gulf of Mexico. Some argue for other causes, including gradual climate change or flood-like volcanic eruptions of basalt lava from Indias Deccan Traps. The extinction killed 16 percent of marine families, 47 percent of marine genera (the classification above species) and 18 percent of land vertebrate families, including the dinosaurs.

End Triassic extinction, roughly 199 million to 214 million years ago, most likely caused by massive floods of lava erupting from the central Atlantic magmatic province -- an event that triggered the opening of the Atlantic Ocean. The volcanism may have led to deadly global warming. Rocks from the eruptions now are found in the eastern United States, eastern Brazil, North Africa and Spain. The death toll: 22 percent of marine families, 52 percent of marine genera. Vertebrate deaths are unclear.

Permian-Triassic extinction, about 251 million years ago. Many scientists suspect a comet or asteroid impact, although direct evidence has not been found. Others believe the cause was flood volcanism from the Siberian Traps and related loss of oxygen in the seas. Still others believe the impact triggered the volcanism and also may have done so during the Cretaceous-Tertiary extinction. The Permian-Triassic catastrophe was Earths worst mass extinction, killing 95 percent of all species, 53 percent of marine families, 84 percent of marine genera and an estimated 70 percent of land species such as plants, insects and vertebrate animals.

Late Devonian extinction, about 364 million years ago, cause unknown. It killed 22 percent of marine families and 57 percent of marine genera. Erwin said little is known about land organisms at the time.

Ordovician-Silurian extinction, about 439 million years ago, caused by a drop in sea levels as glaciers formed, then by rising sea levels as glaciers melted. The toll: 25 percent of marine families and 60 percent of marine genera.

Throughout the history of life, extinction has been a natural and inherent part of the Earth's ever-fluctuating biodiversity. Environmental changes and interspecific competition necessarily produce "unsuccessful" organisms, species not well suited for survival in their ecological niche. The result of such a condition is either evolutionary adaptation or extinction. In the latter case, an evolutionary line is ended, and, as is often the case, new lines emerge to fill the vacated niche space. Thus, life forms appear and disappear and biodiversity is maintained through a complex balance of speciation and extinction.

The only explanation that has been posed, and, perhaps, the only explanation that *can* be posed for periodicity is that mass extinctions have and ultimately extraterrestrial cause. Astronomical forces seem to be the only ones to act with sufficient precision to explain the rather exact schedule of mass extinction events under the periodic theory. The regular timing of the cosmos could possibly inflict mass extinction on the Earth via climatic changes or even regular bolide impact events. In the case of the latter, it has been postulated that periodic disturbances in the comet cloud, perhaps caused by the passage of our solar system through the outer reaches of the Milky Way or by a hypothetical dark star or tenth planet, send comets hurtling toward Earth at regular intervals.

Mass extinctions are often signifiers of large-scale climatic, environmental changes, often global in nature. Many organisms are naturally unfit for these changes and are lost, while some adapt to the changed environment. Mass extinctions often leave behind a great deal of unused niche space and the opportunity for adaptive radiation is great. Trends will of course appear as the fossil record is viewed over the long term. Some taxa will survive well through the traumatic mass extinction events while other forms will be repeatedly lost. Specific examples will be examined later in respect to each major extinction event. One of the most important aspects of the macroevolutionary record is the profound differences found between what adaptations are helpful in regard to "everyday" survival and survival in the midst of a mass extinction event. In this way, these events significantly shape what lines persist and what lines become evolutionary dead ends.

References

Donovan, Stephen K. *Mass Extinctions*. New York: Columbia University Press, 1989.

Ridley, Marc. *Evolution*. Cambridge, Massachusetts: Blackwell Science, 1996.

Stanley, Steven M. *Extinction*. New York: Scientific American Books, 1987.

Now does any of the foregoing support belief in an almighty, omnipotent, omniscient, omni benevolent deity who created everything directly and for a specific purpose and who "numbers the hairs on our heads and notices even the fall of a sparrow"? Of course fundamentalists would argue that the reason for planetary calamities and imperfections in animal and human life forms is all due to Original Sin. However I don't believe that Adam and Eve existed when all of the aforementioned global calamities and extinctions of life took place some 65 million plus years ago.

CHAPTER 8
BLATANT CONTRADICTIONS

Not only is the Genesis account an unsatisfactory explanation of how our world situation came to be the way it is, but theologically, it, and large portions of the Old Testament are a blatant contradiction of other portions of the Bible and especially the New Testament. I John 4:8 tells us that "God is love" or in essense that God is the personification of love. The Apostle Paul in I Cor 13:4-7 defines Love in these words:

" Love is patient, love is kind. It does not envy, it does not boast, it is not proud. It is not rude, it is not self-seeking, it is not easily angered, it keeps no record of wrongs. Love does not delight in evil but rejoices with the truth. It always protects, always trusts, always hopes, always perseveres." (New International Version UK).

Even the Old Testament in Proverbs 10:12 tells us that "Hatred stirs up strife, but love covers all sins." And yet Lev 17:11 tells us that "it is the blood that makes atonement for the soul." Likewise in the New Testament Heb 9:22 tells us that "without the shedding of blood thee is no remission of sins." So which is it ?

If love "covers all sins" rather than blood, then why did Yahweh require thousands of animal sacrifices yearly and why did God The Father of the New Testament require a human sacrifice in the form of Jesus in order to forgive the sins of Adam and Eve and mankind? Why could he not have just forgiven Adam and Eve ? And why condemn the children for the sins of their parents? And if according to the Apostle Paul, Love " does not envy" and "is not easily angered" and "keeps no record of wrongs", then why did Yahweh say: "For I the Lord your God am a jealous God visiting the iniquity of the fathers upon the children to the third and fourth generation of those who hate me." ? Exodus 20:5. Jesus in Matt 18:22 tells us that we should forgive ou brothers up to seventy seven times, yet his Father could not forgive Adam and Eve once ?

These are not trivial contradictions. They call into question the entire nature of God. Is He a God of Love and a God worthy of devotion or is He a tyrant who gives us free will on the one hand while at the same time warning us that the penalty for exercising that free will is death and destruction ? Can God just forgive and forget as his son instructs us to do? Or can He only be appeased by blood? And yet these teachings are the basis for at least three of the world's major religions.

Is it any wonder that these three religions have never been able to effectively co-exist and have in fact been the main source of much of the suffering and strife experienced by millions over the last two thousand years. Is it any wonder that these kind of teachings continue to inspire and be the basis for terrorism and war down to this very day; each of them looking upon the others as infidels ? Like Father, like son. They are incapable of forgiving and forgetting; incapable of compromise; they are only appeased by revenge and the outpouring of blood.

And yet while inseparably linked by their concepts of "The Fall of Man", each of these religions claims to be distinctly and uniquely the "Chosen People" to the detriment of the other two. And of course all three see other religions which do not share their commonality as definitely beyond the pale, they see those worshipers as pagans and infidels. Judaism, Islam and Christianity all claim to be based on a unique revelation direct from God and that they are distinct from other religions in their rites and practices which God imparted directly to them.

The Jews and Moslems claim circumcision as a unique rite imparted to them by God through the patriarch Abraham to set them aside as holy and consecrated to God and unique from all other men. Yet archeological findings reveal that circumcision was practiced by the priestly classes of Egypt and by African tribes way before the days of Abraham. The Jews took great pride in their Ark of the Covenant, the small wooden shrine which was carried with poles by the Levite priests and which contained the tablets of the Ten Commandments. But arks of similar design containing statues of deities were carried in procession by the Egyptian priests long before Aaron fashioned the Ark of the Covenant. Likewise the rituals surrounding animal sacrifice and purification practiced by the Israelites were not all that different from those of their surrounding neighbors, the Egyptians and Babylonians.

The Jews claim to be the first practitioners of monotheism, but that is also untrue as we know that monotheism was first practiced in Egypt under the reign of Pharoah Amenhotep IV (Akhenaten) and his Queen, Nefertiti long before Moses or the captivity of the Jews in Egypt. Many of the psalms written by Akhenaten centuries before the Exodus are identical to psalms purportedly written by King David at a time much later in history. The Epoch of

Gilgamesh, the Babylonian account of the Great Flood predates the Genesis account of the Flood of Noah by many centuries and those writings exist in stone and can be dated as do the ancient Egyptian texts and are far earlier than any of the Biblical writings, existing copies of which only date back to the period of the Babylonian captivity of the Jews in the sixth century BC. So one can be justified in wondering, is Judaism the result of a direct revelation of God to the Hebrew patriarchs or merely a creation of a much later date by Jewish scribes and scholars during their captivity in Babylon and based partly on the monotheism of Akhenaten and the rituals and ancient writings of their captors, the Babylonians? I find it odd that the Israelites, who felt justified in practicing genocide in the name of God on their neighbors, the Canaanites and Phillistines due to those people's practice of child sacrifice, include in their scriptures a laudatory account of their patriarch Abraham in the act of sacrificing his own son Isaac, who but for the grace of God would have ended up as a burnt offering. See Genesis 22:1-12.

Likewise one can ask the question, is Christianity so unique as to be clearly the result of a direct revelation of God through his son, Jesus or is it merely a compilation of faiths extant during the first century in Israel and other areas along the trade routes which connected to Israel? No one is saying here that Jesus of Nazareth did not exist, there is historical evidence that he did. But were his teachings so unique and revolutionary or were many of them in existance before and during his time on earth? We know for a fact that the Essene community which existed in the land of Israel prior to and during the preaching tours of Jesus taught basically the same concepts of purity, piety, forgiveness and brotherhood that Jesus taught because we now have their writings which were discovered in the 1950's. Other facets of what make up our current belief system of who Jesus was, but which he did not clearly state himself during his lifetime and were attributed to him after his death may well have come from other earlier sources.

The Vatican was built upon the grounds previously devoted to the worship of Mithra, one of the greatest gods of ancient Persia. His worship began around 600BC and flourished until the 2nd century AD throughout a large portion of the ancient world. The entire Messianic idea originated in ancient Persia and this is where the Jewish and Christian concepts of a Savior came from. Mithra was considered a great traveling teacher and master. He had twelve companions and performed miracles. He was called "the good shepherd", "the way, the truth and the light"'"redeemer", "savior" and was considered the mediator between God and men. He was identified with both the lion and the lamb, as was the "Lion of the Tribe of Judah" and the "Lamb of God, Jesus. His ceremonies included a sort of baptism to remove sins, anointing, and a sacred meal of bread and water, while a consecrated wine, believed to possess wonderful power played a prominent part according to the International Encyclopedia.

Profesor Franz Cumont of the University of Ghent wrote that the worshippers of Mithra "held Sunday sacred, and celebrated the birth of the Sun on the 25th of December." He added that they believed in a Heaven inhabited by beatified ones and a Hell peopled by demons. They believed in the immortality of the soul, in a last judgement and in a resurrection of the dead and upon a final conflagration of the universe. ("The Mysteries of Mithras", pp 190,191).

In the catacombs at Rome was preserved a relic of the old Mithraic worship. It was a picture of the infant Mithra seated in the lap of his virgin mother, while on their knees before him were Persian Magi adoring him and offering gifts. This is not unlike carvings in the Temple of Karnak in Egypt picturing the young infant god Horus, seated on the lap of his virgin mother Isis. Mithra was purportedly buried in a tomb and after three days he rose again. His resurrection was celebrated yearly. Mithra had his principal festival on what was later to become Easter, at which time he was resurrected. His sacred day was Sunday, "the Lord's Day" and his religion had a Eucharist or "Lord's Supper".

Now is this all merely coincidence or are we seeing here a pattern used by the Church long after the death of Jesus and his apostles for the metamorphosis of Jesus from merely an enlightened itinerant teacher to the Son of God? Let's face it, most of what is taught by the institutional Church of today, far more than what can be found in the gospels, was assembled at the time of Constantine in the fourth century AD including the present Bible canon or list of which sacred writings, of which there were thousands, were to be considered what we now call the Bible. Out of those thousands of writings only 66 were selected to make up the Bible. Is it possible that Emperor Constantine, who saw an opportunity to unite his vast empire through creating a powerful State Religion, engineered which writings and teachings would be acceptable and which would not ? which writings would support the divinity of Jesus and which would not ? And we must not forget St. Helena, the mother of Constantine who was the real star of the time. She went on a pilgrimage to Jerusalem and came back with enough pieces of the True Cross and enough True Nails to build a small condominium complex. She also found Mary's kitchen table, the Veil of Veronica and the original manger from Bethlehem after all of those items had been lost for three hundred years. She even located all of the original holy sites like the room where Jesus ate the Last Supper, even though Jerusalem had been burnt and sacked by the Romans some three hundred years earlier and there had undoubtedly been some reconstruction during the intervening years.

And is this also why the vast numbers of scrolls which were discovered in the mid 20th century, the Dead Sea Scrolls and the Nag Hamadi writings have only recently been translated and released to the general public more than fifty years after their discovery? Were Israeli and Christian authorities doing all within their power to keep those writings from the general public out of fear that they might somehow contradict rabbinical and Church teachings?

CHAPTER 9
THE CHRISTIAN
RIGHT IS WRONG

I give special attention to Steve Allen's book, "Steve Allen on the Bible, Religion and Morality", primarily because it was written with the same intent as mine. Mr. Allen saw the evergrowing specter of fundamentalism as very dangerous; both to democracy and to intellectual freedom and quality education. In the introduction to his book on page 29 he states:

"Many of our nation's fundamentalist Christians, who, by and large, believe that the Bible is reliable as history and science, are no longer content with teaching their freely gathered congregations their theology and publishing their views, which they have every right to do. But just as my freedom to swing my arms about stops at the point of another's nose, so the freedom to preach unscientific superstition deserves to be limited when it attempts to IMPOSE ITSELF on those who have not requested it and who many, in fact, hold contrary religious opinions, or none at all".

Mr. Allen goes on to say: "When, for example, America's fundamentalist believers in the inerrancy of the Bible insist on having historical and scientific errors taught in our nation's public schools, then they must be opposed by all legal means." I agree with Steve Allen 100 %. I saw a special on public television not more than a few months ago perhaps in March of 2005 which exposed how fundamentalists are the ones now censoring textbooks for use in our public schools; deleting any mention of evolution; homosexuality; birth control or anything that does not agree with THEIR thinking. When fundamentalists decide to rewrite history and textbooks to fit their agenda, as Mr. Allen says; they need to be opposed by all legal means. And when they preach hatred of diversity from their pulpits which directly leads to either the suicide or the murder of a gay man or woman; they need to be opposed by all legal means.

I don't believe that either Steve Allen or I could be considered anti-religious, but when religion becomes destructive of our God-given freedoms, then something has to be done about it. And we are among good company. The Christian Right would like you to believe that this nation was founded by devout Christians and that all of our law and government is based upon Christianity when nothing could be further from the truth.

I would like to present for your examination a number of statements made by one of our revered founding fathers, Thomas Jefferson, and other renowned thinkers of the period. I think that their words are just as appropriate now as when they were first penned two hundred years ago.

THOMAS JEFFERSON ON SEPARATION OF CHURCH AND STATE

"The clergy, by getting themselves established by law and ingrafted into the machine of government, have been a very formidable engine against the civil and religious rights of man" (Letter to J. Moor, 1800).

"The clergy...believe that any portion of power confided to me [as President] will be exerted in opposition to their schemes. And they believe rightly: for I have sworn upon the altar of God, eternal hostility against every form of tyranny over the mind of man. But this is all they have to fear from me: and enough, too, in their opinion" (Letter to Benjamin Rush, 1800).

"History, I believe, furnishes no example of a priest-ridden people maintaining a free civil government. This marks the lowest grade of ignorance of which their civil as well as religious leaders will always avail themselves for their own purposes" (Letter to von Humboldt, 1813).

"In every country and in every age, the priest has been hostile to liberty. He is always in alliance with the despot, abetting his abuses in return for protection to his own" (Letter to H. Spafford, 1814).

"Nature has constituted utility to man the standard and test of virtue. Men living in different countries, under different circumstances, different habits and regimens, may have different utilities; the same act, therefore, may be useful and consequently virtuous in one country which is injurious and vicious in another differently circumstanced" (Letter to Thomas Law, 1814).

"As the circumstances and opinions of different societies vary, so the acts which may do them right or wrong must vary also, for virtue does not consist in the act we do but in the end it is to effect. If it is to effect the happiness of him to whom it is directed, it is virtuous; while in a society under different circumstances and opinions the same act might produce pain and would be vicious. The essence of virtue is in doing good to others, while what is good may be one thing in one society and its contrary in another…" (Letter to John Adams, 1816).

"Reading, reflection and time have convinced me that the interests of society require the observation of those moral precepts only in which all religions agree (for all forbid us to steal, murder, plunder, or bear false witness), and that we should not intermeddle with the particular dogmas in which all religions differ, and which are totally unconnected with morality" (Letter to J. Fishback, 1809).

"Are we to have a censor whose imprimatur shall say what books may be sold, and what we may buy? And who is thus to dogmatize religious opinions for our citizens? Whose foot is to be the measure to which ours are all to be cut or stretched? Is a priest to be our inquisitor, or shall a layman, simple as ourselves, set up his reason as the rule of what we are to read, and what we must disbelieve? "(Thomas Jefferson, in a letter to N. G. Dufief, Philadelphia bookseller, 1814.

"The Christian god can easily be pictured as virtually the same god as the many ancient gods of past civilizations. The Christian god is a three headed monster; cruel, vengeful and capricious. If one wishes to know more of this raging, three headed beast-like god, one only needs to look at the caliber of people who say they serve him. They are always of two classes; fools and hypocrites. To compel a man to furnish contributions of money for the propagation of opinions which he disbelieves and abhors is sinful and tyrannical."

-Thomas Jefferson

"Our rulers can have no authority over such natural rights, only as we have submitted to them. The rights of conscience we never submitted, we could not submit. We are answerable for them to our God. The legitimate powers of government extend to such acts only as are injurious to others." (Notes on Virginia, 1785).

Now these last words of Jefferson are especially timely to me because if, as Jefferson said: "The legitimate powers of government extend to such acts only as are injurious to others." Then how, may I ask is my serving my country in the military injurious to others? And if the legitimate powers of government extend to such acts only as are injurious to others, then how am I injuring others by marrying the person that I love? And if the legitimate powers of government extend to such acts only as are injurious to others, then how am I injuring others by adopting a child that no one else wants?

Other great Revolutionary War period thinkers had similar feelings on separation of Church and State such as Thomas Paine:

Thomas Paine

(1737-1809; author of Common Sense; key American patriotic writer)

"As to religion, I hold it to be the indispensable duty of government to protect all conscientious protesters thereof, and I know of no other business government has to do therewith." (Thomas Paine, Common Sense, 1776. As quoted by Leo Pfeffer, "The Establishment Clause: The Never-Ending Conflict," in Ronald C. White and Albright G. Zimmerman, An Unsettled Arena: Religion and the Bill of Rights, Grand Rapids, Michigan: William B. Eerdmans Publishing Company, 1990, p. 72.)

"Persecution is not an original feature in any religion; but it is always the strongly-marked feature of all law-religions, or religions established by law. Take away the law-establishment, and every religion re-assumes its original benignity." (Thomas Paine, The Rights of Man, 1791-1792. From Gorton Carruth and Eugene Ehrlich, eds., The Harper Book of American Quotations, New York: Harper & Row, 1988, pp. 499-500.)

"Toleration is not the opposite of intolerance but the counterfeit of it. Both are despotisms: the one assumes to itself the right of withholding liberty of conscience, the other of granting it." (Thomas Paine, The Rights of Man, p. 58. As quoted by John M. Swomley, Religious Liberty and the Secular State: The Constitutional Context, Buffalo, NY: Prometheus Books, 1987, p. 7. Swomley added, "Toleration is a concession; religious liberty is a right.")

"All national institutions of churches, whether Jewish, Christian or Turkish [Muslim], appear to me no other than human inventions, set up to terrify and enslave mankind, and monopolize power and profit. I do not mean by this declaration to condemn those who believe otherwise; they have the same right to their belief as I have to mine. But it is necessary to the happiness of man that he be mentally faithful to himself. Infidelity does not consist in believing, or in disbelieving; it consists in professing to believe what he does not believe. It is impossible to calculate the moral mischief, if I may so express it, that mental lying has produced in society. When a man has so far corrupted and prostituted the chastity of his mind as to subscribe his professional belief to things he does not believe, he has prepared himself for the commission of every other crime. He takes up the profession of a priest for the sake of gain, and in order to qualify himself for that trade he begins with a perjury. Can we conceive anything more destructive to morality than this?" (Thomas Paine, The Age of Reason, 1794-1795. From Paul Blanshard, ed., Classics of Free Thought, Buffalo, New York: Prometheus Books, 1977, pp. 134-135.)

"Whenever we read the obscene stories, the voluptuous debaucheries, the cruel and torturous executions, the unrelenting vindictiveness, with which more than half the Bible is filled, it would be more consistent that we called it the word of a demon, than the word of God. It is a history of wickedness, that has served to corrupt and brutalize mankind." (Thomas Paine, The Age of Reason, 1794-1795. From Gorton Carruth and Eugene Ehrlich, eds., The Harper Book of American Quotations, New York: Harper & Row, 1988, p. 494.)

"Take away from Genesis the belief that Moses was the author, on which only the strange belief that it is the word of God has stood, and there remains nothing of Genesis but an anonymous book of stories, fables, and traditionary or invented absurdities, or of downright lies." (Thomas Paine, The Age of Reason, 1794-1795. From Gorton Carruth and Eugene Ehrlich, eds., The Harper Book of American Quotations, New York: Harper & Row, 1988, p. 494.)

"The most detestable wickedness, the most horrid cruelties, and the greatest miseries that have afflicted the human race have had their origin in this thing called revelation, or revealed religion. It has been the most dishonorable belief against the character of the Divinity, the most destructive to morality and the peace and happiness of man, that ever was propagated since man began to exist." (Thomas Paine, The Age of Reason, 1794-1795. From Gorton Carruth and Eugene Ehrlich, eds., The Harper Book of American Quotations, New York: Harper & Row, 1988, p. 494.)

The Adulterous Connection Of Church And State. (Thomas Paine, The Age of Reason, 1794-1795. From Gorton Carruth and Eugene Ehrlich, eds., The Harper Book of American Quotations, New York: Harper & Row, 1988, p. 500.)

Despite his pre-eminent role in early American deism, [Elihu] Palmer (1764-1806) is scarcely remembered today. He has been overshadowed by his friend and associate Thomas Paine (1737-1809 [Elihu] Palmer's first major public address after moving to New York was given on Christmas Day 1796. He came out swinging, rejecting the divinity of Jesus as a "very singular and unnatural" event, and condemning as both immoral and incomprehensible the doctrines of original sin, atonement, faith and regeneration. The lecture was well attended and widely read when published. Reaction from the Christian establishment was swift and predictably hostile, but something in Palmer's message caught on with many of his auditors and readers. Invitations to speak poured in from Baltimore, Newburgh and even Philadelphia. The following is part of the text of his public address:

"Twelve centuries of moral and political darkness, in which Europe was involved, had nearly completed the destruction of human dignity, and every thing valuable or ornamental in the character of man. During this long and doleful night of ignorance, slavery, and superstition, Christianity reigned triumphant; its doctrines and divinity were not called in question. The power of the Pope, the Clergy, and the Church were omnipotent; nothing could restrain their frenzy, nothing could control the cruelty of their fanaticism; with mad enthusiasm they set on foot the most bloody and terrific crusades, the object of which was to recover the Holy Land. Seven hundred thousand men are said to have perished in the two first expeditions, which had been thus commenced and carried on by the pious zeal of the Christian church, and in the total amount, several millions were found numbered with the dead: the awful effects of religious fanaticism presuming upon the aid of heaven. It was then that man lost all his dignity, and sunk to the condition of a brute; it was then that intellect received a deadly blow, from which it did not recover until the fifteenth century.

From that time to the present, the progress of knowledge has been constantly accelerated; independence of mind has been asserted, and opposing obstacles have been gradually diminished. The church has resigned a part of her power, the better to retain the remainder; civil tyranny has been shaken to its center in both hemispheres; the malignity of superstition is abating, and every species of quackery, imposture, and imposition, are yielding to the light and power of science. An awful contest has commenced, which must terminate in the destruction of thrones and civil despotism; in the annihilation of ecclesiastical pride and domination....

Church and State may unite to form an insurmountable barrier against the extension of thought, the moral progress of nations, and the felicity of nature; but let it be recollected, that the guarantee for moral and political emancipation is already deposited in the archives of every school and college, and in the mind of every cultivated and enlightened man of all countries. It will henceforth be a vain and fruitless attempt to reduce the earth to that state of slavery of which the history of former ages has furnished such an awful picture. The crimes of ecclesiastical despots are still corroding upon the very vitals of human society; the severities of civil power will never be forgotten". –Elihu Palmer

(Elihu Palmer, Principles of Nature; or, a Development of the Moral Causes of Happiness and Misery Among the Human Species, 3rd ed., 1806; as reprinted in Kerry S. Walters, Elihu Palmer's ÔPrinciples of Nature': Text and Commentary, Wolfeboro, N. H.: Longwood Academic, 1990, pp. 82-83.)

Now, some two hundred years later, freedom, democracy, and education in this country are once more threatened by the same forces of ecclesiastical bigotry and fanaticism which existed then in Elihu Palmer's day, only now they have built up an extensive power base of money and all of the political power which money can buy to further their agenda. They have the ability to manipulate the markets; create shortages; deprive us of our pensions; destroy the economies of nations in one geographical area so that they may boost the economies in another area where THEY stand to benefit the most. It's all within their grasp and there is absolutely no one, Republican or Democrat that seems to be willing to stand up against them. Of course not; it would be political suicide.

Evangelists and Jehovah's Witnesses have been harping for almost one hundred years now about the "Coming End of the World" and the return of the Messiah. They have been pointing to all of the world plagues listed in the Book of Revelation as "signs of the times". What they haven't told you is that they are meticulously and methodically creating these plagues by manipulating world economics and world politics so as to make the prophesies appear to be coming true. And you can rest assured that this Unholy Alliance; this new Trinity of World Commerce, Religion and Politics will not stop until they have dragged us all into an Armageddon of their own creation. In their lame minds, they believe that the Messiah can't come until the Jewish Temple is rebuilt on the Temple Mount in Jerusalem. Of course that is at present a holy site of Islam; the Dome of the Rock. The Dome's existence prevents the Jewish Temple from being rebuilt on that site so what to do? Well, the plan of action is undoubtedly to stir up as much hostility and chaos in that area as possible; create the conditions necessary to institute a "holy war" between the West and Islam if necessary. And if the Dome of the Rock happens to gets accidentally destroyed in the process, too bad.

You see, in the past, the enemy was always identifiable, and a nation would have to limit its assaults to that enemy nation alone; there would be no excuse for going beyond that. But today's world politicians and strategists are sly. By declaring war on a nebulous enemy; "War on Terror", they can instantaneously declare any nation or people or even individuals as terrorists and attack them preemptively with no explanation necessary. Under the "Patriot Act" even you and I can be carted off without any explanation or any recourse to an attorney or defense and without even any explanation as to what we are being charged with, in total violation of the U.S. Constitution. Being in a state of perpetual war allows the President of the United States Presidential Imperatives and the right to over ride the Constitution; to declare Marshal Law if necessary and institute a virtual Police State.

I know that by now you must think that I am some kind of a conspiracy nut, but I am by no means the only one concerned about this unholy alliance between Church and State and along with that, the looming threat of world domination by world trade organizations that will determine your and my fates. So you see, I'm not just some dizzy little queen who's only concern in life is gay marriage rights; not by any stretch of the imagination. I am concerned for all of us because so long as anyone on this earth is exploited and disenfranchised, then none of us is truly free because it can happen to us too and will if the present patterns are not changed.

Just to show you how far Christian Fundamentalists will go to advance their theories and attempt to give so called scientific proof for their beliefs, I present you with the following ridiculous assertions that are made on a website entitled "Amazing Bible Discoveries by Dr. T.V. Oommen". It can be found at: <www.biblediscoveries.com/arkofcovenant.html>.

In the article, Dr. Oommen contends that a Christian archeologist, a Ron Wyatt of Tennessee, discovered the Ark of the Covenant back in the early 1980's in Jerusalem, buried in a cave which he believes was located directly under the site of the crucifixion of Jesus. The article claims that four angels directed Ron Wyatt to the site and allowed him to examine the contents of the Ark, revealing the original Ten Commandments and other related items. He further contends that God miraculously arranged for the site of the crucifixion to be directly above where the Ark was buried for a special reason. You see in ancient times, the High Priest would go into the Holy of Holies in Jerusalem and sprinkle the blood of sacrificial lambs on the lid of the Ark of the Covenant as a special sacrifice to God for atonement of the people of Israel. Both Dr. Oommen and Ron Wyatt contend that there was a hole in the bedrock where the cross was placed with a shaft leading down into the cave directly above where the Ark of the Covenant was hidden and that God arranged for the crucifixion to take place there so that the blood of Jesus would drain down that shaft onto the lid of the Ark of the Covenant, thereby making atonement for all of mankind. Ron Wyatt contends that he took samples of the dried blood on the lid of the Ark of the Covenant and had them analyzed and here are the results:

"Now I can tell you the rest of the story. When Ron found his way to the upper part of the cave in which the Ark is kept, he noticed dried blood above through a crack. This was verified to be the same crack he had seen on the bedrock. Then he found that the stone box in which the Ark was resting had its lid broken into two and separated. The implication is obvious. When the soldier pierced Jesus' side with a spear, his blood flowed down through the crack and drops of blood fell on the Mercy Seat! Later on, when Ron was able to go into the cave and inspect the Ark, he found dried blood on the Mercy Seat, with animal blood on one side and human blood on the other. This was verified by blood analysis on samples he brought back to America. In a two page leaflet Ron issued in mid-1993 and on his video, *'Presentation of Discoveries'*, based on a live presentation a few years back, the blood work results are mentioned. Essentially, it was human blood of a male; there were only 24 chromosomes in the white blood cells (the red cells do not have genetic information). What this implies is that Christ had only half the number of chromosomes normal humans have, half of 46, plus a Y chromosome which had to come from a non-human source, and that source has to be the Heavenly Father! It is possible that further blood analysis will be done in the future, but Ron would prefer the scientific world confirm that the sample he brought is from the Ark, and presently there is no way to do that. So any further blood analysis results would be subject to the same kind of skepticism that Ron's critics have raised."

Now scientifically, this is absolutely ridiculous and beyond any possibility and I now present you with the explanations of genuine scientists, not Christian scientists.

The condition of a living organism having only half the number of chromosomes that it is supposed to have is called "haploid" and this is what scientists say regarding this condition:

"A cell is haploid if it contains exactly half of a species' typical full set of genetic material. Haploid cells are often used in sexual reproduction.

Most cells within a human (and other animals) are diploid, which means they have two copies of each chromosome. Sex cells, however, are haploid – they have only one copy of each chromosome. This is not exactly the same as monoploidy; rather, one of two differing copies of the same chromosome is in the haploid set. A monoploid cell, however, is likely to be identical to the cell it was copied from.

In animals, haploid cells are found only in sex cells. In fungus and certain algae, however, haploid cells are the norm. Male bees, wasps, and ants are haploid because of the way they develop: from unfertilized, haploid eggs.

Spontaneously and induced haploidy were reported in several animal species, including Drosophila, salamander, frog, mouse,chicken et al. Usually haploidy in animals produces physiologically abnormal individuals that die during embryogenesis.

Haploid development is a normal part of the life cycle for some animals, but it has not been observed in mammals. Studies in mice have revealed that the preimplantation developmental potential of haploid embryos is significantly impaired relative to diploid embryos. The reasons for the severely limited developmental potential of haploid embryos in mammals have not been discerned. Development of haploid rabbit parthenogenones is also inefficient. This indicates that the mammalian genome, in contrast to genomes of other organisms, is subject to gene regulatory mechanisms that disrupt the ability of a haploid genome to support early development."

So based on Dr. Oommen and Ron Wyatt's theory that the blood of Jesus had only 24 chromosomes, what does this make Jesus? The "Rabbit of God that taketh away the sins of the world" or the "Chicken of God" or worse yet, the "Fungus of God"? It all just goes to show how far Fundamentalists will go to deliberately lie to their children and to the public in general in order to give some kind of scientific basis to their irrational and historically and scientifically undefendable beliefs.

And if you want to take this all one step further, you might want to read "Mythic Past" subtitled "Biblical Archeology and the Myth of Israel" by Thomas L. Thompson by MJF Books of NY. Mr. Thompson contends that outside of the biblical records, there is absolutely no historical evidence written or otherwise that King Saul, King David, King Solomon along with his grandiose temple, Ark of the Covenant and magnificent empire ever existed. All the archeological evidence supports just the opposite, that what we think of as Israel was never more than a sparsely populated agricultural community which was a vassal of the Egyptians, Assyrians, Babylonians, Persians, Greeks and finally Romans and was never an independent thriving state at all. Jerusalem only became a metropolis after it was rebuilt under Persian and Greek rule.

Mr. Thompson further contends that the Israelite writers and theologians merely created their own glorious history after the fact. He maintains that their theology was based almost entirely upon mythic heroes, Egyptian, Persian and Hellenist belief systems popular at the time of their return from exile in Babylon and when they later began compiling their scriptures which we now know as the Old Testament. Those writings were not in fact based upon any earlier sacred scriptures hidden away in some mysterious Ark of the Covenant; no such earlier writings exist. It's interesting that we do have original documentation for all of the other ancient societies and religions. We have the pyramid texts over four thousand years old and inscribed in stone; we have the Code of Hammurabi inscribed on clay tablets over three thousand years old and yet we have no written records of Israel or it's theology that go back any further than 500 BC or the first century of our common era. Doesn't anyone find that odd? For a society and a people who put the Torah above all else, a "people of the Book", isn't it odd that they would not have preserved any original copies? Unless of course there were none and the Torah and the Pentateuch were all written hundreds or even one thousand years after their purported authors had lived.

CHAPTER 10
WHAT IS LOVE?

In the English language, the word "love" can connote a number of feelings and ideas, but the ancient Greek language was far more precise and had at least four separate words to more accurately describe what kind of love was being spoken of. "Philia" was the Greek word used to denote brotherly love. "Storge" was the word used for familial or love of immediate family. "Agape" was the word used to describe an all encompassing, unconditional love such as the love of God towards mankind. Lastly, "Eros" was the word used to denote sexual or erotic love.

Regardless of what religious beliefs one might hold, or even if one has no particular faith at all, I feel that the definition of "love" given in the Bible in the 13th chapter of Paul's first letter to the Corinthians is excellent and says it all. Beginning in verse 4 he says:

"Love is long suffering and kind; love does not envy; does not parade itself, is not puffed up; does not behave rudely, does not seek its own, is not provoked, thinks no evil; does not rejoice in iniquity, but rejoices in the truth. Love bears all things, believes all things, hopes all things, and endures all things. Love never fails."

With all due respect to the Bible, we might add one more quality to love which Dr. Phil the noted counselor makes mention of often in his TV show and that is: "Love Doesn't Hurt".

I think that most people today, both hetero and homosexual tend to be operating in only one of the four dimensions of love; namely Eros. They confuse sexual attraction and infatuation with love and never evolve or grow beyond that point and that is why their relationships fail in a short time. Sexual attraction is nature's way of propagating the species and it works really well, but sexual attraction alone is not sufficient to build lasting relationships or social institutions like "the family unit". It is a starting point to be sure, but Eros needs to evolve and mature and attract its brothers and sisters: Storge, Philia and Agape in order to become what we would term "True Love". And the participants in a loving relationship need to manifest those qualities mentioned above from I Corinthians 13:4-8 if the relationship is to endure.

If a relationship is based solely upon physical attraction it is sure to fail because there will always be someone else who one or both partners finds MORE physically attractive than their current partner. Also a relationship based only on Eros will fail because physical beauty is only temporary and wanes with time. What does one do when their partner begins showing signs of aging; trade them in for a new model? Unfortunately, those whose love never matured beyond the erotic stage do exactly that. This is what accounts for the 50% divorce rate in this country. But if love is present in all four dimensions, then the other three will sustain it when Eros has begun to dissipate. They will also guard the relationship when the temptation to stray arises. The loving qualities of familial and brotherly or sisterly love, coupled with unconditional love will keep one faithful in a relationship and discourage one from ever doing anything that would bring emotional pain to one's marital partner.

Now interestingly enough, the Bible puts enormous stress on love. I John 4:8 says that "God is Love". Romans 13:10 says that "love is the fulfillment of the Law". I Peter 4:8 says that "love covers a multitude of sins". The Bible repeatedly uses the metaphor of a bride and a bridegroom to symbolize the relationship between God and his Church. I John 4:12,13 states: "No one has seen God at any time. If we love one another, God abides in us, and His love has been perfected in us. By this we know that we abide in Him, and He in us, because he has given us His Spirit."

All of this brings me to question how the Church of today measures up to God's standards? Is the Church today united in a bond of love? Is it manifesting the "Fruitage of the Spirit", namely: love, joy, peace, longsuffering, kindness, goodness, faithfulness, gentleness, self-control" (Gal 5:22,23) ? Or is it fulfilling a prophesy of I Timothy 4:1-3 :"Now the Spirit expressly says that in the latter times some will depart from the faith…forbidding to marry, and commanding to abstain from foods which God created to be received with thanksgiving by those who believe and know the truth. Despite all of the Ecumenical Councils, the Church of today is still very much divided on many issues. Two loving people of differing denominations may not be able to be married in either of their churches. A grieving wife may not bury her husband from her own church if his faith was different from hers. The Roman Church still insists on celibacy for its clergy and most churches with few exceptions will not provide commitment services or bless civil unions for same sex couples, while historic records show us that the early 1st and 2nd century Christian churches did.

Now this is nothing new; the New Testament of the Bible is replete with accounts of differences of opinion between the early Church Fathers, but the Bible also shows clearly how those differences of opinion were resolved and it was not by popular opinion or by voting or long standing tradition, but by evidence from the Holy Spirit. One must remember that even Jesus was accused of breaking the Law for healing people on the Sabbath and for eating with and healing Gentiles, yet Jesus pointed out to the scribes and Pharisees of his day that it was they who were violating the Law by missing its point, by putting man-made rules ahead of the Spirit of the Law. Jesus let the Holy Spirit guide his every decision, which is why he healed the servant of a Roman centurion of great faith and stated: " Truly, I say to you, I have not found such great faith, not even in Israel."(Matt 8:5-10).

Later, as recorded in the Acts of the Apostles, we have the account of Peter being directed by God to preach to the Gentiles. Now it was the common belief of most of the apostles that salvation was only intended for the Jews (the circumcised) and that it was a sin to enter into the house of a Gentile or eat with them. Yet Peter was led to the house of Cornelius, a Roman, and was inspired to preach to his entire household. Acts 10:44 states: "While Peter was still speaking these words, the Holy Spirit fell upon all those who heard the word." Now it wasn't as though Peter did not get flack from his fellow apostles and believers because he did. As recorded in Acts 11:2-18 the account states: "And when Peter came up to Jerusalem, those of the circumcision contended with him, saying "You went in to uncircumcised men and ate with them!"...Peter responded: "And as I began to speak, the Holy Spirit fell upon them, as upon us at the beginning...If therefore God gave them the same gift as He gave us...who was I that I could withstand God?"...When they heard these things, they became silent; and they glorified God, saying "Then God has also granted to the Gentiles repentance to life." So the apostles did not debate the issue or vote on it; they accepted the evidence of the Holy Spirit.

Now admittedly, if the Biblical accounts can be considered historically accurate, some of the evidences that the Holy Spirit approved of individuals back then might have been certain "gifts" like the ability to "speak in tongues", heal, teach, prophesy or interpret tongues. Many of those gifts would dissipate or cease over the centuries as Paul says at I Cor 13:8 : "Love never fails. But whether there are prophecies, they will fail; whether there are tongues, they will cease; whether there is knowledge, it will vanish away...And now abide faith, hope, love, these three; but the greatest of these is love." So what would or could or should the Christian Church use as a litmus test today to determine the Will of God or the urging of the Holy Spirit in their decision making processes? I would certainly say that the manifestation of the "Fruitage of the Spirit" (Galatians 5:22,23) in the lives of those in question, coupled with their deep devotion and commitment should be the ultimate proof of God's approval since such qualities are evidence of God's presence in the lives of those individuals.

So one wonders how the Church thinks. One wonders how someone like a Mother Theresa, who so clearly manifested the "Fruitage of the Spirit" and may soon be canonized as a Saint would not have qualified even to be a priest because she was a woman. One wonders why many fundamentalist Christian Churches will not allow a woman to preach, teach, or even speak in the presence of men, while we recall that Jesus first appeared not to any of the male apostles after his resurrection, but to Mary Magdalene and then sent her to tell the apostles. Wasn't that a speaking and teaching mission? Jesus was later to appear directly to the apostles so why the need for Mary to go ahead of him and announce his resurrection to the apostles? Obviously Jesus specifically chose to reveal himself first to her ahead of all of his followers, undoubtedly due to her immense faith. And he commissioned her to teach and preach before commissioning the apostles. Remember, all of the apostles, except John, ran away and hid after Jesus arrest. Only Mary the mother of Jesus, Mary Magdalene and John were present at the crucifixion.

So one wonders why the Church of today continues to see women as second-rate members and why it continues to persecute faithful, diligent, hard-working, gifted and talented homosexual members of the Christian Community who have manifested the "Fruitage of the Spirit" and who have given their all for the Church. Apparently the Church is still stuck in that age old Patriarchal mind-set and groups homosexuals along with women.

In a largely selfish, hedonistic world where millions of heterosexuals who have the right both through their church and their government to enter into holy matrimony and yet CHOOSE not to; in a world where 50% of children are born out of wedlock or worse yet, aborted; in a world where 50% of marriages are terminated within five years, one wonders why both the church and the state refuse to allow committed, faithful, loving and Spirit-filled same sex couples to marry. The qualities of love and commitment which these individuals possess, which are so lacking in our society in general, are most certainly a demonstration and evidence of the presence of God in these people's lives so why should those "gifts of the Spirit" be thwarted by either the church or the state? To me, the issue of Gay Marriage is a moot point.

Now fundamentalists might argue that same sex attraction is "of the Devil" and if all homosexual relationships were characterized by gross promiscuity, cheating and merely lust, one might believe that conclusion to be correct. But True Love, a love which manifests itself in all four dimensions, does not come to everyone; many don't even want it; still more are incapable of loving anyone; so if and when it comes, it can only be part of the Divine Plan; a gift of God and as Jesus said in Mark 10:9: "Therefore what God has joined together, let not man separate."

Now I know that many of you will say: "Jesus was only talking about marriage between a man and a woman" and in the context of that verse, you are correct. Jesus was addressing a question about heterosexual divorce; homosexuality was relatively unknown in Israel although very common in the Gentile world and Jesus would have known that. The fact is that Jesus never said a word about homosexuality one way or the other anywhere in the Gospels; if it was an important issue to him, and salvation was dependent upon it, I would imagine that he would have addressed the issue. But the principle remains the same. What God has joined together, let not man separate.

Just as in the case of the Gentiles, who were not directly invited into the Church by the apostles, but whose hearts were opened independently by the Holy Spirit and who were led by the Spirit to embrace Christianity, I maintain that anyone whose heart is opened to love by God, be it the love of a man for a woman, a man for another man or a woman for another woman; all are being led by the Spirit and that love should not be discouraged or thwarted. Marriages in Biblical times were not a big thing like they are today; no need for approval of either church or state. The arrangement was made through the families; the man took the bride to his home and once the relationship was consummated they were considered married. The same principle should apply today.

When two people are moved by God and choose to bond in a committed, monogamous, lifetime relationship, then they are really in effect already married by God, so why should not the church and the state be willing to honor and respect that committed relationship? Why should the church and state force them to remain in a state of perpetual sin? It seems to me that they are rewarding promiscuity and punishing love. No one in the Church or state is excommunicated or punished for living together and parenting children out of wedlock, but homosexuals who choose marriage are marginalized and denied equal rights under law. Is this fair? Is this equitable?

Two dear friends of mine, T and W, just celebrated their 10th anniversary. Fortunately for them, they were able to have a religious ceremony ten years ago at the Unitarian Church nearby. The Unitarian Church is to be commended for its Spirit inspired approach to gay men and women, as are also the United Church of Christ and some individual clerics of the Episcopal Church while the church at large remains divided on the issue. T and W are models of faithfulness and commitment both to one another and to the Christian Community.

They have enriched each others lives and the lives of all they encounter. Their marriage has made them better Christians and better citizens, better sons and better brothers. How can anyone deny the evidence of the Holy Spirit working in their lives? Fortunately for them, Connecticut now allows civil unions and they were able to legalize their love and relationship just this weekend as witnessed by their loving parents and friends. Even the Episcopal priest who assisted the Unitarian minister and celebrated the Eucharist at this event admitted that he had struggled with this issue for some time and based upon the love and commitment demonstrated by this fine couple, came to the same conclusion as I, that what God has joined, let no man put asunder. He further stated that the closest that most people will ever come to God is in the context of a loving, committed relationship and that it would be a crime and a sin to deny anyone that opportunity.

Of course if T and W move to another state, legally, their relationship could end up null and void and that is a pity. What a shame that the United States which prides itself as being a bastion of freedom and equality, lacks the maturity and compassion of other States like Canada and Spain in granting gay civil unions nationwide.

And so it was with these deeply held beliefs in the sanctity of a committed, loving, lifetime relationship; one that would be in harmony with my sense of faith and spirituality that I continued to search for the right man. Don't get me wrong, I wasn't a prude; I had not taken any vows of celibacy and did not reject the prospect of more casual relationships "with benefits" along the way as I continued in my search. I was always open to new friendships, hoping that God would guide my steps and eventually bring the right man into my path. And even if a new friend at first seemed to lack the qualifications which I was looking for, hope always sprang eternal in my heart and I tended to ignore their disqualifying characteristics and see only what I wanted to see. I believed that deep down, even the most unrepentant bachelor needed to be loved and that showered with an outpouring of love and affection, even they could learn to respond and change in time.

CHAPTER 11
LOVE COMES ONCE MORE

As you will remember, my last lover, "R" made a quick exit from my life back in 1985, when I had confronted him about his multitudinous infidelities; despite his continuing profession of undying love for me. I asked him why he had told me that he was in love with me; his response: "I didn't think that you'd sleep with me unless I told you that I loved you". Well isn't that special? I had been womanized. You see, this is the danger in dating a bisexual. That's what men normally do to women; tell them that they love them just to get into their panties. So to all of you women out there who feel singularly used and abused by men; you're not alone. Men will just as soon "use" each other when the need arises and lie to each other, just as they do to women; they're all "dogs". I tease about this often with girls that I work with. But of course it's not funny and I have learned great compassion for women as a result of it.

I think that last experience with "R" left me so embittered that I just didn't want to go through it any more and I totally gave up on dating or meeting anyone for fifteen years!. I just did like everyone else; I found people to take care of my immediate needs. Unlike the others though, I was always up front and didn't give anyone any illusions that I was about to "marry them"; it was simply "strangers in the night" helping one another make it through another night. There was always mutual respect and I always left "the door open" to a possible relationship, but I honestly didn't think that I would ever fall in love again; I just couldn't allow it to happen; it was just too painful, never lasted; and always ended bitterly. So I protected myself mentally and emotionally.

Now every New Year's Eve, I always attended a wonderful open house party which was hosted by a very nice gentleman nearby with a large home and lots of room for entertaining. It was always a wonderful gathering attended by 40-50 gay men and women. Each of us contributed wonderful gourmet entrees and there was always plenty of champagne and wonderful desserts. This was certainly far better than spending New Year's Eve in a gay bar. Unfortunately, many of the participants didn't make any effort to keep in touch throughout the year so you only saw some of these people once a year.

One young man who was always at those parties was just such a person. He seemed pretty much to be a loner,who like the others, showed up once a year. But he made a lasting impression on me first, because he was very tall and handsome and second, because he would always "come on to me" with a lot of sizzling sexual innuendos. I couldn't quite figure out what was going on because I was twenty years his senior and I knew that there couldn't be any physical attraction there, yet he kept coming on, year after year. Then I finally concluded that he was just a tease and enjoyed the way that I reacted to his flirtations so I decided to call his bluff and invited him to my home. Well, oddly enough, he accepted the invitation.

We went out to dinner one night and then went back to my place. He asked if I had any porno movies to which I responded :"of course" and threw the video of his choice into the VCR. I thought that he just wanted to see the video and didn't expect anything else, but one thing led to another and things happened. Well, of course, I wasn't stupid enough to think that this was the beginning of some big love affair, I mean I didn't even want that, but I did feel that it might be a promising new friendship with benefits, so I continued to see him on a weekly basis. He was young and handsome; full of life and devilishness. I loved his wit and humor and it was simply refreshing to be with him. He somehow made me feel young again. Of course I didn't take him seriously. I knew that he had a penchant for much younger men, but only on an anonymous level; he never seemed to want to be serious with any of them and didn't seem ready to settle down with anyone any time soon. So I figured, well that's good. We will probably be friends for many years and our friendship will not be impeded upon by any serious outside relationships on either of our parts; so it was a nice workable arrangement.

But I was growing fonder of him day by day. I knew that while he was sexually attracted to younger men, that he found the companionship of older men more to his liking. I began wondering if there might be even the remotest possibility that he could ever care for or settle down with someone like me perhaps a few years down the road after having sown his wild oats. But then, I had no reason to believe that because I had never actually witnessed any tender or romantic side of him; only a raw sexual side. I didn't know if he was even capable of loving anyone so I put all this into my memory bank and onto the "back burner".

Well then came the bomb. "D" had to go away to California for a convention as he does each summer. Whenever he returned I would always get a kick out of all of his "war stories" of his sexual conquests while away; he loved sharing these things with me. He really didn't have any other friends and he enjoyed telling me of his conquests. There was as yet no jealousy on my part because we were just good friends and had no claims on each other. But this time was different. This time "D" advised me that he had met a young man in California and had fallen in love with him. Well, that put things into a different light entirely. First off, I didn't want to burst his bubble, but I though that the possibility of falling in love with someone in three days was absolutely ridiculous; "in lust", yes, "in love", absolutely not. How can you love someone that you don't even know? I figured that there was no point in dissuading him; the object of his affection was 3,000 miles away and I was sure that the flame would soon burn out. "D" continued running with other young local men in the absence of his beloved, but the flame didn't die out entirely and that concerned me.

That Christmas of 2001, "D" advised me that he was sending his new love a round trip airline ticket and that "F" would be spending Christmas with him and New Years as well. I suddenly began feeling fear and jealousy creeping in and wasn't sure what to do with the situation. In fact, I didn't even know why I was feeling fear and jealousy; I mean it's not like we were lovers. But I knew how much "D" detested jealousy, so I tried to keep a lid on it. Once "F" had arrived and was settled in, my buddy wanted me to meet him, so I decided to do the gracious thing and have them over to a nice home cooked dinner. "F" being Mexican, I figured that I would make him feel at home by making a nice Paella Valencia with a nice flan for dessert and a nice pitcher of sangria. I wanted to be a gracious host and I guess I also wanted to impress "D" with what a good cook I was and how much better I could provide for a man than my young competition, who couldn't boil water without burning it.

Well, the meal was a wonderful success, but the evening was absolute agony for me. Every time that I left the table to take things to the kitchen and return with the next course, I would return to find "D" tenderly leaning over the table kissing his boy gently on the lips. Of course the boy was just falling all over "D", leaning his head on his chest and holding hands all evening making certain that I knew that he had "staked his claim". I was absolutely furious and in pain all at the same time. You see, I had never seen this tender side of "D" before. That puppy dog look in his eyes and the way that he held "F" in his arms just killed me. I wanted "D" to look at me that way and hold me the way he held "F". Up until that point, I wasn't even aware myself of how much I had come to love "D" over the year that we had been seeing one another, but now I knew in no uncertain terms that I was in love with him and it was too late; there wasn't a thing that I could do about it. Well, the two of them thanked me for the lovely dinner and left my place arm in arm to go back to his place. I retreated to my living room by myself and cried myself to sleep.

That week was absolute hell for me and New Year's Eve was the worst of my life. I went to the usual house party where I had first met "D" and spent all evening trying to avoid him and his new love. I couldn't bear seeing "D" kissing him and holding him; it was just too upsetting. I got mildly drunk, which was not a very good idea since I had an alcohol problem earlier in my life, but I did anyway and then retreated from the party as soon as the "ball had dropped". Of course all through this, "D" was entirely unaware of what was going on and oblivious to my feelings. In fact he was even egging his boyfriend on to tell me how many times they had "gotten it on" that day and such and it was driving me crazy.

Well, of course, I knew that it couldn't really last. For one thing, "D" although "out" to his parents, doesn't discuss it; his family is very religious so I think that their understanding is that "yes, our son has tendencies, but is celibate." "D" would never allow "F" to actually move in with him and blow his cover; how would he ever explain that to his parents? As it turned out, New Year's day, "D"'s new little lover started making demands. He didn't want to go back to California; he wanted to stay here with "D" and was getting all hostile and suicidal and scared the hell out of "D", so "D" took him to the airport and sent him packing back to California. He called me to tell me what a disturbing time he had gone through and that he was glad that "F" was now gone. Well, I was glad too and knew that I couldn't waste any more time. I had to tell "D" what I was feeling for him, at the risk of losing friendship and all. But it was tearing me apart not being able to tell him.

So I invited him over again for a nice dinner. I knew that he loved duck, so I made a lovely Canard a'l'Orange with all of the trimmings. "D" was once more really impressed with my culinary skills, but now it was time for me to drop the bomb. I told him that I had to talk to him. "D" couldn't imagine what could possibly be on my mind and then I told him that I had fallen in love with him. Well, he was shocked to say the least, but not upset. I think that he was mildly flattered, but didn't want me to get hurt. He pleaded with me not to love him, but I told him that it was already too late; that I had never planned on it, but that it just "happened". He was honest with me and told me that he also had grown to care for me in a special way, but that he could never be attracted to an older man and that any possibility of a love relationship would be out of the question. I reminded him that he had allowed me to be somewhat intimate with him, but he explained that he only allowed that because he knew that it made me happy. Well, at least that was something; he did care for me in a special way and he did want to make me happy; that counted for something. I felt that I could live with that so long as he didn't get seriously involved with anyone again any time soon.

This marked a new point in my evolution regarding love. Up until then, I had always insisted on monogamy and refused to share anyone who I loved with anyone else. But now, for the first time in my life, I was willing to share "D" with all of the young men that he pursued on a regular basis because I knew that made him happy and I didn't want to deprive him of that happiness. I could never give him physically what they could, so I left that to them. I felt that if I could only have his heart, I didn't care where his other body parts roamed; I just wanted his love so badly.

I continued to fall deeper and deeper in love and it was wonderful. I put his picture on my computer as my screensaver so that the first thing that I would see each morning when I booted up was his handsome, smiling face. I somehow hoped that just maybe, somewhere down the line he would see reason and that we would end up together. Being in love was good for me. I had fallen into some pretty serious depressions in the past and was losing my zest for life. But loving "D" brought it all back. Everything in life was brighter as a result of loving him. Even my horrible job at Home Depot, which I hated with a passion, was somehow not quite so bad, when I had time to dream about "D" and fantasize our being together. I put myself through all kinds of fantasies ranging anywhere from our first kiss to marrying him at the local Unitarian Church. I was the happiest that I had been in a long time.

That Easter of 2002, his parents were in Florida and he had no one to spend Easter with so I asked my sister-in-law if I could bring him on up for Easter Dinner. My sister-in-law is always so kind and gracious and was glad to include him along with our small family. "D" was a little concerned about what "title" he was going under; I assured him that I told her a "friend" and had not used the term "lover". Well, "D" hit it off great with my brother and sister-in-law and we had a great time; he fit right in. And he was helpful too and helped my sister-in-law clear the table and such. I just sat there and gazed on him with total admiration and adoration. I couldn't help but think of how proud I always was to be seen with him and what a wonderful partner he would make for me if he could only calm down and see the finer points of having an older lover. I reminded him that no young lover would put up with his wandering eye or be willing to share him, but that I was willing to give him full autonomy so long as he ultimately came home to roost with me. I assured him that no one else would ever make such an offer.

I realize now, in retrospect, that I was doing with him, exactly what my dear friend Linda tried to do with me, namely playing "Let's Make A Deal". She had told me that if I married her I could still have my men on weekends, and I had counseled her against that explaining that there would always be the possibility of my falling in love with one of my weekend men and then what would she do? So it was foolish for me to believe that making a deal with "D" would work any better.

Things started deteriorating; he was spending more and more time with anonymous strangers and less and less time with me and I was hurt. Also he began demanding that I remain celibate if I expected him to allow me to be even mildly intimate with him because he didn't want to catch anything from me. Well, I asked him "Are you asking your anonymous partners to be celibate?" He didn't seem to care if he caught anything from them. We had a really big argument over it and he told me that what he did with his time was none of my business. I explained to him that I wasn't restricting him, but just felt that he wasn't being fair to me and had no right to restrict me. We decided that maybe we needed to stop the intimacies although at this point they were few and far between and see a little less of each other until we cooled down. I decided at that point that I was not going to call him; he was the one that was suddenly changing all of the rules and if he wanted the relationship to survive in any form, it would be up to him to make the next move. I felt that I had begged and compromised as much as I could and was getting nowhere. Now it would be up to him. He could let it die a natural death or do something about it.

After about a week, I got a message on my answering machine while I was out. When I played it back, I heard a timid and very sad voice on the other end saying that he had been miserable all week and unhappy and that we could not go on like this. He said: "I need you in my life; let's talk this over". Well, I played the recording over and over and wept tears of joy. That sounded pretty serious to me. Maybe he had come to his senses. Maybe the time apart allowed him to think and go within and determine that he loved me just as much as I loved him. I couldn't wait for us to get together. We did meet and talked things out; I made him another nice meal during which we talked things over. He allowed me some "liberties" with him, but still not anything of a romantic nature. He never kissed me or held hands with me like he did with "F".

In time, he became neglectful again and the romantic aspect of the relationship was at a standstill. Also he had gone on another convention and this time had fallen in love again with a man from New Orleans. I confronted him about it and asked him if he saw any "pattern" there; like how come he only fell in love with people who lived at least 1,500 miles away? Was that to be absolutely certain that nothing could ever come of it? Or was it just that he needed a "sailor in every port" for whenever he went on these conventions?

I knew that he didn't like smokers, so I figured that maybe if I quit smoking, then he would kiss me; so I quit smoking for a while, but even that didn't do any good. Then he invited me to go on vacation with him in upper New England; well, that built up my hopes. God I would have four full days with him all to myself; it would have to help our relationship. I had always wanted to see him outside of the bar scene and away from the cruising circuit and now I would have my chance. I enjoyed being with him and waking up to him immensely, but it really didn't change anything. We slept in separate beds and there were no intimacies other than one brief incident. I had so hoped to be able to sleep with him; not for sex, but just to be near him and feel his warmth and hold him close to me, but that was out of the question. But it was still nice just to wake up to him and have breakfast together. I watched his every move and adored him from afar but couldn't "push it" or he would say that I was getting "greedy".

Needless to say, in time, the flame of love began to burn down to a flicker. It needed fanning and no one was about to fan it or encourage it. I do not fault "D"; he never led me to believe that he was in love with me. He wasn't like "R" who deliberately lied to me just to get what he wanted. No, "D" was always honest with me and probably remained unromantic and cool so as not to lead me on. I, on my part had done this all to myself. I had actually created a lover in my own mind with whom I was madly in love, but who did not actually exist. The "D" that I saw in my mind's eye was tender and warm and loving and caring, while the "D" that I was actually dealing with was simply frivolous; flirtatious, devilish and promiscuous. I had simply fallen in love with what I thought he "could be" rather than what he actually was. And yet in an odd way, I was attracted to the devilish rogue too, so maybe I'm just nuts. I still love him very much and expect that I always will, but I am no longer "In Love" with him to the extent that I was and have yet to meet my soul mate. I am beginning to fear that may never happen.

I have continued trying to meet someone permanent by placing and responding to adds on the internet, but even though my add specifically states "Long Term Relationship", all I ever meet are married men or gay men already in relationships looking for a one night stand. I can't believe how many married men respond to my add; it certainly puts the Kinsey Reports into a different light. In my appraisal, 50% of men are gay or at least bisexual. And I strongly question how many are truly bisexual. Let me share a report with you from a study which was conducted with supposed straight, bisexual and gay men. All three groups were wired to test equipment to measure their sexual arousal; all three groups were exposed to pornographic images of men and women shown separately. As would be expected, the heterosexual men were only aroused by pictures of women. The gay men were only aroused by pictures of men.

While in the group of self-admitted bisexual men, 75% were only aroused by pictures of men, so in all honesty, one wonders how many bisexual men are truly bisexual or just lying because they cannot admit to being homosexual.

So these are the problems that I am dealing with. Of the available men on-line, a large number are married, gay but already in a relationship and cheating, or lying about their bisexuality so as not to have to commit to anyone. Of the small percentage remaining of actual single homosexuals my age, they are all looking for someone 18-22 who works out seven days a week. So what is a typical middle-aged gay man who is not a gym rat supposed to do? Just curl up and die?

My Dad met my step-mom when he was the age that I am now, but they were sensible people. Dad wasn't looking for a 20 year old sex kitten and my step-mom wasn't looking for a 20 year old stud; they were realistic and accepted each other for their fine inner qualities and their ability to love. But there is no such realism in the glitter palaces of the gay world. If you ain't young and pretty and buff, nobody wants to know about your fine inner qualities. We gay men are often our own worst enemies.

Even though I may have said that I am no longer "In Love" with "D", sometimes I think that I am only fooling myself because I still long to be with him; still long for his embrace; still light up at the sight of him and of course, this makes it very difficult for me to pursue other men. But even if the relationship never grows to the level that I would want, all in all, I am still glad that I met "D" and I hope that we will always be friends. In many ways he helped me grow from a shallow demanding person who was only willing to give conditional love, to a more mature person who was willing to compromise and willing to love unconditionally for the first time in my life. Maybe this new openness will help me to find that special man who will appreciate me for who I am; I certainly hope so. I hope that"D" continues to grow too.

At present, I think that part of his problem is that he has done like so many others who live in fear of discovery; he is not comfortable with being gay and keeps it separate from the rest of his life; only acting on it when he's horny. Even though homosexuality is accepted in his workplace which even sponsors gay organizations, he will not join such organizations for fear of discovery, yet his co-workers are "out" and participate so there would be no need to fear and he could even network and meet other nice young men in his field, but he will not risk it.

Instead, he takes far greater risks of exposure by frequenting "cruise areas" which are under police surveillance and running the risk of being blackmailed, mugged or even worse by male prostitutes. If he were arrested for engaging a male prostitute it would be in all of the local papers and then he would risk losing his job and career, to say nothing of the respect of his family. To me, a stable relationship would be far more rewarding and less risky and most families would accept that far better than a life devoted to promiscuity.

I asked him how he justifies this behavior with his church life. I explained that at least a loving, monogamous relationship with someone would be more in keeping with spiritual values than just using people for sexual gratification. I reminded him of a church service from the Episcopal Church during which we from time to time renewed our baptismal vows. Part of one of the prayers said: "I will uphold the dignity of every human being." I reminded him that we were not upholding the dignity of every human being if we were simply "using them" and encouraging them to lead a life of prostitution. He said that he doesn't allow himself to think about things like that. He simply has compartments in his brain; one for family, one for spirituality, one for professional life and another for sex and none of them overlap; he just keeps them all separate. But I explained to him that one can not live a balanced integrated life by splitting it into four distinct sections; that's almost like a person with multiple personality disorder. He said that it worked for him.

Well it may work up to a point, but it requires a lot of energy and planning to keep four different lives from ever overlapping; energy that would be better spent living a happy, integrated and balanced life. And it deprives him and others like him of one of the most important aspects of life, namely love. He will never be able to have a lover if he has to keep that person separate from his family, work and spirituality; he'd only be sharing one quarter of his life with them and that would not be sufficient, for most people, to keep a relationship going.

CHAPTER 12
PROVINCETOWN

All the while that I have been going through my man problems, a dear friend of mine, "K", a friend for over 30 years has been suffering similarly. "K" and I both were Jehovah's Witnesses at one point and I was shocked years later to rediscover him once more in a local Gay bar. He had met a young man on the internet who he fell head over heals in love with, only to find out that the young man is living with a woman who just became the mother of his child. Similar to my situation, the young man on occasion will grant him sexual favors, but is entirely lacking in showing affection or any emotional response whatsoever and it is tearing my friend apart. "K" has been very generous with him and has been helping him financially at great expense, but he remains cold and aloof to both "K" and even toward the mother of his child. No amount of outpouring of love seems to motivate him or draw any response. But like me, "K" is so madly in love with this guy that he is unable to just walk away from the situation.

I decided that maybe it would be a good idea for us to get away from our men for a few days and distract ourselves so I set up a vacation for us in Provincetown, MA which is considered by some as "Gay Heaven" along with Key West, FL of course. I had been to Provincetown many times in the past but due to complicated work schedules and lack of vacation time, I haven't been there in almost 9 years now and wondered what I would find. Would it be as I remembered it? When I first went to Provincetown back in 1972, it was outrageous and it was a "Gay Heaven". There were just throngs of gay men, gay shop keepers, gay waiters and desk clerks; all of them friendly, full of fun, flirtatious, and campy. It was like an enormous fraternity and there was just a natural camaraderie between all. Even my hetero friends used to love to go to PTown and gay discos back in the 70's because the people there were so frivolous and funny and it was always such a festive atmosphere. There was always a broad spectrum of gay men of all sizes and builds, all ages: all manner of men anywhere from ultra butch, clad from head to foot in leather, to extremely feminine drag queens in outrageous and beautiful costumes; it was just an enormous party atmosphere. But somehow now that has all changed both at home and in Provincetown.

Perhaps there is an advantage to being a small, close-knit minority, misunderstood and avoided by the general populace because it takes courage and commitment to put yourself on the line and associate with such a group of people. One tends to bond easily with like-minded members of such a group and can truly "let his hair down" and be himself, without fear of rejection or reprisals. So back in the late 60's and 70's, gay men and women who went to designated gay bars formed lasting friendships and permanent relationships with one another in those "safe zones". We could be open and genuine with one another and depended upon one another for emotional support and friendship which we could not find anywhere else unless we hid our true identities. But now, with the growing general acceptance of homosexuality, our solidarity and loyalty to one another seems to be breaking down and we are becoming assimilated, which is not necessarily a good thing because it is breaking down our sense of a "Gay Community".

As "K" and I strolled down the streets of Provincetown this time, other than occasional rainbow flags flown from businesses and guest houses, there was little to remind one that this was "Gay Heaven". The streets were inundated mostly with hetero couples and families; the store clerks and waiters were largely young, straight, college students from Poland, Hungary, Brazil, you name it. So there was none of the usual gay banter, kidding or flirtatiousness between customer and service people which used to exist years ago. One was almost afraid to discuss gay issues too loudly over dinner for fear of offending a straight family at the next table.

And the gay men themselves have changed radically. While once, there was that broad spectrum of gay men, now there seems to exist only a sub culture of Abercrombie Boys who are all buff, tan and tattooed and walk like John Wayne. They spend the entire year preparing themselves for their grand appearance at Provincetown only to pose and model and reject everyone who is not a mirror image of themselves. They are an example of narcissism at its extreme. One can't tell them from their straight counterparts except when they open their mouths and that unique feminine nasal tone speech contradicts the extreme masculine, straight image which they are trying to project. One wonders why they are trying so hard to look and act "straight" in "Gay Heaven". I saw hardly any men at all in leather and no drag queens whatsoever other than the female impersonators at nightclubs. So for all practical purposes, I might just as well have vacationed in Hyannis port, Yarmouth or Sandwich and not missed a thing for all the gay culture which was lacking in Provincetown.

And this is the same situation that I find back home. The gay bars are no longer fun places to go to and attendance has dropped markedly. Local gay bars used to have funny drag shows and strippers and comedians years ago, but now all they have are a handful of Abercrombie boys standing and posing and not connecting with or talking to anyone. And if you're over 40, God help you. You are completely invisible and can't even get a bartender to serve you a drink. I'm certainly glad that I made friends and developed a support network back in the 70's because bar people these days don't make friends and are totally lacking in social graces.

Of course I attribute much of the poor attendance at gay bars and gay social clubs to the internet and the invasion of "straight" men into gay domains. Years ago if a straight man wasn't getting exactly the kind of kinky sex he wanted from his wife, he would either have to pay for a prostitute or elicit free sex from a gay man at a gay bar. But of course that meant the risk of someone seeing his car parked at a gay bar or seeing him coming out of a gay bar; plus it also cost money for cover charge and maybe plying the gay man with a few drinks. But now it's easy and totally anonymous to go into chat rooms, hook up with someone based on false information, submit someone else's picture and go to the victim's residence for free sex. Chances are that even though you don't look much like the guy in the picture, once you're there, your host will probably be too embarrassed to tell you to get lost so you'll get what you want, a quickie.

The only part of "Gay Culture" which remains is the sexuality aspect. If you go to a gay bar located in a rural area with woodlands next door, chances are the bar will be almost empty and why? Because no one wants to be bothered engaging in any kind of meaningful conversation in the bar and actually meeting anyone to establish a relationship; that's far too intimate and committal. No, they'd rather bypass the bar entirely and just venture off into the woods next to the bar to engage in nameless, faceless, meaningless, often unprotected sex with multiple anonymous partners rather than invest any time in getting to know someone. Now admittedly, a lot of these men may not even be gay, so of course they don't want to establish a relationship. And they can't take anyone home because what would the wife say? And the gay ones can't take anyone home because what would their lover say?

The same thing proved true in Provincetown. Now here are hundreds of gay men all with hotel or guest house rooms within very easy walking distance to the bars. Do you think that any of these men can connect in the bars and get to know one another and possibly invite their new friend back to their room for a drink and whatever? Oh no, too committal. So they stand in the bar posing all evening and move to a different spot if you try to stand next to them because you're just not hot enough.

Yet when the bars close, they will all make their way down to the rear of the Boatslip Inn and hundreds of them will huddle under the pitch dark deck to have anonymous sex with multiple partners, possibly the very same men who they rejected in the bar; I mean how can they tell? You can't see anyone clearly it's so dark. And they will stay there for hours or until the police chase them out. What is their excuse? They all have rooms to take someone to. Do they simply prefer public sex coupled with the threat of arrest? Is that the only thing that can turn them on ? Do they ever stop to think of what a breeding ground for disease such a situation fosters? Do they have an unconscious death wish? Whatever happened to meeting someone nice, going out to dinner and then making love? Nah, that's too committed and too intimate. You can f—k me, but for God's sake, don't kiss me.

I find myself truly ashamed of most of my brothers of the "Gay Community". Community? What community? It seems more to me like a pack of wild dogs in heat. I can't imagine what all the upheaval about Gay Marriage is about when you can't seem to find someone willing to spend more than fifteen minutes with you, let alone a lifetime. The only thing that made me proud and happy in PTown was the occasional sight of some older lovers who had obviously met back in the hay days when there WAS Gay Pride and had stayed together ever since. I did see several older gay men helping their lovers along in either walkers or wheelchairs and who obviously knew the meaning of the word "commitment" and were still very much in love.

Those older men made me proud, but the vast majority simply appeared to be self-serving hedonists. I suppose I should pity them rather than rail on them since they fail to realize that their time in the limelight is short. Once they hit 40 and are no longer hot, they will have neither sex partners nor friends. If they have money, they may very well be able to buy sex from hustlers for the rest of their lives, but they won't be able to buy love or friendships which they should have been developing and nurturing in their younger years but chose not to. Not many will be able to boast of the circle of friends like I have, many for as long as thirty years. Of course if they persist in their current frenzy of unprotected sex with hundreds of anonymous partners, I suppose they won't have to worry about old age and loneliness anyway will they? Especially if they stick their heads in the sand and refuse to be tested for HIV or STD's since they would "rather not know". Well, not knowing is not the answer. Not knowing can be deadly. Even putting HIV aside, untreated STD's, and there are many of them out there, can be deadly. Even if these individuals don't care about themselves, they should care enough about their wives and lovers to protect them. But then I suppose if they cared about their wives and lovers at all they wouldn't be conducting themselves the way they are anyway would they?

A perfect example of this is the married man that I was seeing from time to time whenever my "beloved" would put me on "probation" and deny me any bedroom privileges while simultaneously consorting with most of the 16-18 year old population of downtown Bridgeport. Yes, "W" was a married man with nine children scattered all over creation because he had fathered them all by different women, but now he was with just one woman who was currently incarcerated. During that period he was lonely and horny and he and I hit it off really well. Unlike my "beloved", he was affectionate; hugged and kissed me all over and he was a tireless and intense love maker; I never experienced anyone like him before or after. He would often make love to me two or three times in one evening and then stay over and sleep with his arms around me all night long; something that my "beloved" would never countenance. So in time, I began to trust him and at least grow fond of him though still deeply in love with "D".

"W" was one of these people who swore that he was healthy, but of course had never been tested so he didn't really know did he? He was one of those who would "rather not know". He also hated condoms, which is why he fathered nine children out of wedlock. But being that he was married, and thinking that I was the only man who had been with him; I gave in to him and allowed him to make love to me without condoms. MISTAKE !!! So now, as a result of the man I loved refusing to make love to me; and the man I trusted lying to me, after years of being STD-free, I am now HIV positive and have to live with this all for the rest of my life; however long or short that turns out to be. Thanks guys.

While in PTown, my friend, "K" met a nice young 37 year old man from Boston. They DID chat in the bar and did get to know each other. That's because "K" is from the "Old School" of gay social graces. The young man had a sad tale to tell about his messed up relationship which he had been in for fourteen years with an older lover. Now one would think that the older man would be more mature and have some brains, but there's no fool like an old fool. The two of them built a successful computer business together and have a nice home, but apparently the older gent thinks that 37 is just too old and now has a 21 year old male mistress on the side who he adores while ignoring his 37 year old partner, so needless to say, the younger man was in town for the weekend in search of some TLC from an older gentleman and "K" was just the right one for him. I'm glad that my buddy had that experience, he sorely needed it, but it still didn't get his mind off of the neglectful man he loves. I also connected with a younger handsome man complete with leather chest harness and pierced nipples. That was nice too; he was very responsive, but more than the sex, I appreciated his kissing and hugs which I did not get from the man I loved.

While in PTown I had purchased a wonderful CD entitled "Amici, The Opera Band" produced by Victor Music. It is a wonderful collection of instrumental and vocal music from operas with very romantic overtones. If you are romantically inclined at all, you will love it. So on our way home I decided to play it in the car. When it came to track 2, "Senza Catene" otherwise known as "Unchained Melody", both "K" and I "lost it" and couldn't stop weeping until I turned it off. I think that when you see the lyrics, you will know why.

"Oh, my love, my darling, I've hungered for your touch a long, lonely time.

And time goes by so slowly and time can do so much, are you still mine?

I need your love, I need your love, God speed your love to me!

Lonely rivers flow to the sea, to the sea, to the open arms of the sea.

Lonely rivers sigh, "wait for me, wait for me!" I'll be coming home, wait for me!"

CHAPTER 13
THE BANKING TRAP

By November of 2005 my unemployment checks were about to run out so I reluctantly began a number of searches for a new job; reluctant, not because I do not want to work, but because I resent the way that 22 year old "dress for success Yuppie interviewers" treat "over 50" applicants. They just sit there stone faced and give no hint as to whether the interview is going well or not; then they say that they will get back to you, but they never do. When you call back they tell you that they hired the most qualified person. Now I have 25 years experience in customer service, which is longer than the interviewer has lived on this planet, yet they invariably hire an 18 year old for the job. Go figure.

At a local job fair, I applied for a job at a local cablevision company; went through 3 interviews and 3 batteries of tests; was assured that I had done well on all the tests and was welcomed by the final interviewer into the company. One week later I was contacted by the interviewer and advised that there was a hiring freeze on and that while I could still begin training, I would have to be hired through a local temp agency where I would now have to go and apply. The rate of pay would of course be lower and I would not be building up any seniority or vacation time with the cable company. Now I ask you, why on earth would a company have a booth at a job fair if they were in the midst of a hiring freeze? I don't like being lied to and toyed with so I declined the job.

Shortly thereafter, I was called in for a battery of interviews by a major bank that I had applied to at that same job fair. At least the bank seemed on the up and up and was willing to hire me direct and at a higher pay so I took the job in their MasterCard department. I must admit that I was very impressed with the bank's stress on quality customer service, which was impressed upon all of us trainees at our orientation. I believe in good and honest customer service and pride myself in giving my best.

The initial four weeks of training was very complex and grueling and I feared that I might not be able to absorb all of the information, but my instructor assured us all that the bank was very flexible and that an associate would have to be guilty of some kind of major deliberate infraction, bad attendance or insubordination to a superior in order to fall under any kind of disciplinary action or termination. I was to find out later that this was not the truth at all and neither was the bank's glowing statement that providing excellent customer service was their first priority as they said it was.

I learned a lot working at the bank though. I wish that I had had access to all I learned about the banking industry when I was a younger man; I might have saved myself a lot of money and grief had I know the deceptive practices and misleading information both given out by banks and withheld by banks. In my earlier years I had fallen into the credit card trap and ended up with several maxed out credit cards which I was paying off for years and years, only to find out that even after all of those payments, my balance remained the same. The fact is that if all you can afford are the minimum monthly payments, you will be paying off the balance for years and years and what started out as simply a credit card, will end up being more like a mortgage.

Here's how it all works. They start you off with some kind of offer of zero per cent interest for 6 months or a year for a balance transfer to pay off other bills. Now it really is zero per cent so that much is truthful. They also admit that there "MAY" be a balance transfer fee imposed of say 3% on the amount transferred, but they don't tell you up front that the 3% fee will be billed at your purchase rate of say 18%. Neither do they tell you that when you send in your monthly payments, that the full amount will always be applied to the lowest interest item or the zero per cent and that nothing will be applied to your purchase or cash advance balances; those balances will just sit there accruing interest monthly until the zero balance item is paid in full. So what happens is this. If you have a total balance of $10,000, $5,000 of which is a zero per cent balance transfer and $5000 of which is purchases, the $5,000 in purchases will be sitting on your account earning 18% interest each month and compounding; therefore your purchase balance will keep growing exponentially while you are paying off the zero per cent balance transfer amount. So you didn't really get zero per cent did you because your 18% balances are growing and growing without any ability to pay them down unless you pay off the entire balance in full.

Another trick that they will play is to offer zero per cent balance transfer checks to customers who already have high balances that they are paying down at high interest rates. So again, if you are suckered into using one of those checks, your existing balance that you have been attempting to pay down will be put on hold indefinitely while you are paying off the balance on the zero per cent balance transfer check which you used. So again your old balance will continue growing and compounding at 18% with no payments being applied to it.

Another trick that they use is to send you out those zero per cent balance transfer checks for 3 months in a row and then in the fourth month send you out a nice little check book with "cash advance" checks. Now if you don't read them carefully, you will use them just like you used the previous zero per cent checks not realizing that these checks are cash advances and will be billed an up front 3% cash advance fee plus the total amount of the checks written out will be billed at 24%.

Also the banks heavily push their associates into selling various forms of credit insurance on your account at a rate of $.79 per $100 of outstanding balance. So if you are protecting a balance of $10,000 your monthly premium will be $79 per month. Many associates do not mention the $.79 per $100 equation in order to make the sale and the customer finds out the hard way when their next bill arrives. Other unscrupulous associates who see that the customer is only $30 away from their maximum credit line will push through the sale knowing full well that this will push the customer over their credit limit and that they will be billed an over limit fee of $39 on their next bill. Also if you are over your limit on say July 5th, you will be billed an over the limit fee immediately. Then, if your billing date is the 6th or 7th you will be billed another over the limit fee for the same overage simply because it has lapsed into a new billing cycle. So your next statement will show two $39 over the limit fees.

The bank's all time best scam is the cash advance since it is billed an up front 3% of the amount of the cash advance plus the balance is billed currently at around 24% and you will never be able to pay it off unless you pay your entire credit card bill in full and suspend all charging on the card for 60 days. Why is this? This is because as I mentioned earlier, all payments are applied to the lowest interest rate items, so if you have an outstanding balance transfer balance or a purchase balance, the payments will always go to those first and not one cent will be applied to your "cash advance" balance; it will just keep growing and compounding at the 24% rate.

I had one customer who called me and told me that he was well aware of that procedure and that was why he paid off his last bill in full and questioned why the "cash advance balance" was still appearing on his newest statement. Well, I must admit, that I was stumped too. It was my understanding that so long as a customer paid the balance in full that this would include the "cash advance balance" as well, but after checking with my supervisor, I found out this was not the case. I was told that since the customer had continued using his card, that his payment in full was applied to the lower rate old balances and to the new purchases, even though those new purchases had not yet actually been billed to the customer on a statement. Therefore, his "cash advance balance" was still owing and still accruing interest at the 24% rate. Needless to say, I was appalled and fearful of how I would explain this to the customer. And needless to say, the customer closed his account; I can't say that I blame him. But I did warn him of one other bank trick. I warned him that if he closed his account and was unable to pay the balance in full within 22 days that the bank reserved the right to raise his interest rate to 28% on the remaining balance. Too many customers feel that they can get even with the bank by closing their accounts, not realizing that the bank has the last word.

Now admittedly, all of these disclosures can be found somewhere in a customer's original application papers, but let's face it, how many people read those disclosures in full and how many are astute enough to grasp all of the subtleties and jargon in those contracts? Even I, as an employee, didn't grasp the entire minutia contained in those multi page disclosures, much less would an average customer with perhaps even a language barrier. The bank really takes unfair advantage of such people. Perhaps there should be warnings on those "convenience checks" much like on a cigarette pack stating: "Use of this check could be hazardous to your credit and financial stability".

One wonders how many of these banking regulations and penalties were even legalized. Well, actually, one doesn't have to wonder; the bank lobbyists have all our congressmen in their back pockets. For example: my balance due is $20, but I sent the payment in late. How can the late fee be $39 when the balance is only $20? Now if I fail to pay the $39 late fee, next month there will be another $39 late fee for failure to pay the first late fee. And what about that earlier mentioned over the limit fee of $39? Now, say you go over the limit on July 5th, perhaps because your most recent payment has not yet been applied; then on July 6th your new bill will go to print with two over the limit fees; one for July 5th when it went over the limit and another because the over the limit balance lapsed into a new billing cycle. Is this fair? Is this just? You were never even given notification or allowed an opportunity to bring the account below the limit in time for the next billing.

And what about the customer who is late with a payment and also over his limit? Well, he gets billed one late fee of $39 and two over the limit fees of $39 each. Nice isn't it? So he is paying $117.00 for absolutely nothing, to say nothing of the interest on the amount due. Of course any money that he may have in a banking institution is earning him an astronomical 1% interest.

So do yourself a favor: DO NOT USE CREDIT CARDS unless you totally know what you are doing. There are some savvy customers who know how to use these cards artfully. I had several customers who took advantage of the zero per cent checks, invested the money in CD's, did not use the card for purchases, paid back the balance interest free before the offer expired and made out well. But those customers who benefit from the bank are few and far between. Most of us end up in a state of indentured servitude and just make the banks richer.

Just stop for a moment and think about even mortgages or car loans. Now most of us realize up front that automobiles are not a good investment and that they immediately lose value as soon as you drive them off the lot. But the talking heads have goaded most people into feeling that real estate is a good investment, but is it? The equation works something like this: if you take out a mortgage, you buy one house for yourself and two for the bank. So back in the good old days, if you took out a mortgage for $100,000 and bought a house, you now feel pretty proud of yourself because you can now sell that house at a profit for $300,000. But is it a profit? By the time you paid off that mortgage you actually paid $300,000 for the house to say nothing of thousands in property tax, repairs and maintenance with a few shekels credit toward your income tax. So who's really making out here? You got it; the banks are the ones making out.

In time, my ideas of good customer service, full disclosure and ethical behavior were to be my undoing in the banking industry. Now since full disclosure is an absolute requisite on the part of banks, my superiors could not fire me for that; they could have gotten into serious trouble if I were fired for full disclosure. So they worked it from another angle. They said that they wanted good customer service while at the same time limiting talk time to customers to 225 seconds per call which included finding out their problem; solving the problem and selling them some product or service. Now many of my customers couldn't even explain their problem within 225 seconds and still others advised me that I was the 4th person that they were speaking to that day because no one else had been able to help them. It seems that a number of service reps had an extraordinary number of disconnected calls, but they were within their range of 225 seconds you see. It's interesting that when I went to my local bank branch with a dispute on my bill for a purchase which was never shipped to me, that it took the manager 45 minutes to determine what to do and set up my claim while I was expected to do the same procedure in 225 seconds and sell the customer some product to boot. But you see managers are not timed and have no time constrictions; only the rank and file have time limits. So ultimately, the bank called for my resignation in exchange for which they promised to find me a different job within the bank that didn't have such stringent time restrictions. Needless to say, I gave them my resignation as they requested, but have never heard from them again. So be it. My honesty and ethics are not for sale at any price. The one thing that I am happy for is that at least during that 11 month period I was able to educate customers and save them from some serious financial problems. Of course any business has the right to make a profit and it has a responsibility to its share holders, but it does not have the right to take unfair advantage of the undereducated and extract fees that amount to usury.

CHAPTER 14
THE AGONY AND THE ECSTACY

The vacation which my friend "K" and I had gone on was intended to wean us away from our unfulfilling relationships was only a minor distraction and unable to erode the deep love and longing which we were still feeling for the men we loved back home.

Once home, my next great event was to be an annual August backyard picnic held by the same generous host who opens his home for the New Year's Eve parties and has for some 20 years now. It was a hot Saturday afternoon so the comfort level was not too great. Of course, my beloved "D" used that as an excuse to arrive at the party in nothing but swimming trunks and spent the afternoon asking older men to hose him down periodically. He seems to love to turn on the older men just to get their reactions; perhaps that was the only reason he ever seduced me was for the attention and adoration that he knows that he can get from older men, but not from his peers. Being the youngest man at gay parties does get one a lot of attention and he loves it. Of course what he wants is attention in general, not specific. He doesn't want anyone to know that he is dating an older man or has given sexual favors to an older man, no, that has to be hush, hush. So the relationship of sorts which I have shared with him for three years now cannot be divulged to anyone.

In fact he approached me on several occasions during the picnic showing great concern that some of the people at the party considered us a couple and he wanted to know how they might have come to that conclusion. I explained to him that some of my closer friends were indeed aware of the feelings that I had for him, but that I had never told them that we were a couple because the love affair was only one-way. Well, he was still very upset and concerned. I was very hurt to say the least. I mean how do you explain a person who is proud to the max of his ongoing affairs with several strangers per week and is willing to brag to everyone about those activities and yet is ashamed and embarrassed to admit that he had ever been intimate with an older man who genuinely loved him?

How am I supposed to feel about this? I put him first above all of my friends for three years; he knows that I loved him; I told him so, but what's more, I demonstrated it because talk can be cheap. I cooked him candlelight dinners; I bought him clothes and other gifts; I sent him Valentine cards; how could he not know that I loved him? I take his father to the doctors and sit with him afternoons so that his mom can have some free time. I put up with all of his dalliances and promiscuity even though I was sick to death of hearing about it. And my reward for all this is that my pure love for him must remain hidden, a secret, something to be ashamed of. I must admit, his little Mexican lover from California was a lot smarter than me. As soon as he saw that the relationship was going nowhere, he didn't waste any time at all, he went out and found someone else who would love him and care for him and left "D" in the dust. "D" had continued writing him and he just ignored the letters, refused to respond to phone calls and found a new lover for himself. "D" even went to look him up while on a convention in Los Angeles this summer. His little friend was cordial, but made no bones about the fact that he was in a happy and satisfying relationship now and was quite content. "D" told me that it was a good closure because apparently his ex had put on 30 pounds and that he would never have been able to love him looking like that. I think that statement alone tells a lot about the person making it. But like a damn fool, I had held on for three years, blindly hoping that if I showered enough love and attention on him that he would eventually rally around. MISTAKE. If he couldn't even continue to love a young man who had put on 30 pounds, then loving an older man with poundage would be out of the question. Beauty may be only skin deep, but apparently so is love with some people.

Oddly enough, "D" did express some regrets that he had not nurtured and grown his relationship with his little Mexican friend. During the period when "D" put him on hold, the young man had gone in search of love and as a result had become HIV Positive. "D"expressed some sense of guilt over that, feeling that if he had only given "F" what he needed, then maybe he would never have become HIV Positive. Oddly enough, it never seemed to enter his psyche or pass from his lips that he was also sad that he had been unable to respond to me, ultimately leading to my becoming HIV Positive also. No, that never crossed his mind. I am not blaming him; ultimately we are each responsible for our own lives, but the fact remains that had he loved "F" and settled down with him "F" would not now be POS or had he loved and settled down with me, I would not now be POS either because he was all that I ever wanted and I would never have cheated on him.

And yet he continued to dangle the carrot in front of me and offer me "favors" if and when he felt like it, but of course he rationed them out giving me just enough to keep me hooked.

At other times he would deliberately withhold favors from me as a punishment if I dared to comment about his promiscuity. But even when he felt, as he put it "generous" our one way sexual encounters had to be under almost laboratory conditions. I would have to ply him first by showing him hundreds of slides of nude young men or keep switching videos of nude young men until he found one that "inspired" him. Eventually I ran out of slides and videos that inspired him since he had seen them all before and needed new stimulation, so I had to keep buying new videos and DVD's.

And even then it was only with the greatest effort and patience on my part that I was able to please him. In the beginning it was much easier, but lately the only effect my touch seems to have on him is to "deflate him". Now one would think that once one was pleased, that they would express some kind of gratitude and then go home, but not my buddy. If I inquired as to whether I had please him or not, his only response was "it was adequate". Then he would give me a brief hug, no kiss of course, and leave to pursue street prostitutes for the remainder of what was left of the night. Now the very fact that even though he had climaxed and there was no longer any physical need left, yet was driven to the streets afterward, tells you right there that it was a mental obsession and not physical need that drove him.

I had to be out of my mind to accept this. I have had a far easier time in the past pleasing total strangers and have received more reciprocation from them and at least a little kissing and foreplay. Those men didn't need hundreds of slides or movies; they were content just to be with me and were adequately stimulated by what I had to offer. They climaxed in short order and thanked me profusely for what I had done for them. They kissed me and went home, not out into the streets in search of more sex. But with the man I loved it was an ordeal with no positive feedback or affection. In fact, it was quite the opposite. When you have just given someone your all and they still need more; it certainly doesn't make you feel very adequate. And then just knowing that he gives far more affection and reciprocation to street hustlers who only want his money and that he can boast of that openly, yet finds the love that I shared with him an embarrassment to be kept hidden is a great source of pain and anguish that leaves me with nothing but sighs and sleepless nights just like tonight as I am writing this.

There is nothing as beautiful, fulfilling and rewarding as loving another fully and deeply and without reservation, but nothing as painful as getting minimal response in return, yet despite the pain, we seem unable to stop loving the beloved. It is the supreme act of immolation that we perform with absolutely no assurance of ultimate reward, yet we are powerless to do otherwise. And yet I feel the love I once held for him draining out of me like blood pouring from an open wound. I feel that I must terminate this before the vestiges of love remaining turn to hatred. I don't want to hate him, yet the thought of feeling absolutely nothing for him seems worse than hatred. At least hatred is an emotion and shows there's still some feeling there. Apathy is worse than hatred; it's just an enormous void with no feeling whatsoever; it's like having your entire body and life anesthetized, leaving no feeling; no desire to eat, to go out, to meet anyone, to socialize; no desire even to live. I just want to sleep and sleep and sleep until the Great Sleep takes me home to, hopefully, rest in peace.

I finally got up the courage to write him a letter; this had to be resolved somehow and it wouldn't be if I just kept silent. I know how much he dreaded what he called my "hostile poison pen letters", but in reality, I had only sent him one and argued with him only once in three and a half years, so I really don't think that I have been all that hard on him. I feel that I have been patient to the extreme and that anyone else would have terminated the relationship long ago. I wrote it in the third person to avoid being confrontational and I wrote it as a short story where he was the victim being mistreated by an errant lover. I included the above paragraph in my closing and apparently he was deeply moved by it.

"D" called me immediately and explained that he sort of thought something was wrong because the last time he had seen me, he felt that I had been very hostile and short with him and he didn't know why. He added that his refusal to be intimate with me that night was neither a tease at all nor a power game, but that I had hurt his feelings by being short and abrupt with him and that's why he left early. I asked him why he thought that I was being hostile to him. What did he think might have motivated it when I am usually very warm and adoring and loving towards him? He sort of figured that it might have been tied in with his sex stories over dinner, but still was irritated at my aggravated response to him that evening. After reading my long letter at least he understood somewhat why I responded the way I did and was regretful that I had suffered so much mentally over the past two weeks. He assured me that he could never just "dump me" as he might have done to others in the past. There was too much between us and he did sincerely care about me but just wasn't "in love" with me and didn't know what we could do to rectify the situation.

I had suggested in the letter that in order to save the friendship, maybe we should see less of each other; cease any intimate contact and definitely stop talking about sex and sexual conquests when in each other's presence. I also suggested that it might be wise not to see each other alone, but to always be in the presence of others. I said this because I felt that however limited my sexual privileges were with him, still they tended to endear me to him and make me love him all the more. Also as is taught in Buddhism, it is unfulfilled expectations that cause suffering. If one expects nothing and receives something, one is pleasantly surprised. But if one expects something and anticipates it and longs for it and then does not receive it; then one suffers. And this is exactly what had been happening with me. I would be longing for intimacy; waiting for intimacy; expecting intimacy, and then when it didn't happen I was disappointed, depressed and angry. So I felt that if the intimacy stopped, I would not be happy, but neither would I ever be disappointed or angry again. I also felt that maybe if the intimacy ceased, that maybe my love for him would wane and I would be able to move on with my life.

But there were problems and contradictions with this plan of mine. First off, the whole reason I was upset was because I felt that I wasn't being allowed to spend as much time with him as I wanted and wasn't being given my fair share of intimacy. So now to spend even less time together and remove all intimacy totally was sort of a contradiction and would leave me getting less than even before. That doesn't make much sense, except from the point of view that it might enable me to break my addiction to him. "D" was not that thrilled with the plan but said that it was up to me to call the shots since I was the one having the problem. His feeling was that what brought us together as friends from the beginning was that he could talk openly with me and tell me things that he could never tell anyone else. And he felt that if now we could no longer talk freely with one another and enjoy porno films and such together and occasionally be intimate that this eroded much of what our original friendship was based around.

I concurred that this did pose a problem, but I also explained to him that I thought it rather sad that sexuality and porno were the only common interests we shared after three and a half years. I have multitudinous interests on every level. I am interested in theater, ballet, concerts, antiquing, craft shows, historic reenactments, Renaissance fairs, ethnic fairs, politics, religion, etc. So I can converse and mix and join in activities with just about anyone. But "D" is very limited; other than going to church with his family, he has no interest in any of the aforementioned activities, which I find a little odd in a well educated college graduate, but none the less, that is the case.

I had tried to get him to share some of these activities with me and over the three and a half year period we did go to one play and one comedy show starring Dame Edna, but that was about it. Most of the time he just wanted to go cruising for men. I had also explained to him on numerous occasions that even though I knew that he wasn't attracted to me and would probably never accept me for his life partner, that if he ever hoped to have a young lover that he could love, that he would have to expand his interests and social skills. Unless he had a relationship with a nymphomaniac, he would never be able to hold their attention if all they had in common was sex. Once the honeymoon was over, the relationship would be too.

I had also explained to him that if he ever found a lover, that I hope he didn't think that he could continue simultaneously to consort with his street boys or have his new lover go with him to pornographic bookstores or take him downtown searching for rent boys. Somehow I don't think that would make for a solid relationship. I had been patient with him, but I doubt that others would have been so patient. So if he ever hoped to have a relationship somewhere down the line, now was the time to learn new interests, develop social skills, and wean himself off of the fast life because I'm sure that he would not just be able to go "cold turkey" once he met someone he thought that he could love.

But of course, he didn't take my advice so now we are left with this gaping void. "D" definitely wants to hold onto the friendship and so do I, but his point is well taken. If we don't engage in sexual activities, intimacy or "visuals", then what else can we do when we are together; discuss world conditions or the weather? But then what is the point in showing him porno flicks and slides if we're not going to be intimate with each other? That would only arouse both of us with no relief other than to jump into separate cars and rush downtown separately to find someone to relieve us.

The fact is that my love for him is the only thing that is holding us together. Well, maybe not. I must be fair; it takes two to tango and obviously he does have some feelings for me, otherwise he would just write me off as "too high maintenance" and walk away. So he is making an effort too in his own way. But the fact is that if I didn't love him, I would really rather spend my time with my other friends since they have more varied interests which match my own. I would much rather go to a fine restaurant and a Mozart concert on a Saturday evening than go to the Bridgeport Flyer diner for their $6. special followed by two hours of cruising downtown Bridgeport. The only reason that I settle for the often bland Saturday evenings that we spend together is because I love him so much and hunger for him all week and will make just about any sacrifice just to see him and be near him and all the more so if I think that he might allow me a little intimacy.

"D" feels that most of our problem is the result of my having fallen in love with him. He feels that if I hadn't fallen in love with him and we had just remained buddies, we wouldn't be having these problems. But that's not entirely true. If I met a perfect stranger at a bar, brought them home, gave them drinks, played porno flicks for them (at their request) and then they just got up and left, I would be disappointed. Now I might not be angry because I might feel that maybe I should have been more aggressive or maybe they were shy. But if they called me the next day to tell me "Wow, those movies you showed me were hot! After I left your place I went downtown and had hot sex with three different guys", then I would be furious. I would think: "Do you think I have nothing better to do with my evenings than ply you with alcohol and show you porno flicks so that you can leave me high and dry and run off with other men?" No, I don't think that you have to be in love with someone first before being offended at their selfish and thoughtless behavior.

In fact, had "D" behaved this way from the beginning, I doubt very much that we would ever have become friends at all. In the beginning he did not flirt with me and tease me only to get up and leave. No, he offered himself to me and I was very touched by that and I began warming up to him. No, we didn't have much of anything in common, but we could talk openly together and exchange sexual fantasies and admittedly, that was fun. I rather liked his devilishness and outspokenness; it was refreshing. We would go out and cruise men together and if we didn't find anyone we liked, at least we had each other to go home with so there was the security of knowing that the evening wouldn't end up being a total zero. There were even times when he would share one of his rent boys with me; somehow he enjoyed watching me with them; a touch of voyeurism maybe? But there was no jealousy on either of our parts.

But then he suddenly changed the rules. He said that he was concerned about catching STD's and consequently stated that if he was to continue to allow me to be intimate with him, then I had to remain celibate. Well, I told him that was ridiculous unless he was going to be celibate himself. Wasn't he concerned about receiving STD's from strangers in video booths? He said "No" because he didn't allow them to make physical contact with HIM; but that wasn't entirely true. So the fact is that he was taking risks with strangers, but would not take risks with me; no, I had to remain celibate to receive his favors. I felt that this was giving preferential treatment to strangers while leaving me shortchanged. And the fact is that I would still have felt this way regardless of whether I was in love with him or not. I think that anyone would have felt the same and would probably have terminated the relationship. So again, I don't feel that the strains in our friendship or relationship came about strictly as a result of my falling in love with him; I think that I would have still seen this as unfair treatment even if I weren't in love with him. The fact that I loved him and was willing to comply with his demands was the only thing that kept the friendship in tact; otherwise I'm sure it would have ended long ago.

So while I know and acknowledge that my falling in love with "D" did complicate the friendship somewhat, certainly for me, and I'm the one that's suffering the most; I'm not so sure that it is the root of all of our problems, in fact it may be the only thing that has kept the friendship together at all. I certainly wouldn't have tolerated nor made excuses for this kind of behavior had I not loved him dearly.

But now the question remains: How do I turn the clock back three and a half years and just go back to being "a cruising buddy" with him after having been in love with him? Without my loving him, is there enough interest and enough in common to keep the friendship together? If we spend those precious Saturday evenings together, but in separate booths searching for other men are we really spending them together? Is that the way to build a friendship? On the other hand, if we go back to business as usual and I continue loving him and being intimate with him, then won't I still ultimately face certain disappointment whenever he "fails to deliver" or when after years of doing this he still hasn't grown to love me anywhere near as much as I love him? Isn't it pointless to continue loving someone who may never be capable or able to return the love? Wouldn't it be far wiser to move on and find someone who can? And yet, I still love him enough not to want to leave him behind. I fear that if he continues in his present pattern that he will have a very sad and lonely life. I feel that I am the only one who loves him enough to put up with his idiosyncrasies and failings and I want to be there for him, and I can't be there for him if I am in the arms of another man. And then too, it wouldn't be fair to the other man if I settled into a long term relationship with him while still loving "D". What do I do? It's driving me crazy.

CHAPTER 15
CLOSURE

"D" suggested that we meet over dinner on Monday, Labor Day to iron out some of these issues in person. I explained to him over dinner that while I took full responsibility for some of the complications that my loving him had brought to our friendship; that still, much of his behavior had been cruel and unfeeling by any standards and that had I not loved him, the friendship would have terminated years ago. I explained to him that while I knew that he could never be "in love" with me; still I felt that if he had any feelings for me even as just a friend, that he would have been more sensitive to my feelings and not rubbed his promiscuity and dalliances in my face. Well, he agreed not to do that any more, but further stated that since sexual talk and visits to cruise areas were now off limits, so too would be any intimacy with him. He claimed that my expectations of him were just too high (like wanting sex once a month) and that if I had no expectations that I wouldn't be disappointed any more. Well, that is true to a point, but what he failed to realize is that since he cut off our one point of contact, what was left? Nothing. Since he lacks interest in anything other than sex, what is left that we can do together? Nothing. So the relationship, if you can call it that, will just wither away and die of starvation.

Then he has the nerve to suggest that maybe if I "accept the Lord as my Personal Savior", maybe that will ease my sadness and help me cope. I felt "What a hypocrite! Have you accepted the Lord? It certainly isn't manifest in your life!" "What do you think that you can just say those few magic words: "Jesus I accept you as my personal Savior" and be saved for all time without making any commitment on your part to leading a better life? I don't think so. Otherwise why did Jesus say at Matt. 24:13 "He that endures to the end is the one that will be saved."? No, I refuse to make promises to Jesus or Buddha or anyone else, when I know that I have no intention of keeping them. While I do not feel that either Jesus or Buddha would have a problem with my loving and caring for another man in a supportive and faithful relationship. I DO FEEL that both Jesus and Buddha would be appalled at both gay and straight men living their lives as merely sexual predators and preying on and abusing innocent individuals who may have actually loved them had they been given a chance. Human beings ARE NOT SEX TOYS to be used and discarded. If that's all the respect you have for God's children, then I highly doubt that you could be "saved" or "born-again". Give me a break!

Well, as if that wasn't silly enough. "D" called me back two days later, I'm sure out of some kind of concern as to how I was doing at that point. But in his usual clueless manner, he made a statement that finally put the lid on the casket once and for all. He asked me how I was feeling, to which I replied: "How do you think I am feeling? Knowing that I invested four years of my life in you and now have no connection to you whatsoever other than seeing you at occasional social events?" To which he replied: "Well, I don't know why you're making such a big deal out of this. All you will be missing is a little nooky now and then, which you didn't get all that often anyway."

Well I was furious to say the least. In one sentence he had managed to totally trivialize and turn into something shameful and piggish, the intense love I had felt for him for four years. Is that all he thought that this was about? Had I not alienated others of my friends on Saturday evenings for four years by limiting their access to me and keeping Saturday evening open for him? Had I not cooked candle light dinners for him; sent him cards; bought him surprises and presents; cooked and sent dinners over to his parents; helped take care of his dad and rendered other multitudinous services to him which I would not have done for anyone else, as in the case of driving all the way to Waterbury and back at 3AM to bring him an extra set of car keys since a street boy had stolen his keys and wanted $500 to give them back. Anyone else would have told him: "Well, you wanted street boys more than me, now take a taxi home." And he thinks that I did all this and hung in there for three and a half years with the sole purpose of getting into his pants, which as he himself admitted was only infrequently? Is that all that he thought that this was about? Apparently, he lacks an understanding of even the most remote concepts of love, longing or devotion and can't conceive of anything pure and beautiful and unrelated to sex. To him, sex is the sole driving emotion and power behind everything. Nobody "loves you", they just want to get into your pants. Well, hell, his pants "weren't ALL THAT; I've had better and passed it up to be with him.

Whatever vestiges of love for him which had remained within my heart, he smothered with that one sentence. So here is my final statement to my beloved "D":

"Yes, I guess you're right "D". All I will be missing out on IS SOME NOOKY, since I never had your love or respect at any point in our friendship. You just toyed with me from the first moment that I laid eyes on you back at those New Years Eve parties; and you continued to toy with my heart for four years just to get the attention and adoration that no one else would give you.

You enjoyed watching all of my porno flicks and requested that I show them to you fairly often. You also enjoyed leafing through all the porno magazines in my bathroom and asking me if I had found any new pictures of young men on the internet.

Now I may be totally crazy, but usually when someone asks you to play porno for them it is with the intent that the two of you will ultimately and imminently have some form of sex together. Usually people do not have the nerve or audacity to ask you to show them porn so that they can just get up and walk out on you and have sex with someone else later in the evening. If you need to be stimulated before hitting the streets, then watch porn at home; don't take unfair advantage of friends WHO YOU KNOW ARE ATTRACTED TO YOU, and just use them and their video equipment for your puerile fantasies.

You liked me looking up all the cruise areas for you on the internet both in Connecticut and out of state whenever you were planning an out of town trip because you were too cheap to get an ISP of your own. You had me spending hours downloading male escort info and printing out pictures and listings of all of the cruise areas in Southern California or wherever it was that you were going and all at my time and expense. And then you got dinner and dessert included at absolutely no cost. Not a bad deal I'd say. Who wouldn't have come over for all of those freebees? But what was I getting out of any of this?

Well Sorry Mary, what did you think I was? the Porn Division of Barnes and Noble? I'm supposed to provide all the porn flicks, magazines and on-line dating and include a snack bar in the deal and get nothing in return other than the honor of your presence? Hell, you can't open and read the magazines and watch free videos in the porn shops; there's a price to pay and you gladly pay it; so why am I entitled to nothing? I know that you made such great sacrifices to be with me for those few hours on a Saturday evening. Your phone was just ringing off the hook with admirers and offers and you passed them all up just to be with me. But it seems to me like you were getting the best of the deal; all that attention and admiration and worship; plus good food, gifts, free porn, and sexually deviant research service all at no cost and even relief if you wanted it. Oh, admittedly, now and then you may have dropped me "a carrot" just to keep me hooked; but you didn't invest much time or effort in me on any personal level. You doled out your favors sparingly and gave me only what you felt you had to in order to pacify me.

In the beginning you were innocent, but once I laid my heart open to you, even though you couldn't respond by loving me, it was still your responsibility as a friend to protect me from further pain. You didn't have to rub all of your sexual adventures in my face. You could have shielded me from that, but instead, you got your kicks out of it. You knew that hearing about your liaisons with others hurt me yet you CHOSE to upset me by telling me anyway. And you knew full well that what you were about to say would hurt me because you always prefaced your stories with the words: "I hope this won't make you hostile".

You loved watching my reactions and controlling me and playing head games with me. You loved giving out mixed messages and dangling the bait just close enough to keep me following you like a sick puppy, while actually giving me nothing of substance. You refused to kiss me or show me any affection; the only physical contact that I was allowed at all was with your genitals. Well, I'm sorry, but I am NOT an electric penis pump. I am a loving human being with feelings. The only reason that I even settled for this very one-way limited sexual activity was because it afforded me the only opportunity that I had to touch you and express my love in some kind of tactile way, all other avenues being denied me.

You delighted in and relished in making me jealous with your tales of conquest, but then whenever I complained that you were treating me unfairly, you would say that I was being hostile and greedy and threaten to withhold your few and infrequent sexual favors from me for indeterminate periods of time; knowing full well what a burden that would be on me since you demanded that I remain celibate in order to qualify to be your "felator cum laude". Well, the games are over and THE PARTY IS OVER" Dearest."

I don't know what "D" will do for attention now. Who knows? Even his popularity for being the youngest man at parties, which are mostly attended by gay geriatrics, will wear thin once they realize that he's just a big tease with no substance; and that they may "get him" once, but never again. I doubt that any of the older men that he comes into contact with will love him enough to hang around for four years waiting for the "crumbs from his table". I doubt that they will cook for him and adore him and wait on him and his family hand and foot as I did.

Of course, he will be able to continue to buy half hour segments of sex on the streets if he doesn't get mugged, murdered or arrested in the process. But he will never be able to buy love at any price. Maybe that's just as well since he seems to value love so slightly and is not willing to make any effort to secure it, once found. He was cheating on his first lover within two weeks of beginning the relationship. Then he met and supposedly fell in love with a young man who he met in a porno theater in Los Angeles while on a business trip. After two days he was madly in love, yet when he came back here immediately went back to his usual rent boys and street behavior while simultaneously proclaiming his love and devotion for his new heartthrob.

Why it never dawned on me that if "D" who had stated that he was only attracted to young men and could never love an older man, could not now love and commit to this young man who was so obviously in love with him, but just left him dangling; how on earth did I ever suppose that he would ever treat me any better? But in matters of the heart, we choose selective blindness; we see only what we want to see; we create a lover in our minds and hearts that actually does not exist anywhere in reality. The "D" who I loved and would have died for was a creation of my own imagination and wishful thinking; he never existed other than in my head and heart. The real "D" is nothing more than a "marshmallow peep" as the term was used in the movie, "Latter Days" to symbolize a man of no substance; just something frivolous, seasonal and temporary and something that melts away leaving one hungry and empty.

It has been over two weeks now since "D" bruised me beyond repair with his thoughtless statements. I have not called him and I have not returned any of his calls until last night; not just to be stubborn or cruel, but simply because I have nothing left to say. Anything that I might say will not be considered; he will not budge an inch on anything so what is there to discuss or talk about? He left me a mildly angry message stating that he had tried to call me on several occasions but was never able to reach me direct and only got my answering machine. He believed that I was purposely avoiding him and screening him out and that if that was the case I should let him know and he will simply stop calling. He said that if he didn't get any response to this message that he would take it that I didn't want to see him or hear from him anymore.

Well that put me in a very difficult position because it's not as though I never want to see him again in my life, but I simply don't know what is to be gained by our meeting one another again over dinner. But I did return his call and admitted that at least part of the time, yes I was avoiding him, because it was just too painful to hear his voice, but that the last two calls I had not screened, but simply had not been at home. "D" said that he felt that it was important that we see each other within the next two weeks or he felt that what was left of the friendship would just crumble to dust. He was probably right, but the question still remains: what is there left to salvage? What does he want from me? Does he think things will be as they were before? They can never be as they were before.

Having never really had any friends before me, I think that he is suffering under a false assumption that casual friends gaze longingly at one another and hug each other warmly and lovingly and make candlelight dinners for each other and send each other loving "thinking of you" cards so on and so on, but they don't. But then he should know that for himself; he certainly never did any of that for me or for anyone else for that matter. If he just wants me to be a friend, then fine, but he has to understand that he will then be treated just the same as my other friends, no better and no worse, but that he has lost forever that special position on the highest pillar in the temple of my heart. If casual friendship is what he wants, then casual friendship is what he will get, but if he is expecting more, he will be sadly disappointed just as I was sadly disappointed in expecting more from him and not receiving it.

Love has a price, and if you are not willing to pay the price, then you should expect nothing. As Kahlil Gibran so aptly put it in his work, "The Prophet":

"When love beckons to you, follow him, though his ways are hard and steep…For even as love crowns you so shall he crucify you. Even as he is for your growth so is he for your pruning…But if in your fear you would seek only love's peace and love's pleasure, then it is better for you that you cover your nakedness and pass out of love's threshing-floor, into the seasonless world where you shall laugh, but not all of your laughter, and weep, but not all of your tears. Yes, love involves giving 100 per cent and sacrifice and effort and faithfulness and putting others first. If a person is not willing to make those sacrifices then he should just remain in the "seasonless world" of instant physical gratification followed up by incessant loneliness, guilt and isolation.

CHAPTER 16
THE COMMON DENOMINATOR

I have been trying for some time now as you well know, to try to establish a long-term, monogamous and meaningful relationship and I strongly question why that is such a momentous problem? I have attended gay social clubs and gatherings where people barely speak to one another or sometimes will engage you in a one hour conversation and then when you see them the next week, forget that they ever even met you. Yet when the meeting is over, they will all race to the nearest gay bar or pick-up area and seek each other out for instantaneous gratification there. What exactly is the problem? What's wrong with meeting someone; conversing; maybe arranging to have dinner together somewhere down the line soon and establishing some kind of dating arrangement? WHAT IS WRONG WITH DATING???

Similarly, when one attempts to meet someone via the internet, the same problems exist and they are mainly twofold. Either the individual wants to meet immediately and strictly for sex, and of course it must be "discreet" because they are hiding either a wife or lover somewhere who they don't want to find out about their indiscretions, or it is the other extreme where they want to chat back and forth endlessly for months and months and make absolutely no effort to actually meet you. Now why would that be? Why would you write back and forth and talk on the telephone for seven months and make excuse after excuse as to why you can't meet when you only live maybe 40 miles apart? Or crazier yet, why would you converse for months with someone who lives 3000 miles away? I'll tell you why. It's because nightly you are going out for instant gratification nearby with numerous faceless, nameless individuals or even prostitutes. It satisfies your sexual needs temporarily and "gets you through the night", but not really; because then you go home to that big empty house and that big empty bed and are faced with your true state of isolation and loneliness.

Now you can't very well take your trick out to dinner or invite him to stay over for the holidays can you? I mean you don't even know his name and you were more than likely given a fake phone number by him at the cruise area. So now you need someone to talk to; someone to unburden yourself with; an imaginary lover 3000 miles away or maybe as little as 40 miles away who can give you the illusion that you are not alone and unloved and isolated, but that there is someone out there who cares that you are alive. So you fill your empty moments (and there are many of them) with this imaginary lover who is really little more than a dishonest pen pal who is playing the same game with you. But neither one of you has the guts or the sincerity to turn this farce into something real. Well, I'm sorry, I am just too old for this kind of adolescent and foolish behavior; I gave up imaginary friends and "let's pretend" when I was a child. What is wrong with these people? Why don't they want a real and genuine life built on truth and honesty and loving and sharing? They have no idea what they are missing out on.

For one thing, sex is far more fulfilling and exciting with someone who you love than with a stranger. Sex with a stranger is simply "fast food" while sex with a man you love is "gourmet" and "haut cuisine". Why are so many willing to settle for fast food; simply because it's easier? Or is it because it's cheaper? You see gourmet food, if cooked at home requires planning and preparation and effort. If purchased out, it is expensive. So is that the problem? Men simply don't want to make an effort or pay the price of time and effort in building a relationship and so prefer to settle for mediocre "fast food"? Well, like anything else in life, you get what you pay for. So if millions of gay men prefer lives of mediocrity; loneliness and isolation, then so be it, but it's not what I want.

I recently placed this add on a gay internet site just as a "wakeup call" and to humiliate the fakers on there. I think that you will find it amusing:

"Looking for decently endowed men to serve; I don't eat cocktail franks. Age, race, looks unimportant; just be functional. I'll do things you'd be ashamed to ask your wife. Me, I am a middle-aged typical robust, heavier man with place to play. If that's a problem for you then try Ricky Martin and see if HE wants YOU. I mean get real; we're not getting married, you're only looking for oral sex because the bitch you DID marry won't suck it; isn't that right? and because you don't have a place to play because you are hiding the fact of a wife or male lover. If you need me to look like a male model or need "chemistry"; then you're not a straight man looking for head; you're a fag just like me. If you have to "be discreet" then stay home; that's really discreet. If you want phone sex, don't be a cheap prick; call a 900 number. If all you do is mutual JO, then stay home and play with yourself or find another sexually repressed and immature person to play with. If you are sexually mature and enjoy full treatment then hit me up; I guarantee you a good time; just be a man, not a wimp."

Now oddly enough, I got some positive responses from that add; one would think that people would have found it insulting. Although I must admit that the responses were from married men who apparently missed the point of the purposely insulting add. And of course this brings me to another point.

I was recently speaking to a good female friend of mine who is alone; having divorced two husbands and not seeking a third and we talked about all of this because the situation isn't all that different in her part of the world or in the straight community and we wondered why? We all grew up with seemingly loving parents and grandparents who believed in the words "until death us do part". What has gone wrong? What is the common denominator here? Well, we finally came to one solid conclusion; MEN. Yes, men are the common denominator and they "are all dogs".

Marianne and I laughed when we came to that conclusion. You see, my ex had often shaken his head at me in disbelief when I told him of my deep feelings for him. He had often told me: "Nobody has feelings like that; Bobby you are such a woman". Oddly I had never taken offense at those words because I fully acknowledged the female aspect of my personality and felt that it was and is the better half of myself. Why? It is because it is my female aspect that is the loving, nesting, nurturing, caring, self-sacrificing, spiritual, creative part. It is my female aspect that is able to create a warm and comfortable and stable home life for myself, my pets and hopefully a lover. Whereas I ask you, of what is my male aspect capable other than "hunting and gathering"; fighting; breeding and moving on to breed some more? The female is really the cement and foundation in any home life, or at least used to be when women were content to be wives and mothers or maybe wives, mothers and career women all at the same time if they were capable. But now that has all changed with the advent of many women wanting to be men and wanting to compete with and effectively emasculate their husbands. This, coupled with men's inability to somehow "keep it in their pants" is what has destroyed family life in this country and has contributed to the 50% divorce rate and the 50% illegitimacy rate. It is what has led to men simply siring colts and women simply having litters instead of building families; instead of evolving; we have regressed to being animals again.

When men simply prefer to litter the planet with their corrupt and unfeeling gene pools and refuse to be responsible fathers; and when women prefer to be artificially inseminated and raise their children as single mothers rather than love a man and build a genuine biological family unit; something is drastically wrong here and we are dealing with an emotionally and spiritually impoverished society. I know this may sound like an odd statement coming from a faggot, I mean God knows that we are all out to destroy family values; but I DO BELIEVE IN FAMILY VALUES. That's why I do NOT want to borrow someone else's husband. I want a husband of my own. If straight people are having sexual problems in their relationships then they should talk it out or get counseling from professionals and not turn to gay men to get their "jollies off". Oh, I know that in their twisted way these straight men console themselves by saying "well, it's not really cheating because it's not like I am seeing another woman", but it most certainly is cheating; it is adultery and many of these selfish men are bringing home presents to their unsuspecting wives in the form of STD's and HIV. Nice guys huh? Still others are infecting gay men like the married man who gave me HIV. Nice going guy! So don't tell me that HIV is a "gay disease" and try to pin it on us. It's simply symptomatic of the general selfishness and unbridled lust of men; ALL MEN.

And I wonder at the ignorance of the religious institutions who seem so intent on bashing gay rights and gay marriage, yet are amazingly silent on the subjects of adultery; sex before marriage; single parenting, etc. Why aren't they speaking out against those ills which are the major causes of the demise of the family. Gay Rights and Gay Marriage are not what is causing the breakup of American family life.

Now I need to discuss another "common denominator" here which I have not addressed before and that is this? What is the common denominator between all of the men who I have loved in this life? Maybe that will tell me how this has all happened to me and where I may have gone wrong. After giving it serious thought, the one common denominator which I have discovered is that each of my lovers was insecure, emotionally unstable and probably unlovable. And in each case, I came forth as the rescuer; the one person who could see beyond the rough surface, the gem that lie within. I felt that I was the only one who could understand or love each of these men and that without me they would probably be unloved and lonely for the rest of their lives. Maybe I have a "savior complex"; maybe I'm co-dependent; maybe I just need to be needed; I don't truly know. But I was successful with many of these men in teaching them to love and bringing out the best in each of them, but unfortunately, I did it all for someone else; someone else became the recipient of all of my hard work and patience and sacrifice. Most of these men went on eventually to fall in love with and settle down with someone other than myself. I suppose that's nice and something that I should be proud to have had a share in, but what about me? Where's the man who will love me? It was probably a big mistake on my part to have taken on all of these "problem children". I should have looked out for myself and chosen someone who could have lifted me up and someone who I could have aspired to be like; someone secure and self-reliant who knew what he wanted out of life. But alas, I did not.

Since that last argument with "D", he came back into my life again, seeming apologetic and agreeing not to flaunt his sexual exploits in my face so I began seeing him again. I "back-peddled" as he put it by resuming having dinner with him and even cooking one of his favorite dinners for him, but minus lit candles at the table. Yes, I wanted things back the way they were and he too, wants what he wants. He wants the cooked dinners, phone calls and the attention, but not the intimacy. He argues that I am not sexually intimate with my other friends so why do I need to be intimate with him? I explained that my other friendships were based upon certain commonalities. I go to fine restaurants and antiquing with my friend "E". I go to the movies and watch "Brit-Coms" and vacation with my friend "B". I go to live theater, art galleries and book stores with my friend "J". We have a lot in common and none of those friends ever flirted with me or offered themselves to me sexually so they have always remained platonic friendships; plus the major factor being that I had not fallen in love with my other friends.

My relationship with "D", however, was based entirely around sex. He crossed the line which my other friends had not by initiating sexual contact with me. At the time I thought that must mean that he had at least some feelings for me, but apparently not. I thought this was a nice and unique situation; a friendship "with benefits", so although less cerebral and intellectual than my other friendships, it did have its own unique quality. And then, of course, I ultimately fell in love with him.

We have little else in common. We do both have strong religious or spiritual beliefs but he won't discuss those with me, I think for fear of questioning his own faith. He claims to be a born again Christian and finds my Eastern Spirituality foolishness. I wanted the relationship to be more than just sex, I wanted us to explore New York museums and galleries together or go see Ellis Island, but all he ever wanted to do was to go see male strippers and engage in anonymous sex at NY bookstores. Since the strip theater closed we have never gone back to New York again or anywhere else for that matter.

So the problem is this: when a relationship is based entirely around sex and then the sex is suddenly removed, what's left? He says: "well we still have the friendship and companionship" and that's true to some extent, but even that is sullied when he continues to expound on his sexual adventures making me painfully aware of all the goodies he is willing to share with strangers but won't share with me. So our evenings of "companionship" ultimately end with my feeling hurt and embittered or "hostile" as he puts it. But then I ask: if he knows that flaunting his encounters makes me hostile, then why does he do it? Does he enjoy making me angry? Does he feel that proves he still has some kind of control over me? I don't know and he's not about to say.

So we had another argument culminating in the conclusion that maybe we just shouldn't see each other any more and I think that is very sad. I reached out to him and did everything I could to please him; there was nothing I wouldn't have done for him. He, on the other hand, offered me four hours a week of listening to his sexual exploits and then infrequently rewarding me with the option of one-way sex. No kissing, no hand-holding, no affection, no cuddling, non-reciprocal sex; none of the things that I wanted. As the relationship deteriorated, I was willing to receive less and less and went along with the program just to hold onto him. But now that he has removed the last intimacy that we ever had, there doesn't seem anything left to hold onto other than a casual acquaintanceship fraught with aggravation.

During all of this, I began seeing an old acquaintance of mine, "F", a bi-sexual who has popped into and out of my life over the years. Oddly enough, even though I have never expressed feelings of love for him nor given him gifts nor cooked special candle light dinners for him, he treats me far better than "D". He is affectionate, cuddly, puts my sexual needs ahead of his own, is reciprocal, brings me little gifts and cooks dinner for me. And he is willing to go to shows or engage in other activities unrelated to sex so he has a much broader appeal. Unfortunately, he is married and will undoubtedly never leave his wife since he is very loyal to her and feels that she could never make it on her own. But at least that shows him to be a sensitive, loyal and warm individual. I can handle being "second fiddle" to his wife of 25 years much better than I was able to handle being "second fiddle" to male hustlers. But despite all of his kindnesses, I still wanted "D" more. Go figure. But now I am convinced that rather than grieve over what "D" won't give me, maybe I would be far wiser to appreciate what "F" will give me, while at the same time continuing to search for a soul-mate all my own; one who I do not have to share with someone else.

CHAPTER 17
WHERE DO I GO FROM HERE?

So now, here I sit; just I and my two cats; lonely, bored, unloved, unemployed, bereft of all faith; stripped of all of my hopes and dreams with no foreseeable future. How am I supposed to deal with all of this? I watch my friends all burying their parents, which I did long ago, but relive each time I go to the hospital or to the wake of a friend's parent. I look at all of these poor souls stripped of everything that they worked for all their lives; reduced to one-room senior housing or worse yet, convalescent homes which are merely ante chambers to the funeral parlor and I see in vivid detail my own future. Although at least they have children who love them; who will be at my bedside to weep for me or see me off to the Elysian Fields?

I often ask myself the question: "Why am I continuing to watch this horrible movie when I already know the ending?" Why don't I just turn off the TV and get it over with? Am I hoping for a happy ending? Well there isn't any; unless one nurses some vague hope of an afterlife and a loving deity. However, I don't seem to understand how anyone could sensibly have much faith in a deity who somehow didn't know that you were alive for 58 years, hasn't kept in communication or made himself known to you, but will now somehow miraculously welcome you home to his heavenly abode that he has prepared for you. I find it very hard to believe that a Deity who has turned a blind eye at the massive suffering of mankind for some four thousand years now; who has winked at the Spanish Inquisition and slept through WWII and the Holocaust; who is oblivious to starvation; famine; disease; floods; earthquakes and other natural disasters of his own creation, has made special motel accommodations for me in heaven. Now granted; some warped fundamentalist will tell you that all of the aforementioned tragedies were the result of Adam's Sin, but that is baloney. How do they account for colliding planets; imploding stars and solar systems; meteor destruction and the extinction of vast numbers of species of life on this planet for eons before man ever set his sorry ass down here?

There is no explanation except that life and creation are simply random; no definite plan; just random. If there were a plan, it would be working wouldn't it? And don't give me the line about some fallen angel son of god with horns that took over the universe. If he did in fact take over the universe, then HE IS GOD. "Oh, but no, they will say; God only allowed Satan to take over temporarily." Well, that wouldn't stand up in court either. If I allowed a criminal to use my car and automatic weapon to rob a bank while I stood outside and watched and allowed it, I would do prison time and rightly so. There fore I accuse and convict God of all of the suffering of humanity and state that HE is just as guilty and culpable as the Devil, if there is one.

Of course none of this helps us down here; being the object of a "tug-o-war" between two jealous but apparently equal deities. It's rather like the famous line from King Lear where Gloucester says: "As flies to wanton boys are we to the gods, they kill us for their sport". I can just vividly see two spoiled brats getting their jollies by pulling the wings off of flies and feeling very exalted in their superior position. To God and Satan, I say as did Mercucio in "Romeo and Juliet", "A pox on both your houses". Neither of them have been very real or tangible in my life; more like Aphrodite and Hermes to me; quaint legends, but of no real consequence. As far as I can tell, man, in his refusal to accept the randomness of life and in his endless desire for control and power, simply created gods he could control by bribing them with sacrifices and such and thereby giving himself some sense of control in an otherwise random world. But the fact is that man's sacrifices are consumed, not by some anthropomorphic deity who will ultimately bless him and avert natural disasters, but merely by a greedy and power hungry class of priests who victimize and lord it over those who are supposed to be under their care and protection.

No, religion, rather than being the salvation of Mankind has proven more detrimental and destructive than constructive. Isn't it the basis of most of the terrorism and human suffering that we are witnessing today? Marx was right; "RELIGION IS THE OPIATE OF THE PEOPLE." It's a mind-altering drug that leads to aberrant behavior.

The other force which is destroying mankind; the Human Family and the earth itself is capitalism in it's present demonic form of world rule by multinational corporations. Not content with exploiting the under educated and disenfranchised in third world countries, it has spread it's poisonous tentacles worldwide to victimize all mankind and bring to ruin all middle classes all for the unjust gain and unbridled avarice of a handful of corporate leaders. But Karma is not a force to be mocked and Gaia or Mother Earth is not an entity to be mocked. Those who victimize others and despoil the earth will all get their just due in time. It may not be in my lifetime or yours, but it will all come crashing down eventually and with a vengeance. Gaia is already feverishly at work creating new viruses and new natural disasters of ever increasing magnitude and violence to destroy those who would destroy this planet and all the ill gotten gains of the rich and greedy will not be able to save them. Gaia and Karma are no respecters of wealth or privilege; they are based on the sure laws of nature that for "every action, there is an equal and opposite reaction."

So where do I turn from here? I have no idea whatsoever. Everything that I have been taught by the educational and religious systems has proven false. The country and system which I once believed in and would have died for, are now bought and paid for by world corporations. There is absolutely no hope in politics; it's all decided before you or I ever even get to the poles; all that we have left is some vague form of "representative democracy" which is in reality democracy to the highest bidder. You and I only have the right to pay taxes, complain quietly, and offer our sons and daughters to the God of War to finance big business and protect it's assets. Science supposedly increases our life span, but we can't get jobs when we're over 50 and end up losing all we have worked for all of our lives only to end up at the mercy of some managed senior housing facility or worse yet, some convalescent home where we will be left to drown like those poor victims of Hurricane Katrina in New Orleans in 2005.

I still have a portrait that was taken of me at age three. My great grandmother was so overwhelmed by it that she took it to the priest to be blessed because she thought that I was a saint incarnate. The portrait shows a radiant, smiling young child with sparkling eyes and an overall image of faith, trust, hopefulness, love, exuberance and a desire to begin this exciting journey called life. I gaze at that picture now and weep wondering where that dear little boy went and how life could have struck so many blows against that face and made such a concerted effort to beat the life out of that little child. I look in the mirror and all that I see is the scarred and aging face of one who has survived; yes, I guess I have to give my self credit for that much, but none the less, one who has lost all hope, all faith, all reason for living and is simply existing on "death row" awaiting the final verdict. What will it be I wonder: AIDS, cancer, a stroke, a heart attack; kidney failure? What will be the method of my execution? Will I be alone or will anyone remember; will anyone be at my bedside to see me off? How dare preachers call life a gift of God. What gift? A gift doesn't have to be returned. I don't see life as a gift anymore. I see it as a death sentence with a few fleeting moments of happiness offset by years of loss and suffering as ultimately everything that you ever loved or held dear is taken away from you. It's a clever con job to keep the species going. Hold out a carrot; make them believe that they will be successful and live happily ever after; it's necessary to lie in order to maintain the survival of the species. I think that if young people really knew what kind of future faced them, they would all commit suicide en masse. That's why our parents lie to us and present a glowing picture of marital bliss and happiness. If they told us the truth, we'd give up.

So why am I watching this terrible movie through to the end? But for a few small details, I already know the ending and it's not pretty. Why wait for the credits to go by? Why put up with twenty or more years of suffering just to see the credits? I don't know. Maybe hope springs eternal; maybe something wonderful will happen within the next five years, or ten years or twenty years. Maybe I will find love, but of course only to lose it to death ultimately, so one wonders is it worth the wait and suffering only to experience love for a year or two or perhaps never? I'm not afraid of "Judgement". If there is a deity, I will go nose to nose with Him at the Pearly Gates and tell him: "I did the best I could with the rotten hand that you dealt me. As far as humanly possible, I loved and respected all of creation both human and animal; I did the best that I could and suffered without retaliation. Where were you though all of it? If that's not good enough, I don't want to hear about SIN. As King Lear said: "I am more sinned against than sinning". So don't even go there."

I would certainly rather leave this life at my own hand rather than at the mercy of some virus or incompetent medical practitioner, or worse yet, some arbitrary deity who feels that I have more to learn from suffering, but I can't say at this point. I feel rather like the lyrics of Peggy Lee's wonderful song "Is that All There Is?"

"I know what you must be saying to yourselves,

If that's the way she feels about it why doesn't she just end it all?

Oh, no, not me. I'm in no hurry for that final disappointment,

For I know just as well as I'm standing here talking to you,

When that final moment comes and I'm breathing my last breath, I'll be saying to myself: Is that all there is?"

CHAPTER 18
LIGHT AT THE END
OF THE TUNNEL

Now I suppose that I could take a different viewpoint of all of this and try to see it all from the Eastern point of view; from the Hindu and Buddhist points of reference which I had told you about earlier in this work. Now I know that you are going to say: "You just got finished telling us that religion is much of the source of human suffering." Yes I did, but Buddhism and Vedanta are not really religions; they are philosophies based upon findings of the science of the mind and not on dogma or scripture. In fact Buddhism in particular does not even postulate any kind of anthropomorphic god. Buddha is not a god at all, but simply "The Enlightened One" and an example of what we can all aspire to.

Now the teachers of Vedanta would say that God is both imminent and transcendent. In simpler terms that is to say that God is both the Creator and beyond creation while at the same time He is also "that which is created" or present in every atom and molecule of creation. What that would mean is that God is not aloof and separate from our suffering, nor is he judgmental and feeling that we deserve what we get, but is suffering along with us and ultimately wants us to come home to Him so that OUR joint suffering will end.

Let me try to explain this concept as best I can in laymen's terms and contrast it with the Judeo Christian concept which I was raised with and which is the source of a lot of my disappointment, negativity and hostility toward God. In the Judeo Christian concept, God the Creator is all mighty; all powerful and all knowing and has the ability to effect change on earth for better or worse and has supposedly done so at various times throughout history according to various scriptures. In his own words from the Holy Bible, he is a "jealous God, visiting the iniquity of the fathers upon the children to the third and fourth generations of those who hate Me..." Exodus 20:5. Deuteronomy 28:1, 15-68 shows God to be, not a God of unconditional love, but just the opposite, a god who will exact extreme justice on those who disobey. In Deuteronomy 28:1 God says: "Now it shall come to pass, if you diligently obey the voice of the Lord your God, to observe His commandments which I command you today, that the Lord your God will set you high above all the nations of the earth."

But then God continues beginning in verse 16 through verse 68 enumerating what would happen if they disobeyed. "Cursed shall you be in the city and cursed shall you be in the country…cursed shall be the fruit of your body and the produce of your land…The Lord will strike you with consumption, with fever, with inflammation…The Lord will cause you to be defeated before your enemies…Then the Lord will scatter you among all peoples, from one end of the earth to the other…and among those nations you shall find no rest, nor shall the sole of your foot have a resting place…" So we see the God of Abraham as most definitely a "conditional God" and not a god of unconditional love.

This creates a great mental problem because we never quite know whether the natural disasters which occur from time to time are just "the earth farting" or if they are attacks by God on a rebellious people. If God is all mighty, then why doesn't he continue to intercede for mankind as he supposedly did in Biblical days? And if he does not intervene and stave off disasters when he has the ability to do so, then what kind of a God is He? And the standard argument or theological theory that God is simply allowing Satan to rule the earth and create havoc and suffering for a set limited time and is allowing him to torture good people as in the case of the Biblical Job, doesn't hold water with me and would not hold up in any court. If you have it within your power to avert suffering or crime or whatever and do nothing, you are just as guilty as the assailant committing the crime. This is the source of my agonizing love-hate relationship with God with which I have been suffering all of my life.

Now in the Eastern way of looking at God, we see almighty God or Sat Chit Ananda or as Supreme Consciousness, Existence and Bliss; limitless, without form; indefinable; unchangeable, etc. Now part of that Divine Consciousness decided to take form and became the phenomenal universe within the dimension of time, space and form or creation as we would say. So the transcendent and eternal part of God still exists beyond creation, while the other aspect of God, namely the phenomenal world and universe exists within the time and space continuum and is therefore subject to the laws of time and space. It is almost as if the scientist who designed the space stations, then journeyed to a space station and became stranded there. Back home he didn't need oxygen tanks and lived life without restrictions, but now, while stranded at his own space station, he is subject to the limitations of being in that time and space.

Likewise, from the Vedanta point of view, Almighty God remains almighty to time indefinite, but He is no part of the phenomenal world or creation and cannot interact with it accept by means of the projected aspect of God found in creation and which is limited to the laws of time and space. Therefore it is only those more highly evolved souls with highly evolved brains and intellects who may effect change for good or bad in the universe. In other words, it is the responsibility of those of us who recognize our son ship and divinity to rise to the occasion and try to help mankind and the universe to advance in a positive and godly direction. If we do not take our role seriously and allow the world to slip into greed and avarice and self destruction, then we have only ourselves to blame; not some distant deity. So God is both transcendent and imminent and in His imminent and limited form, he suffers with us, side by side. He is the homeless person from New Orleans; he is the AIDS patient in the hospital; He is the lonely little old lady dieing in the convalescent home, but also the loving nurse attending her and trying to make her passage as smooth and painless as possible.

So yes, God is with us, but in His limited aspect, which means that He can only effect change when a substantial or critical number of his children recognize their son ship and responsibility and work together for good. And so long as a substantial or critical number of people continue to shift their son ship and responsibility to an imaginary Santa Clause kind of deity who will just miraculously drop down from heaven some day and solve everything in one fell swoop; then positive change will never come; the kingdom of God on earth will simply never come. That's why when Jesus disciple, Philip asked him "show us the Father" his response was: "He that has seen me has seen the Father" (John 14:9) and then he continued on to explain how he was in union with the father and that likewise his followers would be in union with him and the Father and that they would some day perform even greater works than Jesus himself.

Likewise when people asked Jesus about when the Kingdom would come, his response was: "The Kingdom of God IS within you". Luke 17:21. Now he didn't say that the Kingdom of God "will be" within you or will come on March 15th of 2020; no, he said that it is already within you and why? It is because each and every one of us is a very real part of God. It is not something that is given us at some point in time by some priest at a ceremony or sacrament, it is our birthright.

Very possibly the world we know today might have been much better off and much nearer to the realization of Godlike Kingdom conditions had the institutional religions helped the members of the Family of Man to realize and shoulder their responsibility as Sons of God rather than convincing them over and over again that they were wretched sinners and "poor banished children of Eve". It is this kind of negative teaching that is so seared into my brain that has created the animosity that I often feel for God. Sometimes I just need to jostle myself and remind myself that what I am feeling hostility toward is not in reality God, but merely a warped and negative concept of God that I was taught as a young child. But sometimes it is difficult for me to make the distinction and I often end up "throwing the baby out with the bath water". So please excuse my ranting against God in the prior chapter. I am back on base again now. Excuse me Lord.

Now the Buddha taught that the source of all suffering is desire, and in particular unfulfilled desire, and boy I can vouch for that in my case. The Buddha basically taught that while it is acceptable to appreciate food and beauty and the good things in life, that we should just experience them and then let them go and not cling to them. It is the clinging to and the desire to hold on to a moment or person or thing and never let them go that causes all suffering because the nature of phenomenal reality IS change and impermanence.

Now I suppose if I am to be honest with myself and honest with you, then I must acknowledge that I have arrived at the very abysmal and dim view of life that I presented to you in the last chapter precisely because I felt that God had taken everything that I ever loved away from me; my mother, my father, uncles, aunts, friends, pets, etc. And I was also upset because now even my financial security was beginning to fade away and I knew that I would probably have to live in reduced circumstances from those that I was accustomed to. I was upset when I envisioned that someday I might not even be able to walk under my own power and would be dependent on others and lose my independence. But again, the Buddha would say, "but you knew all of that was coming" you knew that physical life was all about change and impermanence and yet you chose it anyway."

I say this because it is both the Buddhist and Hindu belief that we keep incarnating due to either unfinished business or out of desire for something here. So it is our own desire that "does us in" and brings us back and subjects us to transition, impermanence and suffering. How deeply we suffer will depend upon how firmly we cling to people; experiences and things or how loosely, allowing them to pass in and out of our lives without hindering them from moving on. I have to agree that it is precisely our desire to hold on to things that causes our suffering and also creates greed. The Masters say that we should be like an earthworm that allows the soil to just run through its body without hindrance or like a lotus that grows in the mud, yet is pure and unblemished and holds its blossom high above the primordial waters. When I look at it all from this aspect, I must admit that it puts it all in a very different light.

I was deeply hurt because I loved "D" 100% and I felt that he only gave me maybe 5% in return and gave the rest to unworthy people who didn't even love him. But haven't I done exactly the same to God? Haven't I put God at the very bottom of my list of priorities and every other petty pursuit first in my life? Haven't I hurt Him just as deeply as "D" hurt me and then blamed Him for my suffering to boot? Had I sought God as fervently as I have sought sex, money and lovers, perhaps I wouldn't have suffered as much as I did. I certainly wouldn't have ended up with HIV at any rate. I can't help but think of the parting words of Cardinal Woolsey in Shakespeare's Henry VIII, Act II, Scene II, when he says to Cromwell: "Cromwell, Cromwell! Had I but serv'd my God with half the zeal I serv'd my King, he would not in mine age have left me naked to mine enemies."

Perhaps I need to take heed of my own words and my own dislikes and apply them to myself. How many times have on railed on older gay men acting like children and trying to be something that they are not; dressing like teenagers and chasing after young men trying in some vain way to recapture their own youth when it was long gone. But maybe I have been doing the same thing only to a lesser degree. Maybe I should follow the customs of my Eastern brothers and sisters who believe that there are stages to life that need to be followed and lived fully in the correct order in order for one to progress naturally from stage to stage and on to ultimate fulfillment. They believe that there is the childhood stage; then the young adult stage or householder stage when one should marry and raise children and then finally the mature adult stage when the children are gone when the adults should cease from sexual activity and materialistic pursuits and pursue their spirituality and work toward union with God culminating in physical death and transformation. Perhaps that is the natural order of things and by trying to go backward and recapture our youth, we are only wasting precious time and not fully living and experiencing where we SHOULD BE at this particular point in our lives.

Trying to go back and be something that we are not, is part of that clinging process which only leads to frustration and disillusionment when we come to the conclusion that perhaps our young lovers and concubines only love us for our material goods after all and we have made fools of ourselves in the process of trying to gain their love and approval by buying their love. Far better would it be for us to be adults and act like adults. Perhaps we can be mentors to younger gay people and help them in their passage and prepare them for their futures rather than being sexual predators or vicariously living our misspent and lost youth through them. In this way we will be fulfilling our duty to those who will live on after us and we will earn their respect rather than their ridicule. Perhaps in some small way we will even be making the world a better place if we can instill values and honor into these young people which were not instilled in them by their own parents who may have been too busy being friends with their children and also trying to gain their approval rather than being responsible parents.

In a recent episode of the gay TV show, "In The Life" which airs on public television channels once or twice a month; noted playwright, author and actor, Harvey Fierstein elaborated on this same theme how it was his feeling that since gay men for the most part don't have children of their own, that it is our responsibility to younger gay men to be there for them and set an example for them; not to victimize them and exploit them as sex toys. It really is in the best interest of the forward progress of the Gay Rights Movement to do so. I recently attended a meeting which is in the format of a rap session for gay men at a local gay community center and I must admit that I was rather surprised at the amount of fear of discovery and feelings of inferiority that still exist in younger members of the gay community despite advances and progress which we have achieved in the last twenty-five to thirty years.

I mean when I was growing up, homosexuality was "the love that dare not speak its name". It was totally unacceptable and there was absolutely no one who I could talk to about it. But nowadays there are gay groups on just about every college campus; gay coalitions of teachers; gay advocacy groups; many gay related television shows, etc. So over all, even though there is still much opposition from the Christian Right and other forces, at least today there is much more compassion and understanding on the part of the general public with many opinion poles showing as high as 50% of the general public supporting gay marriage and similar issues. So I am rather surprised at the fear that still exists among young gay men and the inferiority problems that in some cases have driven some young gay men to go to such as extremes as to even seek out "healing" and sexual reprogramming from radical Christian Right groups.

With new attacks coming from Rome in the form of pending removal of all gay priests; which are estimated at somewhere between 30-50% of the clergy and continual assaults from Christian Right political organizations; unless we fortify our young gay men and women and instill within them with the courage and fearlessness that our "gay ancestors" showed at Stonewall back in the late 1960's, the gay movement will be over and done with and we will once more be plunged back into the dark ages. There will be no gay community and there will be no further advancement of gay rights; all that will exist will be pockets of gays, bisexuals and sexual predators in general meeting on the internet for "discreet sessions" and living in perpetual fear of losing their jobs; housing; and social standing if they are discovered. Again, if we put physical pleasure first in our lives; and ignore the importance of advancing gay rights and building solidarity in the gay community, then we will have no one else to blame for our loss of freedom but ourselves.

And then too, all gay issues aside, for those of us who do believe in reincarnation, maybe our later years would be more wisely spent working at overcoming habits and cravings and addictions which hold us in bondage and keep forcing us back into this phenomenal world of change, impermanence and suffering; rather than romping through the forest preying on gay youth. Maybe we should be seeking that which is permanent, eternal, unchanging and blissful; maybe we should be working toward returning home to "Our Father" once and for all time. Once a soul has reached a certain level, it is no longer comfortable in this world of name and form it is too sensitive and too easily bruised; it finds lesser evolved souls as unfeeling, often destructive and difficult to be around. It is as the great poet, James Kavanaugh, said in one of his poems: "There are men too gentle to live among wolves".

But somehow I have to either fulfill or conquer this need to be loved by a man. It is all that I have ever wanted all of my life; it is all that I have sought after these last forty years. All I want from this life is for one man to look me dead in the eyes and tell me how much he loves me and that he wants me to be his life's partner and actually mean it. Oh, it's been said to me in the past, but never really meant; it was said to me to get gifts or sexual favors; it was said to me by those who needed a place to live or a sugar Daddy. I want it to be real this time and not just in response to my own words of love toward him. I want him to say it first.

CHAPTER 19
AS THE STOMACH TURNS

Fortunately, "D" and I did make up and continued to be close friends and I was happy for that. I imagined that we would always be close, but not lovers. But then one can hardly undervalue good friendships; they are hard to come by and I figured that there must be at least some love and something there that made us put up with one another and keep coming back to each other. But now I am forced to question it all again.

"D" agreed to go away with me this summer for a short vacation. I suggested that we go on a nice bus tour of the Pennsylvania Dutch country or possibly to New Hope, PA which is a lovely artist colony popular with gay couples. Well "D" had other ideas. He wanted to go to Providence, RI to a sex complex and gay bathhouse. He also wanted to go to Washington DC, of course not to see the Capitol or the Smithsonian but because he had been there on a convention and had found good cruising parks and strip clubs. So I compromised and suggested that we go to Provincetown.

Oddly enough, even though he had hitherto banned our intimacies, before going to Provincetown he put this question to me: "If we are going to be staying together in the same room and I should have NEEDS during the night, would you be willing to take care of them?" Well, I was shocked and felt a glimmer of hope once more that perhaps he was "back peddling" as he always said and that maybe we could be intimate again. I knew that I would have to share him with half of PTown, but if he had a little left to share with me, that would be sufficient. Well, needless to say, nothing happened between us. Plenty happened between he and other men and me and other men, but nothing between the two of us and I must say that I was saddened and disappointed. I had grown very fond of him again over those days in PTown; I enjoyed waking up to him and having breakfast with him and dinner with him and it brought back all of the old feelings that I had earlier had for him. I was very depressed on the way home because I knew that it would be back to the old routine of seeing him once a week for a few hours only and sharing him with his local stable of regular call boys. As soon as we got back I found a note pinned to his door by one of his bisexual tricks who was desperately trying to reach him. He said that he was tired and really didn't feel like sex, but that he better contact the guy because he didn't want to disappoint him and lose his attention should he need him in the future.

Now I find this both amusing and frustrating that he will "rise to the occasion" for fear of losing a trick, but never had any problem whatsoever telling me that he was tired or not in the mood and making me wait for weeks and months until he felt inspired. He obviously didn't give a crap about my needs or losing my attention by keeping me waiting. Now admittedly, he never considered us lovers even though he knew that I was in love with him, so he felt no obligation to me as a lover, but what about as a friend? He knew how much joy being intimate with him gave me and that it was the one thing that made me truly happy so why was it so easy for him to deny me those brief moments of happiness and keep me on hold while making pleasing strangers his first priority? I didn't feel that seeking intimacy with him once or twice a month was asking all that much and I never asked him to give up his call boys or tricks, I only asked that he save a little for me. Was that asking for too much? Apparently it was to him.

Last weekend I made him his favorite dishes for dinner as a surprise, instead of going out to eat. I had also spent the entire week downloading images of beautiful young Latino boys off the internet and put them all into a slide show for his viewing pleasure. Of course, I had ulterior motives, I'm only human. Well, he enjoyed the dinner immensely, got half way through the slide show and announced that it was late and he was tired and would have to leave. Needless to say, I had hoped for more and was very disappointed but I did not let on; I just gave him a warm hug and sent him on his way. I did the dishes and put things away which took about an hour. But of course after looking at all of those slides, I was raring to go so I raced down to the local porno store to see what was going on there and lo and behold, who do I see heading out of the parking lot but "D" who of course looked a little unnerved. I didn't make any snide comments, but I'm sure that he knew that I was wondering why someone so tired and not horny was in downtown Bridgeport cruising the bookstore parking lot instead of going straight home to rest. And of course that's exactly what I was thinking.

Needless to say, I was pissed. So when a nice looking guy in a pickup truck invited me to follow him home, I did. Well that turned out to be a near disaster. Once in his place he hit me up for $20 to get some crack. Well, I wanted no part of that and told him that I had to go, at which point he blocked the door and wouldn't let me leave. He kept begging me to help him get his drugs and that he would do anything to please me, but I wanted no part of it. I finally managed to force the door open with him still attached to it and made my getaway, but now

I was even more pissed. I was pissed because I could have had a lovely respectable evening at home giving pleasure to a man I loved, but because he rejected my advances, in effect he forced me back into the streets again risking my life and self respect to get what he could have so easily given me himself if he cared at all.

The next day he called asking me why I had made that slideshow, to which I responded that I thought it was pretty self-evident why I had made the slideshow. He asked me if I was angry with him, to which I responded that I was disappointed but not angry. I told him of my adventure and how I had narrowly escaped some real danger. I mean what if the guy had gotten hostile and beat me up? He admitted that he met no one that night, to which I responded: "Well isn't that nice? Neither of us got what we wanted when we might have at least shared a good time together had you decided to stay." At that point he got angry and said that I had no right to expect sexual favors from him. I reminded him of how many ways I go out of my way to please him and questioned why he couldn't occasionally give me the one thing that truly pleased me.

He said that I was being irrational and had no right to expect anything of him. He reminded me that he had told me before that our intimacies were over. I then reminded him of his asking me if I would take care of his needs in PTown? He said that was different because we were on vacation then. I asked him "who is being irrational now"? It's OK for me to have sex with you on vacation but not at home?" Does that make any sense? Not to me it doesn't. I told him how he made me feel second rate and how he is more concerned about disappointing strangers than disappointing a good friend. He didn't like that at all, but too bad, because it's true. He said: "I told you before, I am happy with things the way they are with no intimacies." Well that's nice for him but what about me? I'm NOT happy with things the ways they are. Don't my feelings count? Does everything have to be his way all of the time? Can't he bend at all?

He told me that I was giving him a headache and making him sick. I told him that he shouldn't have played with my feelings. If all he ever wanted from me was a casual friendship then he should have never been intimate with me in the first place and I would have respected that just as I do with my other friends. But I assured him not to worry, that I would never ask him again and I won't. I have my pride too and I will not be swept under the carpet like dirt. If he wants casual, then casual is what he will get; no more first priority. He can get in line behind the rest of my friends and wait his turn. For too long now I have neglected my other friends in favor of him, but no more. If he wants Duck a L'orange and crab legs for dinner he better start looking for a good restaurant because Chez Bob's is now closed for the season. And if he wants someone or something to brag to about his sexual conquests (mostly bought and paid for) then he better find a good tape recorder. I was willing to accept the crumbs from his table, but now he doesn't even want to give me the crumbs. What does that tell me?

But I will not give up on my dream, it's just sad that "D" will not be a part of it. At least now I am free to pursue the love of someone who may actually respond and love me in return. Before I was driving with the brakes on and not really trying to meet anyone new because I always hoped that he would eventually respond to my love. I didn't want to abandon him while I felt that there was still some small hope. Now at least it is clear to me that I must move on and not look back.

I can't be concerned about him spending the rest of his life in shallow encounters without ever being loved. He WAS loved and he didn't appreciate it. I can't be worrying nightly that he's being mugged, stabbed or arrested. It's not my problem. He made his choice as we all do and we all have to pay for our choices in life. I would hate to see him scandalized and lose his career, but if he doesn't care, then why should I? If he prefers danger and risk and vice more than love then so be it. I tried to steer him away from all that and encouraged him to meet someone nice on his own level and settle down, even though I knew that would end our relationship, but I genuinely wanted what was best for him. He made some half-hearted attempts at meeting people, but as usual, still spent most of his time pursuing street thugs and still does. Ultimately it can only lead to disaster of one form or another.

CHAPTER 20
DEALING WITH CHANGE

In the meantime, our poor little family keeps getting whittled away. In October of 2006 my sister-in-laws' mom passed away. There was no real cause of death other than the fact that she had just given up on life and wanted to die. She stopped eating and took to bed more and more and then just died. She had totally lost interest in activities that she once loved like going to the casinos and such and had spent more and more time just sleeping. I guess that prolonged bouts with chronic depression can lead to death. Then in November of 2006 my niece-in-law suddenly died after a long bout with liver damage due largely to pain killers prescribed by the medical institution. So now my nephew is a widower at age 40. My brother was diagnosed earlier in the year with colon cancer and is undergoing chemo treatments, so all is not well there either, but it has afforded an opportunity for my brother and I to become closer.

When he first told me about his health condition, I knew only too well how it felt to have an alien invader inside of you which could potentially go wild and cause your ultimate demise. It's so easy for people to say: "I know exactly how you feel" when in reality, they can't possibly know how you feel unless they have "been there". So I decided that was the appropriate time to share with my brother the reality of my HIV+ status and let him know that I truly did understand how he felt. My brother appreciated it very much and told me that I should have told him sooner. He felt that it must have been a terrible burden to carry alone. One good thing that has come out of my brother's health condition is that it has somehow mellowed him and has brought out a more appreciative and loving side of him that I am sure was there all along, but just needed to surface. Since then we have become much closer. In fact, for the first time in 59 years, my brother hugged me when leaving my condo over the Christmas holidays. It came as quite a shock to me, but a pleasant one. My sister-in-law is also very loving and compassionate and has been a real rock at holding the family together; she is a true blessing to our family. I only hope and pray that my brother can beat his cancer and have many years to enjoy with his new found appreciation for life and family.

The Christmas holidays were a bit bleak this year due to the recent losses in our family. It's very difficult to sit at the festive table and not notice all the missing faces of loved ones who were once there. It's also very difficult wondering if we will all be together again the same time next year. We have always known that life is uncertain at best, but I think that we push that reality into the back recesses of our minds, not wanting to face that reality. Losses are at least a wakeup call that alerts us to the fact that we need to live each day to the full and treasure each moment. The past is just that, it is past. The future is unknown and may never be. All we really have is the present and we need to live it fully and take every opportunity to reassure our loved ones of our love and appreciation and as far as is possible, be at peace with everyone since there may not be a second chance. Easter was likewise difficult since my brother had just finished a series of chemo treatments which left his exhausted and frail and not really up to holiday festivities. He had to keep leaving the table to take naps and in some ways it was like he was already "gone from the picture". I really don't know how I will manage if anything happens to him. He is my last living blood relative and the only one who I can talk with who has shared memories of Mom and Dad and growing up together. I want to see him as much as possible during this period, but that isn't always practical when he is tired and worn out. Also it hurts me to see him thin and frail when he was always such a strong and take charge person. Life can be very cruel. Just when he and my sister-in-law should be enjoying and reaping the benefits of having worked hard all of their lives, something like this has to come along and ruin it.

My own health condition of HIV+ status seems to be at status quo. It is three years now and fortunately I seem to be holding my own and am still not on any anti viral medications, but I am suffering from deep depression and don't seem to have any interests or motivation of any kind, I simply want to sleep most of the time. Of course most of it stems from my unemployment status with no hope of any decent kind of job in sight; my unemployment compensation has run out and the cost of living keeps escalating beyond belief. My only short-term goal is to land another useless job, make it last at least six months and then go on unemployment again only to repeat this procedure until I am 65. In this brave new world of outsourcing. with jobs leaving the country at record rates, that's the most that I can hope for. Then too, there is no one special in my life and my friendship with my Ex, "D" is almost non-existent. I might be motivated to go back to England again, but travel costs are now so exorbitant and the dollar is worthless in England and Europe these days so I really can't afford it not knowing if or when I will be able to secure work again. And then there is the "sword of Damocles" hanging over my brother, which tends to sadden and depress me also.

And then too, when I think of England, I think of how charming and unique it was back in the 1950's and 60's. I remember the wonderful little individual shops; the chemist shop (pharmacy), the fish mongers shop, the butcher shops, the fresh produce shops, the open air farmers markets, the bakeries, etc. I remember the ladies in their hats and white gloves shopping and the gentlemen in their blazers and bowler hats and the polite little children in their school uniforms, but I wonder what I will experience if I go back there now. More than likely those shops have all been replaced with super Stop & Shops or their equivalent and due to globalization, the people I see will be largely Indian, Pakistani, Muslim or African or they will be young Englishmen wearing blue jeans, Budweiser T-shirts and sneakers. It will be hard for me to find fish and chips or Cornish pasty shops hidden behind Chinese takeout, pizzerias, Taco Bells, Tandouri chicken and falafel houses. All of the charm and culture and things that made England unique will be gone, just as we are losing our American culture here at home where celebrating the "Cinco De Mayo" has somehow become more important than celebrating the Fourth of July and where there are far more Puerto Rican, Mexican, Brazilian and Portuguese flags flying from houses than Old Glory. So what's the point of spending $800 air fair and traveling 3000 miles just to be in the same scenario that I can see in any US city? If you ask me, globalization has really ruined everything. Of course that's not the case for the Rich and Famous who created this situation since they only travel in their own private jets to Islands that they themselves own and which are off limit to tourists. And they don't mind having native servants because it gives them someone who they can feel superior to and who will work for next to nothing.

Of course one might say: why not travel the US and explore your own country? Well yes, again that might have been nice twenty or thirty years ago when each area had its own distinct culture, cuisine and uniqueness. But nowadays as I travel the US all that I see are either devastated towns and communities with closed restaurants and storefronts due to the loss of industry or sprawling shopping malls and condos, each replete with a Home Depot, Walmart and Target store. Likewise, the indigenous cuisine has been replaced by Chinese takeout, Taco Bell, and Pizza Hut. If I get lost anywhere I will have problems getting directions from either the Pakistani gas station attendants or the Mexican, Ecuadorian or Brazilian service people in local businesses. Just last week it took me 15 minutes to try to place a simple order with a MacDonald's employee who couldn't speak English and couldn't figure out how to use the register or make change. But later, when on break, he did marvelously well with his cell phone. Likewise, last week, I spent a half hour on the phone with a Hewlett Packard customer service rep in India who was of no help to me because I couldn't understand a word that he was saying, yet those jobs are now unavailable to Americans.

I have basic cable TV; it's all that I can afford; it gives me channels 2-26. At least 4 of those channels are in Spanish. When I go to an ATM machine the instructions begin in Spanish and I have to choose English as an option. When my friend recently purchased a cell phone, the instructions were in Spanish only. What's wrong with this picture?

I also notice that most of what I see on Educational TV these days seems to revolve around shows depicting the supposedly rich cultures of Mexico, Peru, the Caribbean Islands, Uganda, Zimbabwe, etc. I see nothing but hours and hours of loincloth native men and topless women building huts and canoes; hours and hours of islanders sacrificing chickens and pigs to ancestors and primeval deities, hours and hours of watching villagers parading around with statues of saints and the Lady of Guadeloupe in gratitude for the fact that she has blessed them with poverty, starvation and no running water or sewers. In an age of space travel and technology, I am not sure that I can consider cultures that have not advanced much beyond the stone age as either rich or educational. Or if not about foreign cultures, the shows are centered around urban ghetto life presenting fatherless households, teen pregnancy, physical abuse and drug addiction as social norms and graffiti as an art form. The producers seem to fail to accept the fact there are many other parts of this once great country outside of urban centers that still do possess family values, work ethics, self-sufficiency, morals and the ability to create real art.

Are all of these shows simply clever media attempts and public relations efforts, prompted by our government to con us into developing an acceptance of the fact that as jobs continue to leave the country and affordable decent housing disappears along with the Middle Class that we will be forced to live side by side with this new breed of Americans? Are they just weaning us to accept the fact that we are fast becoming a third world country ourselves and that we might just as well learn to accept all of our third world neighbors now because we may need to learn survival skills from them in the future and be willing to work for $5 per hour, sleep on factory floors or share an apartment with 2 other families just as they do? Of course not everyone will have to come to this acceptance. The rich and famous who are encouraging and promoting this decline and erosion of the American Dream just so that they can get cheap labor and make bigger and bigger profits will all be safely tucked away in their multi million dollar palatial homes in gated communities designed to protect them from the same people that they expect us to live and work with.

A workmate of mine, Steve, a father of three died on the job, why? He was having recurrent serious headaches but wouldn't go to the emergency room because he didn't have health insurance and didn't want the hospital to attach his wages for payment. Consequently he died on the job of an aneurism while millions of illegal aliens can receive free emergency and hospital services at our expense and hospital workers are not allowed to even ask if they are documented workers or not. Then why are they allowed to ask me if I have health insurance before treating me? What's wrong with this picture?

And this same scenario is being played out all over the world due to globalization. I watched a report on BBC news just last week which highlighted that even greedy British businessmen are refusing jobs to Brits while hiring Eastern European refugees at below minimum wages and then deducting $100 per week from their wages for rent since they allow them to sleep in the factory complex. What's wrong with this picture?

Now admittedly, any company or corporation has a duty to its stockholders and needs to make a fair profit. But we're not talking about fair profits here; we are talking about gouging and absurd profits that are not even reinvested into the companies or paid to the stockholders but merely doled out as rewards to the corporate executives. We're talking about a situation not unlike that of France in 1789 just prior to the French Revolution.

Now many political pundits and news show hosts are saying: "When will the American People wake up?" Well we're already awake but what can we do about it when Congress and every administration since that of Nixon, who opened trade with China, has sold us out? I and many thousands like me have sent letters to our congressmen and signed countless petitions which have all fallen on deaf ears. It doesn't much matter who you vote for because whether Republican or Democrat, they are all in the pockets of big business lobbyists and there IS NO LOBBY for the American People.

So that's why I take no pleasure in traveling around the US. When I visit the homes of the Founding Father's, I am reminded of the bright future that we once had; I am reminded of the limited government which they established and the sanctity of the Constitution which they wrote which Congressmen today give only slight honor to or spit upon outright. I am reminded of great men like Sam Houston and our ultimate victory over Mexico. But now I see that Mexico has defeated us and that we have become a dumping ground for any third world country that can't take care of its own. I see us fast becoming a third world country ourselves where illegals have more rights and benefits than citizens and where our own culture and language are being jeopardized by invaders who refuse to assimilate and who demand that their children be taught at our expense in the languages of their origins. And we are beset by by immigrants who do not intend on making this their homeland or investing in this nation but who send all their earnings back to their own countries rather than supporting the economy of their new homeland. And I suppose why should they? Who is setting the example? Even American corporate moguls are not investing in the U.S. anymore; they are doing all of their manufacturing overseas or outsourcing all of their jobs overseas. I find it odd that Ford, General Motors and other U.S. companies cannot afford to hire American workers and still be able to turn a profit for their investors while Toyota can. Can anyone explain this to me?

And you ask me why am I depressed? I am depressed because everything that I once believed in, everything that I once held dear, family, friends, lovers, financial security, work ethics, opportunity, the ability to travel, my culture, my language, the Constitution, the nation that I once loved; everything is slipping away from me and there's not a thing that I can do about it except retreat into the past into a world of fantasies and fond memories. Of course this should lead me to apply the marvelous truths which I learned years ago attending local Alcoholics Anonymous meetings, namely :

"God grant me the serenity to accept the things I cannot change,

courage to change the things I can,

and (the) wisdom to know the difference."

My elusive search for a soul mate still goes on. Hopefully, there's someone still out there looking for exactly what I am looking for because my desire for the love of a man can be fulfilled in only one of two ways; by actually realizing the love of a man or by relinquishing my desire of my own free will. Of course, I would prefer the first scenario and fear that in my case it is the only one that will work because I simply "fall in love too easily; and I fall in love too hard." I am incapable of loving just a little; it's all or nothing. I have been in this pursuit now for some forty years with no permanent results. I have a lot to give and share and I feel that I deserve love as much as the next man; maybe more since I am willing to give more. I hope to hell that I don't eventually come to the conclusion that "all men are just dogs". But I am beginning to believe that this is the case. God knows that I have tried Match.Com, Gay.Com, Yahoo Personals, Out.Com, etc. etc. and all I have found is total losers who email you upfront and say that they want to get together, but then when you ask them to name a time and place just disappear as suddenly as they first appeared.

Apparently they place those adds or respond to adds only when they are horny and then when the moment passes they are no longer interested. I don't know why it should be so difficult to find a kindred spirit. But then : "Nobody loves a fairy when she's forty" and I will be sixty this June. Has everyone, like big business become so selfish and self centered that no one can relate to anyone anymore? Is this the reason for the 50% divorce rate even among straight people? Is it simply that every mans' first concern is what they can get out of it rather than what they can give or put into it? I think that's the problem these days both in interpersonal relationships and even in the corporate world. "What can I get out of this?" rather than what can I put into this? What can I leave for future generations?

CHAPTER 21
JUST WHEN YOU THINK...

Just when you think that things can't possibly get any worse… they do. As of early June of 2007, my brother's chemotherapy wasn't accomplishing much, in fact, it was having a negative effect on his blood cells and rendering them incapable of retaining oxygen. Therefore he was constantly out of breath and too weak to walk or move around much. The only thing that alleviated this problem was an occasional blood transfusion. The cancer had now spread into his hips and was causing great pain when walking. But in a courageous attempt to bring the family together for perhaps the last time and also to celebrate my 60th birthday, my sister-in-law, Patti organized a night out at an upstate theatre to enjoy a lovely Mozart concert together on the evening of June 2nd. My poor brother could barely make it from the theatre marquis to the entrance of the concert hall. And of course he looked terrible; emaciated, drawn, and donning a baseball cap to cover the fact that he had lost all of his hair.

I walked him to his seat while Patti parked the car and of course people sort of stared wondering what was wrong with him or possibly since he was on my arm, surmising that we were a gay couple and that he was the one with HIV or AIDS. It was very uncomfortable, but I will be forever grateful to Patti and to my brother, John, for having the courage to pull it off. The concert was lovely, but it was tainted with the recognition that this might be our last nice time together, but it wasn't.

I was able to spend Father's Day with my brother and family. Patti cooked a lovely roast on the grill with assorted grilled vegetables and such and everything was delicious. But my brother was very weak and had no appetite and had trouble chewing and swallowing and it was heart-breaking to Patti because she tried so hard to please him. Exhausted from just eating, my brother retreated to the family to his recliner and dozed off. I later joined him in the family room and tried to keep a conversation going, but he just looked so far away, sort of staring into space and not really connecting. He looked really tired and worn and I figured that I should let him rest so I leaned over and gave him a big hug and a kiss on the forehead and departed.

Over the next week or two I kept in touch by phone, but Patti said that my brother was really not up to a visit and that she would be taking him back to the hospital soon for another blood transfusion. I had a bad feeling about all of this and when my phone rang at 5:30AM on June 30th and I heard my sister-in-law on the line, without her saying a word, I knew immediately what had transpired. My brother had passed away around 2AM, quietly and in his sleep. When my sister-in-law had awakened at 2AM to take him to the bathroom as was his habit, she found him lifeless and with no pulse.

I suppose we have to be thankful for small blessings. Had he lived longer he would have suffered more and may have ended up alone in a hospice. At least it was good that he just drifted off peacefully from the home that he loved. But it was a terrible tragedy none the less for both he and Patti and the entire family. Patti and John worked and struggled so hard for so many years in the hopes that they would have a nice retirement together, travel places and do things they had never had a chance to do while raising a family and then suddenly that dream is just snatched away and replaced by Eternal Retirement. It just doesn't seem fair. And yet, I suppose if you look at all the millions on this planet who suffer and starve and meet untimely deaths daily without ever having experienced any of the accomplishments or joys that my brother did experience, he was certainly more fortunate than they. But that still doesn't make me feel any better. I don't think that those others should be starving or suffering either and I strongly question the Divine Plan that allows for so much human suffering with no way out other than death.

As always, Patti was a rock and rose to the occasion and together, she and I made arrangements to give my brother a beautiful and personal tribute and sendoff. We had a nice viewing; my nephews brought displays of all of John's hobbies and accomplishments to the funeral parlor and I displayed a nice portrait of our parents near his casket. Patti made beautiful floral tributes and the wake or viewing was well attended. The following day we had a beautiful funeral at my old church, St. George's Episcopal Church, complete with music that he loved and a bagpiper to pipe him into the church and out. He had requested that several months before his passing so we were true to his request. As it turned out, my three nephews were pall bearers and preceded the casket into the church with the piper at the fore. Patti and I followed behind. As the piper began to play I thought that I would "lose it", but then Patti reached over and grabbed my hand firmly as we proceeded together down the aisle. That was just what I needed, and perhaps so did she; that human touch which said "you are not alone" we share this grief together." Following the service, the piper played outside in front of the church. As the piper played, Patti and I waved and blew kisses to my brother as the hearse sped off on it's way to the crematorium. Oddly enough, the pall that had been placed on his casket at the church appropriately had embroidered upon it a red phoenix rising out of the flames.

So now, aside from Patti and the boys, the fact remains that my original "blood family" has all gone over to the "other side". And I sit here and wonder why I am still here? I almost feel guilty. Wouldn't it have been better had I gone first? I mean, he has a wife and children left behind while I have no one other than my two cats. Why was I spared or was I spared? Will my survival be a blessing or a curse? My friends all say: "It's better to be over-the-hill than under the hill", but is that really true? Is it necessarily a blessing to outlive all your family and friends and end up alone in the care of paid strangers? I think not. As my Dad always said whenever he saw a hearse going down the street: "Well, at least his sufferings and problems are over now, we don't know what lies ahead for us.". And that is true. I mean at this point, all my best days are behind me; what do I actually have to look forward to? Am I going to begin a new, successful and lucrative career at age 60? Am I going to meet the man of my dreams now, when I haven't been able to accomplish that for 40 years when I was younger and more attractive? Is my health going to improve as I get older? Will they find a cure for HIV before I have to go on meds or before my virus replicates itself one thousand fold? Are my finances going to suddenly go up while my cost of living goes down? Or to be realistic (not necessarily pessimistic) am I not rather faced with diminished health, diminished eyesight and hearing, diminished finances, inability to travel abroad or even locally, inability to afford nice restaurants or operas or ballets anymore; separation from loved ones, friends and pets through their passing; loneliness, despair and ultimately institutionalization, suffering and death? What a lovely plan; must be Intelligent Design. Don't get me wrong. I am not saying "Why me?" or "poor me". No, this is our common plight unless we are lucky enough to die suddenly before we know what hit us. I just think it's a lousy plan.

One of my friends keeps telling me that I should see a therapist, but I really can't see what good that would do unless she or he could negate all of the above and assure me that within the next twenty years I was going to win the lottery, get a body transplant and find the love of my life. And yes, I am reticent to try new things like therapy because I already tried things just like it, courses in: "New Age Thinking", "The Power of Positive Thinking", "Loving My Inner Child", etc. with all their catch word phrases like: "I am worthy; I deserve the best in life; good things are coming my way; I love myself; every day in every way I am getting better and better", etc. They are all lovely sentiments or mantras which I repeated over and over, but they never made me successful or changed anything in my life. And if the only other answer is prescription drugs, then I'm not sure that I would really be any happier, I'd just be numbed or in an altered state not very different from when I smoke pot except that prescription drugs are legal yet more expensive. I guess I just don't want to be disappointed again by another false hope.

Now yes, there are a few constructive things that I could be doing. I could quit smoking for the 18th time. I could start dieting for the 20th time and I could start walking daily, all of which would improve my health and I suppose that would be good. But will that get me a job? Nope. Will that get me a new boyfriend? Nope. Even if I lost 100 lbs and was a normal weight, the fact remains that 60+missing teeth+no job+ no money+ HIV=no boyfriend. No one with a good job, who likes to travel abroad or go to the opera or go to fine restaurants is going to want to date someone who can only afford movie matinees, diners and day trips and then make love to them in a full body condom. The fact is that I am "damaged goods" and no amount of exercise or therapy can change that. I guess that's why I don't bother to try because the scales are weighted so heavily against me that whatever little improvements that I could make would be too little and too late and would never tip the scales in my favor. The only "lights that I see at the end of the tunnel" are the lights of a trailer truck coming toward me in the wrong lane.

My friend also advises me that part of my problem is that I lack in self-respect and self-worth. Well that may very well be, but I ask "what during the course of my life has given me feedback that might have improved my self-image"? I think that gay people in particular all have self-worth and self- esteem problems; how could they not? From early on in adolescence when everyone wants to fit in with their peers, we know that we are "an ugly duckling" and are not like other boys. We are afraid to tell our family, friends, church or synagogue for fear of ostracism, rejection or outright physical violence. So how could we possibly feel equal to our peers or as good as them when we know that we are not normal and have to hide our identity? At best, our condition is described as a mental disorder or a genetic aberration, but not our fault. That's reassuring.

So how do we deal with this? Some never deal with it, they stay in the closet for life. Not all, but many marry a woman and have children to cover their identity and bolster their own self image by feeling "Gee, I must be a real man, I mean I fathered children didn't I? ". Some commit suicide. Others get flippant and say "I'm near, I'm queer, get used to it." but inwardly they still hate themselves. Now a therapist would more than likely tell them to do things that build their self image and self worth so they do.

Many spend hours in gyms to look stronger and better than straight men. Others strive to get prestigious jobs and earn more money than straight men. Others join the army to prove that they are just as courageous as straight men. Still others get married or have civil unions with another same sex partner to prove that they are just as monogamous and moral as straight people. Then they may adopt children to prove that they make just as good parents as straight people. Some devote their lives to the Church to prove that they are just as spiritual as straight people. Some buy fancy clothes and big houses and live well beyond their means to prove that they are as affluent as straight people. Others become devoted musicians, athletes, or actors, again, to prove that they can excel and exceed straight people.

Now I suppose all of the above are better than just feeling miserable or committing suicide. But they are all still driven by a lack of self-worth so the patient never actually gained a real sense of self-worth, they just found a myriad of ways to try to prove to themselves and others that they are in some way equal, but they don't really believe it themselves or at some point they would stop trying to exceed everyone else and stop trying to impress other people.

I have a friend who is a perfect example of this and he has been in therapy for years. He was that way when I met him and he still is. That's why he didn't have time for me because he was too busy trying to be "super Democrat", super Catholic, super son, super achiever, etc. Now he has graduated to super spouse, super Catholic, super homemaker, super executive and super decorator. He's spending thousands to try to turn what was already a lovely condo, into a Martha Stewart showpiece just so that he can say: "I don't have tacky linoleum; all my kitchen and bathroom floors are individually made Tuscan terracotta tiles or imported Florentine marble and all of the other floors are the highest grade oak affordable. All my window treatments are hand-made teakwood blinds and all of my artwork is signed oil paintings by a registered Cape Cod artist and all of my kitchen counters are hand cut Vermont granite, etc. etc."

Isn't this a kind of obsessive behavior? and all at the expense of never having time for friends because he is too involved in decorating and has to work hours of overtime to pay for all these baubles. So I think that he still has self-worth problems or at some point in time he would have stopped trying to impress others and trying to be the "Gay Poster Boy" and have come down to earth. Again, don't get me wrong; he's a lovely person, devoted son and devoted long-term companion or spouse and a dear friend of mine, but I simply feel that his behavior is driven and compulsive.

I think that sometimes, attempts to bolster self-worth can eventually evolve into just the opposite, namely a delusional sense of superiority. That's like all of these queens on the internet who are just as old as us and maybe just as heavy, but when they look in the mirror, all they see is their high school yearbook picture and they think that they are better than us and that they can snag a 20 year old muscled boy toy. I don't think that possessing an over-exaggerated sense of self-worth actually makes anyone more worthy or more attractive to others. They are only kidding themselves and need a reality check because others see them as they really are, not as what they imagine themselves to be. These are the 60 year old men who will go to the gay bar in spandex or leather and actually think that they look good revealing their knobby white legs with varicose veins and their naked cellulite butts peaking out of leather chaps while everyone in the room is just laughing at their absurdity. It's one thing to be young at heart, but it's quite another for an old fart to think that he actually looks like a young stud.

To me, no amount of muscles or money or possessions or college degrees makes one person any better than another. What's important to me is how people treat others and how they treat animals. Some of these queens won't even have a pet because it's just too much bother and responsibility and might soil their decor. But if they can't even care for a pet or commit to a pet for maybe 16 years, then I rather doubt that they have the capacity to care for another human or commit to another human for life either. This guy Chris, who I dated, certainly had a sense of self-worth, in fact he just felt superior to everyone, but he was just a big fake and that's why I dumped him. So his sense of self-worth didn't attract me or anyone else. People who actually DO have a genuine sense of self-worth do not need to continually prove it; they just naturally radiate self-confidence and are usually very down to earth and yes, that is an attracting quality when it is real, but it is very rare in deed.

Most people both straight and gay spend their entire lives trying to impress other people, at the expense of their health, happiness, friends, pets and loved ones. They are too busy accumulating symbols to validate their concept of self worth and competing with their neighbors to actually get a chance to enjoy life. What's worse is that they are never really happy either because there is always someone who is just a little more handsome or a little more buff; someone who has a little more wealth or is a little better educated and they feel compelled to strive to be better than that person. If they can only feel good about themselves by feeling better than someone else, then they are fighting a losing battle.

Maybe in that respect, I do have a better sense of self-worth than my friends give me credit for. You see, I have spent my entire life being a friend to the friendless. People constantly ask me "how can you stand being around so-and-so? I wouldn't put up with him or her for five minutes." But that's just it; if I were not the friend of so-and-so, they wouldn't have a friend in the world. I somehow always felt obligated to support the friendless and lonely. I also supported a lot of "lost causes" and movements because at the time I thought that they were important and worthwhile.

Now does that mean that I have no self-respect or does it simply mean that I have compassion and empathy? But if self-worth means being happy with yourself and not trying to be something that you aren't or not trying to give others the impression that you are more than you really are then yes, I do have a good sense of self-worth because I have never pretended to be anything other than who I am. I can loudly proclaim that I am a gentleman who is intelligent, compassionate, loving, devoted, dependable, faithful, artistic, spiritual, clever, witty, generous, a talented speaker, a culinary wiz, a talented decorator and homemaker and a great lover (Are you with me Dr. Phil ? How am I doing?). I do not deny those qualities; the problem is that no one is buying them.

The fact is that employers don't want someone who is customer-oriented, skillful and dependable; they want someone young and stupid who they can pay minimum wage. And men?, and this goes for straight men too; they don't give a damn if you are intelligent, can cook, make your own clothes, decorate, dance, be loyal and faithful and capable of maintaining a home and family. Hell no, their only requirement is that you be young and pretty and put out for them. Gay and straight men are both alike in that respect. They just want a trophy that they can parade around with on their arm because again, that enhances THEIR self-worth, or at least THEY think that it does. In reality, everyone is staring at them and laughing saying: "Look at that damn old fart with his "rent boy"; I wonder how much he had to pay for him?" The same goes for an older straight man sitting in the restaurant with his 20 year old girlfriend. People will stare and say: "Either that's his daughter or a hooker". Of course the young girl only wants him for his money, but that doesn't seem to bother him because he only wants her for a trophy and for sex. It's really just a business deal, not a love affair. Well I am sorry, I need to love and be loved; I guess that I am a rare life form.

Please God, if you are really there or really care at all, and if it be your will, send me a soul mate. Or if that is not your will for me, then at least grant me a transcendental experience of yourself so that You can be my soul mate. Allow me to feel and know your love and know that it is real and that you are the only one deserving of the kind of devotion that I have to give. Maybe that's the lesson that God has been trying to teach me all along, the lesson that Jesus so aptly taught us when he said: "You shall love the Lord your God with all your heart, with all your soul, and with all your mind. This is the first and great commandment. And the second is like unto it you shall love your neighbor as yourself". Matt. 22:40. Maybe I've had it all backward all along in seeking to love men first and God second.

CHAPTER 22
ANSWERED PRAYERS

A wise minister once stated that all prayers are answered, but that sometimes the answer is "yes", sometimes a flat out "no", and at other times "wait". He also stated that if one tries to pursue a beautiful butterfly, he or she will never catch it. One has to remain perfectly still and wait for the butterfly to come to him and alight on him of its own free will. Feverish pursuit of something often has the direct opposite result and ends in loss and frustration because animals and in deed other humans can sense your desperation and will flee from you.

I had prayed to God that He would bring someone worthwhile into my life or if not, that He would become my Lover and allow me to feel and know His love and know that it was real and that He was the only one deserving of the kind of devotion that I have to give. Apparently God, in His wisdom, knew that I was just too earthy and too emotional and physical to ever be fully satisfied with a metaphysical relationship and so His answer was to send someone new and wonderful into my life and it came about in the strangest way.

Someone who I had made acquaintance with at local get-togethers, and who I was attracted to, but felt was totally unavailable, contacted me about concerns he had relating to a mutual friend. He had received numerous despondent emails from a friend of ours and was concerned that our friend was depressed enough and desperate enough to possibly harm or kill himself and he contacted me to see what we could do to help our friend. I assured him that I was not only aware of the problem, but that I had been a sounding board and a friend in need to this person for quite some time and continued to be supportive and available to him at all times, either day or night. I discussed the problem with him at length and assured him that I had known this person for over 25 years and was very well aware of his ups and downs and moments of depression and I assured him that while our friends was at the moment in deed deeply depressed and sullen, that he was by no means suicidal and that there was nothing to fear.

"JD" was very relieved to hear this and apparently deeply impressed with my in depth explanation of the problem and with the years of loyalty and support that I had offered to our mutual friend. His glimpses of me at parties and gatherings had never revealed this side of my nature. Apparently he had always seen me as somewhat flippant and entertaining, but lacking in depth and warmth. It just goes to show that you never know how others see you in public; of course they only see the surface and often miss what lies beyond unless they choose to search deeper. Well, fortunately, "JD" chose to search deeper and asked if he could begin writing and calling me. Well, of course my response was "yes".

After just a few weeks we discovered that we had so much in common: love of music and theater; interest in history, political science, culinary arts, writing, philosophy, ecology, human rights, etc. etc. So "JD" made the first move and invited me to dinner at his home and a concert at Woolsey Hall the evening of September 28th. On the way back to his place we talked and laughed and then JD suddenly reached over and grabbed my hand. We held hands all the way home and it was wonderful. We enjoyed our time together thoroughly and decided to plan on seeing each other again as soon as possible. In between we spoke on the phone for hours to the point where JD said:

"How could you let me go on so long? How could I let me go on that long? I don't even like to talk on the phone. At least I didn't used to like to talk on the phone. What's gotten into me? I feel like a schoolboy with his first crush. Only thing is there's no parent yelling for me to get off the phone. This is crazy".

Well, the long and the short of it is that we have been seeing each other regularly ever since. We even spent Christmas Day together and "JD" gave me some very thoughtful and insightful gifts which showed that a lot of thought had gone into them. "JD" is very resourceful and comes up with so many wonderful activities to share in and he's a wonderful chef and comes up with so many delightful dishes; having dinner at his home is always a pleasure and a gastronomical high. When we are cuddling on the sofa, while listening to delightful romantic piano music, I feel so secure in his arms and it is like a piece of heaven on earth.

I must admit that I was a little concerned in the beginning as to how well I would be able to respond to him physically since I had always associated passion with younger men and he is slightly older than me, but the moment that he first held me in his arms, I instinctively "knew" that it could work; it was magic and still is. I just felt so comfortable with him as though I had known him for years. And the amazing thing is that he seems to feel the same way about me. I don't know how, but he says that I excite and arouse him; I guess this is what they mean when people say: I'll go out with you if the chemistry is right."

"JD" really is everything that I ever wanted in a man: mature, yet at times boyish, intelligent, intellectual, but by no means boring. He's tall and handsome, clever, witty, thoughtful, generous, affectionate and physically demonstrative, naturally masculine, yet not in an affected way; none of that "who you thinks gonna win the series crap". He's simply a man's man. I wish that I could say the same of myself, but "JD" seems to be charmed by my mixed bag of masculine and feminine qualities and is not dissuaded by it at all; he finds me unique and accepts me as I am, which is so refreshing. I can truly be myself when I am with him and when I lay my head on his chest it is just so comforting and I finally feel that I am home at last. It took me 40 years to get to this comfortable place, but better late than never. "JD" really brings out the best in me and makes me want to aspire to be more and better than I am at present. I guess the saying is true: "you always save the best for last".

Of course no one knows what the future will bring; we could drift apart down the road, but I honestly don't see that happening since we add so much to each others lives. Or we could be parted by simple mortality since neither of us are "spring chickens" and we both have some health issues, but you know what? For once in my life I am determined to live in the present. Right now it's really good and I am really happy and I am not going to allow "what ifs" to destroy that happiness. I'm also not going to put any expectations or timelines on him. I have not asked him to be faithful to me, even though I am faithful to him. I have not asked that we live together or get married. If it's meant to be it will happen of its own accord when the time is right; meanwhile, it's fine just the way it is.

Following a birthday party which we attended in April, I inadvertently mentioned something which JD had said about one of the guests to a trusted friend. Unfortunately it got back to the guest and caused some trouble. I apologized to JD over the incident and he lovingly overlooked it saying: "Bobby, no mistake that you could ever make or anything that you could ever do would make me stop loving you." If anyone had told me a year ago that someone as wonderful as "JD" would come into my life I would never have believed them. I guess you just never know what's right around the corner or that someone who you already know on a casual level could end up becoming the love of your life.

JD's life wasn't easy either and he voluntarily put his homosexuality "on hold" for many years because he was and is an honorable man and had pressing responsibilities which he shouldered admirably. But that's all the more reason why he deserves to enjoy the latter years of his life with someone who will truly love him and honor him and let him be himself. I think that I might just happen to be that person. I certainly hope that I am because "Fish gotta swim, birds gotta fly, I gotta love one man til I die; can't stop loving that man of mine."

CHAPTER 23
IF IT SEEMS TOO GOOD
TO BE TRUE...

If something seems too good to be true, it more than likely is. Like so many others, JD is now history. He was NOT an answered prayer. Everything was wonderful for the first eight months. No one could have been more romantic and more reassuring. He was constantly saying things like: "I miss you the moment you leave here.", "It's not right for us to live apart", "We should buy a duplex together", "No one has ever made me feel this way before", Do you have any idea how much happiness you have brought into my life?".

But then the axe fell on June 5, 2008 with an email from him saying: "You need to give me some space; I am very disappointed in you." But he didn't say what he was disappointed about so I called him, at which point he rattled off a caustic list of his gripes, namely that I was too fat, that he didn't like my smoking (I smoke outdoors, never in his home), that he resented my sordid past and thought that all of my friends were losers and idiots, that I talked too much, but said little of any value, that I snored (but then we didn't even sleep in the same room), that I was trying to entrap him and force him into a relationship that he didn't want, etc.

When I reminded him that maybe I, also wasn't getting everything that I needed in the relationship like maybe some reciprocation in the bedroom; he responded that he couldn't bear to look at me, much less reciprocate. I reminded him that all of the qualities which he complained about were known to him from the beginning and yet he pursued me anyway; why? He said that he had thought that he could overlook them, but now he found that he couldn't and that they were wearing on him.

I justified his caustic remarks based upon the fact that at least some of the allegations were true. I promised to work on my weight and smoking if he would just be patient with me. Over the next three months I dropped 30 pounds and cut back drastically on my smoking. But apparently that wasn't enough. He continued to make sarcastic remarks about me, my family and friends and continued bringing up my past. In the beginning he told me that one of the things which most attracted him to me was my intelligence and lively conversation. Now he no longer wanted to hear anything that I had to say. He would abruptly cut me off with words like: "I'm not interested in that", "You told me that before", or just plain "Shut up".

He became totally controlling and domineering. I had to go to his place all of the time; he rarely made the journey here. And once at his place I was a virtual prisoner for 2 or 3 days; we hardly left the apartment other than to go grocery shopping. He would not allow me to cook; he said that I couldn't cook to save my life, yet that's not what my other friends have said who I have cooked dinner for many times. He insisted on doing all the cooking and would then sit down and praise his own culinary skills for the next hour with statements like: "Gee, Bob, these marinated shrimp are out of this world; how did you make the sauce?". Following dinners, I had hoped for some nice quiet time for cuddling with a little soft, romantic music in the background like he had done in the beginning. But now, all he wanted was to watch grade C- Netflix videos back to back. I brought up many academy award winning videos, but he would have none of that, we could only watch his videos and his choice of TV, and listen to his choice of music. Nothing that I ever suggested was ever acted upon. He began sitting away from me in a chair, clutching his remote and engaging in endless channel surfing. I'm not an idiot, I could feel him pulling further and further away from me. Nothing that I did to please him seemed to make any difference.

Despite all of this, when he ended up in the hospital due to a serious bicycle accident, I was at his bedside every day. He was finally released into my custody because I am a healthcare worker. I took him back to his place and attended to his needs for the next four days, taking him to labs and doctor's appointments and pushing him around grocery stores in a wheelchair. He was very demanding, impatient and mean to me during all of that period, but I justified it by saying to myself: "He's in pain" or "Maybe it's the medications". Instead of keeping his medications all in one place, he has them scattered all over his apartment. So whenever he would ask for a specific med, I would have to search every room and read every label to be sure that I was giving him the correct med. Well! He would scream: "Where's my f—king medicine? Can't you read? Are you just totally incompetent?"

Following my four day ordeal, he handed me a check for $300 and said that he felt well enough to care for himself now. I questioned the check, reminding him that what I did was done out of love and concern for him. He responded that he didn't want to be "obligated" to anyone.

At HIS request, I continued seeing him on weekends and sometimes mid-week, but the situation continued to erode. He continued making snide remarks and complaining about my weight and refusing to honor any of my requests. Finally he did come down to my place for one evening. Out of a clear blue sky he made the comment: "You know, when I first met you, I thought that we had a lot in common, but now I'm not so sure." When I asked him what he meant by that he turned on TV and changed the subject. After 3 hours of TV viewing, he announced that he was too tired for any intimacy and went to my bed; I slept on my sofa.

The next morning, while he was shaving, I asked: "Honey, what would you like for breakfast?: French toast, an omelet, scrambled eggs and bacon? His response was, as usual: "Let's go to a diner". Needless to say, I was hurt and insulted. I asked him again why he won't eat at my place and he responded that my place was unsanitary due to the fact that I have cats who have access to the countertops and dining room table. I assured him that I wash down the counters before preparing meals and put new linen on my table each time, but that didn't make any difference. So off we went to the diner. At the diner, I insisted on paying for both of us since I had not been able to provide breakfast for him at home, but he wouldn't have it. Afterward, he just dropped me off in front of my place, without a kiss or hug or anything and went home; he didn't seem to want to spend one more minute with me.

Since JD had never failed to alert me as to all of the things that he found wrong with me, I felt that it was about time that I question just where this relationship was going. So I sent him a very polite email suggesting that maybe he could cut me some slack, allow me to make some decisions, try to meet me half way. I told him that I was certain that we could work these things out and that I felt that he was worth it, but that we needed to talk, not watch TV.

His response was that I was a passive-aggressive bitch just like his ex-wife; that he had been through all of this before and was not going to go through it again. He demanded that I meet him somewhere mid-way near the highway so that he could return my clothes and so that I could return his house keys.

So much for his statement to me in April 2008: "Bobby, there isn't anything that you could ever do or any mistake that you could ever make that would make me stop loving you." Or his more recent statement on Sept 1,2008 : "I love you more than my own children."

So I met him at a diner on Sept. 12, 2008. We exchanged items and then he asked if I would like a cup of coffee; I really don't know why. We sat down to coffee, but could barely look at each other. He talked about his children and I about my friends and then he said he had to go, but that he would call me. I doubt that will ever happen.

After that, he sent me an email saying that I had "insinuated" myself into his heart and that I was trying to force him into a marital relationship, etc. etc. He was implying that I was the pursuer, that I had seduced him, when nothing could be further from the truth. I merely responded to his lead and his reassuring words of love and affection. I told him that I had never set a timeline and had never pressured him along those lines. I told him that the only expectations that I ever had of him were: consistency, equality and respect. He responded by quoting Ralph Waldo Emerson : "**A foolish consistency is the hobgoblin of little minds**" "A great person does not have to think consistently from one day to the next." Well la-de-da. Now he was equating himself with the great and mighty.

I had occasion to speak with JD's last boyfriend at a picnic this weekend and it helped a lot. Apparently he has a long established pattern of wining and dining and then later verbally abusing and controlling the men in his life. The ex-boyfriend's account was identical to my own experience of JD; it was almost like a script. The ex also advised me of another of JD's prior boyfriends who he also verbally abused to the point where he also couldn't take it anymore. Maybe it's his own revulsion and non-acceptance of his own homosexuality that drives him to find vulnerable gays to work his hostility out on, I don't know. All I do know is that I am tired of having to be the patient therapist in every relationship that I get involved in. But you see this is what happens when you try to have a relationship with someone who is part of a major throng of "walking wounded".

Due to our Puritan heritage (the Pilgrim Fathers) and our largely Judeo-Christian religious upbringing, most gay men and women in this country were raised from a very young age and throughout our formative years to believe that homosexuality was unnatural, sinful, degrading, evil and worthy of death. Oh yes, and as if that wasn't enough, even death was to be followed by an eternity of suffering in the fires of hell, rather than "resting in peace".

So how did we handle it? At first we didn't worry about it because many of our peers were also engaged in "sexual experimentation" too so we didn't see ourselves as any different from other boys our age. But then when those same boys "graduated" and moved on to having sexual encounters with the opposite sex and we didn't, we suddenly realized that something was wrong; that we were not the same as other boys. Many of us went into denial and fought it tooth and nail by attempting to date girls and attempting to appear as other boys, but it didn't work. Some of us committed suicide or blocked out our feelings by resorting to enormous amounts of drugs or alcohol or both.

Our dates were uncomfortable and filled with anxiety. Oh, we went through all of the motions; kissing, fondling, necking, exploring, etc. but it was all nothing more than a big act and generated absolutely no physical pleasure whatsoever. It was as though our bodies were anesthetized. How could anyone continue in this practice and continue to use other human beings, namely girls, who may very well have genuinely liked us, just to keep up a front? It was dishonest and cruel and could ultimately end in disaster should the object of our affection figure it out and betray us or worse yet, should they not figure it out, fall in love and expect us to marry them.

Some of us were so frightened of discovery that we didn't care who we hurt and continued down the road to matrimony. Others did care, but deceived themselves into thinking that "the right girl" could cure them of their infirmities. Others became, for all practical purposes, asexual and threw themselves obsessively into careers, the arts, the priesthood or the military so that they would have valid excuses for not being married and no one would be any the wiser. But this was all such reactionary thinking and absorbed so much time and effort and robbed us of any genuine feelings or any sense of self-confidence or self worth. And despite all of our best efforts, the fear of discovery was always just below the surface and created unnecessary stress in our lives.

Any group of people, members of which spend their entire lives in fear that someone will discover who they really are, is obviously living in a constant state of shame and inferiority. Over time, this becomes imbedded in the psyche and becomes a belief system or a script to live by. Psychiatrists tell us that when people are living "by a script", it is nigh impossible to reach them or change them for the better. When a person who is stuck in their script which goes something like this: "I am evil, flawed, inferior and unworthy of love", meets up with someone who falls in love with them and tries to assure them that they are in deed everything that they were looking for, that love and reassurance is only met with hostility and frustration because it contradicts "the script".

On too many occasions to count, JD assured me that he was "a miserable, cruel, son-of-a-bitch" and was unsuitable for anyone and only in relationships for what he could get out of them. Of course, rather than take him at his word, I saw value in him and tried to reassure him, which only made matters worse. When I reminded him that certainly his willingness to stay in an unhappy relationship for over 19 years just to raise his children showed a depth of love, devotion and self-sacrifice, his response was that he got more out of it than he put into it and that his children made him happy, otherwise, he would have dumped them.

So how, I ask you, are any gay men and women able to find enduring and satisfying relationships in this day and age when most of our potential life partners are carrying around all of this baggage which society imposed upon us? Had we been raised in an environment where homosexuality was a valid option no different than being right or left-handed, we wouldn't have these problems, but such was not the case and continues not to be the case. So long as religious institutions continue to condemn us or at best tolerate us and so long as nations continue to consider us as second rate citizens unworthy of military service and unworthy of marriage, these feelings of inferiority, different ness and inequality will continue to persist.

Oddly enough, our plight is not unlike that of many other marginalized groups that have gone before us and had to fight for their rights too, namely women, immigrants and African-Americans. In a nation that has boasted that "all men are created equal" for over two hundred years, I find it odd that true equality was only a given for white, US born males. All of the aforementioned groups had to somehow prove to the nation that they were equal and of course those in power saw to it that those individuals would not get an opportunity to prove themselves.

For too many years to count, African-Americans were not allowed in the military until it became necessary to fill the ranks. But even then they were segregated, used largely as cannon fodder and never allowed to serve as officers. And then if they were fortunate enough to survive after putting their lives on the line to defend freedom and democracy, they returned home to menial jobs, if any jobs at all and segregation without even the right to vote.

Women suffered the same plight: no right to vote for many years and passive acceptance in the military, only given menial tasks and no possibility for advancement. Once home they were paid less than men doing the same tasks. It is only now in 2009 that our new President, Barack Obama has passed legislation to provide for equal pay for equal work; God bless him. And it is only now that an African-American has risen to the highest office in the land that others of his race finally feel equal and feel that there is nothing that they cannot achieve if they apply themselves. I am happy and proud that I and other intelligent white voters helped to make this a reality. But it is truly sad that almost 150 years passed since the Emancipation Proclamation was decreed before true equality could be finally realized. I wonder how many white males in this country can truly comprehend what a debilitating effect the here-to-for lack of equality had on those who were marginalized.

And I wonder, what will it take for gays in this country to achieve full equality; a gay President or a gay five-star general? While the media and entertainment industry have increased the number of TV shows and movies including gay characters and gay themes, we are usually represented by silly, prissy and dysfunctional gay men or overtly masculine lesbian women in comedy sitcoms. Are these to be our only role models? No one seems to realize that homosexuality spans a broad spectrum of behavior ranging from overtly masculine to overtly feminine; most people fall somewhere in the middle. Oddly enough, it has always been the overtly feminine gays who have been the pioneers and leaders in the struggle for equality and gay rights; perhaps because, unlike the others, they couldn't hide. What we need now is for those on the overtly masculine end of the spectrum and those in the middle to show the courage to rise to the occasion and come out and be positive role models. Until that happens, I fear that we will remain where we are.

I recently viewed a wonderful movie on TV, "Prayers For Bobby", which was based on the book of the same name written by Leroy Aarons and published in 1996 by Harper One.

Very painful and personal, this is the story of a mother's struggle to reconcile the tension between her deeply held religious beliefs and the suicide of her gay son. Mary Griffith came from a religious family and raised her four children to believe in God and live a Christian life. Their conservative Presbyterian church was the center of family life for every family member except Mary's husband, Bob. When 17-year-old Bobby confided to older bother Ed that he was gay, the family's life changed. Mary convinced Bobby to pray that God would cure him and to seek solace in church activities. Bobby did it all, but the church's hatred of homosexuality and the obvious pain his gayness was causing his family led him increasingly to loathe himself; he ultimately committed suicide.

As I watched the movie, I couldn't help but identify with the pain and anguish that young man suffered. It took me back to my seminary days when I too entertained suicide as the only honorable way out of my plight. I too had prayed and prayed that God would heal me and felt increasingly more despondent when He didn't and my homosexual urges became increasingly more powerful. I felt that God had abandoned me and I hated Him for it.

The pinnacle of the movie came when Mary Griffith spoke at a town hall meeting and revealed that now she understood why God never healed her son, namely because there was nothing wrong with him, nothing to heal. I wept profusely when I heard her say that; perhaps because it was something that even I, who seemed well enough adjusted to my homosexuality needed to hear from someone else. Maybe now I can begin to forgive God, just as I am sure that He has already forgiven me for abandoning Him. All I can say is what the sticker on my refrigerator says: "God, please save me from your followers.".

No, snakes like the one in the Garden of Eden, don't talk. The whole story of man's fall from grace was merely a metaphor and a bad one at that by some insecure local tribal deity and his followers who wanted to gain dominion over their fellows.

The truth of the matter is that physical and emotional and spiritual maturities are still in the process of evolving. This planet and all that share it are in a continual state of evolution. Hopefully some day all life will reach a state of perfection and enlightenment and all will be at one if self-serving religionists and politicians don't destroy it all. But I'm sure that God knows what he's doing and won't allow that.

Only human serpents like the vipers spoken of by Jesus in the twelfth chapter of Matthew talk; namely religious leaders like the Scribes and Pharisees. In verses 34-37 Jesus said: "You brood of vipers, how can you who are evil say anything good? For out of the overflow of the heart the mouth speaks. 35 The good man brings good things out of the good stored up in him, and the evil man brings evil things out of the evil stored up in him. 36 But I tell you that men will have to give account on the Day of Judgment for every careless word they have spoken. 37 For by your words you will be acquitted and by your words you will be condemned."

Where do I go from here? I'm sure I don't know. Five of my older friends, Marianne, Mary, Neal and Frank, not to mention my ex-lover, Carl, who I had been married to, passed away within this last year. Another friend of mine, Bill, is in a convalescent home with a debilitating disorder much like Parkinsons, but without any known treatment or medications. I have adopted his cat, Bouvier, because I knew he would be crushed if she went to a shelter. She's a sweet little thing.

Had I met someone when I was young and we had been able to share our lives together and if we had shared memories and could grow old together, that would have been wonderful and comforting. But I am sixty-three now and it's really too late. Anyone who I meet now would have spent three quarters of their life building memories with someone else or maybe no one. And I would have to overcome and compensate for the effects of sixty years of bad experiences that the other person had experienced.

All the passion and excitement and spontaneity that young lovers experience would not be there for us to share without the aid of a little blue pill. At most, all we could hope for would be companionship, but I have that with my circle of friends and pets already, so maybe I am not so bad off after all. Maybe despite all the failed loves of my life I am still blessed and need to appreciate that. My sister-in-law, Pat is still there for me; she's such a tower of strength. And thank God for Public Television; it is my mainstay.

I have finally lost all interest in men and sex and am now leading a celibate life. I find much more joy in my pets and feeding my other little buddies, the birds and squirrels on my back deck. I have also lost interest in the acquisition of material goods and antiques; one can only fit so many of them into a four room condo. I realize now that all the years of searching for Mr. Right and for material goods were merely poor attempts at filling a gnawing emptiness within which, in reality, can only be filled by God. I can't help but think of poor old Cardinal Woolsey's words in Shakespeare's "Henry VIII" when he said: "Had I but serv'd my God with half the zeal I serv'd my king, he would not in mine age have left me naked to mine enemies".

Fortunately, I still do have many of my friends who helped shape my life over the years and to whom I am forever indebted. There is Tom, who introduced me to ballet and steered me away from Wicca and back to the Church. And there is Elliot, who introduced me to Opera and fine dining and cooking and has been there for me to feed and care for my furry friends in my absence. And there is Bill, who shared my love of England and history and traveled with me often. Even in his weakened state, he managed to make his way to my hospital bed with his walker to cheer me while I was in the hospital; now there's true friendship. And there is John, who has also always been there for me. He introduced me to reading and literature and fine Renaissance music and it is his unconditional love and friendship and belief in my abilities that inspired me to write this book.

On October 28, 2010, I almost joined my five older friends who had gone before me into the great unknown. I had only been on the HIV "cocktail" of Combivir and Kaletra for 8 weeks when recent blood work revealed that my hemoglobin, which should be at a level between 14 and 17 units for an adult male, had fallen to 6 in a one month period of time. This means that my heart and brain were being starved of oxygen and that I could have had a stroke or heart attack at any point had my doctor not promptly gotten me into the hospital for several blood transfusions and a myriad of tests.

Apparently, AZT, one of the medicines in Combivir has been known to have this effect on 2% of HIV patients using it. I just happened to be of the 2% group. So now I am in recovery, but not on any meds and at the mercy of my virus until my doctor can set me up with a new HIV "cocktail" carrying less devastating possibilities.

So to all my friends out there in the internet chat rooms; those people commonly known as "bug chasers" who are seeking to have unprotected sexual relations with PWA's or persons with AIDS; a word to the wise: don't even think it. I have spoken with several of them in the past who just brushed me off saying: "Oh, it's no big deal. If you get HIV you just take a pill."

Think again my friends. Do you have $1,500 a month for the pills? And what about the side effects as in my case?

Likewise to all of you young heterosexuals out there who think that HIV is just a gay disease; think again. Apparently you are all having unprotected sex or the illegitimacy rate in this country would not have exceeded 50% in recent years; nor would women be having DNA tests on 10-15 different men, trying to find out who the fathers of their children were. If HIV were just a gay disease, then why is it ravaging the heterosexual communities in villages and towns all over Africa and India? Think again my dear ones. An ounce of prevention is worth a pound of cure.

President Obama did not turn out to be the Messiah after all. He had a lot of wonderful ideas and great sincerity, but I don't think that he realized how impossible it would be to "change Washington". No, Washington will not change any more than Rome changed; and like Rome, our empire will fall as we become a bankrupt third world nation of diverse barbarian hordes with nothing in common to unite us, not even a common language or faith since public displays of faith are now unacceptable and a national language would be politically incorrect. It's what happens in time to all empires. As Scottish writer, Alexander Fraser Tyler wrote in 1770 about the cycle of democracy:

"A democracy cannot exist as a permanent form of government. It can only exist until the voters discover that they can vote themselves largesse from the public treasury. From that moment on, the majority always votes for the candidates promising the most benefits the public treasury with the result that a democracy always collapses over lousy fiscal policy, always followed by a dictatorship. The average of the world's great civilizations before they decline has been 200 years. These nations have progressed in this sequence: From bondage to spiritual faith; from faith to great courage; from courage to liberty; from liberty to abundance; from abundance to selfishness; from selfishness to Complacency; from complacency to apathy; from apathy to dependency; from dependency back again to bondage."

I guess King Solomon was right also when he said: "Vanity of vanities, all is vanity." His last exhortation is the strongest and most meaningful to me: "Fear God and keep his commandments, for this is the whole obligation of man." Ecclesiastes 12:8,13.

Politics are so corrupt that I am no longer interested. I vote only to maintain my right to vote, but I really don't expect any change for the better. Not when I know that world corporations and Wall St control Congress and will always do what's best for THEM and not for the country or the people. Most institutional religions are of no interest to me because they come across as either so ignorant, ridiculous and bigoted or so moderate and wishy washy that they don't take a stand on anything or have any parameters or concepts to live by at all. Materialism doesn't do it for me any more and I am convinced that all men are just "dogs" and not in the nice sense either.

But I still love animals and I have ultimate faith in my pets and friends. It's sort of a tragedy that it takes one over sixty years to learn what life is really all about and how to live it properly since at that point it's almost really too late to start over. Now one might say, "Well then pass this wisdom along to the next generation". I would gladly do that, but no one cares and no one wants to listen; the young would rather learn the hard way than take anyone's advise or admit that someone else might be right. So as they say: "Youth is wasted on the young." and unfortunately, each generation will have to reinvent the wheel. As my Dad always said: "Old too soon, smart too late."

But one thing is certain. I am now free to pursue God in my own way, without the distractions of sex, materialism, politics or religious dogma. And I am hopeful that some day soon despite His/Her long silence, or perhaps despite my long spiritual deafness and distractions, that I will hear His/Her "still quiet voice," and not have to depend on questionable religionists to tell me what God has to say; as though they ever actually heard Him or ever really knew His will. What a laugh.

When one looks up into the unpolluted night sky as I did in Peru and gazes at an infinite universe and billions of solar systems just like ours, it is the height of arrogance and false pride for anyone to think that we are so special and chosen and brilliant as to know the full nature of God and Reality and worse yet, to think that we can speak for God and force our myopic views on others.

All mankind would do well to heed the words of Psalm 46:10:

"Be still and know that I am God." As Judge Judy always says: "That's why God gave you two ears and one mouth."

EPILOGUE

To my dear readers, who followed me in the past, I must tell you that much has changed in my life over the past twelve years that has totally changed, not only my "opinions" on many areas of LIFE, but has changed by entire belief system and I would like to share that with you all. While we all may have and are entitled to many "opinions"; still, in the end, we cannot, reasonably have more than one "truth".

Throughout my book, I made a number of incorrect assertions about Institutional Christianity and promoted Hinduism and Vedanta as the Ultimate Truth, because at that time, I was unaware that there were Christian churches that were every bit as sophisticated and enlightened as the proponents of Vedanta, if not more so, and I will endeavor to explain why. I was, at that time, totally unaware that there were Christian churches that promote the very highest and most advanced forms of meditation and spiritual transformation available to mankind.

In my original writings, I was also very antagonistic toward Christianity and labeled Christian Churches as being largely the persecutors of LGBTQ people. But there again, I now have a much clearer understanding of what The Church expects of LGBTQ people, and it's not much different than what they expect of all single members of their churches. I will endeavor to explain all of that as we move on.

In my original writings, I also postulated that since homosexuality exits even in the animal kingdoms, that, ergo, it only followed scientifically that it must, therefore be "natural". Wrong again.

So, please allow me to address some of these issues because I do not want to be the cause of anyone deliberately avoiding many of the beliefs and institutions that I wrongfully attacked in my book, and losing out on the benefits that those same institutions can bestow.

First off, I need to remind both myself and the reader that all of the negative experiences that I suffered under Institutional Christianity throughout my life were suffered at the hands of Western Christianity! While I have always been aware that there are countless forms and denominations within the broad category of "Christianity", I had no idea that it basically breaks down into two major categories: Western Christianity, created by Rome, and Eastern Christianity, created by the Apostolic Fathers from the very beginning of The Church.

As we all know, the "Church", began in Jerusalem in the 1st century, following the Death and Resurrection of the Lord, Jesus Christ. It was founded by Jesus, but administered by the Apostles and the very first "churches" were in Jerusalem and in Antioch. In successive years, other churches were founded in Alexandria, Egypt and in Greece and in Asia Minor and finally in Rome. The structure of the new "church" was already pretty firmly established by the end of the 1st century as can be attested to by the writings of the Church Fathers in "The Acts of the Apostles", and in the Epistles, or instructions to the various young churches such as the churches in Ephesus, Galatia, Thessalonica, and Corinth, which can be found in any Bible, regardless of the translation or denomination of the publishers or printers.

While there was not at that time in the 1st century, any Bible, as such, and there were no Gospels, as we now know them today; the Apostles did have some Old Testament scrolls and the Hebrew Psalms to structure the new Church around. While some may say that it was not the intent of Jesus to found a new religion, that would appear to me to be thoughtless imaginings because, according to the Gospels, Jesus said in Matthew 16:17-19 "And Jesus answered him, "Blessed are you, Simon Bar-Jonah! For flesh and blood has not revealed this to you, but my Father who is in heaven. 18 And I tell you, you are Peter, and on this rock I will build my church, and the gates of hell[b] shall not prevail against it. I will give you the keys of the kingdom of heaven, and whatever you bind on earth shall be bound in heaven, and whatever you loose on earth shall be loosed in heaven."

So, Jesus, was in fact establishing a Church that would endure until his 2nd coming. And while some misapply his words, thinking that Peter was "the rock" spoken of in that passage; the fact IS, that Jesus was referring to Himself as the Rock. And when He spoke of "giving the keys of the kingdom", he was not speaking about giving that power to just one man, but to all of the Apostles, because Jesus had always considered them all as equals. And so that is the manner in which The Church was set up with the Apostles, the "Bishops", all being the spiritual leaders and then, as their assistants, Deacons and what was called Presbyters, or as we know them, priests. Oddly, enough, back then, one of the main qualifications for bishops and deacons and presbyters was that they be "Husbands of one wife, with Godly children! There was no insistence back then on celibate Bishops or priests.1 Timothy 3:2-12

Authorized (King James) Version

A bishop then must be blameless, the husband of one wife, vigilant, sober, of good behavior, given to hospitality, apt to teach; 3 not given to wine, no striker, not greedy of filthy lucre; but patient, not a brawler, not covetous; one that rules well his own house, having his children in subjection with all gravity; for if a man know not how to rule his own house, how shall he take care of the church of God?

The Lord, Jesus, during his last evening on earth, set the precedent for a basic ritual around which all future worship would revolve, and that was in the breaking of bread and the drinking of wine, in remembrance of Him. This was a brilliant idea because the breaking of bread and the drinking of the Passover cup was already central to God's Chosen People on earth, so it was only natural that the Lord, who came to "fulfill the Law and the Prophets and not to contradict them, would want to merge the "old" in with the "new" in creating His New Covenant, which would include the Jews, but which would be much more universal in reaching out to non-Jews as well.

During His many appearances following his death and resurrection, the Lord, was always "known to them", in the "breaking of bread". In Luke 24 we are told that Jesus "took bread, blessed and broke it and gave it to them; their eyes were open end and they recognized him. . . ." . In verse 35 the two disciples report to the eleven and their companions that he was made known to them in the breaking of the bread.

So the "breaking of bread" and the sharing of the cup, would always be central to all worship and liturgy from the beginning of The Church and down until the End of Time. And yet, we see that this is so sadly lacking in most Protestant forms of worship and relegated perhaps to only one Sunday out of each month, if that often.

For several centuries, the Church was all One Holy Catholic and Apostolic Church; "Catholic", meaning "Universal" and not today's connotation of Roman Catholic. But since there were as yet no Gospels or any Bible or codification of scripture or practices, due to years of persecution and the need for Christian communities to be able to flee and hide at a moment's notice, various sects began to emerge, with either mistaken concepts about Church teachings or with deliberate divergences into pagan and Hellenic philosophies, which were prevalent throughout the Roman Empire during the early centuries. This problem needed to be dealt with and these issues were finally taken up by "The Church", once it had become legal and promoted by Emperor Constantine.

The several main churches located throughout the Empire, did not decide these issues independently, but came together in Councils, to sort out these issues together after much prayer and reliance on the Holy Spirit to guide their thinking and decisions. There were several important councils over successive decades, beginning with the 1st Council called by Emperor Constantine in 325 AD. It was known as the First Council of Nicea. It was at that Council, that the bishops from all over the Empire decided on which of the many hundreds of religious writings would make up the "Bible Canon" or the approved list of what we know today as the Old Testament. They also decided on which writings would make up the New Testament and which would be considered the Four Gospels.

Many more Councils were to come down the line as conflicting teachings were being circulated around the Empire, both as a result of error, and some being deliberately taught to destroy the unity of the Church by its enemies. But, as a result of subsequent Councils, "The Church" was always able to arrive at solutions and maintain unity until one of the churches decided that they should take precedence over all of the others.

All of the Christian Churches of Alexandria and Jerusalem and Syria and Asia Minor and Greece agreed on solving doctrinal issues together and the bishops of all of those churches were regarded as "One among Equals", UNTIL the Roman Church began pulling away and just about demanding that THEY be the Supreme Church and that THEIR Bishop be the Supreme Pontiff and Lord over all. And in the year 800, the Bishop of Rome furthered that agenda by crowning Charlemagne, Emperor of the Holy Roman Empire, when the Roman Empire already had an Empress, Irene!! The Church of Rome took it upon themselves to create a New Rome, in the face of the Byzantine Roman Empire, that had succeeded the old fallen Roman Empire when Rome fell to the barbarians in the late 4th century. Charlemagne was crowned Imperator Augustus in Rome on Christmas Day, 800 by Pope Leo III and is therefore regarded as the founder of the Holy Roman Empire (as Charles I). Through military conquest and defense, he solidified and expanded his realm to cover most of Western Europe. He is often seen as the Father of Europe and is an iconic figure, instrumental in defining European identity. His was the first truly imperial power in the West since the fall of Rome.

Needless to say, that did not set well with the rest of the Christian Church. In 1053, the first action was taken that would lead to a formal schism: The Greek churches in southern Italy were forced to conform to Latin practices and, if any of them did not, they were forced to close. In retaliation, Patriarch Michael I Cerularius of Constantinople ordered the closure of all Latin churches in Constantinople. In 1054, the papal legate sent by Leo IX travelled to Constantinople for purposes that included refusing Cerularius the title of "ecumenical patriarch" and insisting that he recognize the pope's claim to be the head of all of the churches.

The Church split along doctrinal, theological, linguistic, political, and geographical lines in 1054 and the fundamental breach has never been healed, with each side sometimes accusing the other of falling into heresy and initiating the division. The Latin-led Crusades, the Massacre of the Latins in 1182, the West's retaliation in the Sacking of Thessalonica in 1185, the capture and pillaging of Constantinople during the Fourth Crusade in 1204, and the imposition of Latin patriarchs made reconciliation more difficult. Establishing Latin hierarchies in the Crusader states meant that there were two rival claimants to each of the patriarchal sees of Antioch, Constantinople, and Jerusalem, making the existence of schism clear. Several attempts at reconciliation did not bear fruit. As time went by, the Western Church, or the Church of Rome, grew further and further apart, creating its own liturgy and its own theology, which ended up being 100 degrees opposite of the liturgy and theology of the early church and of the rest of Christendom or the Eastern Church.

Beginning with St. Augustine of Hippo, a 4th century theologian, the Western Church began formulating a theology very different from that of the rest of the Apostolic churches of the East. In his youth he was drawn to the eclectic (and now extinct) Manichaean faith, and later to the Hellenistic philosophy/religion of Neoplatonism. After his conversion to Christianity and baptism in 386, Augustine developed his own approach to philosophy and theology, accommodating a variety of methods and perspectives. Believing the grace of Christ was indispensable to human freedom, he helped formulate the doctrine of original sin, which was and is very different from the view of the Eastern churches. While the Eastern churches believed in "Original Sin" as having been committed by Adam and Eve, they did NOT believe that their sins were passed down to their descendants or that their descendants were in any way responsible for any sins other than their own. This is why Eastern Christians never rushed baptism of infants because they feel that children, up to the "age of reason" are sinless.

Augustine is recognized as a saint in the Catholic Church, the Eastern Orthodox Church, and the Anglican Communion. Although the Eastern Church did NOT accept all of his teachings. He is also a preeminent Catholic Doctor of the Church and the patron of the Augustinians. His thoughts profoundly influenced the medieval worldview. Many Protestants, especially Calvinists and Lutherans, consider him one of the theological fathers of the Protestant

Reformation due to his teachings on salvation and divine grace. Protestant Reformers generally, and Martin Luther in particular, held Augustine in preeminence among early Church Fathers. Luther was, from 1505 to 1521, a member of the Order of the Augustinian Eremites.

The Western Theology that Augustine began and that others, subsequently added to, depicts an angry deity intent on punishing mankind and it almost depicts the Devil as the "enlightener of mankind" in that it was he, who offered Man the opportunity to know "hidden secrets" such as "knowing good and evil" and thereby becoming "like God". It depicts a deity who now had to cast man out of the Garden of Eden for fear that Man should get to "The Tree of Life" and be able to circumvent God's wrath and live forever. And while some of those elements are, indeed, present in the Genesis narrative, they have been seriously misinterpreted over the centuries. Western Theology eventually deteriorated into a theology of anger and punishment and hell fire and damnation and special places in the afterlife for those who were not good enough to go immediately to heaven, but not bad enough for hell, such as babies, etc. And if you had enough money to pay for priests and monks to pray you out of Purgatory or Limbo, then early exits from such domains were possible.

The truly sad part of all of this is that even following the Protestant Reformation when millions left the Roman Church; they still took with them much of the incorrect and negative theology and incorporated it into their newly created churches. Many Calvinists and Anglicans and Lutherans still maintain those negative concepts of the "afterlife" and confused concepts as to what is necessary to gain salvation. The Protestant Reformation merely "spread the cancer of Western theology" far and wide and made it even worse by instructing the faithful that they could just read the Bible and interpret it for themselves without having to know anything about the ancient languages that it was originally written in or anything about common beliefs at the time that the Gospels were written, or anything about the context of Biblical passages. So, of course, this just opened Pandora's Box and led to the formation of as many Protestant denominations as there were Protestant believers.

AND, OF COURSE, IT WAS THIS NEGATIVE THEOLOGY THAT I INHERITED FROM MY PROTESTANT AND JEHOVAH'S WITNESS BACKGROUND! And it was THIS corrupted theology that prompted me to accuse the Church, in general, for all of the "perceived" inconsistencies and contradictions in Holy Scripture and all of my "perceived" ways that the Church was acting in a cruel and bigoted way toward members of the LGBT Community. It is a shame that I was unaware at that time of the Eastern Church and the vast difference in theology that exists therein. You see, there never was a "Reformation" in the East because the Eastern Church had not fallen victim to Neo-Platonism and pagan philosophies and was not teaching methods of "buying people out of Hell and Purgatory" by means of monetary gifts to the clergy, etc. as in buying "indulgences". The Eastern Church remained in its unadulterated original form as established by the Apostles from the beginning.

And it was even this corrupted theology and corrupted interpretations of the Book of Genesis, coupled with my studies of Buddhism, that brought me to my false conclusions which were the basis of the title of my book, namely "A Gay Epiphany.....". But you see, it WAS NOT an "Epiphany" at all, but rather a rediscovery of an ancient HERESY within the Church that took place centuries back. It was known as "Marcionism"

Marcion of Sinope c. 85 – c. 160) was an early Christian theologian. Marcion preached that God had sent Jesus Christ who was an entirely new, alien god, distinct from the vengeful God of Israel who had created the world. He considered himself a follower of Paul the Apostle, whom he believed to have been the only true apostle of Jesus Christ, a doctrine called Marcionism. Marcion published the earliest extant fixed collection of New Testament books. According to Christian sources, Marcion's teacher was the Simonian Cerdo. Irenaeus writes that "a certain Cerdo, originating from the Simonians, came to Rome under Hyginus and taught that the one who was proclaimed as God by the Law and the Prophets is not the Father of our Lord Jesus Christ" (Against Heresies, 1, 27, 1). Also, according to them, Marcion and the Gnostic Valentinus were companions in Rome.

Study of the Hebrew scriptures, along with received writings circulating in the nascent Church, led Marcion to conclude that many of the teachings of Jesus were incompatible with the actions of Yahweh, characterized as the belligerent god of the Hebrew Bible. Marcion responded by developing a ditheistic system of belief around the year 144. This notion of two gods—a higher transcendent one and a lower world-creator and ruler—allowed Marcion to reconcile his perceived contradictions between Christian Old Covenant theology and the Gospel message proclaimed by the New Testament.

In contrast to other leaders of the nascent Christian Church, however, Marcion declared that Christianity was in complete discontinuity with Judaism and entirely opposed to the scriptures of Judaism. Marcion did not claim that these were false. Instead, he asserted that they were entirely true, but were to be read in an absolutely literalistic manner, one which led him to develop an understanding that Yahweh was not the same God spoken of by Jesus. For example, Marcion argued that the Genesis account of Yahweh walking through the Garden of Eden asking where Adam was, proved that Yahweh inhabited a physical body and was without universal knowledge, attributes wholly incompatible with the Heavenly Father professed by Jesus.

According to Marcion, the god of the Old Testament, whom he called the Demiurge, the creator of the material universe, is a jealous tribal deity of the Jews, whose law represents legalistic reciprocal justice and who punishes mankind for its sins through suffering and death. In contrast, the God that Jesus professed is an altogether different being, a universal God of compassion and love who looks upon humanity with benevolence and mercy. Marcion also produced a book titled Antitheses, which is no longer extant, contrasting the Demiurge of the Old Testament with the Heavenly Father of the New Testament.

Marcion held Jesus to be the son of the Heavenly Father but understood the incarnation in a docetic manner, i.e. that Jesus' body was only an imitation of a material body, and consequently denied Jesus' physical and bodily birth, death, and resurrection.

But, you see, Marcion's interpretation of Genesis was entirely wrong. It, nowhere took into account later scriptures found in the Old Testament that would further elucidate and better explain the very simple narrative of creation found in Genesis. Genesis does not stand alone. It must be seen and understood in the context of later scriptures that would be written to make up the ongoing and progressive history of God's relationship to all of his creation and in relationship to humans and mankind, in particular.

Fr. Alexander Schmemann, Dean of St. Vladimir's Orthodox Theological Seminary in Crestwood, NY, and a leading Orthodox theologian of the early 20th century, best explained the existence of Evil and the personification of Evil in the light of ancient scriptures and in the light of the personal experiences of The Church. He explains it thusly:

In fact, the Orthodox Church has never formulated a systematic teaching concerning the Devil, in the form of a clear and concise "doctrine." What is of paramount importance is that the Church has always had the experience of the demonic, has always, in plain words, known the Devil. If this direct knowledge has not resulted in a neat and orderly doctrine, it is because of the difficulty, if not impossibility, rationally to define the irrational. And the demonic and, more generally, evil are precisely the reality of the irrational. Some theologians and philosophers, in an attempt to explain and thus to "rationalize" the experience and the existence of evil, explained it as an absence: the absence of good. They compared it, for example, to darkness, which is nothing but the absence of light and which is dispelled when light appears. This theory was subsequently adopted by deists and humanists of all shades and still constitutes an integral part of our modern worldview. The remedy against evil is always seen in "enlightenment" and "education."

Such however is certainly not the understanding of evil in the Bible and in the experience of the Church. Here evil is most emphatically not a mere absence. It is precisely a presence: the presence of something dark, irrational and very real, although the origin of that presence may not be clear and immediately understandable. Thus hatred is not a simple absence of love; it is the presence of a dark power which can indeed be extremely active, clever and even creative. And it is certainly not a result of ignorance. We may know and hate. The more some men knew Christ, saw His light and His goodness, the more they hated Him. This experience of evil as irrational power, as something which truly takes possession of us and directs our acts, has always been the experience of the Church and the experience also of all who try, be it only a little, to "better" themselves, to oppose "nature" in themselves, to ascend to a more spiritual life.

Our first affirmation then is that there exists a demonic reality: evil as a dark power, as presence and not only absence. But we may go further. For just as there can be no love outside the "lover," i.e. a person that loves, there can be no hatred outside the "hater," i.e. a person that hates. And if the ultimate mystery of "goodness" lies in the person, the ultimate mystery of evil must also be a personal one. Behind the dark and irrational presence of evil there must be a person or persons. There must exist a personal world of those who have chosen to hate God, to hate light, to be against. Who are these persons? When, how, and why have they chosen to be against God? To these questions the Church gives no precise answers. The deeper the reality, the less it is presentable in formulas and propositions. Thus the answer is veiled in symbols and images, which tell of an initial rebellion against God within the spiritual world created by God, among angels led into that rebellion by pride. The origin of evil is viewed here not as ignorance and imperfection but, on the contrary, as knowledge and a degree of perfection which makes the temptation of pride possible. Whoever he is, the "Devil" is among the very first and the best creatures of God. He is, so to speak, perfect enough, wise enough, powerful enough, one can almost say divine enough, to know God and not to surrender to Him—to know Him and yet to opt against Him, to desire freedom from Him. But since this freedom is impossible in the love and light which always lead to God and to a free surrender to Him, it must of necessity be fulfilled in negation, hatred and rebellion.

These are, of course, poor words, almost totally inadequate to the horrifying mystery they are trying to express. For we know nothing about that initial catastrophe in the spiritual world—

about that hatred against God ignited by pride and that bringing into existence of a strange and evil reality not willed, not created by God. Or rather, we know about it only through our own experience of that reality, through our own experience of evil. This experience indeed is always an experience of fall: of something precious and perfect deviated from and betraying its own nature, of the utterly unnatural character of that fall which yet became an integral and "natural" part of our nature. And when we contemplate evil in ourselves and outside ourselves in the world, how incredibly cheap and superficial appear all rational explanations, all "reductions" of evil to neat and rational theories. If there is one thing we learn from spiritual experience, it is that evil is not to be "explained" but faced and fought. This is the way God dealt with evil. He did not explain it. He sent His Only-Begotten Son to be crucified by all the powers of evil so as to destroy them by His love, faith and obedience.

One must remember that Genesis was only a very basic outline of how God planned on dealing with that original rebellion against Him by his own spiritual creation and then by Man's betrayal of Him by choosing to obey the Serpent, rather than trusting in God's warning as regarded the "Tree of Knowledge".

We must all deal with the reality of inner corruption because our first parents chose the way of the one who is darkness itself. In today's passage, we read of a statement Jesus made to some of Israel's religious leaders in one of the most theologically rich interchanges in the New Testament. Facing those who sought to kill Him (John 7:25), Jesus tells them that their murderous hatred of Him is rooted in their family lineage. They are children of the Devil, who has been "a murderer from the beginning" (8:44). Jesus refers to Satan's temptation of Adam and Eve in the garden, which introduced death into the experience of those who bear God's image (Gen. 3). Since that day, all people (except Christ) have entered this world in Adam, who gave up his loving relationship with the Creator to partake of the corruption of the Devil. Abandoning God as our Father, we took Satan as our father in the garden, and we have been reaping what we sowed ever since.

Like those who opposed Jesus, we are born murderers, liars, and thieves, unable to please God even if we never take these evil desires to their most harmful end. Consequently, we must "become partakers of the divine nature" through faith alone in Christ (2 Peter 1:4). Transformed from the inside out, we are enabled by the Holy Spirit to follow His law as we submit to Him.

So you see, Satan is NOT the great Liberator of Mankind, as he pretended to be. He is a liar and a murderer. The fact IS, that he and those who joined with him from the non-physical or heavenly realms, are jealous of and hate mankind because it was God's purpose to create in mankind, a sort of hybrid creation that would be both spirit and physical or material, so that they could live in and work within the worlds of matter and physical reality and that was something that the angels did not have the ability to do. So they were jealous of mankind and hated both mankind and God for not giving THEM those abilities. And both Satan and his minions continue to hate us down to this very day and are bent on our destruction and annihilation. It is only those ignorant of these facts, who glorify "personal freedom" and freedom from both God and from any laws or restrictions as the be all and end all of life. But they are only fooling themselves because no one is ever truly "free". Either you are a willing servant of God Almighty, who created you in His Own Image and has called you to be like Him, to be both human and divine and to live eternally and perhaps be co-creators with Him in His ever expanding Universe....or you will, by default be a slave of Satan, who has only called you to death and destruction because "misery loves company".

So the choice is YOURS and it has always been yours. Even in God's dealings with the Israelites, and even at the reading of the Ten Commandments, God always offered them a choice, because HE respects the Free Will that he imbued us with. That is why in the book of Deuteronomy, we read: "I call heaven and earth as witnesses today against you, that I have set before you life and death, blessing and cursing; therefore, choose life, that both you and your descendants may live." Deuteronomy 30:19.

Now, that is not to say that if we choose to ignore God's Law that HE will then aggressively "curse us". God LOVES his creation. He does not curse His creation. But HE knows that there are consequences when we break even "Natural Law". For example: If we jump off of a mountainside, we will be dashed to pieces; not because God hates us, but because we have violated the Law of Gravity. Likewise, when we break God's moral laws; there are consequences. If we have multiple sex partners, we are liable to catch deadly STD's. Or if we commit adultery, we are likely to be murdered by the woman's husband. etc. etc. If we choose a life of violent crime and home invasions; we are likely to be killed by the police or the home owners. There are consequences to all of our decisions and actions in life. Yet, somehow, that seems to escape the thinking of most people and especially the thinking of the young, who somehow see themselves as immortal and not accountable for any of their actions. "Let's just party and play" and if you get pregnant, you just murder the fetus....no big deal". Right ???

So you see, the REAL EPIPHANY IN MY LIFE, was NOT my confused multi-god, multi-theology, LGBTQ-Inspired understanding of REALITY and God's Will for Mankind. But it has become something much higher and more profound than that. And even my understanding of how "natural" homosexuality really IS, has come into question now that I am much older and my life is no longer driven by hormones.

I no longer subscribe to the belief or opinion that anyone is strictly "gay" or strictly heterosexual. I think that humans fit into a rather large spectrum and are influenced by far too many outside factors for us to be able to clearly pigeon-hole anyone as distinctly gay or "straight". And I am clearly seeing this today in 2022 as respects the Transsexual Community. Scientists and sociologists now know that an infant's survival instincts will drive a child to be whatever the biological parents want it to be in order to survive, by winning their love and affection and protection. If a couple recently lost their young or infant daughter and desperately wanted to have another daughter…or if they desperately wanted to have a son and the child born to them is a daughter; the child will "feel" or "sense" the disappointment and try to transform itself to meet with their expectations. And that includes acting like the gender that the parents WANTED the child to be born.

I know this FOR A FACT, because I experienced it in my own life. My parents had lost a daughter, who they had clearly loved. And my mother made it no secret that even though doctors had warned her that she should not attempt to have another child due to health issues; that she chose to risk her life this one last time in an effort to have another daughter. And then I came along instead. As you will remember from the early chapters of my book; I was basically raised as a daughter and kept away from my father and from male role models during those early formative years of my life. And while that did not ultimately result in "gender confusion", none the less, it did result in my developing as somehow "different" from my male associates and friends and decidedly more "feminine" and less masculine and aggressive. And it led to my life-long search for acceptance by other males and the need for a strong male relationship, which I felt that I might achieve by "giving men what they want". So was I ever actually a card-carrying homosexual? Or was I merely responding to survival techniques basic to the human species?

And then too, there is always the need in every one of us to be "part of something bigger than us". So, when I was young and in my early twenties, I felt the need to identify with and support the LGBTQ Movement and march in all of its parades and support all of its political agendas. But now, 40-50 years later, I no longer feel any of those needs. I am entirely self-sufficient and I do not have to "play up to other men" to ensure my survival. And I no longer need to "identify" with any organization to feel a part of something bigger. And what is worse, is that nowadays, I feel that the LGBTQ movement, which was once the "victim" has gone way too far and has now become the persecutor and the antagonist and the perpetrator of violating other people's rights in their desperate attempt to achieve social respectability.

Not all that long ago, most gay men made fun of heterosexuality and family life and the rose covered cottage with children running about in the yard. We called them "breeders" and all manner of other disrespectful epithets. And yet now, some 30 year later, we want to copy them and we all want to have either our very own CHURCH or SYNAGOGUE weddings and children by surrogate mothers; either that or we want to adopt South American and Eskimo children (LOL) and become respectable PTA "mothers and fathers". I wonder what made us suddenly dash our own uniqueness to pieces and made us want to "BECOME QUASY-HETEROSEXUALS IN ROSE-COVERED COTTAGES"? And the worse part of it all is that now WE HAVE BECOME THE PERSECUTORS. We "go after" small businesses, specifically to punish and sue and destroy those who refuse to participate in our gay weddings. And now we are attacking women's rights, in that we are supporting a handful of men with gender-dysphoria, WHO THINK THAT THEY ARE WOMEN, but are unwilling to actually get a sex change and allowing them to share bathroom facilities and to compete in women's sports. And the incredible part of this is that our government, that claims to operate under "democratic principles", is allowing perhaps 2% of the population to deprive all women of their rights to safety and privacy in public facilities.

And I feel very certain that the day is not far off when the LGBTQ Community will show their "true colors" and attempt to force through legislation that will allow them to sue and persecute any religious organization that refuses to marry them in their churches or synagogue's. And the day is not far off when gay weddings alone will not be sufficient. They will want weddings for brothers and sisters and weddings for mothers and sons, and weddings for dads and their sons. How far do we want to take this? Weddings for humans and animals? And the Mark of Satan is so clearly stamped on all of this because he wants to destroy the Human Family and make it become extinct. Since he already KNOWS that he will never be able to rule all of Mankind; he would rather destroy Mankind utterly. But thanks be to God, Our Heavenly Father will never allow that.

So please, my Dear Ones; ignore my original "Gay Epiphany" findings. While there is merit to my explaining what life was like growing up gay in the 50-s and 60's. In retrospect, I can no longer say that I would encourage the gay lifestyle for anyone young who thinks that they might be gay. Before making any drastic and permanent life decisions, please, explore all of the other possibilities available to you. And if you are male and simply have no inclination towards marriage or females, or if you are female, but not particularly or obsessively attracted to males, do not automatically come to the conclusion that you are gay. Perhaps God is leading you to a life of celibacy and monasticism and dedication to Him and you will never find a better "Life Partner" than The Lord.

I cannot help but reflect on the wise words of King Solomon found in the 12th chapter of Ecclesiastes as regards the WHOLE OBLIGATION OF MAN.

New King James Version

1 Remember now your Creator in the days of your youth,

Before the difficult days come,

And the years draw near when you say,

"I have no pleasure in them":

2 While the sun and the light,

The moon and the stars,

Are not darkened,

And the clouds do not return after the rain;

3 In the day when the keepers of the house tremble,

And the strong men bow down;

When the grinders cease because they are few,

And those that look through the windows grow dim;

4 When the doors are shut in the streets,

And the sound of grinding is low;

When one rises up at the sound of a bird,

And all the daughters of music are brought low.

5 Also they are afraid of height,

And of terrors in the way;

When the almond tree blossoms,

The grasshopper is a burden,

And desire fails.

For man goes to his eternal home,

And the mourners go about the streets.

6 Remember your Creator before the silver cord is [b]loosed,

Or the golden bowl is broken,

Or the pitcher shattered at the fountain,

Or the wheel broken at the well.

7 Then the dust will return to the earth as it was,

And the spirit will return to God who gave it.

8 "Vanity of vanities," says the Preacher,

"All is vanity."

9 And moreover, because the Preacher was wise, he still taught the people knowledge; yes, he pondered and sought out and set in order many proverbs.

10 The Preacher sought to find acceptable words; and what was written was upright—words of truth.

11 The words of the wise are like goads, and the words of [e]scholars are like well-driven nails, given by one Shepherd.

12 And further, my son, be admonished by these. Of making many books there is no end, and much study is wearisome to the flesh.

13Let us hear the conclusion of the whole matter:

Fear God and keep His commandments,

For this is the whole obligation of man.

14 For God will bring every work into judgment,

Including every secret thing,

Whether good or evil.""

OTHER RECOMMENDED READING

"Steve Allen on the Bible, Religion & Morality"-Prometheus Books

"101 Myths of the Bible" by Gary Greenberg-Barnes & Noble Books

"What the Bible Really Says About Homosexuality" by Daniel A. Helminiak, Ph.D.-Alamo Square Press

"The Church and the Homosexual" by John J. McNeill - Beacon Press

"Prayers For Bobby" by Leroy Aarons-Harper One

"The Mind Of The Bible-Believer" by Edmund D. Cohen-Prometheus Books

"Same Sex Unions In PreModern Europe" by John Boswell-Villard Books

"Homosexuals In History" by A. L. Rowse-Dorset Press

"The Hero With A Thousand Faces" by Joseph Campbell-Princeton University Press

"The Origin Of Satan" by Elaine Pagels-Vintage Books/Random House

"Adam, Eve and The Serpent" by Elaine Pagels-Random House

"The Gnostic Gospels" by Elaine Pagels-Random House

"Who Wrote The Bible?" by Richard E. Friedman-Harper Press

"Faith Of Our Fathers" by Edwin S. Gaustad-Harper and Row

"The Dead Sea Scrolls Deception" by Michael Baigent and Richard Leigh- Simon & Schuster

"Why I Am Not A Christian" by Bertrand Russell, Simon & Schuster

"Bisexuality In The Ancient World" by Eva Cantarella-Yale Press

"The Jesus Mystery" by Janet Bock-Aura Books

"Autobiography of a Yogi" Paramahansa Yogananda-Self Realization Fellowship

"Beyond Words" by Sri Swami Satchidananda- Integral Yoga Publications

"Jesus Perusha" by Ian Davie-Lindisfarne Press

"The Living Gita" by Sri Swami Satchidananda- An Owl Book, Henry Holt and Co.

"Inspired Talks" by Swami Vivekananda- Ramakrishna-Vivekananda Center, NY

"The Jesus Mysteries" by Timothy Freke & Peter Gandy-Three Rivers Press, NY

"Mythic Past, Biblical Archaeology and the Myth Of Israel" by Thomas L. Thompson-MJF Books, NY

"The End Of Faith" by Sam Harris- W.W.Norton & Co., NY

"The Jesus Puzzle" by Earl Doherty-Age Of Reason Publications, Ottawa,ON.

"The Incredible Shrinking Son Of Man" by Robert M. Price-Prometheus Books, Amherst NY

"The Christ Conspiracy,The Greatest Story Ever Sold" by Acharya S-Adventures Unlimited Press, Kempton, IL.

"Nickel and Dimed" "On Not Getting By In America" by Barbara Ehrenreich-Metropolitan Books, NY

"Your Money Or Your Life" by Joe Dominguez and Vicki Robin-Penguin Books, NY

"Merchants Of Misery" "How Corporate America Profits From Poverty" by Michael Hudson-Common Courage Press, Monroe, ME

Printed in the United States
by Baker & Taylor Publisher Services